BROKEN PROTOCOLS 1-3

This set contains:

Broken Protocols
Broken Protocols 2
Broken Protocols 3

by

Dale Mayer

DALE MAYER

BROKEN PROTOCOLS 1-3
Dale Mayer
Valley Publishing
Copyright © 2014

All rights reserved. Except for use in any review, the reproduction or utilization of this work in whole or in part by any electronic, mechanical or other means, now known or hereafter invented, including xerography, photocopying and recording, or in any information storage or retrieval system, is forbidden without the written permission of the publisher.

This is a work of fiction. Names, characters, places, brands, media, and incidents are either the product of the author's imagination or are used fictitiously. Any resemblance to actual events, locales, or persons, living or dead, is entirely coincidental.

ISBN 10: 1927461952
ISBN-13: 9781927461952

Broken Protocols

Dani's been through a year of hell...

Just as it's getting better, she's tossed forward through time with her orange Persian cat, Charmin Marvin, clutched in her arms. They're dropped into a few centuries into the future. There's nothing she can do to stop it, and it's impossible to go back.

And then it gets worse...

A year of government regulation is easing, and Levi Blackburn is feeling back in control. If he can keep his reckless brother in check, everything will be perfect. But while he's been protecting Milo from the government, Milo's been busy working on a present for him...

The present is Dani, only she comes with a snarky cat who suddenly starts talking...and doesn't know when to shut up.

In an age where breaking protocols have severe consequences, things go wrong, putting them all in danger...

DALE MAYER

Protocol 1:3:1 – *You will in no way use technology to damage the life of another – particularly if those actions are to selfishly enhance your own.*

Chapter 1

Dani Summerland was on top of the world. It had taken several years, but she'd finally put her past behind her. A new day had begun. A new job, her first date in a long, okay…in a *very* long time and for once, her future looked bright.

It had been a hell of a year.

She glanced at her watch and realized she was running a little behind after working late. She walked faster on the busy street. Rush hour had peaked, but there were plenty of people racing still to get home. Her apartment was just around the block. For the umpteenth time, she pulled the faded, crumpled photo of her and Lawrence from her pocket. He'd been everything to her. Now, a year after her very public humiliation, she could finally say she'd recovered. It was time to get rid of the picture. She'd hung onto it as a reminder. Of a lesson learned to never be forgotten. Some rules were never meant to be broken – and ignorance was not an excuse. She'd had some inkling that things with Lawrence weren't as they'd seemed, but young love and all the rest of those glorious emotions guaranteed to get her into hot water had overruled her better judgment.

So she'd ignored those little nudges. Until she found him at a company event, the host, in fact – with his wife at his side.

That had been the most disastrous evening of her life. The wife's mocking look and laughing comment to her in the ladies' room later about being her husband's latest side piece hadn't helped. The pink slip from his legal firm the next day was just another insult and another piece of her education.

Never have an affair with the boss – especially when it turns out he's married.

She'd been such a fool. She hated that the other staff had known – and no one had said anything to her. That they all believed she was the kind to have affairs with married men. Now she got the snide comments she hadn't understood. The mocking and disgusted looks she hadn't connected to the truth.

There was nothing like learning about men – life – consequences – the hard way.

There was a garbage can up ahead. She stopped, carefully ripped up the picture – one that she'd once loved and held dear – into tiny pieces, and fed them to the can.

Then she turned, pulled up her coat collar, and walked faster.

It was time to let go and create a better future. And as of today, it looked damn bright.

***

"What the hell?" Levi studied the massive wall of monitors in front of him. They should be locked behind the security field at this point. He glanced around the large empty office to see if anyone had slipped in behind him, but he was alone in the encroaching darkness. Then again, he should be. It was damn late, and it was his brother's office. No one was allowed in but the two of them. Not in this age of computer espionage. His world lived on computers, and his brother was a genius when it came to programming. There was nothing he couldn't build.

Hence the large company that they owned, with a few family backers, and the heavy security measures they used to keep their inventions secure until the official release.

If it weren't for Milo's recent odd behavior, that little kid look of having a secret he desperately wanted to share, Levi wouldn't be here now. Genius Milo – chocolate-munching, green Mohawk-ed, geeky Milo had been acting suspicious for days.

That would give anyone nightmares.

As his partner and older brother, Levi didn't dare let Milo go off half-cocked again. Genius he might be, but he was lacking a certain level of common sense, as proven by their being slapped by the CCDA Regulatory Commission last year. No one doubted Milo's intentions – it was just that they weren't clearly thought out. At the end of the nerve-wracking review, the board had determined that the brothers would be allowed to continue their IT company, but the genius needed to be carefully watched.

A year later, the regulatory overseeing eye had eased – slightly. But the scrutiny had chafed for both Milo and Levi. For Milo more so.

And as Levi stared at the complex coding on the screen mounted in the center of the wall, he realized that Milo was in deeper than before. Levi's heart sank. This last year had done nothing to smarten Milo up. This program looked to be almost complete, if not ready for testing.

"I wondered how long it would take you to check up on me." Milo's quiet voice spoke from behind him.

Levi dropped his head into his hands, wanting to pull his hair out. Instead, he said in low worried voice, "What have you done?"

"It's nothing bad. In fact," Milo's voice picked up enthusiastically, "it's kind of awesome."

"*Kind of* awesome?" Levi spun around to glare at Milo. "This could mean jail time, you know that." He towered over his younger brother. "This could mean losing the company. Years of our time and effort. Years where the family helped us, backed us, protected us. Did you even think of that?"

"No. No, it doesn't." Milo rushed over, wringing his hands. At least the childish delight of the last few days had dimmed. Milo just didn't get that rules and regulations were there for a reason. Levi did. He lived by them. His brother didn't even acknowledge them. And Levi had been bailing him out since he was a little boy – he wasn't going to change now.

Milo loved history. And when he added his crazy geek skills and a complete lack of comprehension of the limits to what he could do, all manner of hell could happen. Had happened. Was possibly about to happen again.

"You don't understand." Milo beamed with excitement. "See, it works this time."

Levi shook his head. "No. It doesn't."

"Yes." Milo hopped from one foot to the other. Passion and joy was on his face and in his voice. "It does. It does. Honest."

"There is no way. You can't just yank a person forward a couple of centuries into our world. Look at what kind of trouble that got you in last time." *Got us*, but he kept that bit quiet. Milo's enthusiasm got him – them – in trouble *every* time. But every once in a while, he came up with something so earth-shattering that most people had no trouble overlooking the problems that came with Milo. Then again, they weren't the ones having to clean up after him.

Milo walked over to the keyboard, his fingers dancing so fast, Levi could barely follow what he was doing on the screen. Colors and figures flashed at alarming speeds.

"Hey, stop. You can't test this right now."

"Sure I can. It works. I actually planned to test it tonight anyway. I just didn't expect to have you here."

Throwing his hands up, Levi gave an exasperated snort. "You were *hoping* that I wouldn't be here. Right?"

Milo shot him a resentful look. "You never let me have any fun."

"Fun?" Levi said ominously. "Going back in time, snagging up any female you want and slapping them down in our time is *fun*? You do remember what happened last time, right?" His glare deepened. "The massive power outage you caused?"

"I figured out how to stop the massive power surge. Besides, I only wanted to brainstorm with Marie Curie," he said resentfully. "She was an intelligent woman. We'd have had a great time."

"If you didn't kill her in the process," Levi snapped.

Milo spun around to face him, his grin once again splitting his face. "No, I fixed that. It's safe now."

"Says you." Levi eyed his brother suspiciously. He didn't know how to get this into his brother's head. This was too important. "This is big. Like seriously big stuff. And the chances of you doing this successfully…you know the protocols are very specifi—"

"Ah, but the protocols are poorly written." His elfish grin flashed and he added, "Besides, they are more like guidelines."

He nudged his brother to the side. "You might want to get out of the way."

"What? What for?" Levi spun around and caught sight of Milo reaching for a button on the side. "No." And he knocked his hand away. Milo stumbled backward, tripped, and fell against his keyboard. The screen went nuts as Milo's elbow smacked down onto the button anyway.

Immediately, a high-pitched whine filled the room. Levi slapped his hands over his ears even as his eyes stared in panic at the monitors dancing with flashing code.

"What's happening?"

"Everything!" Milo danced, laughing like a loon. "But it's nothing to worry about."

A flash of light exploded in the center of the room, blinding them both.

Chapter 2

Dani glanced at the clock, realizing she had just enough time for a cup of tea and a snack before getting dressed. She filled her teakettle and placed it on the stove.

She danced a quick jig across the living room. Perfect day, perfect date, and perfect evening to come. If there were misgivings that her bubble was about to burst, it had to be residual negativity left over from the year from hell. And that Murphy's Law had been formulated specifically with her in mind.

But that was over. She was all about new beginnings. And that meant she could open the bottle of wine she'd been saving for a special occasion. She reached into the back of the fridge and pulled it out. Twisting the top off, she poured herself a glass and held it up to sniff it.

Charmin Marvin, her overgrown orange Persian cat, jumped lightly up onto the counter. She bumped the wine glass gently against his nose.

"Cheers!"

Meow!

She flipped her long blond braid behind her back and laughed. "Right back at you, big guy. Here's to us." Eyes closed, she took a large gulp of her wine. Still too buoyed to relax, she put her glass down and snagged Charmin up. Humming a tune in her head, she twirled him around.

"We're gonna be just fine."

Meow!

She laughed and twirled him again. She wanted to enjoy this moment. It had been a long time coming, but it was all good.

Her life was back on track. It had been a long painful struggle, but she'd made it.

Tonight was going to be good, too. Danny was a cute, *single* guy who had transferred into the company last month. Life was good again.

"I wish you could talk, big guy. Just think how great that would be." She did a quick pirouette with him. Just as she slowed down, a white light exploded in her living room.

Waves blasted her, picking her up and throwing her back against the couch, Charmin clutched fiercely in her arms, his claws digging deep into her skin. Mist swam through her brain and her eyes burned. Her chest squeezed tight. She couldn't breathe. Her ears rang and her lunch was crawling up the inside of her throat.

What the hell had just happened? She could only hope the property damage would be minimal. Otherwise, her landlord would freak.

She sat forward, clutching Charmin tight, afraid he'd take off and she wouldn't be able to find him again. Moving slowly, her muscles heavy and unwieldy, her body in major shock, she struggled to her feet and headed for the doorway. Smoke filled her living room. She stifled a cough and covered her mouth with her sleeve to avoid breathing the reeking aroma.

She crouched low, gasping for air.

Had there been a gas leak? A bombing?

Then she heard voices. *Oh thank God.* She struggled toward them.

A strange voice cried out, "Damn it, Milo, what did you do?"

"Wowza." A cackle filled the air. "Look, it worked!"

Through the mist, she spied two men…or at least, she thought they were men. The one in a purple and turquoise skin suit with a green Mohawk bounced in front of her, a maniacal laugh coming from his mouth. Then her shocked gaze landed on the second man. *Lawrence.*

And that couldn't be.

Her heart slammed against her ribs, and then she really couldn't breathe. She gulped for air as she stared at the one man she'd loved and hated – and had spent the last year trying to forget – who now stood in front of her.

Unbelievably, after all this time, anger rose in a red haze. She stepped into his personal space and smacked him – hard.

His head flipped to the side, then came back around slowly, a red mark quickly rising on his cheek. Shock lit the deep dark depths of his eyes.

Uh oh.

She took a step back, her ribs frozen and locked.

He took a step forward.

Finally, her lungs expanded. She took a deep breath, spun around, and ran.

She raced out the door and headed toward the elevator. And somehow got turned around. There were no walls of elevators. Nothing looked right…nothing looked normal. Blindly, she ran from door to door until she found one leading outside and bolted through.

And came to a skittering stop. Her mind couldn't process what her eyes were seeing. She was on a balcony – a very high up balcony. And that couldn't be, either. Her apartment was on the 3rd floor, whereas from the scenic panorama laid out before her, she had to be at least sixty floors up – if that was even possible.

The view in front of her was like nothing she'd ever seen before. It appeared to be a city. Or rather a metropolis on steroids. Buildings rose in weird space-agey looking domes, and there were rail cars on big circular runs. And God help her – there looked to be vehicles flying high above her head.

It looked nothing like Vancouver, BC, where she lived. In fact, as she shuddered and leaned back against the closed door behind her, this didn't even look like her planet.

***

"Where did she go?" Milo cried out. He spun around and said, "She's gone."

And damned if he didn't look like he was going to cry. Levi threw up his hands and snapped, "What did you expect? You snatched her out of her world and dumped her here. We have to find her."

"Find her? Where else can she go?" Milo dashed up beside Levi. "She can't *go* anywhere. That's the beauty of this."

"Really? I think you forgot to tell her that." Exasperated, Levi raced out of his brother's design room and into the short hallway. There were several more doors ahead and he could only hope she'd gone in a straight line. Actually, he could hope that this disaster was just a bad dream, but knowing his brother…

"We have to stop her before she goes outside." To lose her in that jungle would be a tragedy. And he had had enough of those on his hands with this damn technology as it was. If the government got wind of Milo's latest experiment, they could both be thrown into jail and the technology confiscated, never to see the light of day – unless those in power wanted to use it for themselves.

And that would be disastrous.

The Council had too much power now. Who knew what they'd with something like this technology? Knowing how corrupt the Council was – it would be nothing good.

Levi couldn't believe Milo had finally succeeded with his time travel project. His kid brother was a genius like none other, sure...but to be able to do something like this...Levi kept moving forward and opened every door he came to, and still there was nothing to find. He raced for the front door, his heart sinking. *Please don't be outside. Please...*

"Wait—"

Too late. Levi had already barreled ahead and made it outside before his brother's words infiltrated his frustration. "Okay, this is bad." Levi said. As he watched, the line of buildings in front of him slowly went dark one after the other. Just like last time. "So very bad."

"I didn't do that." Milo said when he caught up to his brother. He held up his new SXC4500 fingerboard computer, and shouted. "I have her on the camera."

Levi spun around. "Where is she?"

"She came back inside." Milo flipped the comp around so Levi could see.

"Really?" That stopped Levi in his tracks. He peered at the screen. "That was actually a really smart move."

Milo grinned. "Yeah. See? I didn't choose a bimbo. We need someone with enough brains to handle this type of switch in her life."

"That's not measured by brains. There is so much more involved here."

"Oops," Milo said, looking back down at the screen. "She's on the move."

Milo's new rocker boots clicked as he raced behind Levi back into the facility. Levi shook his head. Milo needed a keeper himself. How could he possibly determine the type of woman that would not go crazy from his damn experiment? Retracing their steps, they tracked her through the building.

Minutes later, they ended up back in Milo's office with still no sign of her.

"She's in here somewhere."

Levi searched behind the chairs and under the desks. "Please tell me you can send her back." Levi turned to his brother. "That you can reverse this process."

"I don't think so." Milo threw him a sideways grin. "Besides, we don't want to send her back."

"I do," Levi snapped. "And I'm sure she wants to go back, too. She has a life, remember?"

"Hmmm. According to my research, Dani Summerland doesn't have much of one." He clicked through his fingerboard computer and started reading off the list. "No partner. No career to speak of. Failed business after one year. Managed to stay gainfully employed. No marriage. No children. No long-term friends on record."

Chapter 3

They knew her name. Dani sank lower in the open closet she'd hidden in as the painful litany of her failed life washed over her. What a horrible dissection of her life. Surely it hadn't been that bad? Besides, it's not as if her life was over. She could achieve greatness yet. *Couldn't she?*

"It's not that simple, Milo."

Dani heard the discussion despite the doors being opened and closed.

The deeper of the two voices spoke again, "She has reasons for what happened in her life. Sure, she *might* be up for a move a couple centuries into the future. She *might* consider it an adventure. She *might* consider it an improvement on her old world. But you didn't *ask* her. You didn't give her a choice, and that makes all the difference. You just yanked her out of her old life. For all you know, she might have a major plan about to come to fruition and you stole that from her."

"I did not," Milo protested. "I did my research, Levi. I'm not an idiot. She had nothing. She was nothing. She would have become nothing. Now she is something – special."

Her heart squeezing tight, she listened to Levi and Milo discuss her life. As if they knew her. As if they knew everything about her. And she meant *everything*.

"And where in her psych profile, Milo, did it say she'd be up for a complete shock like this?"

"Ahh…" Milo stuttered.

Levi's voice dropped to an ominous level. "You didn't get a psych profile, did you?"

"Well, it's not so easy. They didn't do them regularly back then. They were quite primitive, remember?"

Levi snorted.

Dani's chest locked tight. A couple centuries into the future? They were kidding – right? But from what she'd seen outside before instinct had her spinning around and returning to the one space she knew – this room – it was not Vancouver. At least not Vancouver as she'd known it. And she'd lived there all her life. Her city was gone. Her apartment building was gone. Her living room was gone.

She squeezed Charmin tighter against her chest and buried her face against his thick orange fur. Thank heavens he was safe with her. The two of them could have gotten blown up in the blast. "You're all I have left," she whispered. And got the next biggest shock of her life.

"Hey. What do you mean *all*?" Charmin said, twisting in her arms, his paw reaching out to bat her chest. "You make it sound like I'm nothing. And I'm a whole lot more than nothing."

Dani reared back and stared into her beloved cat's glowering eyes. She shuddered and closed her eyes briefly. "Charmin?" she asked cautiously. "Is that you?"

No, it can't be. She felt stupid for even asking the question. There was no way her cat could talk. Then again, there was no way she'd been yanked two centuries into the future either. She dropped her head back. She was losing it. Tears gathered in her eyes. Why her? All she'd ever wanted was to be happy.

Questions rippled through her mind. Terrifying her. Making her heart stall then race like she was being chased. She squeezed her eyes shut again. One tear rolled down her cheek. She turned her head to wipe her face on her sleeve. She needed some normality here. Something real she could grab and hang on to. She took a deep breath and whispered, "Please, Charmin, don't tell me you can talk."

And oh God…he actually answered her.

In a deep voice unlike anything she'd ever heard before, Charmin said, "I could always talk. Since when did *you* learn?"

She swallowed, opened her eyes, and stared down at her best friend. And found find him staring at her, his face only inches from hers, with a puzzled look in his eyes. Such a human look in that gaze. Such a human-sounding voice.

Except the claws in her flesh were all feline.

Her mouth dropped open, and she shook her head in denial. "Not possible. It's not possible."

"Well, it's not probable. I figured you were too primitive, too underdeveloped to learn such a skill." He brightened, that wide mouth twisting up into a grin. "But you surprised me. You actually learned to talk."

At last she understood.

She was crazy.

She'd finally turned some invisible corner into a complete fantasy world in her mind. She'd always wanted to be able to talk to animals. It had been a secret dream ever since she was a little girl. Obviously, reality had become too much and she'd retreated to her childhood state. It was almost a relief in a way. To have an explanation for this insanity.

It was either that or she was having a crazy dream. And that was all too possible. Not to mention being a better option.

She beamed at her cat. "I'm going to wake up soon and this will be just a happy memory."

"I wish I was dreaming." Charmin snorted. "This little room is nice and cozy and all, but where is the couch? I need my nap."

"Sleep? *You* need to sleep?" She shook her head, staring around the tiny closet. "I was trying to get ready to go out on a date."

"Yeah, great." Charmin gave a jaw-splitting yawn before tucking into her shoulder. "Who needs a date? Well, okay, you do, but really, I need my beauty sleep." And he closed his eyes.

She stared down at her cat and whispered, "Please let this be a bad dream. And please let me wake up soon and find everything back to normal."

"I hope so," Charmin muttered, "because you forgot to feed me dinner before we time-travelled."

At the words *time-travelled*, she forgot to breathe again. "Don't say that," she cried.

Suddenly, the door opened. The same two men peered in, but the green Mohawk, so large and long, was all she could focus on.

A scream caught in the back of her throat. But no sound came out.

"Aha. There you are," said the owner of the Mohawk, Milo, if she'd gotten the names right. "And who were you talking to?"

She wanted to fight. Wanted to kick them both in the teeth so hard they'd never eat again. The older brother, Levi, according to what she'd heard – and not Lawrence as she'd initially thought – peered around the green hair. This close, she could see he looked very similar to Lawrence but there was something younger, cleaner about his features. And maybe nicer. Lawrence had gained a seedy look to his cheeks and a perpetual smirk to his eyes.

As if he was always one up on you.

Which, in her case, he had been. And if Levi wasn't Lawrence, she had just smacked a complete stranger.

Damn.

She risked a look at Charmin, saw the feline smirk as if to say 'Uh oh, now you're in trouble', and shuddered. In a low voice, she said, "You can bite them in the balls while I run."

"Not happening." And damn if Charmin's voice didn't drop low to match hers.

Levi reached down and yanked her to her feet. She tugged her arm back, climbing out of her hiding spot on her own. She shot him a dark look. "You don't have to hurt me."

He retreated instantly, his hands out in front of him apologetically. "Look, I'm sorry. We're not going to hurt you. Please. Let's go sit down and we'll explain everything."

She raised one eyebrow and proceeded to repeat everything she'd heard them say. Their eyebrows shot up. She added, "As you can tell, I can hear just fine. Now I want you to tell me how the hell you're going to fix this." She glared at Milo. "I want to go home."

Milo jumped forward, his face earnest and proud at the same time. "See, that's the thing. We can't. That's the beauty of this technology. It can't be reversed."

"And that's beautiful?" she asked ominously, her heart and mind screaming their protests in sync. "How do you figure?"

While she waited, she realized the men were guiding her into a glass cube she hadn't noticed in the dark room. She could barely see her surroundings, but it looked like a futuristic type of office with huge wall screens she'd never seen before. And some kind of center console. The screen looked kind of see through and had all those weird colors. She couldn't tell from her position.

Once inside, she sank into the deepest corner of the cube to avoid their touch, holding Charmin tight. He was her one link to normalcy. He stared up at her and opened his mouth.

She slapped a hand over it and glared at him. And realized that if Charmin could talk – there was nothing normal left.

Trying to process the situation faster, she studied the men, waiting for something to happen. Levi pushed something on his wrist and the cube took off. She shrieked, reaching out a hand instinctively to steady herself, only to find the ride smooth and quiet.

She couldn't help but be reminded of the old Charlie and the Chocolate Factory story. Except this wasn't likely to have a happy ending. As the glass cube swept around corners, she realized it wasn't on rails. In fact, it didn't appear to be attached to anything. She gasped and squeezed her eyes closed. "Where did the ground go?" she whispered.

"It's there. Below us."

She peeked through her closed eyelashes to see the bottom of the glass cube and nothing else. Just a swirling whiteness – as if they were in the middle of a cloud. Her mind spun, grasping for any reasonable explanation – and came up empty. She fell back against the glass, hyperventilating. "Oh, this is not good. This is so not good."

Milo explained, "It's just a modern elevator."

That didn't deserve a response. His idea of a modern elevator and hers were miles apart. She shifted Charmin in her grasp but dared not loosen her hold. Not that there was any chance of dropping him with the way his claws dug into her arms. She wouldn't be surprised if he'd drawn blood. If she were unlucky, she'd be dripping blood down onto their glass floor.

The elevator changed directions again, sending her lurching sideways. *Oh shit oh shit.* She felt the beads of sweat rise on her forehead.

"It's going to be fine," Milo said with a wide grin. "We're perfectly safe."

At the end of his words, the glass box came to a complete stop. And it dissolved around them. As in here one minute and gone the next. The men exited – if there was a cube to exit. They'd barely travelled. It almost looked like the same building – or maybe the same set of buildings? There'd been no sign of the outside world at all.

She straightened, took one step in their direction and without warning, her stomach heaved.

***

"Oh yucky. That's so…yucky." Milo danced away from her, his face a picture of morbid fascination. "I'm calling someone to come clean that up."

"Fine, but let's not be here when they arrive." Levi knelt by the woman's side, trying to ignore the reek from the mess at his feet. Sweat had beaded on Dani's forehead, at least that's the name he thought Milo had called her, and her color had gone pasty gray. Probably a delayed reaction. Rushing forward a few hundred years had to be tough on the stomach, if not the rest of her. That she could even walk and talk and…look half as sexy as she did was amazing. And he shouldn't be noticing. Now she'd curled into a small ball, her slim frame rocking back and forth. The massive furry critter in her arms was making a horrific howling sound that set his nerves on edge. He might have sympathy for her, but that animal…

Through the noise, he heard her whispering into the animal's fur, "It's okay, Charmin. It's going to be okay, baby."

"I know it's hard to believe, but you are right. It will be okay," Levi said, hoping he wasn't lying to the poor woman, "but there is no way I can agree with you calling that…that thing *baby*."

And damn if that furry thing didn't rear back and glare at him. As if it heard and understood.

Dani froze, lifted her head to stare at him, and then she did something that completely disarmed him.

She started to giggle.

Chapter 4

Dani couldn't stop giggling. She tried, but laughter came in never ending waves. She had to stop. If she didn't, they'd turn into tears soon. And that would be bad news. For everyone.

"Oh brother. What an ass," said Charmin in that low guttural whisper. "You can pass on this one."

Her laughter rolled out freely. She caught sight of the two men and the combined shocked looks on their faces. They might have managed to toss her forward a couple hundred years, but she'd managed to shock them. And she planned on keeping them off balance.

She had to find a way home and she needed their help. But she'd be damned if she'd let them walk all over her. Knowing what was outside the building scared her shitless, and for all she'd been trying to shake off her old life, she hadn't meant to shake it off this far.

And who was this Levi? With each new look, she realized Levi looked so similar to Lawrence, she had to consider he'd come forward in time as well. But there were just enough visual differences, too. Then again, she hadn't seen Lawrence in over a year. That could account for some of the differences in appearance. No, Levi was younger, much younger. Besides, how likely was it that the two of them were dragged forward in time? And if they had, were there others like her here?

"It's not the same guy," Charmin muttered.

She wiped the tears from her eyes as her laughing spell ended and whispered, holding Charmin so the men couldn't see her talking to him. "Why do you say that?"

"Because you're in the future. That means he's not the same man." He shot her a look of disgust, adding, "Duh!"

She pursed her lips at the sarcasm and stared up at Levi. He had the same tall, lean build, the same jet-black hair as Lawrence. The same quaky smile. But like a younger brother. Still, she had to know. "So did you come from my century as well?"

Levi shook his head in a slow movement that made his slightly long hair curl on his shirt collar. If they were two hundred years in the future, the men still wore shirts and pants. His weird looking friend could have been from any number of places in her time so he looked odd, but not *that* odd. Outside of the technology like the elevator, and God, how creepy had *that* been, the rooms she'd seen so far looked almost normal. It's what had been outside that had shocked her.

"I'm sorry. I don't know you." He tried for a friendly smile and added, "Yet."

She rolled her eyes. "You would say that."

He gave her a hand to help her stand up, moving her away from the mess. "You are mistaking me for someone from your time."

"Yeah, right. Like you aren't the spitting image of Lawrence Blackburn."

Levi stiffened. "That is my last name. And Lawrence was a black-hearted ancestor of ours. I'm sorry if you were harmed by him. I can only assure you that I am not him in any way."

She stared at him. "Doesn't that figure? Well, at least tell me he's dead? That would almost make this worth it."

"That I can do." He smiled and held out his hand as if to shake hers. "I'm Levi Blackburn, and Lawrence is definitely dust by now."

The younger guy bobbed his head up and down. She wondered if he had an iPod or something in his ear because he seemed to move to some inner beat. He gave her a huge grin and said, "I'm Milo. Levi is my brother."

Her gaze widened. "That is so wrong."

The smaller guy narrowed his gaze, confusion clouding his eyes. Levi said, "Well, it's true. Milo is a genius."

She snorted at that. "Oh right. That whole genius thing about creating some kind of time machine that snatched me out of my own life. Well, thanks for nothing. So before we go too far down this road, how about you reverse the results and let me return to the time where I belong."

A long strange silence filled the room. She narrowed her gaze suspiciously. "Why did you say that's the beauty of this – that this isn't reversible?"

And Charmin gave voice to her thoughts. Thankfully, it came out in a garbled whisper. "Uh oh."

Milo looked down at his feet and shuffled from left to right and back again. Yeah, he was guilty as hell. She switched to Levi. And he was staring at Milo.

"You didn't figure that you needed a way to reverse the process." She motioned to the nonexistent glass elevator around her and said in an ominous voice, "You figured anyone – any girl – would be delighted to find herself yanked away from everything she holds dear into a foreign world where she has no way to support herself?" Her voice rose at the end to shrill tones. "Dependent on you two for my living?"

Both men winced in sync.

She lowered her voice and continued in an angry whisper. "And seeing as how I'm running up a list of questions, here is a biggie." She paused. "Why me?"

***

Levi didn't know what to do. She knew his ancestor, a man who'd left a horrible legacy of infidelity and distrust. That she mistook him for *that* man was a huge insult. He tried to remind himself that he didn't know her and she didn't know him, but she'd jumped to one hell of an assumption. And she was pissed. The tears, the loud voice, and the death grip she had on her pet also said she was terrified.

And that he could understand.

She also looked familiar. Like very familiar. At least her facial features. That tiny delicate body and luminescent skin, no. But he hoped she'd become familiar. Then it hit him. He reared back to study her closer. Was she the girl in his favorite photo? There were differences, but she was close…oh so close. He wanted to pull it out of his pocket and compare it to her but didn't dare. He turned to stare at his brother, wanting to question him on the spot. But it wasn't the time. And left him wondering…was it her?

She looked ready to cry, and a woman's tears broke him every time. "Please. Let's go to our place. We can explain the facts and come up with a plan of how to fix it."

His words appeared to make all the stuffing and ire drain from her body. Her shoulders sank and she buried her face in the animal's fur. He reached out gently and nudged her forward. She moved as he directed. Home was right around the corner. Thankfully, it was in the same block as his office with aboveground and underground access between the two. He liked to live close to his place of business.

He walked her forward a few more steps. "Please. Let me just get you in a place where we can talk privately."

At his wording, her compliance stalled and so did her footsteps.

He wanted to pick her up and carry her, but that damn pet of hers glared at him. He'd claw Levi's eyes out if he gave him a chance. With another firm push, he added, "Come on, you're safe with me."

And then they were there. Milo entered first, the girl followed. Levi brought up the rear and re-engaged the alarms, locking them in.

"Privacy on."

The buzzes and clicks told him that the security system had scanned the space and found it clean.

Feeling a tad better, he strode forward and poured himself a large shot of whiskey. And downed it.

"Jesus, Milo. What are we going to do?"

Milo had collapsed onto the couch. The air couch lifted and fell as he settled into his preferred space somewhere in between. The girl stood immobile in the center of the room. Ash blonde hair, fine boned, but she moved well. Maybe she was a dancer? There'd been ire in her voice and fire spit from her eyes. So there was spirit in there. In spite of the circumstances, Levi admitted he was intrigued.

"Welcome to our home," he said gently. "Now, I introduced the two of us. Please, won't you tell us – what's your name?"

She spun slowly. "You brought me into your world and you don't even know who I am?" The shocked horror in her voice hit him hard. Then he saw the hurt in her eyes. Contrarily, he wanted to enfold her in his arms and hold her close. To tell her that it was all okay. To let her know he wouldn't desert her. That it would work out fine.

But he'd never been a liar before and he wasn't about to start now.

"I didn't choose you. Milo did." He motioned to his wacky brother, floating suspended in the middle of the room, his Mohawk hanging over the edge of the deep purple airbed. His eyes were closed as if he'd dropped off to sleep.

"Milo did? And what the hell is he lying on? Whatever it is, I want one, too." Her body swayed in protest to being vertical. "It wasn't purple and it wasn't floating when we walked in."

"No, it wasn't." He sighed. Life had changed a lot since her era. "That's only a few of the things you're going to have to get used to now."

She shook her head and said in a forlorn voice, "That's just it. I don't think I can."

Chapter 5

"Never mind. Let's just shelve this for the moment." Dani tried to straighten up, but her legs had taken on a rubbery sensation and refused to hold her properly. "I don't know if this is a delayed reaction, different oxygen in the air, or..." and her brain shut down. "I don't know," she whispered. "I don't feel so good."

The room swayed and circled around her.

"Easy." Levi grabbed her and led her toward the side of the room. "You can stay in here. You need rest. I don't think travelling through time was easy on your system."

"You think?" She laughed brokenly, but even her voice sounded odd. "Did your genius brother consider the damage to my DNA? That the reconstituted cells of my body didn't pull together the same way that it was taken apart?"

"There wasn't supposed to be anything like that happening." He motioned to the doorway on the side. "The bedroom is through there. And chances are your body is fine. It just needs time to adjust."

She didn't have the energy to argue. And with every step, her body was getting heavier. The effort of lifting one foot after another almost beyond her. Before she understood what was happening, Levi was dragging her to a long white surface. She desperately wanted a bed to sleep in, but being horizontal on any surface would do. The sleep would follow regardless.

"I think I need a doctor," she whispered.

"We don't have doctors anymore," Levi said. "At least not like you mean."

"Great. In the future, there are no doctors. Now really make my day and tell me there are no lawyers, too." After all, Lawrence had been a lawyer. Suddenly they'd reached the white object, and damn if he didn't push her on top of it.

"A hero you're not."

She felt more than saw his surprised look, then her own shock took over as the white surface softened and stretched, supporting the contours of her body like she'd never felt before. "What is this thing?" she whispered.

"A bed."

How that could be she didn't know, and she no longer cared as her eyes drifted closed and she let go.

Into a deep sleep.

***

Levi stared down at the impossible woman, proof of this impossible situation, brought on by his impossible brother. Dani didn't look well. But he didn't have an exclusive medical unit here. If he had, she'd be lying in it right now. There was one in the building. His friend Johan Strand owned it. If he was away, Levi would have taken her there instead of here. But Johan was home and he'd be entertaining – like he always did.

Walking to the door, he cast a last look at the sleeping beauty. Compared to today's enhanced and cosmetically perfect women, she had character. She wasn't stunning. But she was pretty. Huge eyes that showed every emotion, a nose that turned up at the end ever so slightly, and a mobile mouth that caught his attention and held it whenever he was with her.

What was he going to do with her? "Damn it, Milo. What are we going to do?"

No answer. He walked over to find his brother either deep in contemplation or…asleep.

"Milo?"

No answer. He walked closer to find that his brother had his headset strapped to his head with his virtual reality goggles on. Damn. He was in the zone. Now was it the game zone or the creative zone? Except with Milo, there was often no difference. Only this was no time to duck out. He reached across his brother's body and pulled the goggles off.

"Hey." Milo tried to reach up and snag them away from Levi.

But Levi held them out of reach. On a hunch, he put them against his eyes and gazed through them. Two young lithe females cavorted in front of him with come on gestures, enticing him to join them.

"Hell, Milo." He tossed the VR set down on his brother's chest. "This is hardly the time for a sex romp."

"Hey. It's always time, bro." Milo went to put them back on his face when Levi grabbed them again and tossed them across the room.

"Damn. Get serious." Levi planted his hands on his hips and glared at his brother. "We have a problem here. A big one. You know she's sick, right. Like she could be dead by morning."

"Nah. She's fine." Milo stood up and stretched and sidled over to where his goggles were. "I'm going to head to bed now."

"Touch the goggles and I'll lose them permanently the next time you are out of the room."

Milo froze. "Hey, that's not fair. I do some of my best thinking when I'm sex…in a playful mood."

With a snort, Levi shook his head. "Like hell. You say you do your best thinking as an excuse to do whatever the hell you want." He reached his brother in seconds, grabbed him by the shoulder, and gave him a shake. "Stop kidding around. We have to solve this problem."

Milo cringed and stepped back out of his brother's reach. "We don't have a problem. I brought her here for you. Therefore, *you* have a problem." With that, Milo snagged his goggles and walked out of the room.

For him? Levi stared after him in shock. And once again brought up the question of Dani's identity in relationship to the photo.

But his brother was gone. Walking away from something he didn't like. Didn't want to deal with. Dumping the problem on someone else's shoulders. In this case – his.

Being sixteen forever was getting old. At least for those that had to live with Milo.

Levi tilted his head back and closed his eyes, waiting for the anger to drain and some reasonable next step to rise up from the depths of his own impressive brain.

Bottom line, she was hurting. And he was indirectly responsible. How could he help her? There really was only one way. She needed a medical pod. And fast.

That meant Johan. His long time friend walked a fine line between legal and illegal business activities. So far he was doing well with it. They both had a hatred for the Council and the multitude of government regulations that were being stuffed down their throats.

He glanced at the time. Maybe, just maybe, Johan hadn't started partying yet.

It was worth a try. In person or by com? Com would be faster.

He punched in Johan's name. And closed his eyes briefly when Johan's face filled the screen. "Hey. Glad I caught you."

"What's up, Levi?" Johan's bright inquisitive grin popped out. "Looking to hook up tonight? I've got some prime flesh coming by soon."

"No. No. I've got some of my own here, but she's sick. I was hoping to use your unit." He waited a moment, and then in a quiet voice, added, "Please."

"Sure. No problem." Johan nodded agreeably. "You know the code. Go for it. With any luck, I won't need it tonight."

Levi wiped a shaky hand across his forehead. "Thanks, Johan. I won't forget this."

"No big. If she doesn't pick up and you're still looking for some action, there will be plenty here all night long."

"As usual." In an effort to appease his friend, he added, "We'll see. I might pop by later on."

"Pod is empty now so go for it." Johan's face blinked out.

As he closed his com, Levi wondered about the sensibility of waiting until later. But how would he get her up there when she was out cold? Levi walked back over to where Dani slept. He frowned at the critter guarding her. How could he get her up to the healing pod without that?

Then the critter dropped its head on Dani's chest like the weight of his head was too heavy to hold. And he realized that the critter had endured just as harsh a trip as Dani. It probably needed the healing pod, too.

That could really be tricky. He could use the elevator to get them all up there and the healing pod had a room all to itself, but would the critter cooperate? Would Dani stay asleep for this?

It would be best if she did.

He really was out of options. And out of time. He opened a cupboard and pulled out a wrap. With some difficulty, he managed to wrap the two newcomers up. He lifted them both into his arms, more disturbed than he realized when neither moved. Maybe they were badly injured internally. His gut twisted. He should've done this earlier.

He raced outside his apartment. "Stealth mode on." The elevator swooped down, encompassing them all. "Johan's healing pod."

The cube took off silently.

They'd made it this far. He hoped the rest would be so easy. The elevator delivered him outside Johan's pod room. He stepped in, relieved to find the room empty and the pod open. He laid his lightweight burden down gently, realizing as he did so how delicate her frame was. Even the critter was light for all that he looked big and bulky. He carried so much fur and the face appeared to have been flattened in the birthing process, but as far as actual poundage went, it had nothing.

And maybe muscle and bone density loss was a side effect of the time travel. He didn't know if the pod could heal that. It was a little out of the generic pod's scope.

He walked over to the door, closing and locking it behind him. Then he turned his attention to the two comatose patients on the table. He closed the lid on them, blanket and all, and walked to the diagnostic table. "Start scanning," he instructed the computer.

The machine made a weird beeping sound, then said, "The blanket and outer clothing of the patients must be removed."

"Scan patients in the condition they are in," he said.

"We cannot," chimed the robotic voice. "Something is stopping the scan from initializing. Please remove the blankets and outer clothing."

"Damn." He returned to the pod, opened the lid and with difficulty, he managed to tug the blanket free. Dani was wearing pants of some stretchy material and a short sleeve shirt. He didn't want to remove it if he didn't have to. "Start scan."

The beeps picked up and a blue laser light started at Dani's head and swept down to her feet. He breathed a sigh of relief. Good, it worked with her dressed. "Scan results?"

"Patients are experiencing extreme reaction to the atmosphere. Muscle weakness, rapid heart rate, and irregular breathing indicate reaction to high stress."

"Tell me something I don't know," he muttered. "Is she going to be all right?"

"Patient is exhausted. We are giving her high doses of vitamins and lowering her vital signs. Sleep is paramount. Her body has undergone a great shock. We are adding her condition to our database."

"No," he snapped. "Cancel that. Do not add her condition to the database."

"It is protocol," stated the computer. "This is a condition we have not encountered. It must be added."

"Shit. Shit. No!" he said urgently. "Do not add at this time. Should the patient not recover quickly, then it can be added. Everyone reacts to stress differently. This is hers."

"This is most unusual."

"Yeah, that's me." Levi walked over to Dani. "What about the critter? What is its condition?"

"He appears to be suffering the same muscle weakness as the woman. Also the same increased heart rate." The computer stopped, then added. "Interesting."

"Do not add this to the database," he snapped.

The robotic voice spoke again. "We must. It is protocol."

Frustration rolled through him. "And yet like the woman, the critter will likely be fine."

"If that is true, why did you bring them here?"

And what was he doing, arguing with a healing pod? Computers had taken over his world. They now argued and chastised and nagged like an old wife.

"I wanted to make sure that there was no internal damage," he muttered.

"We did not scan for that."

He stopped and turned to look at the console. "Why not?"

"You did not remove her clothing. We could not go through all the material."

"That's crap. Of course you can."

"We do not know this particular blend of materials. We must add it to the databank."

He was going to pull his hair out. "Do *not* add it to your databank."

"We must. It is—"

"Protocol, yeah, I know." He walked over to the pod. "If you are done with the booster shot, I'll take off her shirt and pants then you can do a deeper scan."

"Acknowledged."

At least that wasn't breaking protocol. He opened the pod and tugged her boots off her feet. Then opened the closures on her pants and tugged them off. He swallowed at the sight of the purple underclothes. Yeah, lingerie hadn't changed much in the last couple of centuries. It was as sexy back then as it was now. Walking to the side of the pod, he opened up the buttons that held Dani's shirt closed and spread the material apart. He could feel his own heart rate race at the sight of her firm breasts rising from the matching purple bra. Crap, he felt like a pervert.

But she was something.

"Can you do a complete scan with her like this?" He rearranged the critter down the long lean length of her, its head resting against her ribs. If she woke to find the critter dying or missing, then there would likely be hell to pay.

"We can."

"Good. Then please complete the full diagnostics."

The pod lid closed and the blue laser light swept slowly down the length of the bed. Then it reversed all the way back up.

"Scan complete," said the computer.

"And the scan results?" Levi asked.

"The patient has no severe internal damage. There have been some recent adaptations to her physical body that we have not seen before."

There was a hum. "We have added that information to our database."

"No," he shouted. "Damn it, don't do that."

"It is protocol."

He dropped his forehead against the glass top of the pod, wanting to smash his fist against the smooth unyielding surface. "And what of the critter?"

"The same odd changes have also recently been done to its body. We have added this information to the database."

He didn't bother arguing. He'd try to wipe the memory after he was done. "What kind of changes have been made?"

"We do not have a scan from before these changes in order to be able to say." The robot was not being helpful.

"Right. Then how do you know changes have been made?"

"There are signs of new tissue," continued the computer. "Signs of healed muscle and skin. The DNA has been altered."

He swallowed on that last bit. Milo had said that wouldn't happen. Then he'd probably worded it in such a way to avoid an outright lie and still not tell the truth. "Are these changes dangerous?"

"Not that we can see at this time." There was a series of monotone clicks as if the console was shutting down.

"So is she healthy?" Levi asked urgently before it turned off. "Good to leave."

The clicks paused. "She is exhausted. She must rest for 24 hours minimum." The robotic voice stopped as if considering its next words, before adding, "Maybe longer."

He didn't want to consider how this console's actions imitated human thinking. "And can you help her do that?"

"It is done."

With a sigh of relief, Levi opened the pod, gathered up her clothing, and wrapped both Dani and the critter in the blanket, along with her clothes. And stepped out into the hallway.

Just as she woke up.

Chapter 6

Dani let her eyes drift open. Heavy and unwieldy, they didn't want to obey her orders. But the juggling woke her up. The sensation of being carried. Only to find she was tucked up against a man's chest, carried like a precious child.

She'd been sleeping so sound, then nightmares had kicked in and she'd surfaced feeling like she'd been through the worst night of her life.

As the memories drifted in, she wondered if she had.

Except for the male carrying her. Levi. His name drifted through her consciousness. He smelled so wonderful. And the strength, the ease with which he carried her…he wasn't even breathing hard.

His heartbeat pounded under her ear. Slow, steady, and strong.

She sighed happily. She didn't know who he was or where she was, but this part was good.

Until the pain penetrated her consciousness. Everything ached. Had this person hurt her? Was she in danger? It didn't feel like it. But then…

Her body was jostled again…and that set parts of her to hurting in the worst way. Bones ached. Joints throbbed. Muscles burned. She tried to shift away from the pain. She moaned.

"Easy, Dani." Lowering his head slightly, Levi whispered, "Take it easy, we're almost back. Just lie still."

"Where," she murmured. "Back where?"

"Back to bed. I took you to the healing pod. It should have helped."

"I hurt. Everywhere." She shifted her legs restlessly. She wanted it to stop. "Put me down." Then her voice broke at the pain. "Please."

"Shh. It's all right. You're going to be fine. We're almost home."

Home sounded good. She felt the urgency in his movements as he moved faster. Then the air changed, calmed. Levi slowed down.

In the background, she heard him call out, "Stealth on."

She was taken into a darker room. She could hardly open her eyes, but it was slightly easier here. Her body was shifted and laid down on a hard surface. She cried out as pain radiated into the corners of her body. "Oh, it's hard. It hurts."

The surface softened, cradled her, eased her pain. She sighed in relief.

"It's okay now," he said. "You're back in bed. Just rest."

She tried to shift, her arms struggling with the blanket, until something big and furry was placed in her arms. She whispered happily, "Charmin."

There was no answer, but she knew it was him and his soft gentle breathing reassured her that he was well. Now if only her body would stop screaming at her. She rolled over, felt something tugged up and placed over her shoulders, and soft, gentle music filled the room.

"Sleep. You'll feel better in the morning."

That made sense. She let herself drift away.

Until a few hours later, when she woke up. Pain radiated throughout her body. She'd never done much jogging but her body felt like she'd done a full marathon. And it complained bitterly. She stumbled to a doorway that led to the bathroom, tears running down her cheeks. By the time she was back in bed, she could barely move. With every step, her muscles had seized up a little more. Charmin lay in the bed motionless, his huge eyes wells of pain.

"I know how you feel, buddy." She stopped and considered what she was doing. "I had to use the bathroom, what about you?"

He had to go sometime. If he hadn't already. She didn't want to check the corners of the room too closely. "What could I do about a litter box for you, Charmin?"

She looked around but there was nothing resembling a decent container that would work. She thought about the bathroom. "Charmin, can you use the toilet?"

He shuddered and gave her a horrified look. "There's water in the toilets."

She winced. Actually she wasn't sure there *was* water in the bowl. She'd noticed a blue jelly substance she'd refused to check out any closer. "I know. But there is no sand or litter here. I don't know what to do for you."

Charmin stood up and jumped off the bed. He landed then fell to his knees. She cried out and reached over to pick him up. "Our muscles don't work right here."

"Yeah, I got that," he grumbled. "How about that litter box thing?"

"How about a water one?" she asked hopefully.

The horrified look in his eyes made her laugh.

"I have to go," he growled. "Let's take a look at it."

She carried him into the bathroom. It had taken her a bit of time to figure out the system. She had no idea how to help him understand. There was a seat that seemed to adapt to the size of the butt sitting down. Kind of like the couch and the bed. She opened the seat so he could see, then perched him on the top.

"This is what there is. You go pee in the hole."

He stared at her.

She gave him a winning smile, and said with bright encouragement, "You can do this."

"So not."

"I'll just leave you so you can have some privacy."

And she escaped.

Oh Lord. What was she doing here? They both wanted to go home. They didn't belong here. They couldn't even move properly. How the heck were they supposed to survive? They had no papers, no identification numbers, no family or friends. No job and worse yet – no money. If such a thing still existed. And then there were the two idiots who'd brought her here. They weren't to be trusted.

On the heels of that thought, she remembered the strength of those arms, the soothing tone in Levi's voice as he told her to rest. He'd been gentle. Caring. That was very sexy. A man who looked after you when you were hurt and hurting was something special.

If only he hadn't been part of the plot to bring her here.

He said he'd had nothing to do with it, but…

And speaking of which, she planned to nail Milo tomorrow and find out how and why she'd been chosen.

She had no great skills. She was no beauty. She had left no legacy – at least at the time of her kidnapping. And that was on top of the dismal list Milo had read off earlier. How had they even known who she was to swoop down and scoop her up?

A weird scratching sound came from the direction of the bathroom, followed by a heavy thud, which hinted that Charmin was done with his business. As he strolled out, heavy limbed, his head dipped lower with every step. She winced. "See, it wasn't so bad."

"It so was," he said darkly. "What kind of place is this that they don't have a decent dry litter box?" He walked over to her and twined around her legs. "Do you realize how long it's been since we ate?" He plunked his furry butt down on the weird tiled floor and stared up at her. "Do you think they know what food is? If they haven't heard about litter boxes…"

How typical. His stomach was always a priority. "I'm sure they know what food is. Chances are good we might even recognize some of it."

He shot her a horrified look, jumped up on the bed, and proceeded to turn around in circles before collapsing. "I'm going back to sleep. Maybe when I wake up the next time, this nightmare will be over."

"That's actually a good idea."

All she could hear was his heavy breathing. She scrambled up beside him and curled herself around his pudgy body. She really wanted her life back. To be back in her tiny apartment getting ready for her date.

How could they take that away from her?

And she fell asleep.

***

Levi groaned and rolled over yet again. His mind wouldn't shut off. He had no idea how to stop the mess from changing life as he knew it. His brother had done the unthinkable. At the same time, it was a major scientific achievement – and no one could ever know.

And what was he supposed to do with Dani? This charming young woman hadn't asked for her life to be destroyed on Milo's whim. He didn't even know how she'd been chosen. She wasn't Milo's usual choice when it came to women. There were no visible piercings and her hair was all the same color.

Then again, Milo had mentioned he'd picked Dani for Levi. That brought the old photo to mind again. Was he so pathetic that his kid brother felt he needed to get Levi a girlfriend? Sure, Levi was going through a dry spell, but that was by choice. He didn't like Johan's party scene. It had been fun once or twice, but he preferred to be with a woman because he liked her, not because she had the requisite body parts. And – he twisted his lips in a dour smile – he was a romantic. Old fashioned. He wanted to love and be loved. Was that so impossible?

He rolled over again. How could he stop the world from finding out about Milo's accomplishment? He also had to stop Milo from repeating his actions. And he needed to find a way to send Dani home. Although he wouldn't mind if she stayed for a bit – if she wanted to.

Was it wrong of him to want her to stay? Instantly he crushed that thought. She wasn't meant to stay here. He didn't dare get attached to her. She wasn't a pet. He couldn't just keep her.

But a part of him was considering it.

Just as morning light drifted into his room and he thought he might finally be able to go to sleep, there was a pounding on his front door. Groaning, he pulled on a shirt and pants. When the noise came a second time, he stumbled to the door, calling out, "Hang on. I'm coming. "

He pulled open the door, his hand hiding a yawn. And froze.

Two suits were standing there with Johan sandwiched between them. He glanced over at Johan, a question in his eyes, but asked in a genial voice, "What's up, gentlemen?"

One man said, "You're wanted for questioning at the Council." The tone was stiff, uncompromising. Just like the look on the first man's face. Levi glanced at the second man's stone face. Council henchmen. Great. He was in trouble again. He cast his mind back to see where he messed up. And how to recover...

Levi frowned at his friend. "Johan, what's going on?"

Johan shrugged but wore his customary careless grin. "Damned if I know. I'm being hauled in, too."

Not good. Levi straightened, looked at the first man, and said, "Do I need my lawyers, gentlemen?"

"If you feel you need one, you may certainly call in representation as is your right. However, at this moment, while we are requesting your presence at the Council, it is not an order."

The unspoken "yet" hung in the air.

"Right. Give me a moment. I'll get dressed and meet you there."

The first suit, who'd yet to speak, said, "No. We will wait and escort you there."

So this was serious. Levi nodded and returned to his bedroom. He swallowed a booster, hoping to make up for his lousy night. He walked to his wardrobe where he pulled out a suit and dressed carefully. Milo did creative. Levi did power and intimidation.

After a quick glance around, he pocketed his comp and walked out.

Johan at his side, the four men travelled to the Council building and were escorted into the inner office immediately.

No waiting. No coffee offered. Immediate reception.

This was *very* serious.

They were led forward to face four Councilmen all seated on a raised podium, watching as Levi's group approached.

Levi recognized all four of them. His stomach sank. He didn't exactly have a good relationship with the Council after Milo broke protocol over a year ago. Except for one member, Stephen Cavendish, a junior member who was also an old friend. As a junior member, his presence on the Council was sporadic.

There wasn't a sound for a long moment as the Councilmen assessed him and Johan. One of the two Councilmen in the middle finally spoke up. "Johan and Levi, thank you both for coming. We understand that there was a disturbance on the health pod registered to you, Johan."

Ah shit.

So much for his orders to that damn computer. It hadn't wiped the data and had instead submitted it as per protocol, and that had raised flags. He'd expected the power outage to have done that. Although there'd been several of those lately, unrelated to Milo's work. He frowned. Or were they? Had Milo tested his program out earlier?

Johan raised his hands, palms outward. "Anything is possible. It experienced heavy use last night as several of my guests took advantage of my personal unit. In fact, there were likely a dozen or so that could have used my pod. I had a big party and many people, not having their own pod, come specifically for that purpose. I don't mind. I never have."

"You will have no problem supplying us a list of your guests then?" The speaker asked, who Levi thought was called Carlson, peering over his glasses at him.

Levi wondered at the glasses. No one used them for vision anymore. Chances were good the speaker was running all kinds of scans on Johan right now. From financials to health statistics. The speaker settled back with a frown, removing the glasses.

That was interesting. Levi turned slightly to study the man at his side. Did Johan have a way to block the scan?

"As many as I can, but I have an open door policy with regards to guests." Johan gave them a fat grin. "The more the merrier." He held his hands up in appeal. "What is this about?"

"Data from the pod proposed a few questions last night. We are obligated to check it out further."

Johan's eyebrows shot up. "Interesting." He glanced over at Levi and shrugged.

"And I'm here why?" Levi asked coolly.

"We have information that you asked to use the pod last night."

Not good. Levi tilted his head slightly. "That is correct. And what regulation did you violate to find that information?"

Johan snorted. "That's a damn good question. Are you recording my calls?" he asked in outrage. He pulled out his comp and jotted down notes. "That is something I will be looking into."

"In the case of issues of national security, we are within our rights to record calls."

"National security?" Levi spluttered. Inside, his nerves jangled. "What are you talking about?" He pulled out his comp and sent a nudge to his own lawyer, John Driscoll. With any luck, he could keep this tied up long enough to solve the problem. He also checked to make sure his comp was recording the session.

"We don't have enough information to complete a full analysis of the problem. The data stream from the pod was corrupted. There was also a massive power outage that we must investigate."

"Ha, corrupt data is the norm half the time. And lately there have been more power outages than not. You know that." Johan laughed. "Any one of my many guests could have broken it." He shook his head. "You will also be able to check that I have it repaired on a regular basis."

"We will follow up on the list you supply. If you have no further information to offer, you are dismissed."

And that tone of voice had Levi's back going up. He glared at the four men staring down at him, identical looks on their faces. But this was not the time or place to start an all out war. He'd warred with these men before. Milo often got into trouble.

And Levi always worked to get him out of it.

He wasn't sure that was possible this time.

Johan tugged his arm. "Come on, buddy. It's time to get a coffee. Let these guys worry about national security." He laughed. "Coffee is on me."

Levi let his friend tug him outside. They went through the austere building in complete silence but once outside, Johan lost it. "They were monitoring our freaking phone calls? They are not going to get away with that."

"Sorry if I got you into this."

"Ha, it probably wasn't even you. Dozens of people were in that thing last night." Johan shook his head. "Besides, I'm glad you did. I need those bloodsucking lawyers to earn their retainers. I've been paying them for years and they do nothing. This..." he held up his comp, "is not allowed."

He glared at Levi. "Do you know how many laws they've broken? Do you have any idea how many secrets of mine they might have uncovered?"

Levi was surprised at the sheer level of fury in his friend's voice. Maybe he had a reason. Maybe he was hiding something. Levi didn't care. He was hiding something himself.

Light rain drizzled down on the two men. Levi looked up, surprised to see a storm gathering above the buildings.

Flash storms were unusual here when the weather was computer controlled.

Johan motioned to the sky. "It's been going on since late yesterday." His face twisted as he studied it. "Wonder what the hell is going on."

Levi's stomach knotted. Please let it have nothing to do with Milo's damn experiment. *Please.* "No idea," he said lightly.

Johan motioned across the street where the coffee shop was. "I know I mentioned coffee but if you don't mind, I'll take a rain check."

"Not a problem. I've got to get to work as it is."

Johan slapped him on the shoulder. "It's been a weird morning already. Let's hope it improves." And he walked away. His long legs ate up the distance. Johan had a specific goal and temper was still riding his emotions.

Levi hoped he was going to his lawyer to raise a little hell. Levi planned to do just that himself.

After he checked up on Milo and Dani.

Chapter 7

Dani woke up slowly, her eyes drifting open then sliding closed again. Only to come awake to wild green hair framing a looming face. She screamed and bolted upward. Tripping over the wrappings, she fell sideways onto the soft mattress. Expecting to fall and still trying to get away, she crab-walked backwards to escape on a bed that seemed to grow in the direction she moved. *Criminy*.

"Calm down. I was just looking to see if you were awake." Milo danced back as Dani retreated a little more. "Hey, I'm not here to hurt you."

Dani took a deep breath and tried to shake off the panic of waking up to a strange face looming over her. "Why couldn't you just call out to me?"

"I did." He held his hands up in front of him. "Sorry. I should have called out louder."

She shuddered and slowly sat up. "Yeah, okay. I'm awake." She pushed her long hair out of her eyes. "Now why did you wake me up?"

"I didn't want to." He stepped back. "I was just taking a look."

She stared. "At me? While I was sleeping?" She glanced down and gasped. She only had her underclothes on. And the fallen blanket had left much of her exposed. She snatched the blanket and clutched it to her chest before glaring at Milo.

"No. No. I wasn't looking. Honest." He shook his head, a blush climbing up his neck and face. "Levi called. Wanted to know if you were up. So I came to look. That's it."

"Well, I am now." She stared at the weird bed. And caught sight of Charmin curled into a still fur ball. "Charmin," she cried and scrambled over to him. Gently, she stroked his still form and almost bawled when she realized that he was breathing. "I was so scared that you'd died during the night," she said to him.

"He shouldn't die," Milo interrupted their cuddle to add, "His DNA may have changed a bit, but he will live a long life."

Dani shot him a disgusted look. "You have no idea how he's changed."

"And he won't ever know if you don't tell him," Charmin muttered in a strangled yowl. He opened his eyes and glared at her. "I could use some more sleep."

He stretched out his front leg and yawned, then tucked up into a tight ball and went back to sleep.

Still smiling, she turned to stare up at Milo. Only his gaze was whipping from the cat to her and back to the cat. *Oh shit. He'd heard.*

"You can hear the cat talk," he whispered in awe. "And like wow. It talks back."

"Right. Charmin is special." That he'd heard Charmin wasn't perfect timing, but it's not like there was a good time. And he'd have found out sometime. She snorted and shoved the bedding back to free up her legs. "Now if you don't mind, I have to go to the bathroom."

Flushing wildly, Milo backed up. "Sure. No problem." He gave one last fascinated stare at Charmin and bolted toward the door. At the doorway, he paused. "Do you need anything?"

"You mean like all my clothes from home? The shampoo and soap I love so I could enjoy a shower? Oh, and how about some food for me and Charmin. And if you guys know what coffee is…"

Milo's eyes lit up. "I can do the coffee part. We have awesome coffee here."

"Well, that's good. At least you have something decent," she muttered as she pulled herself to the edge of the bed. Her legs were slow and shaky, but at least they held when she tried to stand up. Only the bathroom looked damn far away.

When she was done, she all but collapsed on the bed.

She'd barely covered up again when Milo returned carrying a tray with both hands. She eyed him suspiciously. Was he trying to make her feel better or was this normal behavior in his time? If so, there were obviously a few good things about living here. Still, she figured he was working that whole 'keep her happy theme' so she didn't explode on him. She could work with that.

"Here is coffee and a snack. Levi is on his way home. We'll eat then."

She stared at the pretty setting and tiny cup on her tray. If she didn't know better, she'd have thought she was in Europe having a cup of espresso. She picked it up and took an experimental sniff. It smelled like coffee.

"It's safe," Milo said. He started to bounce from side to side. "Go ahead, try it."

She eyed him over the rim of her tiny cup. Why was he so excited? She eyed the rich liquid suspiciously. Then took a tiny sip. And sighed. Oh joy. They actually had *real* coffee. She almost melted with her second sip and by the time she'd reached the bottom of the miniscule cup, she was looking for more.

Milo disappeared and returned immediately with a small silver pot. He refilled her cup and took a step back. She glared at him. Then at the pot. And back at him.

He swallowed. "Sure. I'll just leave the pot here. You can have as much as you want."

"Thank you, that's very generous of you," she murmured, keeping a close eye on him. "And you're right, it is good coffee."

He beamed. "Thank you.

"Did you make it?"

Confusion made the smile go away. "Umm, I guess."

Okay, smaller steps. "Did you grind the beans and pour water into a pot, measure the coffee, and start it dripping?" At least that's how coffee used to be made at her apartment and at most of her jobs.

He shook his head so fast the bright green Mohawk waved in the wind like a hand. "No. No. I just pushed a button."

Interesting. Then again, it was to be expected that everything here would be computerized, technological advancement being what it was. She should probably be grateful she hadn't been dragged into the Flintstones era.

Coffee like this with a push of a button definitely had something going for it.

"Hello? Dani?" Levi called out. "Are you here?"

Really, where else would she be? That was one huge world out there and she had no money and no ID. It would take a braver person than her to venture out there alone.

Milo bubbled out with, "We're in her bedroom."

Yeah, like she always entertained men in her bedroom.

Just then, Charmin sat up and stretched out a paw. She watched as he hooked the treat Milo had added to her tray. It appeared to be a sweet bun of some kind, but she'd yet to try it. She wasn't sure her stomach could handle anything solid right now. But she wanted to. Her last meal had been a long time ago.

Levi filled the doorway.

"Isn't this awfully cozy looking," he said coolly, his clear blue eyes taking in everything, assessing it all.

She lifted her chin. "Milo offered me coffee and I took him up on it."

"Levi, what happened this morning?" Milo asked worriedly. "I heard the door and just like that, you were gone."

Dani studied Levi's face. He looked everywhere but at her.

"It was about me – wasn't it?" And she knew. Somehow, someone had found out. "What did you tell them?"

He looked straight at her, then walked forward several steps. "Nothing."

Milo stepped between the two of them. His gaze darted from one to the other. He asked his brother. "What did you say?"

"Nothing." He ran his hand through his dark curls. "They asked a few questions and I answered. They didn't ask about you specifically so I didn't have to lie."

Milo bounced forward. "What did they ask about?"

Looking very uncomfortable, Levi said, "They asked about the pod."

"What pod?" Milo stepped forward to look into his brother's face, "Levi, what pod?"

"Johan's healing pod. I took Dani up there last night. She was hurting. I figured if she had sustained internal damage due to the time travel, the pod could heal her."

"Oh no. Oh no." Milo danced backwards in horror. "No, you didn't. Please say you didn't."

"Considering you refuse to have a pod of our own, I didn't have much choice. Also considering you dragged her through a wormhole and dumped her here, her body is suffering. Did you even consider the impact on her physical body?"

Dani watched the brothers. Levi the older and more responsible. Milo, the younger incorrigible genius with little sense of reality. He'd been protected so much that he wasn't held accountable for all his actions. Like what he'd done to her.

And Levi was doing his best. She spoke up. "I'm sorry for the trouble taking me to this pod, but thank you for thinking of me and my health."

Both brothers turned to stare at her. She gave a little finger wave. "Yeah, I'm here too, remember?"

"So if we'd had a pod," Milo said slowly. "This wouldn't ever have happened."

Levi snorted. "No, if you'd listened to me in the first place, this wouldn't have happened."

Milo's face twisted in thought. Moodily, Levi kicked the door. "Besides, there is a pod being delivered today."

"No, no. I hate them." Milo backed up, shaking his hands wildly in front of him. "They are dangerous. We can't have one."

"Well, too bad," Levi snapped. "You should have thought of that before you hurt Dani."

Milo spun around to look at Dani. "I didn't hurt her."

"Yes, you did. And she's still suffering. For all we know, she could have long-term health issues. She needs our help now."

"But a pod is going to be connected to them…" Milo hissed.

"No." Levi smiled. "This one is unregistered."

Milo gasped, hot color flooding his face. "But that's…illegal!"

It was Levi's turn to stare at his brother. "A little too late to worry about that now," he said.

Dani laughed at Levi's glare. "You two are obviously brothers."

Both turned to glare at her.

She shrugged and took another sip of coffee. "So when is this healing pod arriving, because you're right, I could sure use it. Not to mention some food."

"You just had a snack and coffee." Milo protested.

"How about real food now?" Dani stared down at the crumbs Charmin had left her and sighed. "Like eggs, bacon, some hash browns?" At Milo's disgusted look, she smiled hopefully and added, "Even toast sounds wonderful."

"We don't eat garbage like that anymore. We care about our bodies here. We drink synthetic and highly nutritious shakes now. "

"Only shakes?" she asked in horror. "What about real food? Like fruit, veggies, fried chicken, cheesecake…and other essential foods."

Milo shuddered in revulsion. "I'm a vegetarian. As we all should be."

"See, that's just not going to work for me." She sat up in bed. Charmin rolled over and stretched his paws. "I like food. Real food."

"And we have food," Levi said. "Real food. My brother has been this way since infancy. I, however, still eat real food."

She brightened. "Awesome. Any chance of some…" her stomach took that moment to grumble and growl very loudly. She smiled hopefully. "And soon?"

Levi stared at her. His eyebrows shot up and a big smile overtook his face. He said, "I can do that. I'll be a few minutes." He turned and left. The room seemed lonely, empty.

"Oh, that's great." Milo grinned. "He loves cooking, now he has you to look after food-wise, too."

Dani stared at him then broke out laughing. "You mean you guys are so advanced but you still have to cook?" For some reason, that struck her as funny. She laughed and laughed. "If I were home, I'd have picked up the phone and just ordered in."

"We have take-out, too." Milo bounded closer. "High-end food."

"Yeah, sure," she scoffed, smoothing the pleats in her bedding. "Like the rest of your supposed advanced lifestyle."

"We do! Healing pods. Awesome elevators." He motioned to the tray with the coffee. "The best coffee ever."

"I'll give you that on the coffee, but your lifestyle seriously sucks. Look at this tiny-ass apartment, the monster cities…"

"Ha! Look what I did with you." Milo did a fast two step. "See, gotcha there."

Immediately the air cooled and her smile fell away. She dropped her gaze. "Yeah, that's a big gotcha."

"Uhmmm, yeah, I'll go make more coffee." He scooted backwards out of the bedroom. Escaping…

She let him go.

If Dani could get up and walk into the kitchen, she would help cook, but any movement seemed to steal all her energy. She sank back against the pillows. She felt like a fat slug whose body had grown so big, so heavy it couldn't carry its own weight. Considering the look on Charmin's face, she had to wonder if he didn't feel the same. She bent to scratch the back of his head. He rolled over slightly and stared at her, but the look in his eyes made her shift and tug him, blankets and all, into her arms.

His head fell back.

"Don't feel so good, do you? Do we?" she corrected. She nuzzled his neck, reassured when his engine kicked in and his heavy purr filled the room. "At least that much of you is working."

"Yes, but I'm tired." He closed his eyes and laid his head back down.

"Me too." She wondered what the pod had done for her last night when she still felt so rough today. Then again, maybe she wouldn't have woken up today without it. Apparently they had an unregistered pod being delivered today. What kind of a government system had pods register the medical knowledge and defects of its contents without the people knowing? There was such a thing as too much government intervention.

And would having an unregistered unit get them into more trouble?

Then again, if they were found with a non-registered person…she couldn't imagine having to explain her presence. Hell, she had no answers, she'd have to tell the truth of what she did know. And likely end up in a psych ward.

Who'd believe her?

Who could?

At least they could have brought her clothes with her. Then again, as she stared down at Charmin, they *had* brought the most important part of her life. Presumably because she'd been holding onto him at the time. And, as she thought about it, when she was whooshed away from her apartment, she'd been wishing he could talk. Coincidence?

What had happened to her old life? Had anyone reported her missing? Did she just disappear forever? Was she a missing person in the history books? Or did the apartment blow up and Milo's little time travel trick cause the deaths of a couple of hundred people? Could she find out? Would she be able to do a search on the Internet and find herself? Did they even have Internet here?

And if they did, would her search be reported to someone that she was researching this person in history? Did the government keep that close an eye on its citizens?

If they kept that close an eye on everyone's health – maybe.

She had a lot of questions and no answers. The biggest one was still unanswered – was this really a one-way trip?

***

Levi worked in the kitchen, quietly and competently at a counter. She needed food. It would be these mundane details that would keep him focused. Maybe while doing the mundane, he'd come up with a solution for everything else. He glanced up at the screen on the wall. Still a half hour until the pod was delivered.

He didn't want anyone else to see it. He'd asked for a call when the delivery left the warehouse so he could put on the special effects. Special effects he'd set up after Milo's genius started to show. And the lines he started to cross.

Innocently of course. *Yeah, right.*

Just as he took the scrambled eggs off the heat, his comp buzzed.

He checked the message. The pod was en route. Good. "Milo, engage the privacy mode setting out front."

"Woohoo." Milo jumped up from the table and raced over to the control unit. "I never get to do this."

"Well, this time, it's necessary." He checked the digital readout on the screen. "Good, it's all working." He set the plate on a tray. "Take this to Dani. I have to go and accept the delivery."

Milo looked at him. "Are you sure about this?"

Levi stopped, the plate in his hand, then laid it down on the tray. "It's a little late to be asking, isn't it?"

Milo's lively features twisted in regret. "I'm just realizing that this is all my fault."

Levi stared at him. "Really, just now?" He leaned on the counter to stare at him. "You really don't get it, do you? This isn't some game. This isn't a rush to beat the technology. This isn't something you can just do then forget about." His temper fired as he thought about all he had to deal with. "You have damaged lives – in ways we can't begin to know about. And you have ruined Dani's."

"I haven't ruined Dani's at all. Don't you see this is beautiful? She has a great life waiting for her here. We'll make it great."

"But you didn't give her any choice. You did this to her. You made her a victim of your mechanisms. And that's just wrong. She should never have been brought into our world. You didn't ask her if she wanted this. You didn't care."

He stopped and stared, wondering what it would take to get through his head. "What you did was wrong. On so many levels. And you've left me to deal with your mess again."

"She's not a mess. She's a miracle." Milo stepped in front of Levi. "Look, I'm sorry for the problems right now. I'm sorry for any that might still come, but damn it, Levi, I did something that no one else has done." His eyes glittered with excitement. "Can't you see the greatness here?"

Levi choked. "And that's all this means to you, isn't it?" Would Milo ever see what he'd done? "And what about Dani? Do you think she's going to consider this greatness?"

A buzzer sounded.

"Damn it. They're early. I hadn't expected them so fast." Levi raced to the door, leaving the food behind on the plate. He opened the door to see his delivery.

"Bring it in here." He stood by as the pod was floated toward him. He led the way to where it would stay. He'd planned on getting one a year ago but had a hard time with the registration requirements. "Thanks."

"No problem. You'll pay through the nose for this, but hey, it's worthwhile."

"I hope so," he muttered. He took the paperwork, glanced at the bottom line, and said, "So we're good?"

"We are. As long as I get that software, we're done."

"It's already in progress." And it was. Levi smiled at the man who would prefer to not be named. He knew him vaguely. He'd had to go to a friend of a friend to make this happen as it was. So he'd taken his first step to the wild side. Then again, Milo had pushed them all over there already.

But Dani needed healing. He couldn't leave her like she was.

Speaking of which, he went through the simple process to open the pod and check it over. "Dani," he called out loudly, "Do you think you can walk over to me?"

He didn't hear an answer. He walked back over to her room to see her struggling to get out of bed. Just that much effort had her sweating. Damn Milo.

And she still wasn't fully dressed. He cursed himself for looking. As she struggled to tug the blanket around her shoulders, he cursed himself again for not taking a better look while he could.

He raced over. "Here, let me help."

She gasped from the effort. "I thought I'd be fine. I got up on my own this morning." Her face flushed then paled.

He frowned, hating that she was hurting. "And you will be fine again. Let's get you into the pod. That will help."

He half-carried her to where the machine waited then helped her lie down inside. While he watched, the pod fired up and started taking her statistics. That stage could take awhile. He glanced down at her, wondering what he'd forgotten.

Mentally, he went through the process from the previous night and brightened. "Right. The critter."

He ran back to her bedroom and winced. The cat didn't look very good at all. It only opened its eyes and stared at him, huge chocolate eyes wells of deep dark pain. "I'm so sorry," he whispered. He scooped him up and carried him over to Dani. She lay with her eyes closed, never moving as he approached.

Carefully, he lay the critter down on her stomach,

Her eyes flew open, saw her pet, then her gaze shot up to stare at him in surprise. He shrugged sheepishly. "He looked to be suffering too."

"He is," she whispered, her gaze gentling. She studied his face and then smiled. A real smile, no sarcasm, no anger, just a slow blossoming movement that he couldn't tear his gaze away from. And then the smile hit her eyes.

He was enthralled.

She might be mad sometimes, and she might be sarcastic, but now that she was smiling at him, he realized how honest she was. There was no artifice with her.

She was who she was, and to hell with what anyone thought of that.

He realized how unique she was. And how much he was falling for her – damn it. Milo had been right. He was interested.

Chapter 8

Dani soaked up the warm healing rays. This pod was amazing. She needed one of her own. She'd skip the bed and sleep in this every night. She wanted to sleep now but at the same time, she didn't want to be unconscious and miss this experience.

Charmin snoozed beside her. She wondered if he was worse off with this time travel thing than she was.

At least she could talk and walk. Charmin was more or less flat out. She reached down and scratched the back of his head. He was definitely more laid back right now. No nagging for attention. No nagging for food. And speaking of food – the pod had arrived before they could eat.

Her heartstrings tugged at the thought of losing her best friend. She had nothing left of her old life but him. He'd been with her for four years and was a major part of her life. To see him hurting like this...

Charmin raised his head and gave her a pitiful look. "Food?"

She smiled in relief. "There will be food soon."

He groaned. A long slow guttural sigh that made her laugh.

"I'm glad to hear you are feeling better."

"Feel awful," he whispered in a low throaty voice.

"I love how you can talk now." She tilted her head in thought and added, "It must be a side effect of the time travel."

"I love how you can talk now, too." Charmin mimicked. "It must be a side effect of the time travel."

She gasped, then laughed and laughed. And maybe he was right. Maybe she'd been the one to learn to talk cat and not the other way around.

She relaxed, her hand resting on his ruff, letting the hum of the pod do its thing. Whatever that was. The lights were a soothing blue and there was no computer voice to disturb her peace and quiet. Food and more coffee would be good, but barring that miracle, for the moment she was doing just fine.

She closed her eyes and fell asleep.

***

Levi walked into the newly designated pod room and smiled. Both guests were sound asleep. The pod would work better, faster if they stayed that way. At least until it was done doing its job. Getting her healthy was just the first stage of this process. Time to work on the second.

He opened his comp and dialed a number that was likely to be popular over the next few days.

When a computerized voice answered, he read off a series of numbers he'd memorized. When a voice came on the other end, he stated, "I need an ID for one young female."

Silence.

He held his breath. There was no guarantee that he'd get his request fulfilled, but he didn't know where else to go. Dani needed a solid ID to go anywhere. And she needed to be tagged. Thankfully, he and Milo made a lot of money. Because taking care of Dani was starting to become a major expense.

"Anything else."

"Yes." He winced. It was from here that things could get dicey. "I need a tagging completed."

The person on the other end sucked in his breath. But when he spoke, his voice was calm. "That is an expensive process."

"I know."

"You have the funds."

"I have the funds." There was no point in elaborating. They either believed him or they didn't. And he'd pay the price, regardless. He had no choice.

Silence. He waited. If this person refused, it would be one person more who would know his secret. And such a secret would be dangerous, especially for Dani.

"When?"

"As fast as possible." Then he reconsidered. Maybe not so fast. Dani was still healing. He didn't want these people to know why she had no ID or tags. And they might if they saw her now. If it could be in a few days, that would give her longer to heal. He had no idea how long it would take, but she needed every day. He'd have to take her out of his place soon. But she needed to be strong enough to handle everything that was coming.

His world was not for the faint of heart.

"Tomorrow morning. No food or water for 12 hours prior."

And the voice rang off.

Levi stared down at the comp in his hand. "That went well." Maybe. They didn't give him a price. They didn't ask for his address. They didn't ask any medical details about who was being tagged. Were they going to contact him again or just show up on his doorstep?

He walked back over to where Dani slept in the pod. She'd taken to the pod as if it were the answer to her prayers, and given the fact that it was easing her pain, it probably was. Stunningly beautiful in sleep, Dani was both a problem and a gift. He stood, enjoying the sleeping beauty when he realized he really didn't want to leave. That more than anything sent him bolting from the room.

Back in the kitchen, he came face to face with Milo.

Milo, dark overtones in his young voice, asked, "Did I just hear you correctly?"

Levi's stomach sank. Milo would need to know eventually, but Levi didn't feel up to a fight now. "What did you hear?"

Milo looked around furtively. Levi rolled his eyes. "We're in our home, stealth is on. No one can hear us."

"You can't be sure of that," Milo cried. "What if someone has this place bugged?" He reached up to grab his hair with both hands.

Levi stared at his brother in disgust. "You care now?"

Round glazed eyes stared back at him. "You don't understand. I can't have people knowing about her."

Levi narrowed his gaze. "Why?" he asked, his tone ominous.

Milo shifted uneasily. Not quite a bounce, but neither was he standing steady. And that wasn't good. "Milo, what are you talking about?"

He leaned forward. "It's my technology. My design. My invention."

"And?"

"And if people find out, they will steal it." He wrung his hands.

"Damn it, Milo, this isn't about keeping your code secret. This is about a young woman whose life you destroyed. You do realize she could die, don't you?"

Milo stared in the direction of the healing pod. That he seemed to be considering the pros and cons of Dani's death pissed Levi off. His brother was naive and simple-minded over some things, but he was also incredibly focused on his stuff.

"No," Levi snapped. "That is not a good outcome."

Milo slid him a sidelong glance. "I wasn't going to suggest we kill her for God's sake, but if she should happen to die…"

"Which I'm trying my hardest to avoid happening, if you hadn't noticed." Levi strode over to the liquor cabinet sunk into the wall. He couldn't believe the bizarre turn of the conversation. He poured himself a hefty whiskey and threw it back. He shuddered as the fire water coated his throat and prepared to do battle in his stomach. He had been doing this a lot lately.

"You really shouldn't drink that stuff. It's bad for you."

Levi choked. "You're worried about my health while you talk hopefully about Dani's death?"

Throwing his hands in the air, Milo snapped, "I'm just saying that now that I know it works, she's the proof. If she dies, I'll still know that it works but we won't have to deal with the evidence." He shrugged. "No biggie."

Levi poured a second shot and took a sip while he stared at his brother. Forced to question his kid brother's ethics…his morals. His conscience. And that was an alarming step. He swirled the golden liquid in his glass. While Levi had been bending over backwards to keep Dani safe and make her as comfortable as possible, his brother was contemplating the advantage of his experiment dying.

How did that work? In his world, not very well.

"Milo," he said, in a deep hard voice, "I don't ever want this discussion to come up again."

His brother pouted. That was the only description Levi could come up with. His brother was actually pouting.

Again reminding him that for all his genius, Milo essentially had the mind of a sixteen-year-old male trapped in a twenty-two-year-old body. Maybe one day the two would match up, but he hadn't seen any sign of the gap closing in years. Milo had hit sixteen with such enthusiasm, it was as if he'd found a way to not age again.

That concept startled him. If Milo had found a way to haul in some poor woman from a couple centuries ago, had he also found a way to slow or stop the aging process?

If so, if anyone found out, neither of them would ever be safe again.

Chapter 9

Whispered conversation slipped under the edge of the pod's hum, disturbing her rest. Something about her dying? Really? Worriedly, her hand automatically searched for Charmin, reassured to find the warm body snuggled up against her. He was still alive. She waited for his chest to rise with his next breath then relaxed. Was she close to death? Or was that a hypothetical statement if the pod didn't do its job?

Dry-eyed, she studied the running green light shifting along the edge of the pod. Was she so badly damaged by Milo's experiment that she wouldn't survive? Assessing her own situation, she realized that outside of a deep permeating fatigue, she didn't feel bad. Walking was a problem though. As if every step required too much effort, like she weighed hundreds of pounds more than she had before her time travel trip.

That had to be due to the change in atmosphere – as if she were living on the moon.

Only she wasn't. But time had obviously changed the atmosphere in the future. Or her body felt it had. And maybe the why didn't matter. If she couldn't go back, she had no choice but to go forward. If she could ever get up.

She shifted her legs tentatively. They didn't ache the same as they had. So maybe the pod was doing its job. Her arms worked fine, her mind was clearer. She didn't know if she was supposed to live in here until she was fully healed – if such a thing was possible – or if there was a day to day booster thing going on.

She wasn't opposed to coming in here daily. She did feel better in the pod. Maybe it was a weaning off thing. As she strengthened, she'd need it less. She was truly grateful they had such technology. Too bad she couldn't take a unit back home. The people there could use this technology.

And this time period needed better food. Her stomach growled again. It had been getting worse since she first woke up. She'd lost track of time and didn't know if it was day or night, and her stomach didn't care. It needed sustenance.

She glanced at the partially closed door. Were they still talking about her impending death? More likely she'd die from starvation at this rate. Should she search for food herself? And would she recognize it if she saw it? Or did the cupboards hold mostly shakes and booster like Milo had threatened?

That sent her stomach careening to almost heaving. Almost immediately, the racing lights warmed and slowed. Probably in response to her discomfort. She closed her eyes. In truth, she didn't want to leave the pod. She was warm and comfortable and pain free. But very hungry.

"Levi?"

No answer. She called out louder. "Levi?"

Still no answer. Damn it.

She tried to push the top of the pod open and found it wouldn't budge. Shit. Was she locked in here?

And if so, how was she going to get out?

"It won't open unless it is done with its work." Levi stopped at the doorway, "Or if you need to go to the bathroom or another physical discomfort. It's set to automatically shut off when the patient has other needs that supersede the healing." He frowned. "But I can adjust the settings so you can open the lid just by pushing on it."

She stared over at him. "The only body function that is paramount at the moment is my appetite. I'm incredibly hungry."

He approached the pod and pressed some buttons on the console. After a moment, he glanced down at her and said, "I raised the height of the lid so you can lie sideways easier." He stared at her. "I guess you didn't get anything to eat yet?"

"No." She gave him a tentative smile. "And if possible, I'd really like to change that."

For the first time all day, a real smile lit his face. "I can do that." He winked at her in a surprise move that left her doubting what she'd seen.

She watched him leave, feeling happier than she remembered in a while. The resemblance was only a passing glimpse now to Lawrence. Levi was a different person. She no longer felt any animosity towards him. He wasn't responsible for this. She understood he was trying to help.

He was his own person and was starting to be someone she really wanted to know better. He'd been nothing but kind to her and patient with his brother. There was something so very attractive about that kind of caring.

Being pampered like this was addictive.

But Milo…now him she wasn't so sure about.

As she came to terms with her new reality, she felt better emotionally. Sure, she'd lost so much, but maybe, just maybe, she'd also gained something.

According to Milo, her life as she'd known it hadn't ended up too special. As in she'd never married, never had children, and she'd never had a major career that he could find.

That was quite depressing. She'd just been approved for a special Internet Security program at the company she'd worked for. It had taken her years to get there. In more ways than one.

If she could return to her own time, she'd try harder to make something of her life there. But if that was no longer a possibility, she wanted to make the best of whatever life she had here.

Maybe she could make a success of it.

She didn't know how society worked here, but with Milo and Levi around to help, maybe she could make a difference.

She'd overheard Levi say something about tagging. She didn't know what that meant, but if it allowed her to be one of them with proper ID – she was all for it.

She was so busy making plans, it was Charmin that let her know something was different.

He pushed himself up on his front paws, yelling, "Food!"

Dani struggled to get out of the pod. It seemed to resist her efforts at first, then all of a sudden the lock released and it opened. She really didn't want the two men rushing in here to find Charmin screaming like he was. But the poor thing did need a square meal. So did she.

When she stood on her feet, a chill settled in. Already? How did that work? She cast another glance at the pod. Charmin had collapsed on the top of the blanket, and the most god-awful sound was coming out of his mouth.

"Food. Fooooooood," he moaned and rolled over sideways in a dramatic movement. He was proving to be a major prima donna.

"I'll go and see what I can find." She tugged the blanket from the pod and wrapped it around her shoulders before she stumbled forward, her gait unsteady. She leaned against the wall and made her way to the unusual doorway. Tall, almost to the ceiling, the doorways were narrower than she was used to. Maybe the people were skinnier today than in her time. Lord knows that would be an improvement.

She staggered into the next room, trying to sort out the layout. How had she gotten into this place? And where the heck was the kitchen? Her stomach growled loud enough that if anyone was in the apartment, they'd hear her coming.

Good. She slipped her hand over the wall, but there was no light switch. "Of course. That would be too easy."

With one hand on the wall, she kept moving forward. The hallway opened up into a large spacious room. Something along the lines of a living room. "A big ass living room," she muttered. For some reason, she'd thought the apartment was tiny. She hadn't seen much of the apartment since she'd been here, but where was the damn bathroom again? Then she needed food. And so did Charmin.

Slipping around the corner, she stopped. There was another bathroom. A monster-sized room and different from the last one she'd used. She used it, then after washing her hands, she stared into the mirror and shuddered. God, she looked pathetic. Even seeing that, she straightened her spine and tried to put a smile on her face. That looked better. She took a couple of deep breaths and smacked her cheeks lightly to put some color on them. Having done what little she could do, she opened the door and shrieked.

"Whoa. Take it easy." Levi reached out to stabilize her. "Come on, let's get you back to bed."

"I need clothes and food. So does Charmin," she whispered. "I'm so hungry."

"I'm preparing food. Wait a second." He disappeared, only to reappear with a long flowing robe. He quickly dropped it over her head. Immediately, her body warmed.

"Now, hold onto my arm and I'll take you to the kitchen. After you eat, it's back into the pod."

"I do feel better and warmer. Thanks for the robe." She gave him a small apologetic smile. "Just not that much better."

"The pod will do its job, but it's going to take some time."

"Like a lifetime?" She stumbled forward, every step a triumph.

He laughed. "Shouldn't be that bad."

"I hope not." She managed a tiny laugh. "Thanks for helping."

"Not an issue. I'm just sorry that you're hurting."

By the time he'd finished talking, he was helping her into a chair at a table. She stared around and realized the kitchen was more or less normal-looking. After Milo's talk about shakes and nutrients, she was scared to imagine what food he'd come up with. "I'm just so hungry. I wonder if it's a side effect of the time travel," she said.

"Maybe. You need it for healing." He opened a section of the wall before she had a chance to see what he'd done. "Is that a refrigerator?"

He turned to look at her. "It's a cooler." He placed a clear plastic jug with eggs and something resembling cheese on the counter. Her mouth started watering. "Could I have a piece of cheese?" she asked, her voice faint with hunger.

He brought a thick slice over for her. As if he knew she had food, Charmin started meowing steadily from the back room. She winced, feeling guilty over her cheese. "Is there any chance you have something for him?"

He grimaced. "I don't have anything resembling cat food, but there is some ground chicken in here."

"Ha," she said. "He'd love that."

And he did. Instead of taking the food to the pod, Levi brought Charmin to the kitchen table. Charmin howled pitifully the whole time. Once at the table, Dani wrapped her arms around him, trying to keep him calm until some food arrived. But he wouldn't be calmed. He definitely wasn't living up to his name.

Finally, Levi brought a bowl of minced chicken over. "Will he eat it raw?"

"I think he'll eat your hand as well if you don't give that bowl to him."

Levi lowered the bowl and Charmin damn near jumped into it. Dani was actually embarrassed. "Sorry, he's usually better mannered."

Charmin stopped eating and turned to look at her. "Get over it. I'm hungry."

Her gaze whipped over to Levi to see what he thought of Charmin's speech abilities. He took a step back. Then a second step and a third until he'd come up against the counter. His gaze went from Charmin to her and back again. "Did he just talk?"

"Oh, I'm so glad you and Milo can hear him, too." She grinned happily. "I was afraid I was going nuts."

Levi stared at her in shock. "Are you serious?"

"Oh, I'm serious with being happy I'm not the only one who can hear him." She leaned forward and said in a conspiratorial whisper. "He's only been able to do this since Milo's little trip. This cat could never talk before."

Charmin snorted and shook his head, spraying flecks of raw chicken across the table. "Yes, I could. *You* couldn't hear me."

She raised one eyebrow and stared at Levi. "Is that possible?"

"What? That the cat talks? Hell no."

She grinned, enjoying herself. "No – that I'm the one that is different. And you two are more advanced – maybe that's why you can hear him? Or did the trip through time make him able to speak?"

"Or both. If one of you has a change like that, then it's quite likely that both will." He ran his hand through his hair, leaving it looking wonderfully tousled. And damn, she wanted to go and run her hands through it, too. Her stomach growled again.

And didn't Charmin start to inhale the food faster, as if he thought she was going to get close and eat his food?

She leaned closer on purpose. "Hey. Don't worry. I won't be eating your chicken."

"Oh crap." Levi straightened, staring at the eggs. "I forgot about your food." He exhaled sharply. "I'll make a cheese omelette." He grabbed a bowl and cracked two eggs.

She coughed. "Uhm, I don't suppose you could make that a big omelette, could you?"

He raised his gaze to stare at her, as if asking if she was serious. At her hopeful look, he cracked two more eggs. "I think your eyes are bigger than your stomach."

"No problem. I'll help her." Charmin sat on the table cleaning his paws. At the odd silence in the room, he looked up to find them both staring at her. "What? I'm still hungry."

While Levi whipped up an omelette, and she was amazed to know that they were still making omelettes this far in the future, she found a cloth and wiped up Charmin's mess. She had been afraid they'd replaced food with pills. And to a certain extent, they might have. If she could take a pill and make her stomach feel like she'd eaten a roast chicken with all the trimmings, she'd swallow a half dozen and maybe feel like she was back to normal. Right now, her toes were so empty she was pretty damn sure she wouldn't make the walk back to the pod.

Just when she was thinking she'd actually start crying from hunger, a plate was placed in front of her.

Melted cheese filled the inside of a golden omelette. She could taste it already. Cutting up a section into small bits to cool, she forked up the first bite and closed her eyes and moaned. "Oh, that's good."

She opened her eyes to find Charmin whacking at the piece closest to him. He caught it in his paws and dragged his prize toward him.

"You get that piece because you got it covered in raw chicken, but that's it. No more."

Charmin ignored her as he tried to eat, but the piece was too hot. He meowed and batted the piece a couple of times, then tried to bite it. Whining, he gobbled it down anyway.

"Geez. Aren't you full yet?"

Charmin stared, his gaze never lifting from her plate. "I'm hungry."

"Oh man." She cut him another piece and slid it toward him. "That's it. The rest is mine."

She wrapped her arm around the plate protectively. She glared Charmin into backing up.

Levi laughed, a refreshing, open laugh.

Dani ignored him until she'd finished her plate. Unfortunately, she was still hungry. She turned woeful eyes to Levi. He stared, switched his gaze to her empty plate, then back up to her face. "Really?"

She nodded.

Blowing out his breath, he turned back to his kitchen and brought out a loaf of thick crusty bread. Her eyes lit up at the sight of it. "Now that would be great."

He cut two thick slabs and brought it over for her, then went back for cheese and butter. She munched happily as

Charmin worked through a chunk of cheese. "That feels so much better," she said when she was done.

An odd sound rang through the apartment. She stiffened. It sounded like an alarm. "Is that a fire alarm or something?"

"I don't know what it is." With a sharp look in her direction, Levi said, "Stay here. I'll be right back."

He disappeared. Dani looked at Charmin, but he'd taken off. She didn't blame him. Feeling scared and hating being alone in a place she knew nothing about, she retraced her steps to the healing pod as fast as she could. And sure enough, she found Charmin hiding between the layers of blankets.

"Good idea. Maybe we can hide away in here until this calms down." The noise was horrific enough to hurt her ears while in the kitchen but as soon as she crawled back inside the pod and closed the lid, the noise disappeared. "Oh, thank heavens," she murmured as the assault on her ears stopped. Just as she started to relax, the lid lifted. Milo, his face twisted with urgency, said, "Come. You have to leave. Now."

She was dragged out of the pod. At the last moment, she snatched up Charmin before she was shoved ahead of Milo. "Where am I going?" she whispered. "I have no place to go."

"Levi has a place for you. Hurry."

Within minutes, she was being hustled into a room she'd never seen before in one of those weird tubes she hated and spinning at a speed her body couldn't stand – upward.

"Where's Levi?" she asked angrily.

"He's coming." Milo chewed on his fingernail and shifted on his feet anxiously.

"Not good enough. If you think to dump me somewhere and hope I'll take care of myself, you're sad—"

"Dani. I'm here." Levi appeared on the other side of the glass. Then while she watched, the glass between them disappeared. Damn, she wished she knew how that worked. "What is going on, Levi?"

"It's a security inspection. My system warns me when trouble is coming." He pushed her ahead of him. "Milo, go back and let them in. Be natural."

"Got it." Milo took off.

"I don't think I like your world," she said.

Levi tugged her forward, making her hurt as she tried to move faster then she could. "Stop pulling on me."

Spinning to face her, he stopped at the look on her face. "Please hurry."

Looking at the worry in his face, she realized this was big. Dangerously big. If anything happened to separate her from Levi, she'd be lost. And with Charmin having his unique ability to speak...he'd be taken away from her, too.

Ignoring the pain, she started to run.

***

Thankful that Dani finally seemed to understand the urgency of the matter, Levi followed just slightly behind. He didn't want her to collapse when she ran out of energy. And if she did, he wanted to be there to catch her.

The pod appeared to have been working as she held the pace steady. He slipped past her to open a door. Inside was the rooftop elevator. With the three of them inside, he sent it to the top beside Johan's place. He kept a worried eye on Dani. She was breathing hard and her color was pale, but she was still standing.

Charmin looked up at him. Levi glanced away, still not able to reconcile what he'd seen and heard. *A talking cat.* Holy crap. He couldn't even begin to think about the ramifications of that. If the cat talked as a result of the time travel, he could just imagine what the scientists would say. And what they'd want to do to him.

It would be disastrous for society at large.

And this feline gave him the creeps. Those huge green eyes seemed to see into his soul. And who was to say it didn't? If it could talk, what else could it do? He shuddered inwardly. He really didn't want to know.

At the rooftop, he could hear loud music at Johan's. Should they blend into one of his constant parties or try for the private rooftop garden that, in theory, the others didn't know about? The only problem was that the garden was damn small. It was a space he used when he needed a few moments away from everything. It would be a tight squeeze for the two of them. And he was almost looking forward to that.

His gaze caught sight of Charmin.

Okay, the three of them.

But given the sudden raised voices at Johan's and the now silent music, he'd take a squeeze over trouble. Dani couldn't be seen yet. He led the way quietly around the rooftop garden to the back maintenance section. Slipping around several large vents, he stepped out onto his tiny private deck.

Dan gasped and spun around. "Oh my! You can see the whole city from here."

He smiled. "Not quite. I do like to come up here. It's pretty spectacular." Levi stood by Dani's side. "I guess this doesn't look like what you are used to?"

She stood, shocked, and stared out at the city. It was a replay of what she'd first seen after escaping the office. Oddly shaped dome buildings that stretched out as far as she could see. Gemstone colors glowed off the sides of some walls with multiple green spots dotting the area…and the air traffic…she shuddered at what appeared to be loads of air traffic. Her gaze flitted from one thing to another. "It's beautiful," she said, "But it's so…so…foreign looking."

"In what way?" Levi asked, looking at her.

"It's surreal, like a science fiction movie set. Foreign. Alien." She shifted Charmin in her arms. "It's nothing like what I'd expected. Huge buildings in weird shapes and colors and lights." She shrugged. "It's just so bizarre to think that I'm actually here."

Levi grinned. "It is. Don't tell Milo, but it's also great."

She stared at him. "We'll see. That he managed to do what he did is pretty amazing. I'm not sure I appreciate it still, but I do understand the genius required to make this happen."

He stood in front of Dani. "You aren't afraid of heights, are you?"

She shook her head. "I'm fine," she murmured. "It is pretty spectacular. Scary but beautiful."

"It is." He glanced around. "It's also private."

"I presume we're hiding here until it's safe to go home again?" At his nod, she rubbed her temple. "It's because of me, isn't it?"

"In a way. You don't have ID or tags. If anyone were to find out about you at this stage…"

Levi hated to admit that the government was corrupt and getting worse every day. He'd love to reassure Dani that this world wasn't worse than the one she'd left. But it would be hard to find proof of that.

Still, her world wasn't perfect either. And as long as one kept a low profile in his world, everything would be fine. Most people never had any run-ins with the authorities and life continued in an easy way.

If he didn't have Milo to contend with, his life probably would have been easy, too.

"How long do you think it will take? I'm getting tired," she asked. And for the first time since they arrived, he took a good look at her. She'd slumped against the wall and her color had all but disappeared. She appeared to be doing a long slow slide to the ground. She pressed her lips together and shifted the huge cat in her arms again.

"Do you want to sit down?"

She looked around. "There isn't a place to, is there?"

"On the floor."

His comp emitted a beep. He pulled it out and smiled. "That's Milo. All clear. The suits came, they visited with him, asked a few question, got a few answers, and now they've left." He smiled. "Hopefully satisfied enough that they won't be back."

Dani smiled. "Good. Let's go."

"Not so fast." Levi clicked through his comp, searching his security readouts to make sure his place was empty. It appeared to be. He did a search throughout the building. Checking for an anomaly, something else that was illegal. There were a few people in the building, and like Johan, most had secrets. Authorities were not welcome here. He checked his wrist unit. "This building is supposed to be exempt from those raids. Lord knows we pay enough for that, but we still seem to have one or two." He looked up. "Okay, it looks good."

"Go back the same way?" Dani asked, heading toward the corner.

"Yes, but slowly. Just in case."

They made their way back to the rooftop elevator. Loud music was once again blasting from Johan's place. If it weren't for Dani, Levi would suggest they blend into the festivities. But with the cat and her current level of exhaustion, she'd stand out as new and different. It also wasn't safe to bring her into a social situation yet. She needed to learn about this world.

Within seconds, they were in the elevator and scooting back to his floor. He led the way back home and as soon as they were inside, he set up stealth mode again. As far as anyone outside this place would know, the place was empty. There would be no power readings, water usage, lights, or heat showing up on scans. It was about all he could do. And considering Milo, it wasn't enough. But it was more than most had. He walked into the kitchen and set up coffee. When he turned back, it was to see two sets of eyes staring at him. Fatigue in both, but also hope. He was stumped. He tilted his head and asked, "What do you want?"

Dani grimaced. Charmin had no such problem. "Foood."

Chapter 10

Dani watched the shock settle on Levi's face. "Sorry, but I'm hungry again, too. All I want to do is eat and sleep."

He shook his head and motioned to the bread still on the table. "I have some cooked meat in here somewhere." He turned to rummage in the fridge.

After placing Charmin on the kitchen table, back where he'd been sitting earlier, Dani picked up the knife and started cutting. Milo walked into the kitchen and stared at her.

"See, I told you shakes would be better," Milo said. "Her body needs nutrients. She's going to need a lot of food to make up for what she could get in a vitamin drink."

"If that's the case," Dani said, "A shake *and* food would work. Just a shake, no way."

Behind her, Levi said, "That's actually a good idea, Milo. Make them a booster. Get the data from the pod and fix one for each."

Charmin, staring at the bread in her hand as she buttered it, said, "What's a booster?"

"A shot of vitamins in this case, to help your bodies adapt," Milo said.

"Ah. So food." Satisfied, he sat back and watched every move she made.

"If possible, Milo," Dani said, "Could you make Charmin's very small and with cream as a base? He's not likely to drink anything else."

Charmin nodded. "Cream. Cream is good."

"Cream is *not* good for you. It's fat. And not a good fat." Milo made a disgusted sound. "It's awful and it will kill you."

He stalked off in the direction of the pod. Dani turned to look at Levi, who appeared to be slicing a hunk of meat. She just didn't know what kind it was. And she hated to ask. She was so hungry that if it was cloned, she probably wouldn't care. Tomorrow was a different story. "Milo has strong views, doesn't he?"

Levi looked up with a smile. "Always has. Not to worry. He has a big weakness for chocolate." At her surprised look, his grin widened. "Makes him seem more human, doesn't it?"

"What about your parents? Are they alive? Live close by?"

He stacked the meat up on a plate and brought it to the table. "They died when Milo was little. I've been looking after him for a long time."

"That must have been tough." She couldn't imagine. She'd had a hard enough time looking after herself. She'd had parents though they'd never been close. And now…she stared down at her bread. She hadn't spoken to them in over five years. Would they even know she'd disappeared?

She wondered. "Is there a way to research the people who lived in my time?"

"There is. The record keeping of today is something quite different than in your time. So you'd need training, but we can certainly do that. You'll need to learn our way of life. In fact, I had considered taking you to Johan's while we were up top, but I figured you'd need to familiarize yourself a little more with our ways before socializing."

She stared at him. Took a bite of bread and meat and chewed. Her mind reeled with the implications of all she'd have to learn. The pitfalls waiting for her. She swallowed.

"I can't imagine." A shudder slipped down her spine. "It's hardly like visiting a foreign place."

"That's exactly what it is." He dropped a piece of meat in front of Charmin to go with the other pieces already lined up. Charmin showed no sign of slowing down or being distracted from his food. "You will be fine. There are a lot of things to learn, but it could be worse."

She stopped and stared. "In what way?"

"We all speak English."

He had a point.

Milo returned with a large glass of something fuchsia pink and a small bowl of something much less bright. He placed the glass in front of her and set the cream down in front of Charmin.

Charmin said, "What is it?"

"Cream," Dani said helpfully. "Their version here. Try it. So far you've eaten everything else."

He sighed, leaned in, and sniffed. "Doesn't smell like cream."

Feeling like she was trying to get a two-year-old to eat his spinach, she said, "It will be good. Besides, it's to make us feel better. Help us heal."

He looked over at her, his huge green eyes staring at her unblinking. "Then you try it."

She should have seen that one coming. Shooting Charmin a disgusted look, she picked up her glass of pink, took a deep breath, and swallowed a big gulp. And felt her throat close and her eyes water. She gasped for breath, desperate to keep her reaction minimal as Charmin watched her with a smug look.

"It's different. Hot almost. Definitely different." She gave him an encouraging smile. "Try it."

"Yours is much stronger than his as you are bigger and the damage to your system is a little more extensive." Milo slumped at the far side of the table, a glass of something rich and creamy with a light green tinge in his hand. He held his drink up. "Mine is an everyday dose, whereas yours is intensive."

"I'll say," she muttered. With a grimace, she picked it up again. Resisting the urge to plug her nose so she couldn't taste the drink, she downed it in one gulp. It was the only way she would get it down. She just hoped it would stay there.

She placed the empty glass on the counter and gave Charmin a fat grin. "Your turn."

He glared at her then at the glass before slowly approaching his bowl, nose first. He sniffed several times, then reached out and licked several times. And missed the cream each time.

"Oh no you don't. You drink it all up, just like I had to." And she hoped she'd never have to again. She leaned in closer and watched as Charmin tried again. This time he got some of the pink stuff and froze. He licked his lips several times and said in surprise, "Hey, it's good." He lowered his head and lapped at the cream.

"Damn. How come his tastes decent and mine is so strong I feel like puking?"

"Yours had to be stronger." Levi stood up, walked to a cupboard, and pulled out a glass. He held it to a wall and it filled automatically. She hadn't even noticed a spout. He brought it back to her. "Plain water."

She reached for it and drank the whole thing, then held it out asking for more.

"Wow, she drinks like she eats. Told you she'd be perfect for you." Milo grinned up at his brother.

Levi quietly brought a second glass of water back to her. She accepted it and turned to Milo.

"Did I just hear you right?" Dani asked, a new hardness, coldness in her voice.

Charmin sat back and stared at Milo. "Ha. You are so going to get it now."

Milo took another sip of his drink. He shrugged his shoulders nonchalantly. "What's the problem? I said he'd like you. So what's the big deal?"

She stood up. "Did you actually go back in time…snag me…for your brother?"

***

Levi was about to join them again when he heard Dani's question. And he really wanted to hear his brother answer it.

Milo's face twisted like he'd sucked on a grapefruit. Dani eyed him suspiciously. "You did, didn't you?"

He shrugged and stared down at his drink.

"Why me?" It was the burning question in her mind. Like how had he come to choose her?

"I had to find a target…er…a person to use for the experiment. Levi has horrible taste in women." He gave an exaggerated shudder and a quick sidelong glance at his brother. "So I figured I could do two things at once. Find a lovely woman for him, add a few enhancements, and try out my experiment at the same time."

Levi winced. While he mulled over the pathetic state of affairs, Dani spoke up.

"Enhancements?" she said in a low dark tone of voice.

Milo shrugged. "That part didn't work out the way I expected it to."

"In what way?" Levi stared at him. It was the first he'd heard anything about enhancements. "What did you do?"

"Hey," Milo held out his hands defensively. "I was just enhancing her communication abilities."

Levi stared at him in shock. "Why?"

"Because you're deep, man. You like to talk. You like to communicate. I figured that if she wasn't much of a communicator, that's something that could be easily enhanced."

Somewhere in the background as Levi tried to work his way through the maze of thoughts crowding his brain, he heard laughter. As in maniacal, off the wall laughter. He stared at Dani.

She was bent over, and damned if there weren't tears rolling down her cheeks.

He waited. Charmin reached out and smacked her with a paw. She appeared to slow down after that. Finally, she choked back the last of her giggles.

"Care to explain?" he asked.

She took a deep sobering breath and pointed at Charmin. "Milo's enhancement did work. It worked on Charmin." She giggled again. "Thank God he didn't add bigger boobs or something just as ridiculous. Imagine how Charmin would look then."

"Really," Charmin sniffed the air. "That would be preposterous."

The two men stared at her then at Charmin.

"You were supposed to come alone," Milo said slowly, staring in fascination at the cat. He opened his mouth as if to add something, then closed it and just shook his head. "And I thought that enhancement was minor for your body size, but if they…it…" he corrected quickly, catching Levi's attention for a moment, adding, "went to him…considering his size…it would almost make sense." He slumped down on the closest chair. "Wow. Just like…wow."

There was a long silence while everyone stared at Charmin.

He preened.

Dani couldn't believe it. "Those must be some enhancements," she murmured, then turned her attention to Milo. "There are a couple of other problems with your logic." He raised an eyebrow. She shook her head, overwhelmed at the casualness of his actions. "First off, what if you did choose the perfect partner for him and destroyed her in the process?"

He blinked.

She snorted. Such a thought hadn't even occurred to him. "Did you even think about failure?"

He laughed. "No. Nothing is a failure in life. There are just times where I've learned something didn't work. And if this didn't work, no one would know. You'd have just been vaporized or something."

"And what if only half of me made it?" She felt sick inside. "What if I was lying from the belly up in a gory pool of blood on your floor?" she said in an ominous voice.

His skin took on a greenish tinge. Then his lips twitched. "Nah. It was either all of you or none of you."

"And how could you know I wasn't some kind of serial killer you were bringing for your brother?"

He grinned. "We have all kinds of DNA markers for that sort of thing. Serial killer material you're not. You actually pick spiders up and put them outside so they don't die."

She frowned, a little weirded out that he knew that about her. "But I won't touch them with my hands."

He laughed at that. "See, that's perfect. Caring, but careful."

"And a personality profile?" she asked. "There's no way you could have done one of those on me. Not when I lived hundreds of years ago."

"We have advanced profile markers for many traits today. Sure, it was a gamble, but you had the same general look that he loved, you fit the other parameters I needed, so it was a good gamble." He straightened. "And you're here all in one piece, so it's time to move on."

Move on? What did that mean? She tilted her head. "Move on?"

"Time to adjust. Time to adapt. Time to deal." Milo levelled a look her way. "This is your life now."

And he walked out.

Levi moved closer. "Time to go back into the pod. Tomorrow could be stressful."

"More than my life already is?"

"Unfortunately," his face turned grim. "Yes."

Chapter 11

Back in the pod, Dani and Charmin slept, woke, and slept some more. When Levi walked in the next morning, she felt much better. Until he said her specialist was here. He dropped a stack of clothes on the bed and walked out.

Like what the hell was a specialist? And why was he hers?

She frowned at his retreating back but struggled upright, gasping at the lingering aches and pains. "I'll be there in a minute," she called out as she stumbled to the bathroom. Once out, she dressed in the unusual but cool clothing. That they fit like a glove was a little disconcerting. How had he known her size? Still, they looked good on her. She smoothed her fingers over the silky black material of the cropped top, loving the exotic feel. The half skirt along the back of the shorts was like nothing she'd ever seen before. Then neither were the interesting gem-like diamonds decorating the top.

She made her way down the hallway, doing a quick twirl to watch the back flare out. *Nice.* She grinned. Not only that, she was grateful that although hungry, she didn't feel like she was going to die anytime soon.

She walked into the kitchen. As she caught sight of the stranger, her breath caught at the back of her throat. Two hundred years into the future made no difference. There was a specific look to those that walked the shady side of life. Not saying anything, he motioned at her to sit down. She glanced over at Levi uncertainly. Immediately, he stepped closer and motioned to the chair, a gentle smile on his face. "Sit, Dani. It will be over in a moment."

Uncertain but willing, she took her place. And waited. Behind her, the specialist was unpacking a bag and laying items out on the counter.

She looked over at Levi, and whispered, "Is it going to hurt?"

He shrugged, his gaze on the man behind her. "Maybe a little. You can go back into the pod afterwards."

Dani twisted around, but the specialist showed no signs of hearing their conversation. Considering he hadn't said a word yet, he might be a deaf mute. She turned back and waited.

She shifted restlessly when nothing happened after several moments. She twisted around again to see what the stranger was doing, but this time Levi stepped in her line of sight. She glared at him. Just then, the specialist stepped forward and grabbed her arm. He searched the soft tissue above her wrist, the rough skin of his fingers almost scratching hers. After a moment, he dropped her hand and checked the other one.

She frowned. "Anything wrong?"

He never said a word and just returned behind her. She opened her mouth to speak again when Levi picked up her hand and pressed her fingers into the same place on his wrist. And she felt some kind of hard material inside.

Her gaze widened in fear as she understood. This specialist now knew she didn't have one. Her mouth fell open and she leaned in close. "But now he knows?"

Levi nodded, bent lower, and with his lips against her ears, murmured, "He's here to give you one."

"But isn't that dangerous? For you?"

"More for you. Don't say anything to him. Cry if you need to, the pod will fix any damage afterwards."

"Oh God, it's going to hurt, isn't it?" And her heart started to race. She clenched her fists. She was such a baby with pain. Tears burned in the back of her eyes. She couldn't do this.

As if understanding, Levi wrapped an arm around her shoulders and squeezed gently. "Easy."

She swallowed hard. There was no choice. She had to have whatever that thing was Levi had. She couldn't even ask for details without letting the specialist know the extent of her ignorance. And that would only bring more questions. And more problems. She hated the subterfuge, the necessary lies. She'd never been any good at those.

Not to mention the way words tended to blurt from her mouth without warning.

Levi started to massage her shoulders, making her realize she'd frozen in place, her muscles locking down.

Just when the wait seemed interminable, the specialist walked over again – holding a gun of some kind in his hands. She gasped in shock, and Levi gripped her shoulders. Not quite forcing her to stay in place, but letting her know he could if needed.

She didn't want to watch what happened so she kept her gaze forward. The stranger snagged her arm and turned it palm up.

Something cold was placed against her skin.

She closed her eyes and held her breath.

There was a hard pinch then nothing. She frowned. Was that it? All that worry over nothing. Just as the thought filtered through her brain, her head lolled to one side and she blacked out.

***

Levi let his breath escape slowly when Dani's head drooped to the side.

"Hold her still," the stranger said.

Levi grabbed her shoulders to stop her from slumping down in the chair, then crouched down and slid his arm under her head, his other arm wrapping around her ribs to hold her still. "I've got her, go ahead."

The specialist nodded and proceeded to do the quick laser surgery to open her wrist. Levi knew he was taking a chance doing this. At birth, the newborns were tagged within the first hour of life. When they hit sixteen, the tags were switched to the ones they'd have for the rest of their lives.

At birth, it was easier as the bones and tissues were soft, pliant. The initial tags were easily replaced as the body was already well accustomed to their presence. Dani had never had a foreign object implanted under her skin. Her nerves were fully grown. Any damage at this stage and she could lose the use of her hand. Scar tissue was yet another problem. He could only hope to get this over with and get her back into the pod quickly.

He watched the man work fast and efficiently. When Dani's wrist was open, he had to look away. There was little blood with the high intensity laser, but holy crap. He gritted his teeth, and being unable to help himself, he dropped a kiss on her head. After another long moment, he risked a second look at the surgery, relieved to see the tag lying nestled in the muscles. He could only wonder how the body adapted to such a thing. But his society had been using ID implants for a long time. They appeared to be the answer. They couldn't be lost, transferred, or stolen – when removed from the body, an alert was automatically sent to the Registrar.

"Is this going to work?" Levi asked. At least the specialist appeared to be competent.

He nodded. "Should."

"It's registered?" He couldn't help asking questions. If this didn't work, Dani's life was in danger. And that was unacceptable.

The specialist nodded again. "It is. When I get this closed up, I'll start the programming."

Ah. Right. The whole computer world that his society ran off of. Dani had to be included or else she'd always be an outsider. A fugitive. And that would be very difficult. There were fringe groups in his world, as there have been in every century. They lived free of the government restrictions and regulations but barely eked out a living, always on the run from the military. He sighed, staring down at the gentle soul in his arms. She didn't deserve that. She didn't deserve any of this.

"Done."

Levi looked up, relief flooding through him. "Are you?" He studied Dani's wrist. The laser had closed the wound. It was red and puffy but surprisingly healthy looking. The man waved a healing wand over it, and that improved the look of the skin again. He exhaled. "Will she be in pain when she wakes up?"

The specialist shrugged. "It's possible. The body needs time to adapt. Her wrist will ache. The fingers could go numb off and on and could potentially swell."

All things the pod could help her with, so it was minor in the scheme of things that could go wrong. The specialist stood and collected his instruments. He repacked his bag then opened a side pouch and removed a comp unlike anything Levi had seen before. The man pulled a chair forward and sat down. Using an odd-looking antennae, he angled the comp so it faced Dani's wrist. He clicked a few buttons and a series of lights under her skin lit up. Levi's eyebrows shot up. He hadn't realized how much programming went into this.

But the stranger seemed to relax back into his chair now that he realized the system was active. He bent his head and worked his thumbs on the keyboard. The lights on Dani's arm continue to beep and flash, then settled down to a steady pulse.

Levi looked down at his own arm. There were no lights. No beeps. But if he bought anything, there was a series of lights as the system went through its security checks. He wondered how long this would take and how much information he'd need to give to make Dani a history. She had to have a full background for the databanks to be happy.

He waited quietly for the stranger to work.

The man looked up. "Her name?"

"Dani Summerland."

The stranger keyed it in. Without looking up, he asked for her birth date.

Doing the math quickly from the little he knew, Levi picked July 1st, 24 years earlier.

There were several other questions as to gender, which he could easily answer. Then came the harder ones. Family history. He stalled. He could give Dani's real parents' name. He'd seen their names in Milo's file, but he had no dates for them. He gave up their names willingly enough and waited, hoping more wasn't required.

"We'll put down that the records were destroyed in the Felonia Crash, shall we?"

Relief washed through Levi. So much information had been lost in that disaster. It was the perfect answer. "That works."

The specialist switched to a series of questions about her medical history. He, of course had no idea, but the pods hadn't found anything major so he presumed she had none. At least as far as the database was concerned, she was incredibly healthy.

He had no idea what other information was being placed in Dani's fake background. And he didn't care as long as it was neutral and wouldn't raise any flags if checked. She needed to have flaws, just not big ones.

There were a few more questions about her education and schools. Not knowing many, he used the same schools that he'd gone to and gave her a degree in IT systems. At least that was something he could train her for. And since so many people had a similar education, it was a common course for her to have completed.

Then finally it was done. Dani was a single orphan female, twenty-four, educated, healthy.

The specialist said, "Last section. We have to connect to her financial information."

Levi nodded, ready for this. Last night when he realized what this process was going to mean, he'd opened some accounts under Dani's name. He punched in his access code on his comp then brought up the account. With a few swift clicks, Dani was connected to the credit system of his times. He'd transferred a moderate chunk of money to help her get established, but not enough to raise any alarms. He had no idea what she was going to need over the next year, and he knew he'd use what money he had to make her life as good as he could make it.

That was the least he could do.

But she'd need so much more.

The specialist packed up the comp and closed his bag. He turned to Levi and held out a porter. Levi stilled. This would be the first time he would see the price for Dani's tagging. He reached for it, took a look, schooled his features to not react, then held the unit to his own wrist and pushed the buttons, allowing the payment from his account. He wanted to laugh at the mockery of the company name on the bill. He'd just paid for cosmetic upgrades for Dani. How true. It would be hard to consider any other body modification that would match this expense.

When it was completed, he handed the unit back to the specialist, who nodded, put it in his pocket, and proceeded to walk out of the apartment.

Feeling odd, yet relieved about the whole thing, Levi reengaged stealth mode on the apartment. There was a part of him that wondered if he wouldn't be better off relocating so as to not be found again.

He'd paid the bill. But he'd also opened himself to potential blackmail in the future. And Dani, now safe from the government, was in danger from the very men who'd helped save her. There was one other thing he could do to protect her – but it was a last resort. And it would involve his family. He wasn't quite ready for that step yet.

His mind raced for ways to protect them both. She moaned just then and he realized she needed the pod. He could work the rest of the details out later. Surely Milo could find something on these men to help balance the scales.

When both had secrets to hide, the playing field was levelled.

And that would best.

But first he had to see to Dani.

Chapter 12

Dani woke to tears rolling down her cheeks. She tried to swipe them away and cried out, instinctively hugging her hand up to her chest. She was being carried in strong arms again. A protective caring set of arms. Levi.

"Easy, Dani. It's over." Levi's comforting voice washed over her.

She tried to understand what was going on. Levi was speaking, but she didn't understand what he was saying.

"I'm taking you back to the pod. An hour in there and you'll feel much better."

The pod. Healing. Her sore wrist. And then she remembered. The stranger. Tagging. For some reason, this injury, this injustice done in an attempt to make everything right…had become the last straw.

Maybe because she was tired, maybe because she hurt, and maybe it was just because it had all become too much, but once she started, she couldn't stop the tears.

"It's going to be all right, Dani," Levi's worried voice whispered in her ear. "I'm so sorry we had to do this."

"It's all right," she sobbed as the tears poured out. "It's not your fault."

"And yet it is." He sighed as they entered the pod room. "Milo is my brother and he brought you here for me. I certainly didn't ask him to do this, but because of his actions, your life has been ruined." He laid her down on the pod. She moaned as her arm was jostled.

"I'm so sorry," Levi said. The pain in his voice was so evident she wanted to reassure him it was fine – only it wasn't fine. Her wrist throbbed.

"I am, too," she whispered, lying back and shuddering. "I had no idea it would hurt this much."

"It shouldn't," Levi said quietly. "He gave you something for the pain, but I'm not sure your body can handle the drugs of today."

Not a nice thought. "The pod might help." She curled into a ball, her injured arm lying on her side so that the pod's rays could gain access. She closed her eyes, tears still leaking through.

"I'll go mix a pain cocktail." He lowered the pod lid. "I'll be back in a moment."

She could hear his footsteps retreating. Thank God. She was set to have a royal bawl. She'd been holding back but now that she was alone, the sobs rolled free. Everything hurt and it seemed like her life was the absolute worst it could be. She cried and cried, letting the tears and stress and pain drain from her overwhelmed system.

She'd always been proud of her ability to adapt. She wasn't sure she could in this situation. She'd try hard, but damn, this was a mind bender to set anyone's balance off. Oddly enough, by the time she stopped bawling, she felt better. Just to be able to let go like that had helped her ease back the stress levels.

Sure, her wrist still hurt, but the coiled sense of being too full, too hurt, too…whatever was gone. She let the last of the sobs hiccup out before she took several deep breaths.

"Are you okay now?"

Levi's worried voice came from the open doorway. Damn. She sniffled back the last bit of the tears. "Sorry," she whispered, her voice thick and ragged, still clogged with tears.

She knew her face would be red and puffy. She could only hope he didn't open the pod. She didn't want him to see her this way.

At the reminder of the pod, she brightened. Maybe it could heal her puffiness the same as it worked to heal the time travel damage. She turned slightly so her face was directly under the pod's flashing lights. She didn't know if it made a difference, but her skin immediately started to lose the tight hot sensation.

"Don't be." Levi stood there beside her and lifted the pod's lid.

She rolled her face into the blanket. It was an instinctive yet childish reaction.

"Hey, don't do that," he whispered softly. "You don't ever need to hide from me."

That surprised a laugh out of her. "Sorry, I just know what I look like after I've been crying."

"Crying is a great way to release all that pent up emotion. You've been through a lot." He smiled down at her. "Give yourself a break. I think you've done wonderfully well."

He lay down beside her and tugged her into his arms. Was he for real? Could any guy be this good? Or was it the men of this century, because if so, then wow!

And inexplicably, his acceptance brought on more waterworks.

Through her gentle sobs, Dani heard Levi's distressed voice. "Please don't cry, Dani. We'll make it work out. I'm so sorry Milo did this, but I promise...I'll do what I can to make it as good as I can. This really is a wondrous time to be alive. There are so many things I want to show you."

He kept talking and murmuring gently as if the sheer mass of words would help calm her down.

It was working. She wiped her eyes, surprised to find the pod had adapted its size to accommodate the two of them. Truly there were many innovative things here. And maybe it was time she stopped being such a wet dishrag and realized what an opportunity she had.

"I'm sorry," she whispered, though he'd told her not to be sorry. "I don't normally cry like this."

"It's like the physical effect on your body. There has to be some kind of emotional reaction, too. Tears only make sense." He smiled at her. And damn if she wasn't starting to like that smile. A little too much. He was worming his way into her heart. She really wanted him in her life.

She snuggled in closer and sighed happily. Maybe life wasn't so rotten after all.

He dropped a kiss on the top of her head. She smiled. He really was a protector. Another kiss landed on her side of her head. She shifted slightly at the same time he slid down a little, and she found herself staring into his eyes. Huge, deeply magnetic purple eyes. Like how could that be? She so wanted eyes like that. Just gazing into them made her insides melt.

A tiny sigh escaped. He was so damn beautiful.

His eyes darkened.

She caught her breath.

Then he lowered his head…and kissed her.

***

The sweetness of her lips disarmed him and made the next kiss inevitable. His lips moved gently on hers. Tasting, exploring, feeling a response that set his pulse pounding. He deepened the kiss, needing more. Needing to know she wanted more.

That she wanted him.

Like he wanted her. He couldn't believe how much. He hadn't even known of her existence a few days ago, and it galled him to think his brother had actually found her and retrieved her for him. Even worse to know that Milo had been right – she did look perfect for him – at least at first glance.

She twisted beneath him, her feet sliding up his calf, hooking under his pant leg and stroking his skin. He shuddered, sliding his hand around her back and down across her bare midriff. He'd chosen the clothes without realizing how sexy they'd look on her. Small and delicate, the clothing looked like they'd been created with her in mind. Add her almost ash blonde hair, and she looked like a slave girl from centuries ago.

He paused. She *was* from centuries ago.

She moved, twisting her body until his hand rested just below her chest. His breath caught in the back of his throat. As if his hand had a life of its own, his long fingers smoothed upward to cover her small rounded breast.

She gasped and arched into his hand.

He bent his head and lapped at the pouting nipple through the soft as silk material.

Her moan turned to a groan, and she shuddered.

God, he shouldn't be doing this.

It wasn't fair.

She needed to heal.

She didn't know what she was doing.

She couldn't know what she was doing.

She was dependent on him.

Argh. He pulled back, panting. "No," he groaned in a harsh whisper. "You're hurt."

"I'm hurting," she corrected. "And it's going to hurt more if you don't kiss me again."

He raised himself higher so he could look down into her blue eyes. "Are you sure?"

Her gaze widened. "I get that you're trying to think of me. Giving me a chance to change my mind. But…" She arched her back, brushing her breasts sinuously against his chest. "Unless you've done away with sex in your time…"

"Lord no." His voice was filled with desire, and he lowered his head again. This time, he held nothing back. He wanted her and he wanted her to know how much. All the reasons why this wasn't a good idea no longer mattered.

He wanted to show her how much he cared. Show her how good this could be between them. Instead, it seemed like his fingers were all thumbs and his normal suave skill had taken a hike. He was considered a skilled lover. But today, with her, it mattered too much, and he couldn't seem to get it right. And she didn't appear to notice.

He was all heat. Animal passion and raw need.

He couldn't get enough of her.

Chapter 13

Dani couldn't think. She didn't want to try. Sensations rolled through her, lighting nerve endings, sparking a hunger she hadn't expected. Her body shifted restlessly, rolling from side to side, following his touch. Needing his touch, needing his kisses, needing...everything.

"Dani? Are you sure?"

She stilled. Her eyelids drifted open, the haze of desire parting just enough for a little comprehension to slip in. She stared up into his deep purple eyes. She wanted him. Did it matter that she barely knew him? Not right now. Did it matter the circumstances of how they came together? Not when she already knew him better than she'd known his ancestor.

Levi had shown heart in a tough situation. He came from a position of caring. He'd shelled out a lot of money to help her, and he'd been looking after his incorrigible brother since forever.

She'd enjoy getting to know him better, but she already knew everything that counted.

She felt him pull back, withdrawing. Shit, she'd taken too long.

"Yes," she whispered, her gaze deepening. "I'm sure."

He stilled then shifted, searching her eyes. Whatever he saw made his own warm, deepen. He smiled tenderly. "Good."

And he lowered his head. This time there was nothing hesitant about his touch. He stroked her breasts, cupping them to explore their weight, brushing the hard pebbles with his thumb. As she shivered uncontrollably beneath him, he learned her body with sure strokes, stopping when something fascinated him before carrying on to the next spot. She cried out, wanting the same freedom to touch him, but every time she reached for him, he shifted back or did something else to drive her crazy.

"Just lie back, relax." he whispered.

"Only if I get my turn later," she murmured back.

Deep laughter filled the pod as he said, "My pleasure."

She smiled and stretched out beneath him, her arms above her head, letting him do as he will.

And he took full advantage. He slipped her top over her head to toss on the floor beside them. His breath caught in the back of his throat as he stared down at her breasts.

She gave a cat-like smile and arched upward.

He bent to take one pouting nipple into his mouth and suckled. A deep, pulling sensation started in her lower belly.

Levi stroked down her ribs to rest at her tiny waist, his fingers flaring out to wrap around the swell of her hips. She felt a shudder run through him.

Lifting one foot, she stroked up and down his leg.

"Aren't you wearing a few too many clothes for this activity?"

A wicked grin crossed his features. He slipped out from under the pod lid and stripped efficiently. She watched as his shirt went flying to the left and his pants and, oh nice…boxers…dropped where he stood. If he had socks on, she didn't know or care. She was fascinated as he stood proudly in front of her, fully erect.

She pushed the lid of the pod up higher and patted the bed beside her. Instead he leaned over, slipped his fingers under the waistband of her half short half skirt ensemble, and slowly removed everything, even her panties.

She lay under the glowing pod's healing rays and stretched under his heated gaze. While he stared, she whispered, "Are you planning on just looking," she asked, her voice husky and deep, "or are you going to join me again?"

He walked to the end of the bed, grabbed her ankles, and gave a tug. She slid, legs open, all the way down until the heart of her was pressed up against him with her legs wrapped around his hips.

She laughed. "Nice."

He grinned and dropped down on top of her, his elbows taking his weight. She wrapped her arms around his neck and kissed him. His lips opened, his tongue wrangling softly with hers.

Swiftly he built up the heat between them, his hands restlessly stroking her body while his tongue drove her crazy. He slipped his hands down to her hips and held her firm.

And plunged deep into her center.

She gasped and arched. Shifting to ease the unexpected fullness, she wrapped her legs around his waist and tightened her inner muscles.

It was his turn to groan. Slowly, he withdrew, paused, only to plunge back in deeper. He ground his hips tightly against her for a long moment, then started to move. His rhythm took over her thoughts and mind as he drove her quickly to the edge. She cried out, "Levi!"

"I'm here. Fly with me." He grabbed her hands and stretched them above her head. He kissed her hard and plunged inside once more.

His guttural groan sounded above her. Then a kaleidoscope of sensation exploded inside, overwhelming and filling, but still something wouldn't let her fly free. An edgy nervousness rippled through her.

Levi's hand slid across her palm to entwine with her fingers. She was no longer alone.

And they flew off the edge together.

***

Levi pulled Dani close to his heart. He could only hope this had been the right thing to do. He didn't want her to regret this step in their relationship. In fact, he wanted to love her all over again. And wasn't that a word to scare any single male?

Dani nuzzled against him and gave a happy sigh. He cuddled her closer. "Are you okay?'

"Better than okay. I'm also not sore. Making love in a healing pod – unique concept."

That startled a laugh out of him. "Thanks. Spur of the moment and all that."

"Spontaneity is good for the soul," she murmured sleepily.

"Do you want to stay here and sleep longer?" he asked against her ear.

Her arms squeezed tight. "Only if you stay, too."

"I will until you fall asleep." He shifted down slightly, grabbed the remnants of the blanket hanging off the edge, and wrapped it around her. "Just sleep."

She gave a deep sigh and closed her eyes. She fell asleep almost instantly.

Levi relaxed beside her, a slumberous warmth in his heart. It had been a long time since he'd held a woman like this. Sex, sure, but not the wonderful aftermath that came from making love with someone special.

"Levi," Milo called through the intercom that piped through their home, interrupting his sated mood. "I think we may have more company coming. They just left the office after serving a warrant there."

Levi froze. "Friendlies or unfriendlies?"

"Unfriendlies."

Levi rolled over. "I'm coming. Make sure stealth is on."

He dressed quickly, his mind twisting with possibilities. "What now?" he whispered into the silence. Dani didn't need any more trouble – and neither did he. He just wanted time to spend with her. To get to know her without all the stress in their lives. And…time to spend making love with her.

Instead, he had to handle yet another headache. He dressed quickly, his movements controlled and efficient.

"Milo, did we get notification that they were raiding the office?"

"About an hour ago. But…er…" Milo snickered. "You were busy…so you probably didn't get the messages."

"And you didn't interrupt me for something as important as a raid?" he asked incredulously.

Milo's voice dipped in embarrassment. "Yeah, I was a little involved in my VR unit at the same time."

"Damn it. Not the best timing." He could hardly blame Milo.

He walked out to the kitchen and opened his scanner. When the pod had first been delivered, he'd placed it into a stealth container so that any scanners from outside the building would not be able to see inside. That would keep the pod and Dani secret. He'd have to bring her out of hiding at some point, but hopefully not until she was ready. His comp jangled. He opened the screen to find the Council henchmen once again at his door. His heart sank.

Levi walked over and opened the door. "Good morning, gentlemen. This is becoming a habit."

The guard held up a red comp unit. Shit. His nerves tightened. A court order. "I presume that's for searching the premises?" He reached for the unit, read the details, and sighed heavily. "Of course it is." He stepped aside while clicking through the screen, checking to see what the orders covered. "You're looking for the source of a power surge? In my home?"

"That is correct."

Hard to believe they secured a warrant based only on suspicion. Levi shook his head and leaned back against the door. "Go for it. Although maybe you could explain to me why this supposed power surge is of interest. It's not like they don't happen many times a month."

"The Council is concerned that your brother Milo may be up to his usual tricks."

As if. Levi snorted. "Only he doesn't work at home."

At least he didn't normally. In fact right now, Milo appeared to be putting on coffee. Good. They were all going to need it when this was done.

"We checked your office building already and couldn't find the power issue there." He nodded at the techs doing a quick search of the home. "This is just to follow up."

"Okay." Levi waited with casual nonchalance. Deep inside his head was screaming with warnings. Had they found anything at the office? Was there anything to find here? He'd been so careful, but it was easy to slip up on the little things. Damn Milo for missing that transmission. Instantly he kicked himself. He'd been just as absent as Milo. That he couldn't regret. But seriously, the timing sucked.

After ten minutes, the techs all filed out, shaking their heads. "Are you satisfied?"

The guard nodded. "We will continue searching the other residences." He motioned to the team. "Johan Strand's place is next."

"Wait, what?" Levi asked. "Why would he have something to do with the power surge? And I thought you were searching to see if Milo had something to do with it."

"We had to eliminate any chance of Milo's involvement first." He turned and walked away, presumably to go to Johan's place. Undecided on his next course of action, Levi realized he should warn his friend but at the same time, the guards could find out he'd done so and that could implicate him again. He couldn't risk placing Dani in trouble.

He closed the door and reset the security before leaning back against it. "Shit." He closed his eyes, trying to sort out what had just happened.

"Yeah, more trouble. All brought on by your brother."

"Whoa." Levi turned to see Charmin cleaning his paw on the ledge behind him. "That's not true."

Charmin looked up, smiled, and said, "Really, which part?"

"It doesn't matter. I'm not arguing with a cat." Levi walked past him.

"No, you'd rather mess around with Dani, I suppose."

Levi froze. Not so much that it was the cat talking, or even the words. No, it was the edge to his voice. Like an older brother looking out for his younger sister. A younger sister Levi had been caught dallying with. He even felt heat crawl up his throat.

"Are you saying Dani isn't allowed to have a special friend?"

"Is that what you are?" Charmin's tone of voice was anything but friendly. Levi looked around, hoping for some help, but Dani was sleeping and Milo, per Milo's usual behavior, had taken off. Probably gone to his bedroom. Cornered, Levi tried to think of a way out of this conversation. Then decided on the truth. "I'd like to think so," he said quietly.

Charmin stared at him intently, that gaze locked on his, searching as if he could see into the heart of him. Then he dropped his gaze and shot one leg into the air and started to clean it.

"Uhm..." Levi wasn't sure, but he was going to assume that he'd passed a test of some kind. He backed up quietly. Thankfully, Charmin didn't appear to notice. Levi checked on Dani, happy to see her sleeping soundly, and made his way into the kitchen. He contacted Johan.

Johan's face came on screen. Levi could only see gray walls behind his friend but had no idea where he was – except that he was not at home. "Are you okay?" Levi asked. "The guards just left my place. They're looking for the source of the latest power surge."

"I'm on the move. I slipped out the back and escaped." He grinned. "The guards said they were there to confiscate the pod – and anything else they deemed necessary. Or at least they are trying to. I have the pod set to self-destruct...so if you hear an explosion..." Johan walked forward, the scene behind his head shifting with his every step. "They will find some stuff. Although not what they are expecting."

He laughed, but there was a nasty edge to it.

"Take care of your woman, Levi. I don't know where she came from, but you need to stop the Council from finding out about her."

Levi winced. "What do you know?"

"Not much, except from the pod. Also I recognized your visitor this morning from the rooftop cameras when I did a quick check around." He sighed. "Look, there's a reason we live like we do. We have secrets. Protect yours. I'm going to take a trip. I'll be gone awhile."

As Levi watched, he could see the scenery shift behind his friend. "And a final word to the wise, the tagging, the unregistered pod, anything else you might think you've done to protect her, it won't be enough. You have to give her the protection of your name." His voice deepened. "Power needs power or you won't survive."

And he clicked off with a mock salute.

There was a heavy rumble overhead. That was likely the pod doing its self-destruct thing. Shit. Did it blow up in time or did the Council henchmen get the information they were looking for? And if they had, what recourse was there at this point? His mind flipped to the other shocking point. Johan knew about Dani's tagging? That wasn't good. If he knew – who else could find out just as easily?

Levi's mind raced from one possible problem to another.

What Johan had said was true. He belonged to a long, powerful family line. And that was one thing that the Council couldn't squash. Although his parents were dead, his uncles had kept them relatively protected for decades. Levi tried to be as independent as possible. Milo had pushed the limit, but in a world where applications had to be made and accepted for children to exist, they were treasured. And families stood strong.

Powerful families stood for and against the government. He'd been trying to keep his brother out of any government involvement and so far that had worked, but Johan was right. The easiest way to protect Dani was to enfold her in the family.

If she lived with anyone but Levi and Milo, she'd barely be of interest and could likely live out the rest of her life without raising any flags, but being here with them…

So the easiest answer was to set her up elsewhere away from him. And that he couldn't do. Wouldn't do. Refused to do.

He'd done the best he could with Dani's fake background, but how would it hold up under close scrutiny?

Therefore, there was only one option left. If he'd had two minutes to think, he'd have realized it himself. He had to marry her.

Chapter 14

Dani woke to the sounds of an argument. She was deliciously warm and her body limber and relaxed. In fact, she felt pretty darn good. Even her wrist. She lifted it and rotated her hand experimentally. A low level ache set in, but it wasn't bad. She ran her fingers across the surface and pressed gently. The ache deepened, but considering what surgery had been done, it looked and felt amazing. She rolled over and shrieked.

"Damn it, Charmin, why are you sitting there staring at me like that?"

His whiskers quivered but he stayed quiet. She frowned, reaching up to stroke his back. "Charmin, are you okay?"

"Yes." He paused. "Are you?"

She frowned. "Yes, I'm feeling much better." She held out her wrist. "See, I'm chipped now." She laughed. "Stupid, huh?"

"He's not Lawrence," Charmin said, "but how do you know he's not *like* Lawrence?"

Heat rose on her cheeks. It was stupid to be embarrassed. Charmin was a cat, what did he know about relationships?

"I know he's not. I'm not trying to relive a dream," she said earnestly. "By the time my relationship was over, he wasn't the same man he'd been in the beginning."

"Lawrence was always the same. You just finally opened your eyes and saw him."

Wisdom from a cat. Wow. It was going to take some doing to get used to this.

"You're right. But Levi is hardly the same type of man."

"And yet…"

She stiffened. "What's your problem with me having a relationship with Levi? Cat relationships last all of ten minutes."

"Except with you."

She smiled and reached for his chin to give him a good neck scratch. Charmin was as insecure in this new world as she was. A relationship with Levi would put his nose out even more. His eyes crossed in joy. Seconds later, his engine started up. She lay there rubbing Charmin and thinking about her convoluted relationship with Levi.

Milo raced into the pod room. "You have to get dressed. We all have to appear in front of the Council." And he bolted away.

Fear stabbed her stomach. *Oh no.* She couldn't do this. But there was no choice.

Charmin spoke up abruptly. "Remember how you always dreamed about marriage and kids one day?"

She looked at him. "Yes?"

"Well, you just might be in for a surprise." And he hopped down and moved stiffly to the doorway. He turned to look back at her. "Remember to keep your dreams fluid."

And he left.

Even more concerned now, she got dressed and made her way out to the kitchen. Levi was standing there, talking in a low voice to Milo.

"What's going on?"

Levi spun, smiled at her, and took a deep breath. "The first night you were here, I took you to Johan's pod. I tried to erase the information, but it caused some issues on the machine and sent corrupted data to the Council. Johan had some of the information still in the unit. When he was raided this morning, the Council gained access to the bulk of his place. He's gone travelling to avoid the Council. He had his own reasons for not wanting the Council to gain access to his place."

She shook her head. "So we're safe?"

"No. In fact, there is only one way to make sure you are safe." He paused, and Milo spoke up. "Make sure you know what you are doing, Levi."

Levi spun on him, his anger turning his face red. "You brought this on. Not me. Not Dani. Yet we are the ones that are taking the hit."

"You don't have to. We can find another solution."

"Really?" Levi asked, bitterness in his voice. "You've had time to utilize that magnificent brain of yours – what solution did you come up with?"

Milo looked downcast. "Sorry, bro, I hadn't thought this through far enough."

"Yes, that's exactly right."

"What does this have to do me?" Dani crossed her arms over her chest, wishing they'd get to the point. "Milo said something about having to appear in front of the Council?"

"Yes. The occupants of my residence have been ordered to appear. They already suspect there are three of us here, therefore the three of us will show up. It also means they'll know that you were the one in the pod." He paused. "The thing is, I don't think you are ready. There are too many pitfalls that you could get into trouble over."

"But there isn't an option, is there?" She studied his face even as her stomach sank. In fact, panic settled in on the edge of her consciousness. "I *really* don't want to go if I don't have to."

Milo nodded. Levi said, "My family is wealthy, powerful, and we have members in big business across most sectors."

She waited.

"With all the problems…past, present, and potential…" He took a deep breath. "The best way I can protect you is to give you the benefit of my name. I can stand in front of the Council on your behalf that way." He paused, then added, "There is only one way to do that."

Her heart stopped. *What did that mean?*

"Dani, will you marry me?"

***

Levi held his breath. Inside, he wanted to wrap her up and rush her to the opposite end of the planet. Only that would just delay the same ending. They'd be found. There was no way they wouldn't. But she looked so lost. So forlorn. It broke his heart.

He walked over and tugged her into his arms. He didn't love her, but he knew he was well on his way to that state. But she hadn't had a chance. To understand life here. To understand her options. To understand what any of this meant.

"I just want to go home," she whispered, her words a dagger to his heart.

Charmin hopped up onto the table, whispered, "Me too."

"I'm sorry," Levi said to them both. "That's the one thing we can't do for you."

"Well, at least not yet." Milo said, "I might be able to build a new program, but they took most of my computer equipment from the office during the raid. It will take years to recreate my work."

"Do they know what they have?" she asked, peering around Levi's shoulder.

Milo shook his head vigorously. "No, the program was set to corrupt when anyone else accessed it. My records show it's gone."

She stared at him suspiciously. "And you didn't have a backup? A half dozen backups? Some modern way to make sure you didn't lose everything?"

He gave her a sheepish grin. "I do, but it's not that simple. It's in pieces and everything is encrypted." He frowned. "Chances are I could put it together again, but knowing that it succeeded and that they are now looking at it makes me less likely to want to even try. It could take years to make it functional – even worse – there's no way to test if it works." He glared at Dani in a challenging manner. "Are you going to want to try it under those circumstances?"

She shifted her gaze to Levi. "I have to make a decision today?"

Levi winced. "We have to be at the Council in an hour."

She stared at him. "And what? We're going to tell the Council that we are engaged?"

Charmin snorted. "Engaged? You?"

Milo and Levi looked at each other. Milo grinned. "Nope. You're going to be married." He started to laugh.

Levi growled, "Milo, stop."

But he laughed louder. Between his giggles, he said, "Except for the final formality, you're already married. He just didn't bother asking you."

Chapter 15

Dani stared at the two men. One howling with ill-placed humor, oh so typical of a teenager. And the other shuffling uneasily on his feet.

Charmin, his eyes bright and lively, stayed quiet, watchful. *Smart.*

"Are we married?" she asked in an ominous voice. Could something like that really have happened without her permission or her knowing? Of course it could. These two could do anything.

She studied Levi's stance. She didn't believe he'd done it for a bad reason. After all, he could marry anyone. Why her? Unless he cared about trying to keep her safe. Of course, keeping her safe also meant keeping his brother safe – so that made a kind of sense.

But that was the last reason she wanted to get married. All she ever wanted was to be loved. For herself. Not because she was a problem.

She gazed out the window, realizing it was uncovered. She wasn't sure she wanted to look out. To see what was outside. She'd loved the bit from the rooftop space, but she knew there would be more out there. She'd wanted to stay inside and avoid the reality check of her new…reality. She was in hiding like a victim. And she was damn tired of feeling that way.

Ignoring the two men, she walked over to the window and stared out. Even though she'd seen little bits and pieces before, she almost turned around and ran back to the healing pod. With no frame of reference for what she could see outside, the thought of going out there terrified her. The odd-shaped buildings appeared even closer from here. More alien in shapes and color. And...the flying cars – if they were flying at all, which they weren't – at least not in any way she understood flying. The cars had no wings. They all proceeded in an orderly fashion – at breakneck speeds!

A shiver ran through her. She'd seen this all before. Something about this time...brought the reality of her situation closer to home. It had been fun, maybe getting to the point of being exciting. But now that she'd have to appear in front of the Council...everything was suddenly magnified. This was not her world. She didn't belong here. She spun around and closed her eyes.

There was no way she was going out there.

She could hardly breathe. She gasped for breath. Levi rushed over. "Easy, Dani. Take it easy. It's not that bad."

Her head shook and the words wouldn't come out. She pointed out the window. He winced and pressed a button. Instantly, the light in the room darkened as if he'd closed the curtains. Only there'd been no whoosh of material sliding across the window or blinds being dropped.

"I'm sorry. This is just the same view that you saw on the rooftop garden." He reached out to rub her shoulder. "The blinds have been closed for the last few days. Milo opened them this morning."

"It's one thing to see that out there when I'm safe in here, but to know that I will be forced to go into that world...to face the Council...it is not easy to be so detached."

"I hate the darkened room." Milo said cheerfully. "Felt like we were living in a prison."

His high-pitched voice paired with his words made her turn her head and stare at him. His bright purple air boots shone weirdly in the half light. She wondered if he was as harmless as he liked to appear. She hoped so. He could do a lot of harm to her if he chose. She gazed over at Levi. He was glaring at his brother, obviously not liking his word choices. Then again, neither did she.

She asked quietly, "Are we already married?"

"Not fully. We need your acceptance."

"But the preparation, the paperwork, the legalities?"

"All done."

She shook her head. "When did you do this?"

"This morning." he said quietly. "After I realized that it was the only answer."

"After the raid." She nodded, starting to understand. "After the Council went to Johan's."

"I called Johan to warn him, but he had already slipped away. He told me about the possibility that the Council may have some information I didn't want them to have."

"Why would your name protect me?" She shook her head. "That makes no sense."

"Only because you don't understand how our government works today. We can protect you. But I need the family to help. Once you're family, they will surround you. Shield you. You can have me represent you in front of the Council as your legal partner. I already have the papers drawn up. Then you'll be safe."

The thought of leaving the safety of the apartment made her feel faint. The thought of facing the Council brought on the nausea. She couldn't face strangers. Not now. Not yet. She shuddered inwardly. Maybe never. She studied Levi's serious face. "And will you be safe, too?"

"Yes. We will be, too." He nodded.

"Then your logic is flawed. Because if that were the case, you'd be protected now. You two already have the family name."

Milo snorted. "She's got you there."

"No. She doesn't understand." He shot an exasperated look at his brother before turning back to face Dani. "The family has been protecting us. But at the same time, Milo keeps crossing the line. This time, there is more than just us at stake. I couldn't live with myself if anything happened to you. When the family closes ranks around you, we can make all this go away."

"You hope..."

A weird musical sound filled the air. Levi looked frustrated for a moment. He ran his fingers through his hair. "It's time."

"Time for what?" Dani asked, looking around for the source of the music.

"Time for you to say yes or no." He took a step toward her. "Please, say yes."

She stared at him, confused but realizing that he wanted – needed – the process finalized before she showed up at the Council. Something that mattered to keep her safe. To keep him and Milo safe. She didn't care about Milo, but she didn't want anything to happen to Levi. She hadn't known him long, but what she did know, she liked – a lot. She could fall in love with him. But that could only happen if she agreed to his plan. A plan that was deeply uncertain. But what were her choices?

None.

Damn.

"I need to know something first." She couldn't get over the feeling that there was something here that she didn't know. Something they weren't coming clean about. And she needed them to. "Why me? I understand that stuff about picking me because I was close, etc. But there had to have been thousands of other women who would do."

Milo laughed. "I can tell you the truth about that now that you're almost family." He pointed at Levi. "My big brother here carries a picture of a woman around. I saw it a long time ago and asked him about it. It's originally from our family archives." Milo's grin widened. "He told me he didn't know why, but there was something about the woman's smile that struck him as special."

She turned to stare at Levi.

Milo beamed. "Show her, Levi."

Dani walked closer. "May I see it?"

Levi frowned, then reluctantly pulled a square metal-looking thing from his pocket. He unfolded it several times before handing it over.

She gasped. "Where did you get this?"

"I told you," Milo said, "From the family archives."

Dani stared at the very same picture she'd ripped into little pieces and tossed into the garbage – or would be the same image except that the part with Lawrence had been cut away, leaving just a shot of her face. She couldn't believe what she was looking at. Coincidence? Fate? Destiny?

How much had her life changed in what – one day? Two days? She couldn't tell anymore.

She lifted her stunned gaze to Milo. "Based on this, you brought me here?"

"That image was the start of my research. I ran the tests, probabilities, scans, more tests – and you passed – so I figure why not do something for my brother – who's always doing nice things for me?" He patted Levi on the shoulder. "You were meant to be a gift for Levi."

Bells chimed again. Levi looked at her, his voice low, urgent as he said, "Dani?"

Her gaze went from one brother to the other. Levi had taken the first step with the photo.

Milo the next.

This step was hers to take.

She swallowed, held out her hand, and said, "Yes, Levi. I will marry you."

And Charmin, who'd been silent up until now, added, "Finally…"

Broken Protocols 2
By
Dale Mayer

Broken Protocols 2

The future is a dangerous place...
To save her skin and the skin of her new lover, Dani Summerland marries Levi Blackburn. That's the good part. The bad part is that she and Levi realize they're pawns in a game with no rule book.

Levi Blackburn can't believe he's married – but he's a lucky man and he knows it. Now he needs to find out who is after Dani and why so they can start their honeymoon.

As they struggle to find out who's targeting them and what they want, the danger escalates and people around them start dying.

It's a good thing Charmin Marvin, her talking cat, is helping them.

More protocols are broken and if they can't win this game, their lives will be broken, too.

Dale Mayer
Valley Publishing
Copyright © 2014
Cover model - Mirish (http://mirish.deviantart.com)
Cover designer - Jason Mayer
ISBN-13:9781927461891

Protocol 2:3:5 – *You will in no way use force to damage the life of another – particularly if those actions are to selfishly enhance your own.*

Chapter 1

Married? To Levi Blackburn? Just like that. Dani Summerland's sense of humor kicked in. How typical of her crazy life. She couldn't find a man on her own in the 21st century but was already married after a couple of days in the 23rd century. That was some matchmaking trick.

And not by choice.

Well, technically that wasn't true. The marriage part was by choice. At least it seemed like a great idea at the time. All of five minutes ago.

Dani Summerland stared suspiciously at the odd looking adornment on her finger. It looked like a ring. It didn't feel like one. In fact, there was almost no weight to it at all. And given the size of the deep purple rock on top, she thought she'd have noticed. Even the metal was soft – comfortable to wear.

She held her fingers splayed wide and shifted her hand in the age old movement of women ever since rings were invented.

"Is it all right?" Levi Blackburn, her new husband, and yet still a stranger in many ways, stepped a little closer to her. The clear glass cube, or what stood in for being an elevator of this time period was almost normal – but there was no way she'd become accustomed to it as it disappeared into thin air when they arrived at their destination.

She flashed him a quick grin. "Sure. I'm just not used to wearing big rocks that appear to be made of nothing or that adjust automatically to any size."

"It's the new alloys," Milo, Levi's brainy child brother, piped up. "Gold fell from grace when the shortage came about 90 years ago. This was the answer."

"And the supersized rocks?" she asked, playing with the rock to make it twinkle in the light.

"Most are synthetic." Milo judged his brother in a joking manner. "But not this one."

She frowned, pretty sure that the rocks in her day came in a synthetic variation as well. But they still had weight.

Then she had no time to wonder as they arrived at their destination. "Now remember, just smile," Levi said. "Hold out your arm when requested to do so, but don't say a word." He shoved his arm outward to demonstrate.

She imitated his actions.

With a nod, he said, "If anyone asks where you're from, tell them you're from Felonia and that you arrived just a couple of days ago."

"Felonia," she repeated dutifully, dread congealing into a nasty ball in her stomach at the thought of anyone speaking to her. "Are you sure I can't just go home?"

"I wish you could. But after this, no one will question your presence or your absence in the future." Levi wrapped an arm around her shoulder and led her forward. For all appearances, he looked like the doting new bridegroom. She shivered inwardly at the remembered passion they'd shared. Now if only they could head off on a romantic honeymoon.

But apparently not. She managed a warm glowing smile. He was her lifeline right now. And had quickly become the love of her life.

And for that, she'd even put up with his brother Milo. Whom she had yet to forgive for dragging her into this century. Using an amazingly advanced computer program, he'd gone back in time, snatched her up, and brought her here as a gift for his brother, Levi.

Talk about a mind bender.

That he'd also brought Charmin and accidentally enhanced Charmin's communication abilities, which was originally intended for her, was beyond anything she could have imagined.

The tube disappeared and Levi, his arm wrapped around her, led her forward into a large room with a clerk standing at the ready. "Good morning. Dani Summerland," Levi said. "Levi Blackburn and Milo Blackburn reporting in as requested."

The clerk frowned. "Only your presence was requested. Not your brother." He glanced up, saw Dani, and his frown deepened. "Not your girlfriend."

Dani straightened in outrage. Levi squeezed her shoulders. "My wife and brother are here because everyone living in my house was requested to attend."

"Wife?" Now the clerk's frown deepened. He clicked madly away on his weird tablet computer. Dani couldn't help but be fascinated as the lights flashed and pages shifted in a wildly erratic pattern she suspected was anything but erratic. She'd always loved computers. She hoped that she'd learn how these worked soon.

"Why do I have no record of that? I should have been notified." His voice rose slightly.

Control freak much? She eased out a shaky breath, trying to appear natural. As if showing up in a futuristic Council to answer for something she had nothing to do with was completely normal. She'd wanted to bring Charmin with her for comfort, but both brothers had shot that idea down instantly.

Charmin hadn't liked it much either.

Even now she wanted to go back and hug him. He was her only link to her old life.

The clerk finally looked up and studied her. Whatever he saw made his lips curl. "Don't tell me, she's from the outer areas. From a fringe group."

Cutting words bubbled up on Dani's tongue, but she bit them back. She had no idea what the outer areas meant, but she didn't deserve to be treated as a lesser person because of it.

Levi nodded comfortably. "She is."

The clerk rolled his eyes. "Whatever. I'll put her down."

Levi nodded his thanks politely and led Dani into a huge chamber room where the ceiling appeared so high up she couldn't see the top. "Wait here. I shouldn't be long."

She reacted instinctively, reaching out to grab his hand. "Are you sure you can't sit here beside me?"

He leaned over and dropped a kiss on her forehead. "You'll be fine." He looked up and nodded his head at someone. "Here's my lawyer. John Driscoll."

Dani turned as the stranger approached. He wore a uniquely tailored suit in glowing blue patterns. The styles might not have changed a lot, but the colors of today sure had. She smiled a polite greeting and shook his hand, charmed at the old style greeting.

"Levi. Are you ready?"

Levi nodded. "I was just settling Dani here where she'd be comfortable."

John smiled at her, and damn if one of his teeth didn't wink out at her the same color as his suit. Wow. Tooth jewelry. Her gaze widened and her breath caught in the back of her throat. It was all she could do to not say something. Instead, she turned to look around her to see the room filling up. Several people took seats. She decided the best thing was to do the same. She watched one man sit down on a black pole that instantly widened to accommodate his butt.

Taking a deep breath, she promptly sat down on the closest pole, her breath whooshing out when it opened successfully into a seat to support her butt. *Thank heavens*. She smiled up at the brothers. "Go on, I'll be fine."

Milo gave her a weird finger salute she guesstimated meant something similar to 'right on' and turned and walked forward. He'd certainly dressed up for the occasion, wearing a black and white striped skin suit. She shuddered at the jailbird look. It didn't matter how long she lived here, she was never going to wear a skin suit like that.

As if understanding her thoughts, Levi bent over and whispered, "You'd look better in that than he does." He kissed her cheek, winked at her, and walked away.

The lawyer, thankfully not sporting painted-on skin pants, waited a few steps ahead for Levi to catch up. Heads bent deep in discussion, they strode out of the room.

And left her alone.

***

Leaving Dani in the waiting room was one of the hardest things Levi had ever done. She knew no one, nothing about the world she found herself in or the pitfalls that awaited her every time she opened her mouth to speak. But he had no choice. He quickened his pace to catch up to Milo strolling on ahead. His brother's flagrant disregard for the rules had put them in this situation. Only Levi had compounded the situation by using his friend's healing pod to help heal the damage done to Dani and Charmin from time travelling.

He could only hope that his friend's attempt to destroy the pod Levi had used to heal Dani would make today's Council visit more of a maintenance check up than an actual investigation. He'd had John meet them here just in case, but he hadn't had time to brief him.

The legal fees that his company paid to keep John's law firm available for times like this was exorbitant. As they were checked at the door and led into a smaller chamber, Levi spotted his old friend Stephen Cavendish on the Council dais. Relief swelled inside. This might have started as a witch hunt, but it wasn't going to end up that way. Stephen, young and only a junior council member, was on Levi's side when it came to Government meddling. And played the game well.

He smiled at his friend, relaxing even more when Stephen winked at him. This would be just fine.

Stephen opened the discussion. "I hear congratulations are in order, Levi?"

Levi beamed. "They are indeed."

Milo bobbed at his side, his headset in. He rarely spoke at these meetings. Probably just as well. What came out usually didn't bode well for Levi.

In a genial let's-get-this-over-with-so-I-can-get-back-to-my-honeymoon tone of voice, Levi asked, "What is the problem that you needed to disturb me during my time of celebration?" He kept his face curious but amiable – at least he hoped it was. One sign of fear and these vultures would pounce.

"It's your friend Johan Strand. He's wanted by the Council. When his request to appear was ignored, a team was sent to retrieve him. Unfortunately, he'd set up some kind of self-detonation on several of his equipment centers. Suspicious behavior at best," said one of the senior Council members. "As your residence is known to be associated with him, we requested everyone there to appear here for questioning."

That's not quite the way Levi understood events to have gone down, but it wouldn't be the first time that the Council had twisted things to suit them. "First, Johan is an acquaintance, not a friend," Levi said in a what-has-this-got-to-do-with-me voice. "Second, I don't know anything about his equipment. Nor do I know where he is, if that is what you are looking to me for answers about." He stood tall and straight. "And my wife knows even less."

The Council stared at him. Even Stephen. Then again, he'd always been good at playing the Council game.

Levi waited patiently. Ever since Milo had gotten them in hot water a year ago, whenever there was a question the Council wanted answered or information they needed to collect, he and Milo were dragged down to appear in person. As if they couldn't lie or cheat their way through these sessions in person like they might be able to through a HoloKomp. He suspected that the Council ran illegal scans on every person that entered these rooms. Hence the reason for keeping Dani out. She might not pass the scans.

He needed the Council to find nothing wrong for a few more months. Then he could start asking them to back off before he involved the lawyers at a more in depth level. As it were, today was one step from harassment. And John had brought that up more than once. But Levi needed to keep a low profile while Dani settled in. No one could take a closer look at her right now.

He couldn't imagine the shock of what she'd been put through. He didn't think he'd have handled it half as well as she had if he'd been in the same situation. In fact, he knew he wouldn't. He looked around, seeing Milo and his lawyer...his extended family only a call away. He'd lose everything familiar and dear.

Just like Dani had.

For the first time, he had a little insight to all that she'd lost.

And how little he could do to make up for it. He'd done his best to protect her, but he could never replace everything.

"Levi?" John nudged him. With a startled look at his old friend, he realized the Council was talking.

"We need to know any information," the elder Councilman, Carlson, said in a tone that demanded obedience. "Any names or locations that you may have heard Johan mention to try and track him down."

Levi frowned while he stopped to consider the request. "In truth, I'm not sure I ever heard him mention anyone or any place in particular. He was notorious for his parties, and serious talk didn't happen then, nor were there any party goers who wanted to talk."

"And yet, he mentioned the two of you going out for coffee after your last appearance here."

Levi's eyebrows shot up at the reminder. However, he answered smoothly, "He did invite me, but the coffee never happened. He wanted to go and see his lawyers instead so he asked for a rain check."

That at least was the truth. He suspected they already knew what he'd done that day. A drone would have noted his and Johan's actions at the time and submitted a report on both men filed away for future reference. The Council muttered between them for a long moment.

"Your answers have been recorded. Should you have any further information to offer regarding the issue, please contact the office."

A different Council member spoke. "We notice that Milo has not added anything to the conversation."

Levi shrugged. "He has nothing to say. He had nothing to do with Johan."

"Not one of the regular party goers?" Eyebrows shot sky high and amused twitters rippled through the Council members.

Milo was an anomaly to them. He lived in his own world and wouldn't have attended one of Johan's parties if his life depended on it. His parties were always private with his other geek friends. Levi highly suspected they played more computer games than sex games when they were together. His whole group was more active sexually in VR than in real life. But that might also be his age or his perspective on other people. Milo was light years ahead of others. While they were looking into a coffee cup and wondering at the pretty pattern the cream made as it was poured, Milo had already analyzed the composition, calories, health detriments, and health benefits for everyone in the damn room as well as who could tolerate that level of fat and who should be running in the opposite direction.

No one was like his brother.

Councilman Carlson said, "And the other occupant in your residence?"

"My wife, Dani?" Levi hated the way Carlson spoke about Dani. "You know her name is Dani. She isn't an *occupant*."

"Is she here?" The speaker ignored his comment, choosing instead to stare at him in a cold manner.

"She is waiting in the outer chamber." Levi curled his upper lip. "I speak on her behalf. All documents have been filed as per protocol."

After a moment where the men clicked away on their comps to verify his statement, the men nodded. Stephen smiled at him.

Levi's breath whooshed out. So they'd skated by safely again.

But for how much longer?

He pushed Milo ahead of him as they walked out. Now to collect Dani and get her home, safe and sound.

As he walked back into the anteroom, he realized she was no longer sitting where he'd left her.

In fact, there was no sign of her. "Shit."

Chapter 2

Dani sat in silence, watching in wonderment as the kaleidoscope of people walked by. Just like in her time, there was a mix of races and ethnic groups. Skin appeared to come in a few more colors, like a light mauve, teal, and copper shades. She didn't know if those were medical enhancements, cosmetic changes, or something genetic. The copper-toned skins were beautiful, but the purple and pink ones were fascinating. Hair was another anomaly. It appeared as if anything went here. Colors from glittery black to Milo's wild green appeared on men in business clothing similar to what Levi's lawyer wore.

The artist and female in her was fascinated and a little jealous of the women here. Every color from the rainbow was represented – plus some she swore she'd never seen before. The skirts appeared to shift and almost wrap around the women's legs as if it was some kind of intelligent material. And maybe it was. The fashions were unlike anything she'd seen before. It wasn't like old styles coming back around again. Instead, this time frame had made huge leaps in terms of fashion sense. She glanced down at her own interesting clothing, realizing she did fit in, but likely with a younger group than those she saw here.

Another thing that caught her eyes was the lack of purses or bags or even briefcases. How could that be? Everyone had to carry something.

Odd.

How did they carry laptops, tablets, or whatever the modern version was? Where did women put their makeup?

As she pondered life in this century, a beautiful businesswoman sat down beside her. Dani started. Dressed with severely coiffed hair in an almost purple-black one-piece skin suit, very little was left to the imagination. Dani stared. The woman's eyes were a deep emerald green. And her smile was nothing like anyone she'd seen before.

"Hi, Dani."

Dani shrank back. Her tentative smile dropped away in shock. *How did this woman know her?*

"I'm Lina Stewart. John is my boss," the woman said reassuringly. "Our law firm represents Levi and Milo," she added.

Relief caused some of the tension to slip away. "Oh, they've all gone into that room." Dani motioned behind her.

The woman nodded. "That's normal." She paused, studying Dani's face intently. "But there's nothing normal about you, is there?

Dani's gaze widened, her stomach sinking. "Pardon?"

"Oh come on, that innocent lost girl look might work on Levi, but I know better." She settled more comfortably, but her sharp gaze never left Dani. Studying, probing, as if trying to figure out something. "You managed to marry one of the most eligible bachelors around. It's not like I can do anything about that." Her smile turned glacial. "At least not right now."

Dani just stared. She waited for the woman to say more. If she wasn't careful, this was a conversation guaranteed to get her into trouble. Like what the hell? Was this woman jealous? Her last comment had sounded almost threatening. Too bad women hadn't changed with the time. There'd been ambitious cats in her century, too.

When the other woman didn't speak again, Dani plastered a cool confident smile on her face and said, "I'm sorry, I don't understand."

The other woman snorted and sat back, an irritated edge to her features. "Right. Fine. Be that way if you want." She looked around at the crowd. "Hopefully the men will be done soon and we can leave."

Dani murmured something but even she didn't know what it was. She was still struggling with her reaction. Relief and worry had taken over her bloodstream and a headache like she'd never had before was building quickly. Too quickly. Where was a healing pod when she needed one?

"Are you all right?"

"I'm fine. Just a bit of a headache is all."

That brought the other woman's head around, her sharp gaze locking on Dani's face. "Why the devil would you allow one of those? Levi really fell for this back-to-natural stuff, huh? Never thought he'd be such a dupe." Lina snickered and stood up. "Later."

And she walked away.

And what was that about all natural? Had people managed to do away with headaches completely here? But in a non-natural way? How confusing. More questions to ask Levi.

Dani was left mulling over her words, her gaze on the woman's retreating back, when Lina just…disappeared. No cube surrounded her, nothing. She was there one moment then gone the next.

Dani stared at the spot Lina had disappeared from to see a series of circles on the floor. She couldn't help thinking of the Star Trek movies from her day and the transporter system. Was that possible here? Or was the system even more advanced?

There were other circles on the floor, with people stepping in and out just as suddenly as they arrived and left. She hadn't noticed them before, but people were arriving and leaving on that odd circle system. But where were they going to and coming from?

And how did they not crash into each other in transit?

She got shivers just thinking about it. What kind of a world had she found herself in? Her headache grew. She wished Levi was done. All she wanted was to be back home safe in the healing pod with Charmin.

And damned if her wrist didn't start to flash weird colors right then. Flustered, she dropped her arms into her lap and slapped her right hand over the lights. But they flashed brightly between her fingers. She had no idea what any of it meant. Neither had she seen anyone else's wrist start a light show.

Even as she thought that, it seemed as if everyone suddenly noticed her. Plain Jane Dani was getting way too much attention than was good for her. She tried to hide the bright lights against her belly but nothing seemed to do the job.

She searched behind her, desperately hoping for Levi or Milo to show up.

There was no sign of either of them.

Suddenly her arm was grabbed and she was jerked up and out of her chair and pushed toward one of those weird circles.

Lina Stewart. "You're coming with me," the older woman snapped as she pushed Dani forward. Dani stumbled and would have fallen but for Lina's grasp on her arm. "What are you doing?"

"Shut up."

Dani pulled back and managed to get free of Lina. Lina snorted, gave her a short shove, and…the room disappeared.

Oh no. Dani could hardly swallow. Her throat convulsed, and it was all she could do to keep the food in her stomach. She didn't know what had happened, but it hurt like hell.

"Jesus, what is wrong with you?" The disgust in Lina's voice had the effect of pushing the nausea up a notch, sending Dani almost to her knees.

"I'm sick," Dani whispered, bending over and trying to take deep breaths. "Where is Levi?"

"They're almost done. If you throw up in my office, I'm charging Levi for the damages."

"It wouldn't be in your office if you hadn't shoved me in here." Dani snapped with as much backbone as she could muster, helping regain her equilibrium. "Take me back to Levi."

Lina shook her head. "I don't get it. He actually married you? I can see partying for a day or two, but marriage?" She turned on her heel and opened her comp. "John, I have Dani at the office."

She clicked off her comp. "Sit down for heaven's sake. They should be here soon."

Shudders rippled down Dani's spine. She cast a quick glance around the gleaming iridescent room. There had to be something to sit on – just not something she recognized as a chair. "I'll stand," she said quietly.

That only earned her another disgusted look. "Whatever." Lina walked out of the room, leaving Dani alone.

Thank God.

A window was open on the far side. Not trusting that she was truly alone or that she wasn't being recorded in some way, she walked over to the window, schooled her features, and looked out. Another traffic scene. This time she was able to look at the vehicles and the pattern of controlled pandemonium. She didn't think she'd ever drive in this lifetime. The sheer speed of the chaos outside the window shook her. That she didn't know the rules of the road was one thing, but she didn't think there'd ever come a time when she'd be comfortable enough to follow whatever passed for rules here.

This place was just too...out there for her.

And where the hell were Levi and Milo? They shouldn't have left her alone. At least not for this long. She understood on one level, but on another...how was she to know about the Lina's of his world or the weird circles on the floor and the non-existent furniture she was supposed to sit on? She hadn't had a chance to do or see or *learn* anything. She'd been concerned with healing enough to just be able to walk.

There was an odd whoosh in the center of the room.

She spun around, her hand going to her chest. *Now what?*

***

Levi turned in a slow circle, his gaze darting from side to side. "Come on, Dani, where are you?"

Milo stared at him. "What did you say?"

"Where's Dani?" Levi muttered softly.

Milo's gaze widened in horror and he spun around. And continued to spin in a slow movement as he searched the room a second time.

"Maybe she had to go to the washroom," he suggested.

John approached the two of them. "I'll file a motion when I get back to the office to have any further Council meetings done by comp. It's ridiculous that we have to continue to show up in person to answer a few questions."

Levi pulled his attention back to look at John. "Good. Please do that. And thanks for your help there." He watched as his lawyer walked away, the blue of his suit shimmering in the brilliant colored crowd.

As soon as he was out of sight, Levi spun to find Milo on his comp. "Tell me you found her."

"There's no sign of her anywhere." Milo swore under his breath before sucking it in sharply. "Wait. Incoming."

Where the hell could Dani have gone? Levi lifted his shoulders. "Incoming what?"

Milo gasped then choked. "Incoming message. From Charmin Marvin?"

Levi turned so he could see Charmin's feline face over Milo's shoulder. "Dani is in trouble. Tracking...now on."

"What the hell?" His words, even voiced low, caught the attention of curious passerbys. Damn. The place was crowded. Still, their curiosity was a good reminder that anything they did and said was likely being recorded.

"Yeah, he's good." Milo clicked a few more buttons. "Got her. She's at John's office."

"How the hell..." Levi raced to the ports.

"Lina took her there," Milo called, running behind him.

He stepped into the port and appeared at Lina's office, Milo right behind him.

And there was Dani.

She stared at him in shock. When she realized he was there in person, she raced toward him. He caught her in his arms and hugged her tightly. "It's okay," he murmured. "I'm here."

She couldn't stop shaking or burrowing closer. Her arms locked around his waist and wouldn't let go. He held her close and continued to whisper comforting things in her ear.

"As you can see, she's fine," Lina snapped. "Lord, all this fuss over nothing."

It was Milo who came to Dani's rescue. "Really? You remove someone from the Council offices without anyone's permission, including that of the woman you kidnapped, and you say it's nothing?"

At the word kidnapping, Lina gasped and Dani burrowed deeper into Levi's embrace. "I did no such thing." Lina stormed closer. "Dani was attracting attention. What did you expect me to do?"

"In what way was she attracting attention?" Levi asked.

"She sat so damn still. So perfect. Like a statue," Lina snorted. "She didn't move, no comp, no nothing. Just an oddness that stood out." She shrugged. "Then her ID started to flash. It was too close to the Missing Person's Alert. Like really." Lina rolled her eyes. "I had to stop her from making a spectacle of herself."

"So because she wasn't you – you figured she was odd." Milo mimicked her voice so perfectly that Levi had to bite back a grin. "And there's any number of reasons for her ID to flash."

"It wasn't so much that it flashed, it was the look of shock, horror, and confusion on her face that was so ridiculous." Lina glared at them. "She was fine when I first saw her. So I left her alone. It was only after I returned that I realized she was causing such a commotion."

Milo narrowed his eyes. "And you couldn't leave it alone. Not because she was garnering attention, but because you weren't. For some reason, he married her, not you. She had him, you didn't. It was all about jealousy, wasn't it?" Milo snapped forward from his sixteen-year-old self with a wisdom beyond his years. "Levi partied with you and you wanted more.

He didn't. Next thing you know, he shows up with this natural girl and is married to her."

Lina's voice turned cutting. "Go back to bed, Milo. It's a little late for you to be up, isn't it?"

Dani lifted her head from against his chest and in low tones, said, "Can we go home now?"

He hugged her gently. To the others, he said, "You two can stay and fight if you want. I'm taking her back. She's been sick and needs rest."

"She could get that fixed. Playing on your sympathies, you know." Lina threw up her hands. "Whatever." And she strode out of the room again.

Milo glared at her receding back. "Bitch."

Dani giggled. "Glad to hear that word is still used nowadays."

"Especially nowadays," Milo said with a smile. "Let's go home."

"Yes, please. By the way," she said, "how did you know I was here? She left a message on John's comp or whatever that thing is, but I didn't see her call you two."

"That's because she didn't," Levi said, loosening his arms and turning her gently.

Milo bounced on his heels to his toes. "You aren't going to believe what *did* happen."

She twisted slightly to look him in the face. Levi kept her walking forward. "Why? What happened?" She looked up at Levi. "Not John?"

Milo shook his head, almost dancing with glee now.

Levi gave a low deep rumble of a laugh. "Charmin Marvin told us."

She stared at him. "What? Really?"

They both nodded.

Her sense of humor kicked in and she giggled.

Levi grabbed her up in his arms for a hug, stepped into the same circle Dani had popped out of earlier and led her out into the Council anteroom within seconds. Her joy was a light in his life. She had to be feeling rough enough without feeling the cutting edge of Lina's tongue, but it hadn't gotten her down. She was a survivor.

Lina had been a mistake years ago. He should never have hooked up with her. After she'd joined his lawyer's firm, their first business meeting have been slightly uncomfortable, but then he'd promptly forgotten about her and the weekend party. An easy thing to do.

To think she'd gone after Dani, regardless of her motives, concerned him. She'd said it was to protect him, to protect Dani, but there'd been no need to remove Dani from where he'd left her. And if she'd said something to John, why hadn't his lawyer said something to him?

Levi mulled it over, not liking where the information was taking him. Innocent miscommunication? Or something more sinister?

Milo's com beeped again. The three were back in the Council room where Dani had originally been waiting for them. They exited through security. On the other side, Milo stopped and tugged Dani toward him. "Could you please look into my com?"

She shot him a startled look. "What?'

He held out his arm and the tiny screen flashed in front of her. Obediently, she stared into the com. Immediately, it flashed. Then the screen cleared and Charmin's flat face filled the screen. He gave her a huge cat grin.

She gasped in joy. "Oh, please, let's go home?"

"Right now." Levi stepped into the elevator tube with the other two crowding close. The trip back was fast and efficient. Dani appeared to have relaxed about their travelling system, and that was good. It was just one of many things she'd have to learn to do on her own. Just as he had other things to learn. Like how to deal with a cat who could send an alarm about Dani. What Levi didn't understand was how Charmin knew there was a problem in the first place.

It would be the first thing he'd ask the talking feline.

Chapter 3

"Her vitals had gone off the wall," Charmin explained in between licking the nutrient-rich cream off the plate, his tongue making little *snick, snick* sounds. "There was a flashing button labeled SCAN, so I pressed it and didn't like the results." He shrugged. "It was obvious she was upset. As there were too many variables to pinpoint the reason, I figured you should be the one to deal with it."

Charmin lifted his head, pink cream dotting the fluff of orange fur sticking out in a high cloud around his face, and asked Dani, "What was the problem anyway?"

"Oh, nothing," she said tiredly. "Just an old girlfriend of Levi's who decided to kidnap me."

Charmin spluttered, sending pink cream all over the table. "What?" He lifted his head to stare at her, shock widening his gaze.

Relieved to be home, her fear slowly subsiding now that she was safe and back with Levi, she gestured in Levi's direction. "He'll give you the details."

Charmin turned to face Levi. When Levi didn't jump in with an explanation, Charmin stalked across the table closest to where Levi stood and glared at him. "Levi, explain."

The look on Levi's face made Dani choke back a giggle. He looked like he'd swallowed a sour candy.

"What's the matter, Levi? Not used to having to explain yourself, especially to a cat?" she murmured as she walked past him to stare out the window. He gave a snort but she ignored him, choosing to study the outside world again, this time with a jaundiced eye.

Behind her, she heard Levi explain about the short relationship he'd had with Lina a long time ago before she worked for his lawyer. Damn, she knew that whatever happened in Levi's life before her arrival should have nothing to do with her. But somehow her rules didn't sound like they'd apply in this case. Lina wouldn't let them.

"Why would she do this to Dani?" Charmin asked.

"I don't know," Levi admitted. "It makes no sense."

"Yes, it does," Milo piped up, adding, "She's jealous. She heard about your marriage just this morning and reacted badly. Opportunity presented itself and she snatched it."

Dani winced. That woman's damn superior tone had said more about Lina than Dani cared to know. She was a bitch. If she'd dated Levi that was one thing, but according to Milo, he'd had an affair with her. At least that's what she thought partied meant. Like really? That was what he considered his type?

If the other women of this century were the same as the barracuda lawyer, no wonder Levi hadn't hooked up with anyone permanently yet. She wouldn't have either. Maybe Milo had done Levi a favor in bringing Dani here.

"But she didn't do anything other than take Dani to her office," said Levi, his frustration and temper starting to show in his voice. "It's not as if she hurt her or demanded money. It's more like she wanted to check Dani out for some reason."

"She kept calling me natural or something like that." Dani spun around to look at the men. "What does that mean?"

"Ha." Milo laughed. "Everyone is improved these days. Babies are born with the preferred genetic markers so there is no illness anymore...or very little. Brain power can be chosen. Looks. Things like that. But that's the parent's choice. When the child grows up, they can also choose their own enhancements. Similar to cosmetic surgery from your day," Milo added. "Every society has fringe groups. Naturals are one of ours. People who eschew any non-natural improvements."

"So because I don't have any enhancements, I'm natural looking so that's something to laugh at?" Dani asked. "Really?"

Charmin snorted. "Some of us don't need enhancements."

Levi smiled and reached out to scratch Charmin under the neck. Charmin's eyes crossed with pleasure.

"Not all enhancements work or are an improvement. Many times the person looked better before the enhancement. But there will always be those that have to push the edge."

"And Milo?" Dani asked, "Are you one of those genetically chosen brains?"

He smirked. "I am that and so much more. Something different happened with me, and I ended up with more than expected."

"Meaning he was likely a genius naturally," Levi said, "By genetically choosing more intelligence, our parents had no idea they'd get someone at the far end of that spectrum."

"Did they understand his nature before they passed away?"

Levi nodded. "Yes, they did. Milo could read before his second birthday and do calculus before his fourth. He hasn't stopped since."

"And you," Dani said gently, "How do you feel knowing that your parents gave Milo all those brains but they didn't give them to you? Presumably it was an option."

"One can ask for genetic markers to be enhanced, but no one can guarantee the results. They chose different markers for me." He shrugged. "And I'm happy with who I am."

He didn't mention what the other genetic markers were and left Dani trying to guess. There was nothing obvious to say either way. He'd tell her when he was ready.

She turned back to the window. What kind of world could already determine what their children would be like before they were even born?

"Where is Mother Nature in all of this?" she murmured. "Does she still have a role to play?"

"That's the thing about Milo. If you take ten different fetuses with all the same genetic markers like his, you won't get ten Milos. Mother Nature still rules."

That made her feel better. She hated to think that everyone was now preordained to be a specific way.

And she refused to believe this was an improvement over the rules of her old society. She couldn't argue that there were some things she'd love to be better at. Speed reading was an example. She'd wanted to go back to school, had just been accepted into an IT Security program before Milo so rudely yanked her out of her life. Now that little training program would be laughable to what she'd need to learn for a successful life here.

She stopped in her tracks. Was it possible? She turned slowly, realizing even Charmin was better suited to life here, due in part to his enhancements. Were there some enhancements that would help her to adapt – learn what she needed to know to thrive here?

"Is there something you can do to enhance me, too?" she asked slowly, studying their faces. "Some way for me to learn what I need to know about your society? About how to live here safely. About your government. Your monetary system. There's so much I don't know. Is it possible to get some kind of…I don't know…microchip downloaded to my brain or something?"

Milo stared at her in fascination. "Wow. That would be so cool."

And she realized there wasn't. She sighed. "Damn. If I could speed read or something, I could whip through all the schooling of your times until I caught up with my age group. Surely I'll be able to understand how this time period functions by the end of that."

"That's not a bad idea," Levi looked at her in surprise. "Milo, you can set her up with a VR system that will walk her through the lower learning levels."

"No one does grade school anymore," Milo said in surprise. "What good will that do?"

"It's going to be the little things that trip me up." Dani explained. "Things that every child will know."

"But they are born with most of that knowledge. Or they already have it by the age of 5."

"So how can I get the same knowledge then? You didn't enhance me – you enhanced my *cat*."

"Hey, how was I to know you'd bring a critter with you?" Milo protested. "I'm not taking the blame for that."

"No one is blaming you," Charmin said with a sniff. "Personally, I like it."

"You would," muttered Dani. She wanted to run back into the pod and forget about this place. Maybe she'd wake up in the morning and this nightmare would be over. But she'd asked for that before and it hadn't happened yet.

"I think Milo can help you," Levi said calmly. "We do have virtual reality learning models. He also has boosters to help you learn faster and retain what you learn. It won't be so bad. We can get you through most of the basics in a few weeks."

Weeks? With a tired nod, she walked back to the small room that had the pod. Fully dressed, she climbed inside and closed her eyes. Hot tears threaten to pour out. Instantly, the pod hummed as it worked to heal her. Only there was no healing this.

How did one heal a lack of self-confidence, a feeling of being overwhelmed, and a knowledge that she was always going to be the stupid relative from the fringe society in which others thrived?

She closed her eyes, curled up in a fetal position, and sobbed.

***

Levi reached out a hand as Dani walked past. She didn't see him, and his hand dropped away. He didn't know how to help her.

As she disappeared around the corner, he was afraid he'd seen her shoulders shake. She'd had an incredibly trying couple of days.

"Well, go fix it." Charmin gave him a flat stare that made Levi pause.

"And how would you like me to do that?" he asked

Charmin's gaze never blinked. "How about the same way you fixed it last time?"

And damn if heat didn't climb up Levi's neck as he realized just how much Charmin understood.

"How did you fix it last time, bro?" Milo asked, walking closer, as if that would help him understand the solution.

Levi groaned silently. "Never mind." He spun on his heels and hurried after Dani. He wished he could fix it like last time, but somehow he knew it wouldn't be that easy. Not now that Lina had become involved. He'd avoided her after that one weekend because she'd become possessive. Meddlesome. Unlike Dani, Lina *was* the kind to push herself into situations where she wasn't wanted. And laugh while doing so. But her actions today…he'd have to contact her and sort it out. And he also needed to talk to John as he hadn't passed on the message about Dani's whereabouts. Not for the first time, he wondered at the loyalty of those he employed.

Dani's subdued sobs reached him in the hallway. Shit.

He bowed his head. He had to stop putting her in situations where she ended up in tears. They were obviously her coping mechanism. But how sad that she ended up crying as often as she did right now.

He walked to the pod and opened the lid. He sat down at the end and tugged her into his arms so he could look into her teary eyes. "First, I'm sorry you had to go to the Council this morning."

She blinked those wet baby blues at him.

"Second, I'm even more sorry that you had to deal with Lina this morning. I'll get to the bottom of what she was up to. I promise."

She blinked several times.

He waited curiously. When she didn't say anything, he continued. "And as for helping you to learn the world around you, I'm going to take the next few days off work to go over the basics. Then we can hook you up to an education system and go through the lower levels first. Milo will be able to help you learn faster."

"Faster," she asked cautiously, a glint of curiosity peeking through the waterworks. Thank heavens.

"Yes, we have modules you can listen to while you're asleep, and you should be able to assimilate the information at a rapid rate."

Her curiosity turned to excitement. "Now that would help,"

He smiled. "I'm not going to leave you in the dark about my world. I should have taken a few minutes earlier to make you understand the ports. They are in all major centers like the Council. As long as the circle is empty when you step into one and you are tagged," he lifted her wrist as a reminder, "Then the ports take you home or to work. If someone is already in transit, the arrival is delayed to sequence landings in the proper order. Ports read your tags automatically."

"But I didn't go to either of those places."

"No. Lina's tags were coded for her office and the Council as part of her work. Not everyone can use them all the time." He paused, wondering how to clarify it. "The Council is an important part of the system and requires easy access for people in law enforcement. People working in police stations, lawyer's offices, parole board, the jail system, and others in the same field have to have access so they can bring someone with them. They have an override. So even if you wanted to go home, because Lina was there in an official capacity, she would have automatically overruled you – unless you knew how to change the coding to come home."

"Then learning how to change the coding is what I want to learn first."

He paused. "That's actually not a bad idea. You were in computers before, weren't you?"

She shrugged. "Only in a small way. And nothing like your computers of today."

"No, but it shows an aptitude. And that's something we can build on."

Without realizing it, he'd shifted her position so she was in his lap, cuddling her against his chest. He dropped his chin to rest on the top of her head. "We will make this work."

"There are so many pitfalls out there," she muttered, but her tone was softer, more relaxed.

"There are, but we can teach you."

"And Lina, is she likely to be someone I have to see a lot?"

She pulled away slightly, as if withdrawing into herself. He tugged her back. There was no way he was going to let her go. Or give her a chance to squeeze more distance between them.

He dropped a kiss on her forehead. She stiffened slightly then melted. She wasn't completely comfortable in his arms, but she wasn't against it. He, personally, didn't think he'd be able to get enough.

Chapter 4

Dani hated it when she'd behaved badly. Crying was getting to be a habit, and she had to stop it. She wasn't weak, just overwhelmed. As in she'd hit the wall.

Sure, she'd had a shock. Sure, she'd been scared, but she also knew people, and this wasn't going to be the last time she came up against someone who didn't like her presence in Levi's life. The fact that he'd married her would add to that disgruntlement and disbelief from other women.

Lina had wanted more from Levi than he'd been willing to give – she likely still did. Dani didn't know what had been on her mind this morning, but she'd just as soon avoid seeing her again. "I don't get how Charmin sent you a warning. Even if he did get the enhancement." She wasn't sure how to reconcile the amazement and jealousy she felt over that bit. "How did he alert you?"

"He called Milo on the house com. We had just returned to the room where we left you and with Charmin's info, Milo could track you easily. It's because of Charmin that your wrist went crazy. He noticed your vitals were rising so he ran a scan that set your wrist off. He called us after that. I have no idea how he thought to do that, but he did somehow."

She didn't know what to think. "So Charmin didn't know where I'd gone?"

"Not really. He only knew that you'd moved and that your vitals had gone off the wall." He grinned. "To put it mildly."

"Yeah, the meeting with Lina wasn't exactly a warm bonding experience."

He laughed. "Lina was never into warm or bonding. She's into *what's in it for her.*"

"Nice. Not." Dani said, "You have interesting choice in women."

"Not my choice," he said almost absently.

"What?" She froze and gave him a wide-eyed stare. "You mean Milo chose her for you, too?"

He started. Then a rumble started deep inside his chest as his laughter rolled freely. "No, he didn't," he gasped when he could. "Sorry, I meant to say I met her at a weekend party. I had nothing to do with her after that. She called many times but I wouldn't go out with her. Never had any intention of doing so."

"Well, guess what? The silent treatment isn't working. Because you never said no, she's still working that angle thinking that maybe this time you will say yes."

He glanced down at her in surprise. "This was a year ago. She's not still interested."

"If she's not still interested, then she's happy to get a little revenge instead." Dani did understand women. And that was something in her experience that men never seemed to get. Rejection was a bitch. And some bitches never forgot.

"I'll make sure she stays away from you."

Dani wasn't so sure. "She's a lawyer and could make a lot of trouble for us if she chose to." She knew to her regret how some lawyers acted. Not all of them were the same, but Lawrence had been bad enough to give her a warped perception.

"No," he said with such surety that she started to relax. "She won't."

"Yeah, I hate to bother you two, but John is calling, bro." Milo's voice filtered overhead from the built-in sound system. "You need to deal with this."

"Damn," Levi said. "You stay here in the pod, and I'll go talk to John."

She tried to slide off his lap only to find herself being lifted then laid down on the wide bed. He lowered the lid, clicked a few buttons, and walked away.

Immediately the pod started to hum again. Disappointed that he didn't kiss her good-bye, she rolled over and closed her eyes. Suddenly the pod opened again and he was there in front of her. With a heated look, he lowered his head and kissed her.

Heat licked down her spine, her toes curled, and her mouth surrendered to his onslaught.

Then he was gone.

She sighed happily, tucking up into a contented ball.

"Really? Do you have to moon around like that?" Charmin said from the floor level. He jumped up and padded toward her. The lid slowly closed over them.

She laughed. "Moon? I think they need to work on your vocabulary, Charmin." She shuffled backwards to give him more room, her hand instinctively reaching up to pet her best friend. "Thank you so much for telling the brothers where I was this morning. That was a horrible experience."

He leaned into her hand, rubbing his head against hers. "They shouldn't have taken you out there."

"I agree," she exclaimed. "But the orders were explicit."

"Hmm." He padded in a circle before curling down in a ball. "I wonder why?"

She tilted her head to look at him closer. "Charmin? What are you wondering about?'

He started to snore.

She frowned. "Are you just pretending to be asleep?"

"No." But he kept his eyes closed and the snores kicked in again.

"Right." He might not be pretending at this point, but he was only one step away from making it reality. She rolled over, giving the pod access to her back.

She could feel herself getting sleepy. Nothing like nerves, shock, and then recovering under soothing warmth to wear one out.

She closed her eyes and slept.

***

"John, what's up?" Levi stood in front of the HoloKomp, trying to remain cool and collected when all he wanted to do was go back and finish what he started. Dani was warm, wet, and willing. And he was a newlywed. He wanted to get back to his wife.

That thought brought a smile to his face.

"I don't understand the humor in this situation." John said stiffly, his gaze hardening in the holographic image in front of the wall. "Glad you think this is all a farce."

Now what? "As I don't understand the situation, perhaps you could fill me in." He kept his voice cool, professional, and just on the edge of pissed. That was the thing about lawyers, they seemed to always forget who paid their paychecks. John more than most.

"Lina quit the firm. She says she can't protect you and your new wife in any court scenario. She is citing irreconcilable differences between her and…" John looked down as if reading from a sheet of paper. "Dani."

Levi wanted to cheer. That was perfect if she quit. "I'm delighted to hear that. I can't say her behavior this morning was anything but one step short of criminal."

John's eyebrows shot up even as the look of anger receded slightly to be replaced by confusion. "What? Did I miss something?"

"I have a question for you that pertains to this morning's issue. Did you receive a communication from Lina stating that Dani was with her in her office?"

John frowned. "Not that I know of. Why? Wait, Lina's office? Why was Dani there?"

"Exactly what I'd like to know. Apparently Lina grabbed her arm and shoved her into a port and took her directly to her office. She treated Dani like a criminal, offering no explanation for her actions. Dani was traumatized by the actions of a woman who is supposed to be helping me and mine." His voice gained a sharp edge at the end. "I hardly see that as appropriate behavior. I left explicit instructions for her to be in that seat when I returned. I don't care if you don't like my instructions, John, but I do expect them to be carried out."

John's face shifted from frustrated to startled to worried. "I have no idea what she was thinking. She said the girl was making a spectacle of herself and she tried to calm her down. When that wasn't working, she went back to the office."

"Spectacle?" Levi said in an ominous tone. "In what way was she making a spectacle of herself?"

"I don't know, honestly. Just that many people were staring at her. She's odd, you know," he said apologetically. "Different."

"*Natural* is the insult that Lina used." And now that he had a better idea of what Lina thought about Dani, he was delighted she was leaving. Levi watched the rush of emotions slide across the face of a man who had worked for him for a long time.

"Levi." Milo worked on the big 3D monitor in the kitchen beside Levi and just out of John's sight. Milo was on one of the many computers in the house. He'd been clicking like a madman for a few moments, then he punched a fist in the air.

"Look at this." He punched a couple more buttons and suddenly the feed from this morning showed up on the HoloKomp where both Levi and John could watch.

All three men watched as Lina approached Dani, sitting quietly in the chair, oblivious to Lina's approach. After a short conversation, Lina checked her watch, glancing around at the crowd. The crowd moved past Dani but in no way was she making a spectacle of herself.

Lina left. Dani's wrist started flashing. It was apparent that she was trying to cover it up. Lina returned, said something, then she tugged Dani upward, almost dragging her to the ports. Lina pushed Dani into the closest one. Levi's gut clenched as he watched the shock and fear on Dani's face before she disappeared from the screen.

"Jesus," John's shocked exclamation came through clearly before he managed to cover it. "I don't know what was on her mind, but I will be speaking with her about this."

"And will she still be working for your firm after this?"

"I had planned on asking her to reconsider her resignation." At the sound coming out of Milo's mouth, John winced. "She's very popular with our clients."

"Male clients," Milo said in disgust. "I bet she doesn't work with any female ones."

They both watched surprise light up John's face before his features twisted as he considered the issue. "You know, I think you might be correct." His lips twisted downward. "Let me talk to her."

"And get back to me with an answer. Then I can make my decision as to how I will proceed."

Before John could respond, Levi disconnected the HoloKomp.

As the screen went black, Levi turned to Milo. "Send him a copy please, and keep that recording in case we need it again."

"Done." He was busy tapping the flat counter screen, obviously searching for something. Levi watched his brother work. When Milo went on the hunt, there was no hiding anything from him. "What are you doing now?"

Rather than answer, Milo grabbed the corners of a small window and stretched it enough for Levi to see Lina's office clearly. Then Milo switched the time clock, backing it up to when Dani should have arrived. Last, he clicked on the speakers.

Levi grinned. Milo had tapped into Lina's security feed.

There was a weird popping sound, and all of a sudden Dani arrived in the office. Scared and stumbling to maintain her balance – in more ways than one as she bent over suddenly, her face green.

They watched the next few minutes in silence until the two of them arrived at the office after Charmin alerted them. At one point, Milo stopped the feed, enlarged it, and backed it up so they could replay the section when Lina sent a message.

Dani was right, at least as far as she understood. Lina had left a communication for John, but the name wasn't clearly audible. Was it for the same John or a different one? Or was it a fake communication? A coded message? Levi lived in a world of corporate espionage. He didn't take anything at face value.

Milo voiced his doubts. "I wonder who she left that message for." He switched cameras and zoomed in on her wrist com. There were a series of numbers. None of them were

John's code. So she'd left a message for a different John. Milo immediately started a search. Within seconds, he had a name.

Johan Strand.

Not John but Johan. His old friend. One on the run himself. And one who was taking way too close an interest in Levi's affairs. With one of Levi's lawyers.

Was he a friend? Or not any longer? Had he ever been?

The one thing he knew about Johan, the man was an opportunist.

So what the hell was he up to now?

Chapter 5

Dani surfaced to a feel good stretch with warmth bathing down on her. These pods were something. She was so happy to be in here. Registered or unregistered, the pod was a huge help and she was grateful. She could just imagine those with arthritis lying here after a long day and feeling the healing rays beat down on the swollen joints. Or those with physical jobs. It used to be that having a Jacuzzi tub was the best way to end the day, but with one of these babies…wow.

Then she had to wonder if there was such a thing as physical work anymore. Did labor jobs exist? And that just took her to labor. Did women still go through labor or did they give birth in a pod? Or did they go to sleep and wake up with a newborn? She laughed. Most likely there was no such thing as pregnancy or labor. Kids were probably created in test tubes now.

"Did that mean computer nannies as well? Daycare Dummies, Kindergarten Komputers." She laughed. "Better not be that way. Right, Charmin?"

"A cat computer would be good," he murmured sleepily. "Cat Custom Chef would also work. How about a Computerized Cat Scratcher? I do need someone to take care of me when you're not here."

"Ha." She smirked. "I am not going anywhere ever again."

"Little do you know."

She sat up, pushing the pod lid up and away so she could slide her legs over the side. She stopped to look down at Charmin, now sprawled across the bed. He was seriously relaxed. "Are you feeling better now? Back to normal?"

He lifted his head to look at her. "Still tired, but better." And he dropped his head down.

As long as he wasn't screaming for food anymore, they were good. She could use some of that wonderful coffee though. She walked slowly to the door, happy when the room looked normal and the walls stayed straight. She used the bathroom then walked into the kitchen. And stopped.

"Holy crap," she cried out. Charmin must have heard her for he raced down the hall toward her. "What?"

They both stared.

The countertop had been converted to some kind of large screen, and both brothers were bent over searching through various windows that at the touch of their fingers moved and shifted, changing form and colors. Fascinated, she walked forward, her eyes on the computer windows as they rippled past. Charmin followed at her side, his gaze locked on the colors and images as they winked on and off, mesmerized.

"What is this?"

"A computer." Milo looked at her. "Surely you've seen one of these?

"I've seen many, but nothing like this." She searched the massive countertop for something recognizable in terms of commands. There was nothing. Neither was there a keyboard. She watched pictures of offices and buildings flash by. "What are you looking for?"

"Who, not what." Milo answered absentmindedly. "Johan."

"Your friend? Why?"

Levi snaked an arm around her waist and tugged her closer. Smiling, she wrapped her arms around his waist and snuggled in. "He's the one Lina contacted in the lawyer's office. It was Johan, not John."

She frowned. "Are you sure?"

"Very. We watched the numbers as she coded them on her personal com device. We managed to get a recording. It was Johan."

She shook her head. "You guys have a feed of that room from that specific time?"

"Milo found it."

Of course Milo did. She wondered what the Council would say if they knew he appeared to go wherever he wanted to electronically and retrieve any information he wanted. Nothing good, she was sure.

"Milo is on our side, and that's a good thing," Levi murmured.

"I'll say." She watched the screens flash by. Up on top of the screen there was some kind of counter. She didn't understand, but it appeared to be connected to the flashes.

Suddenly there was a beep, and a single window surfaced and started to flash.

Levi leaned forward. "There he is."

***

"Good, we found him." He watched Milo concentrate as the windows flashed faster than the human eye could see.

"No, we haven't."

"What? What do you mean? He's right there." Levi tapped the picture that had shown up. "That's his location."

"No. It's the location he's letting us see. He's not there now. In fact, I'd probably say he set that up as a decoy."

Levi groaned. "Not good." He turned away to glare around the kitchen. "What reason would he have for hiding like that? What is he afraid of? And why from me?"

Charmin laughed. "The same reason you hide away. Because you are involved in something you want no one to know about."

Milo stared at him. "In which case, he's likely the one behind all this. Maybe the one who actually supplies the pods." He turned to his brother. "Levi, what does Johan do?"

"Deals in trading. But I don't know what."

Dani made an odd sound. He turned to look at her, but she was staring at Charmin. "Like Lawrence Blackburn. Part of the reason he was so oily was he used information like a weapon."

Levi stared at her. "What does Johan have to do with my ancestor?"

"Ah," Milo said. He turned back to the computer system. "That assumption is probably correct."

"What is correct?" Levi stared at the three of them. "What am I missing?"

It was Charmin who filled it in for him. "Johan and the pod and his disappearance all make sense if he is trading ...buying ...selling ...information."

"Ah hell."

Chapter 6

Dani wondered what kind of mess she'd fallen into. "I don't understand what Lina would gain by taking me to her office."

The two brothers shrugged. "I don't know. Unless we weren't supposed to get there as fast as we did? Maybe someone else was arriving and we beat them," Levi said thoughtfully. "Milo?"

"Already on it." Milo's fingers flashed so fast, Dani could hardly see what was happening. Understanding was a long ways away.

"Ah, here it is again. I'll let it stream longer. Should have thought to do that in the first place."

Before her was a recording of Lina's office. In silence, they watched as the video continued. She couldn't see a time stamp, but it hadn't been more than a couple of minutes after the time she'd left with Levi when there was another pop and two men arrived.

She gasped. They looked dangerous. Unsavory. Then again, it was a law office. They dealt with the criminal element all the time. Both men wore leather skin suits with heavy boots and chains hanging from the pockets. They were so typical-looking of the thugs from her day that she started to laugh.

Milo shushed her. "Let's listen."

The speaker replayed the conversation.

"Where is she?" The younger of the two men asked.

"How should I know?" said the older one. "The boss said she would be here."

She? Dani or Lina? And who was the boss?

While Dani tried to figure out what the men were talking about, Lina walked into the screen. She stared at the room and spun around in a full circle. In a shocked voice, she said, "Please tell me you have her stashed somewhere."

Levi sucked in his breath. Dani looked up at him, watching as fury darkened his skin and tightened his features. But he never lifted his gaze from the screen. She turned her attention back to the men talking.

"She wasn't here when we got here. Figured you had her in your private office." The man looked behind her. "Are you sure she didn't go in there with you?"

Lina glared at him, tiny beads of sweat forming on her brow. If he hadn't been watching so closely he doubted he'd have seen them. "Of course I'm sure." She spun around once more. "Damn it. Where could she be? There's no way those idiot brothers could have gotten to her first."

"Check the log. Then you'll know for sure."

She walked over to a wall just off the screen. The two men turned to watch her, but they weren't close enough to read the log.

"Damn. It was them." Lina turned back to face the men. "How could they have known she was here?"

Dani was confused. Lina knew she'd left with Levi and Milo. Why was she lying?

"The obvious answer – she told them," the first man said. "How else?"

"I scanned her when she arrived," Lina said. "She had no personal com on her."

"Really? How bizarre is that?" Thug One said. "Everyone has one."

"She must have left it behind at the Council," Thug Two said.

"What, so the brothers would find it and know that she's here somehow?" Lina asked sarcastically. "That makes no sense."

"Well they knew, somehow." Thug One looked bored.

"Tracker," Thug Two said. "She must have a tracker on her."

The three stared at each other.

"They wouldn't track just anyone," said Thug One in consideration. "She must be valuable."

"What she is…is different," Lina said. "We need to know in what way"

The two men shrugged. "She can't be that different."

"Oh, she is. We just don't know much or why."

And the video stopped.

Silence ensued.

Then Milo exploded. "Idiot brothers?"

***

Levi grinned. Dani laughed. Welcoming a chance to lighten up after all the lies and deception. "Of course that would be the one thing out of that entire conversation that you'd remember."

"I remember everything," he snapped. "I am *not* an idiot."

Levi watched Dani and Milo spar. He listened with only half an ear. His mind was consumed with what he'd heard. How did anyone know about Dani? And what did they know – or think they know?

He'd been so careful. It had to be Johan, but what good would that knowledge do for him? He had his own troubles. Snatching Dani wasn't going to help his case.

And why kidnap her? Ransom? Levi had money, but not millions. As far as he understood, Johan had more money than Levi did. Johan knew about the tagging, so that was probably where the leak had come from. He'd been afraid of problems from that corner but hadn't expected it so quickly. He'd done everything right. Dani should have been safe. She needed to be safe.

But apparently she wasn't even close.

Damn.

That Lina had been lying through her teeth was also worrisome. Was she trying to save her own skin so no one would know Dani had disappeared before the men arrived to take Dani away? Or was she playing a different, more dangerous game?

His mind spun. "Milo, we need to track Johan's movements. Find out who he's associating with, who he lives with now. Details on his business pursuits. Things like that. I hate to think he's behind all this, but we have to consider the possibility."

"For what purpose?" Dani asked him. "Would he have any concept of where I've come from really?" She lifted her shoulders slightly and dropped them. "Honestly, unless he knows the truth, and that's too bizarre for anyone to believe, what difference would my story make to him?"

"That's what we have to find out."

Milo tapped the screen, and a picture of Lina appeared. "She's the one who will know. We have to get this information to John and corner her. If we show her the evidence we have on her, she'll break." For the first time, Levi saw a mature look come over his brother's features. "I refuse to let this bitch do this to us."

"I don't know what penalties she'd face for this, but surely she'd turn on the others to save her skin." Dani glanced over at the photo. "Women like her are always more concerned about squeaking out of trouble themselves."

"True enough." Levi walked over to a blank wall and brought up his private HoloKomp system. "I'm going to get John on the line. Milo, can you package up the section of video where the two men arrive in John's office? Cut it after where she checked the log to see if we'd managed to get there before her henchmen. We'll show John how she's been lying to both sides."

"Done," Milo said almost absently. "I've also isolated the henchmen's faces. Their tags have been shut down, so we can't identify them that way. I'll run a facial recognition program to identify them."

"Let's show their faces to John as well. He might recognize them."

"Speaking of John, make sure you initiate a body scan to see his vitals. He might be a good liar, but his body will show the effects of your questioning and seeing the men's faces. No better lie detector in the world."

Dani gasped. "You can do all that?"

"And so much more. Watch and learn, sweetheart." Levi sent a link to John. "He'll be online in a moment."

Chapter 7

Dani watched as John's face appeared on the wall again. On the wall yet out of the wall in a very life-like 3D image.

"What now?" John snapped. "I'm still trying to get ahold of Lina."

"This." And Levi set the video screen to play show. "It's just after Milo and I left your office."

In front of Dani, the two thugs appeared in Lina's office almost magically. Another projection but large enough for John to see. She really wanted to learn to use ports. She would love to travel if it was instantaneous. She'd had some stomach reaction, but presumably it would get better over time. At least she hoped the physical reactions would calm down.

She studied John's face, wondering at the clarity of the image that made it seem like he was right inside the room. It was on the tip of her tongue to ask. Maybe they even had interplanetary travel. Now that would be so cool. Honestly, what she'd seen outside had scared her, but at the same time it was exciting.

As long as she was safe inside. Though by this time she realized that she'd only seen a tiny portion of what the technology of today's world could do.

As the video played out in front of him, John gasped in shock, his skin turning a pasty gray. Once he spoke, he didn't waste any unnecessary words. "That's Paul and Tommy Defino. They're on the run after escaping prison transport.

Both are wanted for breaking and entering, armed robbery, and a host of other charges."

"Did you represent them? Lina? Is there any other viable reason why they'd be in your offices and communicating in this manner with your business associate?" At Levi's cutting tone, Dani turned slightly so she could see his face.

She had never seen this angry Levi. He stood tall and arrogant, arms crossed over his chest as he challenged John. Angry but in control. Someone had messed up and he'd know the reason why.

He handled power well. It emanated from him in long, reaching waves. He knew what he could do and how to get what he wanted in life. There was something very attractive about that.

She understood he ran the large company founded by him and his brother, and that had to have molded him. For the first time, she could see the businessman who'd carved a place for himself in the corporate world.

John shook his head. "No. I won't have that element in my company. I've been trying to locate Lina but so far she's not answering her personal com, her home, or her car's communication system. I don't know where she's gone."

Levi shot Milo a look. He grinned and shambled over to the large countertop, flexed his fingers, and got to work. Dani was torn between watching Levi verbally bat John around and racing to Milo's side to watch him perform magic. She'd always had a love for technology but hadn't realized her interest was this strong. And the stuff she was seeing...

Her fascination won out, and she raced to Milo's side. He was moving windows and clicking parts of the countertop that she couldn't see had any buttons. She presumed he was busy tracking down the bitchy lawyer. Dani didn't want to cause anyone else trouble – "live and let live" was her motto.

But if they weren't going to leave her alone, then all bets were off.

Still, she wished she understood what Milo was doing.

He pounded on the countertop, making her back up, afraid the monitor thingy would break. Instead, the huge 3D monitor opened up like a huge box rising up out of the counter. Milo went into action, sweeping windows to the side and bringing up more. His hands danced in and out of the blue-green images that flowed from the box. She recognized that Milo had some kind of facial recognition software running down on one side. He was looking for the missing lawyer. And she wanted him to find her.

She bent over and studied the pictures as they whipped by. Now he was flicking the pictures like a movie stream and the computer was tossing in ones of males from the search for the Defino brothers she'd seen in the video. Her mind saw it before her eyes recognized it.

She reached out and stabbed a picture before it disappeared off the side of the counter. "That one."

"What one?" Milo dragged it down toward him and blew up the image. It was the profile of one of the men. Oddly enough, it had been the snake's head earring she'd recognized.

A long, low whistle slipped out of Milo's lips. "Nice. That's the older one, Paul. Now to source his location."

Once again screens went flying. Just when a headache from the flying images was starting to settle in for good, Levi turned off the video and joined them.

He stood on the other side of Milo. "No sign of her?"

"Not yet. We've found him though." Milo reached up and tapped the image in the corner. As he did, Charmin jumped up.

"Whoa. No cats on the monitor."

Charmin backed up slightly to the edge but did not jump off. He stared at the images, his whiskers vibrating.

She didn't know if he was planning on jumping on the flashing images or if he understood what they were looking for and could help. She didn't want to ask, but her attention was caught as he stared at the fast-paced screen in front of him. Then his paw flashed and he dragged an image back toward him.

"Hey, no scratching the monitor," Milo cried.

"I didn't scratch it." Charmin sniffed. "Besides, I can't. It's holographic." He released the image. "I believe this is who you are looking for." He sat back and proceeded to clean the paw he'd touched the monitor with.

Everyone leaned over the screen. The image was too small for her to see. Levi reached over and tapped it twice. The image blew up.

Lina.

Milo stared at Charmin. "Wow. Like seriously good."

Levi snorted. "And who made him like that?"

Milo snickered. "Good point. We're all good."

"Yeah, right," Dani said.

"Hey, you found this guy. I didn't." Milo beamed at her as if she were a prized student.

"Really?" Levi looked over at her with respect. "That's great. Trying to find images when Milo gets going is not easy."

She grinned. How could she not? At least she wasn't a complete loser.

Charmin shot her a direct look. She flushed. Surely he couldn't read minds now, could he? He went back to his grooming. As she looked around the kitchen, she realized that what she really wanted was some of that awesome coffee. She'd come out looking for some earlier, but with everything going on, she'd gotten distracted.

She walked around behind the men. At the other side, she studied the flat wall, looking for anything to denote cupboards, coffee makers, or even a water spout.

And found nothing.

***

"Dani, what do you need?" Levi asked, circling the counter to stand beside her. He wanted to take her in his arms and kiss her, but something stopped him. Maybe it was the fact that she'd done well with Milo.

Not everyone did. Maybe it was Charmin, who'd shifted his position so he could stare right at Levi. Stupid to be nervous of a cat. But there it was.

Even odder that the cat had managed to snag Lina's picture out of the thousands floating past. He'd have to talk to Milo about what exact enhancement he had given the cat.

"I was looking for a drink."

"Water?" He walked to the wall. "Watch." She stepped closer to see a break in the paint. It was a scrolled-style circle. He pressed his hand flat on the wall and pressed down. Instantly, a cupboard popped out. He removed a tall, skinny glass and moved over several feet. While she watched, he pushed another section of wall and a small fountain slid out with a hand attachment. He squeezed the attachment, and her glass filled with water. "See, it's easy. Every space in today's world is designed to multi-task."

"Like anything new, it is if you know how. Is this filtered?" she asked.

"Absolutely." Like everything in their world, water was severely regulated, being one of the last few natural resources left to them. They had to protect it. But she didn't need to know that right now. She'd quickly be overloaded with information.

She tossed back the drink and held it back out again. He refilled it and handed it over. She sipped the second glass. "Is there any chance of getting coffee?"

His face lit up. "Oh, good idea. That's exactly what we need." He turned around to make the first of what he expected would be several pots. He'd have to look into buying a bigger unit.

Yet none of the changes were anything like the ones Dani had gone through, so he couldn't complain.

He ordered coffee with a push of a button. Dani was quiet behind him. He wondered at the conspicuous silence over the marriage deal. He'd avoided the topic altogether. He'd almost brought it up in the pod room earlier, but it hadn't been most pressing issue so he'd held back. Maybe she was hoping it would go away.

He was hoping to resume the honeymoon. He couldn't help but think about the many benefits of being married. And how hot and willing she'd been in his arms. God, he wanted that again. And soon. Like now. He slid a gaze her way. She'd settled back to watch him, her eyes intent on his motions. And damn if that intensity wasn't a turn on.

Just then, her stomach grumbled. At first he didn't recognize the sound. Then it sank in. He froze. Uh oh. Dani had been pulled from bed, taken to the Council, kidnapped and returned home to recuperate in the pod – all on an empty stomach. Checking the comp on his wrist, he winced and said, "You missed another meal, didn't you?"

"Two meals," Charmin whined from the monitor counter.

Levi nodded. True enough. "Right. Coffee first. Then food."

Charmin started howling at the sound of food being placed second. "How can you put coffee first?" he moaned. "I need foooood."

Chapter 8

Dani chuckled at Charmin, walking closer to him to scratch his neck. "You hadn't even noticed that you were missing a meal until it was mentioned."

"Of course I noticed." Charmin said, turning his neck for her to get at another spot.

How did a cat manage to look affronted? Dani shook her head and scooped him up. She stared down into those eyes, so familiar and yet so different now. She recognized her wonderful old tomcat in there, but at the same time there was someone different. Someone better. Her heart swelled as she held him close. "I'm so glad you survived that trip."

"Me too," he whispered, rubbing up against her neck. "Like what would have happened to me if you came here and I was left locked in the apartment?"

A shudder swept through her. "That would have been horrible. You'd have died without me to take care of you."

"And yet today, I took care of you." He reared back and pinned her with a beady eye. "So I should get your share of lunch."

She laughed. "So not going to happen." She carried him over to Levi, who appeared to be making sandwiches. At the sight of the thick slabs of bread and cheese, Charmin moaned louder.

"With all the technology you have available – how is it you are cooking?" Dani asked.

"It's a hobby." He flushed then shrugged uncomfortably. "It's a bit of a joke to my friends actually."

"So there is an alternative."

That made him laugh. "Yes. We have machines that create complete meals now. I just don't want to have one around."

"Oh." She personally would love a machine that could do it all. Then again, if he was happy to cook, she was happy to let him.

"He's into retro stuff. Like food and cooking." Milo spoke up. "It takes work and it's disgusting."

Dani laughed. She looked over at Levi and shared a look of understanding. "Unless it's chocolate, I suppose."

Milo scowled. "Chocolate is different."

"The food is almost ready. Give me another minute." Levi reached for a large block of something. She leaned in, then realized what it was. "Oh yum, that looks like roast beef."

He gave her a strange look. "Did they have that in your time?"

She stared at him. "Of course." She frowned. "This is from an animal, isn't it?"

He looked at the block of meat and then back at her. And she realized it was square. As in very square. As in too square. "Oh damn. This isn't meat, is it?"

"Meat is bad for you," Milo said from the other side of the counter. "I've told you that. Boosters are better – in all ways."

"Except that Charmin is a carnivore," Dani reminded him. "And so am I."

"He could drink boosters, too." Milo appeared to be warming up to one of his favorite subjects.

Charmin said in a low voice, "Let's go back to the meat."

"Except I'm not sure it's meat."

"Oh, it's meat," Levi said, "And it came from an animal, but not a live one."

Dumbfounded, Dani could only stare at the block of gray stuff. "Like cloned meat?"

"Ha, 3D printed meat more likely," Charmin said with a snicker. He sniffed the air experimentally, caught a whiff, and started to wiggle out of her arms. "Except that would be old tech here. And this smells delicious."

"Hey wait. You're going to fall." She tried to tighten her grip.

"Let me go and I'll jump." He tried to sneak out of her arms, but she clamped down tight and said, "No animals where the food is."

"We'll sit at the table. He'll bring food when it's ready." She walked him back over to the table where they'd eaten their first meal.

"Ha. I could be dead by then," Charmin groaned.

"And they might happily kill *you* if you don't behave yourself," she snapped. "Remember your manners."

"And maybe they should remember theirs," he retorted, "Considering that we are the guests and they are the hosts." He peered around Dani's body to stare at Levi's back. "Lousy hosts at that."

She gasped in horror. "You apologize right now. That is not acceptable. You know perfectly well that he's preparing our meal. Now be appreciative of that fact before you lose out completely based on your bad behavior."

"Harrumph." Charmin stared up at her. "I'm not a two-year-old. You can't treat me like that."

Milo started laughing from behind her.

She tilted her head toward the sound. "Do you hear that? That's because although you're not that age, it's how old you are acting."

Charmin's marble eyeballs hid behind his suddenly slitted eyes. He started to howl deep in the back of his throat.

"Stop it. Communication is new for you, I get it." She dropped a kiss on top of his head. "That's okay. You'll get the hang of it, and besides, you'll always be my adorable kitty."

"Oh brother." He turned away from her to pad over to the furthest point on the kitchen table. "This could get embarrassing if you're going to get all mushy."

Her laughter pealed out to ring around the room. Without warning, she reached across and scooped him back up in her arms. She started to dance, holding Charmin in her arms as if he were a human-sized partner with one paw up. "It so could get mushy. Because I love you. I always have. You are my best friend. And now that you can talk, I so want us to have a tea party and play dress up…"

At his shocked shriek, she bent over giggling, still holding him in her arms. He dug his claws in, probably as a punishment. She straightened, the odd giggle still pouring out. "You are too funny. I was only kidding, by the way."

"You'd better be," he threatened, curling his claws ever so slightly.

"Watch the nails," she said in warning.

"Why? You have a healing pod now. I can cause all kinds of damage and you'll be just fine." He stretched up to stare into her eyes. Would she ever get used to him being able to talk like this? She hoped so, but she also didn't want to lose the pet she'd had since forever. Emotion washed over her and she wrapped him up tight. Against his fur, she whispered, "I'm so glad you're mine."

His engine kicked in and made the tears once again burn her eyes.

But it was his whispered, "Me, too," that made her heart melt.

***

Levi stopped to watch the two interact. He couldn't believe the language coming out of Charmin's mouth. Damn, he needed to corner Milo and asked him about those enhancements. He remembered Milo's slip of the tongue earlier. If he knew his brother, it was to know he wouldn't stop at one enhancement if there was a chance to slide more in. Considering how quickly Charmin had locked on that image on the screen, he had to wonder if eagle vision or super quick reflexes might have been one of the other enhancements. And that would suck for Dani if the cat had received all the benefits. Imagine knowing that your cat was smarter, faster, and more intelligent than you were.

Talk about a major burn.

He remembered Dani had snagged a picture from Milo's fast-moving stream as well, so maybe they'd both received enhancements. They could have shown up stronger on Charmin due to his size.

He watched the two cuddle and for the first time in his life, he saw something lacking in his. He'd never had a pet. He'd had a teddy bear for his first couple of years until he'd been deemed old enough to go without. And now as he watched Dani cuddle Charmin, he realized how much the cat enriched Dani's life. And quite possibly that worked both ways.

Just then, Charmin's head popped up over Dani's shoulder and that golden gaze locked on his.

Even before he opened his mouth, Levi knew what was going to come out. He held up heaping plates of food and walked closer. Charmin's eyes rounded in delight and he scrambled to get out of Dani's arms and onto the table.

"He's got food," he said urgently when Dani resisted.

She laughed and dropped him on the table. "Let's eat then."

As she took her place at the table, she asked, "Levi, can I help you do anything?"

"It's done. Not to worry, you can help next time. These are just simple sandwiches."

Milo walked past. "And I'll make boosters for both of you while I get mine."

Levi happened to be watching both Dani and Charmin, so he saw them wrinkle their faces in disgust. Catching his eye, they both grinned. Dani said, "We'll drink it because we need it but honestly, food is more our style."

She motioned to Charmin, who was busy gnawing on thick chunks of ham that Levi had finally found for him. "I need to go and get cat food for him."

Charmin lifted his head and stared at him in horror. "I eat protein. Not cat food. Protein. Chicken. Fish. Lamb. Mouse." He stared more intently, just to make sure Levi understood the seriousness of the issue. "Understand?"

Levi raised one eyebrow and nodded "Got it."

Chapter 9

Dani had finally filled up enough to know that she was going to make it another day. She wasn't so sure of Charmin, as he'd finished his second helping and was plowing through a third right now. For herself, the fatigue had returned in triplicate. The pod seemed too far away to reach, and her eyelids were already drooping.

Before she had a chance to decide if sleeping where she sat for a few moments was a good idea or not, she was scooped up and carried into the tiny healing room. She snuggled against Levi's chest. "Sorry, just got so tired all of a sudden."

"Hey, it was a tough morning for all of us." He shifted her in his arms. "An afternoon nap is perfect."

She heard a series of buttons clicking then a low hum. The healing pod. She so wanted to be in there. And just like that, he laid her down inside and dropped a kiss on her forehead. She smiled sleepily, closed her eyes, and let her mind drift off.

She heard the door shut behind Levi as he exited. In the distance there were sounds of conversation, but it was far enough out of her hearing that she couldn't make out the words.

Drifting was nice, easy. She heard a weird sound then felt something small hit her arm. She rubbed her arm then rolled over to get more comfortable, loving the way the bed adjusted beneath her. What a marvelous invention. Several small noises outside the pod bothered her, but there was a buffer created by the pod's humming noise that filtered those out. It was great.

But maybe not quite great. Her eyes opened. Something didn't feel right.

She didn't feel right.

But she didn't know what was wrong.

"Charmin? Are you here?" He'd said he'd follow her in a few minutes when Levi had carried her in this direction – but had he?

It felt like...someone was here.

And as that knowledge filtered in, she realized that someone definitely was, but it was not someone she knew. Or rather, wasn't someone who was supposed to be in here.

Shit.

Her breath caught in the back of her throat. What was she supposed to do? She could slip out of the pod and make a run for the door, but it wasn't like that would be a subtle move. They'd see her. And maybe that was okay. Just because there was a stranger in here didn't mean they were out to get her. Except everyone that had been a stranger so far had been out to do just that.

She could lie here and pretend to be asleep.

Gently, she rubbed a sore spot on her arm.

Slowly, she pulled her feet up toward her chest. She felt exposed. What if this person grabbed her by her feet? That thought whirled inside her head, making her almost blind with fear. Her breathing became raspy. The more she tried to control her breathing, the worse it got. The pod lights changed from blue to purple, and immediately more heat beat down on top of her. The pod knew she was under stress. Her vitals had to be off the wall. At the same time, she knew that had to be a signal to whoever was in here with her. There was no sign of Charmin.

Would he recognize that her vital signs had gone crazy again? Or was he still eating like he wasn't ever going to get another meal? She closed her eyes and starting calling him in her mind. *Charmin, please help. Charmin, can you hear me? Please, someone come.*

She took another long shuddery breath, surprised to find she'd curled up into a fetal position. She'd feel like a fool if everyone came racing into the room and she was actually alone.

But she'd rather that than the opposite. She wondered how she could bolt out the door without getting caught.

Then a noise sounded behind the pod. *Oh God. Oh God. Oh God!*

She froze. And couldn't catch her breath. She had never had a panic attack, but this was starting to be a full on scream-for-her-life-and-run moment.

As quiet and as naturally as she could, she slid over to the edge of the pod bed.

Stiff, barely breathing, she readied her muscles and slowly pushed the pod lid open just a little bit.

Three, two, one…

She slid under the edge of the pod and bolted for the open door, screaming at the top of her lungs.

***

"What is that?" Charmin sat up abruptly from his cleaning to stare in the direction of the pod room. Levi and Milo raced down the short hallway where Dani ran smack into Levi's chest. He caught her in his arms while trying to see what had scared her. "Milo, check the room out."

"No, no, he shouldn't go alone," Dani cried out, "There's someone in there."

"What? Impossible." Levi shook his head as he held her close. "No one else is here. It's not possible."

She shuddered in his arms. "It's not only possible, it's real. I could hear their breathing and weird noises." She slapped her hand over her arm. "I swear something hit my arm."

"What?" Levi stopped back and lifted her arm so he could see. "There's no way."

But there was. A slight red spot showed on her upper arm. He tucked her close to him and moved her into the kitchen. "Stay here." He walked to a wall and brought up his security system with a few commands. "Milo, where are you?" he said.

The intercom broadcasted his voice. He set the computer to show all the occupants in his house. Immediately, the gray screen lit up several orange hot spots. He easily identified himself and Dani. Charmin had to be the smaller one.

And there was Milo in the pod room.

"I'm right here, Levi." Milo said as he walked into the kitchen. "There's nothing there."

Levi shut down the intercom, sealed off the pod room, and motioned his brother to come over to him. He tapped the monitor at the red image in the pod room and in a low voice said, "Then what or who is this?"

Chapter 10

Dani huddled at the kitchen table. Charmin sat in front of her, but his attention was on the brothers behind her. She'd rather be back in Levi's arms. A chill rippled up and down her arms. She rubbed them, wishing she understood what they were talking about. Had she just imagined an intruder? The pod room was barely big enough for anyone else to stand in, let alone hide.

And why hadn't she seen someone if they were there?

None of it made any sense. The fact remained; her arm stung from whatever had happened to it. Milo walked over, ran a gentle finger over her arm, and frowned. He said, "The healing pod didn't fix this?"

"Not sure it had time," she admitted. "And I'm not going back in there until I know it's safe."

"We need to know what caused it."

"And how do we do that?" She stared down at the puffy skin on her arm. It was a tiny injury. Not worth making a fuss about. Still…"Whatever this was, my body doesn't like it."

Charmin jumped up on the table beside her and rubbed his head against her shoulder. "Hey, Charmin. Wished you'd been in there with me?"

"I hate strangers – you know that."

"True, you used to always run away." She rubbed her cheek against his head. "Except you like Levi and Milo just fine."

His engine kicked in when she kissed the top of his head.

"They are different," he said with a yawn, dropping his butt on the table and looking around with interest. "Do you think they have any leftovers?"

"Probably, but keep eating like a crazy man and they will be forced to keep canned cat food around for you."

He looked at her through slitted eyes. "You mean canned shrimp and tuna – right?"

She shook her head. "I don't know why they would. Besides, you loved canned cat food before."

"Sure, but they don't have that food here. And," he leaned in, tilting his head so he was whispering in her ear, "what if Milo picks the food? It's likely to be green and full of boosters."

At that, she giggled. And boy, did that feel good. From fear to laughter in a heartbeat. She caught a glimpse of the satisfaction in his eyes. "You did that on purpose." she accused.

"Did not." He twisted and started grooming his back.

"Did too," she muttered.

"So what? Someone has to do something to keep your mind off the intruder."

Intruder? It sounded worse when he said it. More real.

"Nope. It wasn't." Charmin continued to clean, sounding completely unconcerned.

"Then who was it?" she asked in an ominous tone of voice.

"Not sure," Charmin said, "But I think it was a what, not a who."

Puzzled, she stared at him, wishing he'd pay attention and stop cleaning his butt. "How could that have been anything but a person?"

"Holograph," Charmin said.

Wordless, she stared at her four-year-old cat, who appeared to understand things way beyond her comprehension. Into the sudden silence, he paused what he was doing and lifted his head to pin her gaze with his. "What?"

"How would you know that?"

Damn if his nose didn't go up in the air before he returned to his cleaning.

Apparently she didn't warrant an answer.

***

Levi strode down the hallway, Milo close on his heels. At the pod room doorway, he stopped and gently pushed the door open as wide as it would go. He couldn't see anything, but the computer scan wouldn't have made a mistake like this.

"I don't see anything," Milo said. He almost pushed Levi into the room as he craned to see over his shoulder. "There has to be a glitch."

"I wouldn't be so sure about that." Levi stepped into the room and bent down to look below the pod. He couldn't see anything with the naked eye. But…he clicked through the windows on his comp and found the same disturbing hot spot. Above and behind the pod.

He walked around until he was directly under the spot. He twisted his head, trying to see into the dark corner, when a light shone directly at the spot. Startled, he turned to see Milo shining a light at the spot in question. He turned when something beeped behind him. "What the…"

"It's my new toy." Milo held up the base of the light to show him the flashing buttons that accompanied the beeps. "It's a bug finder."

Levi stared at his brother before switching his gaze from the device to the high corner of the ceiling. "Bugs?" he asked in a hard voice. "Here? After all the sweeps and security measures we have in place?"

Milo leaned closer and whispered in his ear. "Probably came in with the pod."

Damn. As he thought about it, it made perfect sense. He'd been so worried about taking this step and hoping it was the answer to help Dani that he'd not run through any of the special security checks. The normal ones, sure. But who had time to consider beyond that? He hadn't had a chance to think about anything...let alone act on the thoughts.

He stared, wondering what to do next. Milo motioned him to retreat the same way he did. Back out in the hallway, Milo closed the door and pressed several buttons on his little gadget. Levi had built in bug sweepers that he used often. His office and home were wired to catch any that made their way inside, but this one...

He smiled reassuringly at Dani, Charmin in her arms, standing hesitantly at the end of the hallway. They'd obviously followed him and Milo to see what they'd found.

"It's very high tech." Milo muttered as he popped open a 3D screen. Then he stepped back to walk around the image. "These are the blueprints of the bug."

Levi stared. "It was inside the unit. Meant to break off as the bug was released from its hiding spot." He turned to face Dani. "The casing is what hit her arm."

"It has audio." Charmin sauntered closer, making Levi want to back away. "So it can hear us...meaning we should be able to hear it."

Milo spun around and stared at the damn cat in excitement. "That's right. I can track it back using its own programming code."

And damn if that cat didn't sit back on its haunches and nod his head approvingly at Milo. Levi felt like the dummy in the class – again. Milo hadn't been the easiest brother to live with. "Can you find out who sent this?"

"Not only that, I might be able to listen in on what's going on in their office or wherever they are holding the receiver for this unit."

"I didn't see a bug in there." Levi hated to bring it up, but... "How small could it be?"

"It's holographic and invisible."

Levi, in the act of walking back to the kitchen, froze. "What did you say?"

"It's an invisible holographic bug," Milo said impatiently.

"And that doesn't sound incredibly wrong to you?"

Milo shook his head slowly, as if to clear his head so he could focus. "We have invisibility and we have bugs and holographs. Someone put them all together."

"And that someone wasn't you?" Maybe that was the biggest surprise here. Levi had never known anyone to get the edge on Milo in a field he loved, and espionage toys were one of his specialties.

"Nah, no point in adding holograph stuff. Just a waste of time."

That almost more sense. It wasn't a practical application. With a smile, Levi continued down the hallway, gently moving a very confused Dani ahead of him, until he realized what his brother didn't say. He spun around and continued to walk backwards. "Wait, what about the invisible part?"

"What about it?" Milo was busy with his little toy.

"Have you managed to make an invisible bug?" Levi tried to hang on to his patience, but his brother could try a saint. "Like this one?"

"Not like this one."

Levi waited.

"Better." And Milo shot him a quirky grin of success. He didn't punch the air with his fist, but it was damn close.

"Better how?" He couldn't see how an invisible bug could be improved on. He waited, but Milo was busy chuckling and clicking away on his fingerboard comp and matching it to something happening on his bug finder. He waited a moment then nudged his brother. "Milo, how could you make a better bug than an invisible one?"

Milo looked up in surprise. "I just expanded on your idea."

As he looked to be returning to the toys in his hand, Levi quickly interjected, "What are you talking about?"

"Stealth technology. Duh. On a micro scale."

And he walked back into the pod room, leaving Levi to stare after him in shock. He'd developed the home stealth technology system to cloak what they were doing in the company and at home. It was a military type of application, but he'd refined it for their purposes and apparently Milo had refined it yet again. He trailed behind his brother. "So you can send in a bug that is invisible AND have it receive and send data without anyone being able to pick up its presence with any tracking device?"

Milo stopped and threw his head back in frustration. "That's what I just said, didn't I?"

Levi snorted. "Not really."

"Well, it's what I meant. Now if you don't mind, I'd like to listen in on our uninvited visitor." Shooting him a dark look, Milo walked forward until he stood just below the spot. Adjusting the monitor, strange voices filled the room.

"I can't tell what's happening. There's been only static for the last bit."

"Any chance they found the bug?"

A snort. "Hell no. This baby isn't even on the market."

Levi cocked his head, trying to figure out who was speaking. He brought up his own comp and set up his tracking system on the next bit of conversation.

"Maybe it's broken."

"And maybe you should pull your brain out of your butt and use it once in a while."

"Watch your mouth. You might think you are the best of the best, but there is always someone better out there. You can be replaced."

That sharp retort was followed by footsteps and a door slamming.

"Ass."

Levi checked his comp to find he had enough to run a voice recognition program. He started it and looked over to see what Milo was up to. He'd held up his bug finder as high as he could to the ceiling.

A weird ear splitting sound filled the room.

And then there was dead silence.

Chapter 11

Dani didn't understand what was going on. A virtual invader? Like how was that possible? It was hard to be scared of someone jumping out and attacking you if he was just an image. She'd followed the two brothers as they'd wrangled their way down the hallway. She heard their discussion and some other voices. It didn't make complete sense, but it appeared that something extra had come in with the pod. And that wasn't likely to be good.

Then the room filled with a horrific noise. She clapped her hands over her ears and crouched on her heels. Just as suddenly, the noise stopped and the silence was almost as painful. She shuddered when something touched her. She turned to see Charmin rubbing up against her leg. "That didn't bother you?"

"No, not the same way it did you."

"And I thought animals had better hearing."

"Sure we do, but I also knew it was coming, so I had time to prepare for it."

"You knew it ahead of time?" She shook her head at her cat. "How is that possible?"

And damn if he didn't give her that look that said she was too stupid to bother explaining it to. She shot a glare at his back and stood back up as the brothers came out.

"What was that?"

Levi wrapped an arm around her shoulder, turning her toward the kitchen. "Milo just killed a bug."

She twisted so she could see his face. "You mean an espionage type of thing?" At his nod, she raised her eyebrows.

"Are you two so heavy into this stuff that people are trying to steal information about Milo's inventions, or is this about me?"

"I don't know. Both are possible. I just don't know how they knew the pod was coming here to have something like that ready in time."

Charmin galloped down the hallway in front of them. He called back. "What's to understand? The bug and pod came from the same person. If you needed an unregistered pod, they needed a bug in here to find out why!"

"That's getting old," Dani muttered, glaring at her beloved know-it-all pet.

His tail flicked in several sharp motions as if to say "get over it".

"He's right though." Milo sauntered past. "It had to have been ready to go before you ordered the pod – or right at the same time. I told you it was a bad idea."

Levi pulled up short. Dani turned, about to ask him what was wrong when he said, "This is getting damn old."

She grinned. "Milo might have brought me for you, but it looks like he brought Charmin for himself."

Levi's gaze widened and he broke out laughing. "That is so true."

They entered the kitchen to find identical looks on Milo and Charmin's faces. As if reading each other's minds in tandem, they turned their backs on Dani and Levi.

She giggled freely, loving it when Levi hugged her close. "Let's go see if the two geniuses can figure this out."

Still smirking, they stepped up to the side of the big holographic monitor that the two smarties were studying.

"My facial recognition hasn't found anything yet," Levi volunteered.

"And it won't most likely. You don't have the latest software."

"What?" Levi stared at his comp. "Sure I do. This was just updated last month."

"And I updated it after trying to find Lina's henchmen buddies." Milo lifted his head to Levi's glare. "What? I sent it you. It's not my fault if you didn't do the upgrade as you were supposed to."

"There aren't supposed to be any. It's supposed to be seamless, remember?" The deceptively soft tone had Dani searching his face, not understanding the undercurrents.

She asked, "Updating computer software was constant in my world. Is that the same here?"

"No." Levi said, his voice more resigned than hard. "It's part of Milo's mockery of my retro preferences."

"Not totally. It's fun to bug you, but it is safer right now to do things manually. You know that. If we have a problem, we have to go into blackout mode. And that means taking everything offline and updating manually."

"Damn."

Milo laughed. "See. You forgot."

"Well, I've had other things to worry about."

Milo reached out, flicked a couple of holo buttons, and pulled a holo headset out of the monitor and wrapped it around the back of his head. He brought up some kind of white screen and with his hands not touching the monitor or the keyboard, words started to appear.

"What the heck," she muttered, leaning closer. "What's he doing?"

"Recording his observations and planning what to do next."

Dani shook her head. "But his fingers aren't moving."

Levi stared at her. "What does his fingers have to do with it?"

"Ah...typing?" She gave him a look that should have made him understand the problem, but instead he grinned. "At least audio for speech."

He laughed. "Sorry, typing is old school."

"Just like me apparently." She watched as paragraphs of text appeared on one side of this big monitor. "So you can just think what you want onto that screen?"

"Sure. Works much better."

"I can see that." She stared, trying to figure out how it worked. "It must be set up for his neural impulses."

"Exactly." Charmin looked at her in admiration. "I didn't think you could figure that out."

"Watch it," she warned. Then had to smile as his face split into a huge feline grin. "You were teasing me, weren't you?"

He nodded before turning around on the spot and lying down. Just before he closed his eyes, he whispered, "Nap time."

"I wish."

Levi reached an arm across her shoulders. "You can go back in the pod."

Wistfully, she considered the idea. "Is it safe?"

"Absolutely. Come on, I'll take you back."

She let him lead her back into the small room. "It doesn't feel the same."

"No, but it is fine. It's safe and secure. The sounds you heard were coming from the bug."

"But it sounded like heavy breathing."

"Probably just the initial sounds as it went live. The bug had no visual on it, so it couldn't see into the room. But it did have audio."

At her shocked look, he rushed to reassure her. "They didn't hear much. It just turned on now while you were in there."

"It could have been on then, too." She leaned in and whispered, "You know, when…"

"No." He shook his head. "The bug would have showed up earlier if that was the case. I had to run all sorts of security programs with the raid and the warrant. No. It was turned on just a few minutes ago."

"Are you sure?" Because she wasn't. "What a horrible thought to think someone was listening in like that."

"They weren't," he reassured her. "It was installed in the pod, to detach at the right time."

Inside the room, he opened the pod. "I have something special to make you feel better."

She slid him a sideways look, wondering what he meant by that. But he appeared to be studying the computer dashboard on the pod. "Go ahead and lie down," he said, his fingers dancing on the keyboard.

Desperate to have the soothing sensation the pod could provide, she scrambled inside and immediately felt better. She had to trust that the Blackburn brothers knew what they were doing.

Then again, she didn't have much choice.

***

Levi waited until Dani had stretched out in the pod. He needed her to relax enough to be back in here. Afraid or not, she needed the pod still and likely would for a long time to come.

He played a gentle music track and set the pod to give a massage.

She moaned. "I don't know what you did, but it feels wonderful."

"It will massage whatever surface you lay on the pod. So a back massage or a chest massage."

"Then I'm good here for a long time."

He smiled. "It will help you to sleep, too." He backed away towards the door when she said, "You're sure it's safe?"

"I'm sure. Just rest."

He waited a few moments, studying the small room and realizing how unimpressive it was. He could fix that. He could also make the room bigger. His head reeling with ideas, he snuck out of the room and headed directly to the big computer.

There, working on the opposite side of Milo, he brought up the dimensions of the apartment. He had paid extra for the adjustable space and so far they hadn't used all of it. He enlarged the space of the pod room, incorporating the bed she'd slept in the first night to make a bedroom big enough for Dani and the pod. As much as he'd love to have her in his bedroom – she was his wife, after all – he wanted that to be her decision. So until that time...he opened the decorating program, studied the settings, and selected a Pacific island hideaway. He started the program, hoping she was asleep already. Otherwise, the changes might freak her out. He should have thought of it earlier.

As it was, he realized he'd better check up on her. He quickly raced back down to the room and watched as the colors changed and the holograph appearance shifted so the pod was in the middle of a South Pacific island. The walls also slowly adapted to the new parameters he'd set, allowing the imagery to have more punch. He thought the sand was a nice touch. Too late, he noticed that Charmin had followed him into the pod room.

"Ohh, a litter box." Charmin jumped in.

"No! That's not a litter box," Levi whispered in a harsh tone.

"Looks like a litter box." Charmin walked forward and sniffed. "Smells like a litter box." He turned in a circle and started to dig. "Feels like a litter box." And he squatted.

"No! Don't do that." Levi hurriedly opened his link to the comp programming back in the kitchen. "Program. No sand. No sand!"

Too late.

Charmin flicked his butt, lifted his nose in the air, and sighed happily. "Nice litter box." He studiously buried his mess then bolted past Levi.

Levi groaned. "I can't believe you did that," he yelled after Charmin. "You know better."

"Who knows what better?" Dani stuck her head out from under the pod, frowning at him. "I was asleep. What happe—" she stopped, her eyes went wide, and she gasped. "Oh my. What happened in here?"

"It was supposed to be a surprise."

"It's a fantastic surprise," she exclaimed. "But why? How?" She pulled herself further out to stare in happy amazement. "We're not really in the South Pacific, are we? If we are, I'm all for staying here."

He smiled at her innocence. "No, we aren't. But if you want to go, just say the word."

"Word," she cried. "Word. Word. Word."

He stepped over Charmin's heaped sand pile and opened the pod. "Sorry, I didn't mean today. Later, we'll travel. There are a lot of things to take care of here first."

She stared up at him, lying back on the pod bed. "Really? It's not expensive?"

His eyebrows shot up. She really had no idea what kind of wealth he and his brother had accumulated or that she herself had for that matter. "Let's just say it's definitely doable. And…" he thought about the benefit of taking her somewhere where no one else would know who they were until she learned more about their world. "It might not be a bad idea. I'll have to think about the ramifications."

"No, you have to work. I understand. You can't just take time off whenever you feel like it."

She really didn't understand. He needed to fill in her education and fast. "There's a lot you need to learn but for the moment, I can work anywhere in the world. I can show up to work in holographic form. That's how I attend most meetings. Yes, we have offices, as you know, but if I want to spend a month on the top of the mountain resort, that can be arranged as well. I can also use special ports to come back to work on a daily basis if I choose."

Her eyes went even wider as she absorbed what he was saying. "Everyone can do that? Not just rich people? Cause wow!"

He laughed. "Not everyone. Obviously, if you are in a field that requires your presence, then you can't take off all the time. But this is a normal in the business world and it's common to port from one place to another this way. Go for lunch in Europe with a business partner or attend a meeting in South America in the afternoon. Time zones are a bit of a problem at times, though."

"I bet," she said with feeling. "And there must be currency issues."

"No, we now have a global currency and a global financial group that keeps track of the international monetary scene."

"That makes sense," she said slowly. "In my time, there was talk about doing something like that."

"It happened somewhere around the same time that English became the global language."

"Do you still have banks?"

"Financial centers, but you can access the same one all over the world. Makes travelling much easier."

"Do you have to pay to use ports?"

"Oh yes, like the Internet, we pay for usage. It's expensive, but nothing like plane travelling would have been in your time."

"That's a relief." She smiled up at him. And damn if that simple movement of her lips didn't make his groin tighten.

"First, you need to heal." He went to close the lid of the pod, letting her go back under. "Then we can explore. There are a lot of things I want to show you here. It really is a magical world."

"Wait." She pushed the pod lid back up. "Can you join me?"

"What?"

She gave him a slow sexy quirk of her lips. "Remember the last time?"

"Oh God, yes, I do." He hesitated, hating that he felt like he needed to ask. What if she said no? "Are you sure? You need to rest."

"I believe we went over this once already. Sex in a healing pod helped in many ways."

Part of him wanted to correct the use of the word sex. It wasn't just sex for him. He didn't really want to know if it was for her. He hoped not, but this was not the time to discuss such things. Not if he wanted a chance to make love to her again.

She smiled, a warm enticing smile that heated his blood. Damn, she was something.

He grabbed his shirt and tugged it over his head, tossing it to the far side of the room. "Make sure you miss the litter box," she whispered with a smirk.

"Ha. It's gone. Bet he didn't know that the rooms clean themselves."

And didn't that make her stare. "They what?"

"Absolutely. Housework is a thing of the past."

"My past apparently." She reached out a hand and stroked down the front of his thighs, pausing before slowly climbing back upward.

Hips surged into her palm, willing her to explore further.

"Remember last time, you said I could have a turn?"

He'd barely thought of anything else. "Yes," he muttered, struggling to open his pants and step out of them. He finally managed to stand in front of her, his eyes watching her face as she studied him with a fat grin.

"So let's trade places." And she scrambled out of the pod to stand beside him. He was now fully nude and she was fully dressed. And didn't his knees start knocking? He wanted this. Damn, he wanted this very much. He lay down on the warm bed, self-conscious for the first time as his erection stood tall and proud. He watched her watch him. He waited with bated breath as she reached out a hand and grasped him gently with one hand. He groaned softly and closed his eyes.

When he felt her wet tongue, he almost lost it.

"You do that and it's going to be all over before we've even started."

She gave a low throaty laugh. "Oh, I don't think so."

Chapter 12

She loved that he lay there so accepting. With all the problems she'd brought with her, he'd done his best to keep her safe. And now he was trusting her like she'd never had anyone else trust her. And she wanted to make it good for him. For them both. She took her time stripping off her new clothes, loving the feel of his heated gaze, the appreciation. He had the ability to make her feel beautiful with just his eyes. When she pulled her tank top over her head, finally as bare as him, he sat up and reached over to cup her breasts.

"Hey," she teased, "I thought this was my turn to run the show."

"Too late," he said thickly. "I can't wait. I need you now." He tugged her forward until she rested on top of him. "I swear I've been waiting for you forever."

Sliding his hands up to clasp her head gently, he pulled her down for a kiss.

And what a kiss it was. Fireworks and liquid heat fought for supremacy, lighting up nerve endings while melting her insides. Lord, he was a hell of a kisser. And she had to admit, there was an odd sense of homecoming attached to this moment. As if she'd been waiting for him, too. And didn't that train of thought take her down a direction she had not thought to go. He was here and so was she. That was good enough for both of them right now. And she wanted him. She'd never been a one-night stand type of person and didn't plan on being one now.

Besides, he was her husband. And they'd yet to have a wedding night.

"Do you have a bedroom?" she murmured when she could.

"Of course." He reached up to clasp her head and tugged her down for more drugging kisses. She twisted sinuously against him, dragging her breasts from one side to the other, then flexing her hips and pressing her pelvis hard against him. He moaned, sliding his hands down to grab her hips and ground his pelvis up against her.

"You know, we could try a bed out one time."

He smiled beneath her lips before moving to trail kisses down her throat. "Next time."

She tilted her head back, letting her long blond hair fall down around them. "That's what you said last time."

He laughed and flipped her over to lie down beneath him. She stared up at him in wide-eyed surprise when he came down on top of her, just where she wanted him.

She spread her legs, making a place for him. He settled in deeper. She arched beneath him, offering her breasts. He bent his head, tugging first the one then the other into his mouth and suckling. He stoked the fires until she twisted beneath him, crying, "Levi, now."

"Not yet."

"Now." She wrapped her legs around his thighs and gripped him tightly. Then she wiggled beneath him.

He roared, lifted his hips, slid his hands down to hold her hips steady, and plunged deep.

She gasped at the invasion. At the fullness. At the rightness. Again. A tiny corner of her mind worried that it was dangerous to think that way, but the rest of her reveled in it. All her life she'd been trying to find her place. Trying to find her home in the world. Apparently she'd just been behind the times.

Levi lifted his hips, pulling back and back and…

She dug her nails into the smooth rounded muscles of his buttocks to stop him from slipping away from her completely.

He drove inside.

She wrapped her legs around him as he set up a rhythm that she was desperate to match and more frantic to increase. He picked up speed. Throwing her head back, she held on for the ride.

Inside, her blood heated as her body raced to the finish line.

She twisted her head, crying out as tiny explosions started to go off, but she wasn't quite there. He lowered his head and claimed her lips, his tongue slipping inside as he drove in one last time. His body stiffened above her and he threw his head back, a long low groan sliding out from deep in the back of his throat.

Then she wasn't aware of anything more as her own body exploded.

***

Nice. Actually a hell of a lot more than nice. Levi lay listening to the strong, steady beat of her heart. The pod started humming around them. The lid was still up. He wondered if it had the ability to take over and help even when it hadn't been closed. Then to his amazement, it dropped into place and set up healing rays all around them. He'd never heard of them being able to open and close on their own, but it didn't really surprise him. It was, in fact, very helpful.

Especially right now, when he couldn't possibly move.

"Wow." She sighed happily, her breathing only slightly calmer. "You are soo good at that."

He grinned, loving the lighthearted intimacy with her. He tugged her up close and closed his eyes. How had Milo known that this is what he needed? That he missed loving someone. Being part of a special twosome.

His kid brother was many things. Intuitive was the one thing he wasn't.

As Dani nestled closer, her leg sliding over his, he could feel her body settle into the gentle rhythm of sleep. That she could trust him after all that had happened made him feel good. He knew she'd had little choice over these major changes in her life, but he hadn't forced her into this step. And although he needed her legally bound to him to keep her safe, she hadn't seemed to have a problem with that.

He twisted slightly so he could look down on her dark blonde head. Who'd have thought she'd find a way into his heart?

He almost winced at the thought. He hadn't thought to find a partner anytime soon. He'd looked for one years ago and gave up when all the relationships seemed superficial and dull. He'd made what he thought were a lot of friends back as a young adult, but the friendships hadn't lasted and the girlfriends had disappeared even faster.

He'd always been looking for something…more.

Dropping a kiss on Dani's head, he realized he might have just found it.

Chapter 13

Dani woke up, cozy and comfortable with the sound of surf breaking close to her head. Her eyes popped open to find Levi's decorating system still in place. She loved it. And she was so going to enjoy being part of his world with these types of perks. She pushed the pod open and sat up.

And laughed.

The sand was gone. Instead, there was a long deck stretching from her pod out into what appeared to be water. She couldn't imagine it being real water, but Charmin had apparently used the fake sand just fine, so who knew?

She tilted her head back to see blue sky and sunlight shining high above her head. This decorating stuff was incredible. She not only could see the surroundings, but she could feel a gentle breeze and even smell the heavy blooms of the tropical flowers. She spread her arms and flopped backwards in delight.

"I love it here!"

"Ha. I wondered when you'd get around to saying that."

She laughed and rolled over to see Charmin walking along the deck as if the water was going to reach up and grab him. He did so hate water.

"You won't get wet, you know."

He glared at her. "What was wrong with the sand here? It was perfect."

"Ah, except I don't want the pod room to be your litter box. If I have to adapt, so do you."

"What can I say?" He hopped lightly onto her pod bed. "It was done in a weak moment. A nostalgic moment."

She shook her head. "As much as I can understand that…"

"It's done, so forget about it." He head-butted her. "Think about loving me for a bit."

She stroked his beautiful fur. "As if I don't love you."

"Maybe, but it seems like you are loving Levi a little more."

"Not more than you!" She gasped in horror. "Never."

"Aha! So you do love him." He half fell, half sprawled on her.

She barely noticed. Her mind was spinning with his words. And that L word. Did she love Levi? How could she? She didn't even know him. But she'd already acknowledged that she knew him better than her major asshole ex — and she'd loved him.

Damn.

"Stop thinking so loud, you're disturbing my beauty sleep," Charmin grumbled. "With all your activities, you might want to grab some shut eye as well."

"Hey."

"If you're going to be kidnapped, you'll want to look your best. Just sayin'."

She bolted upright. "Why did you have to say that?" she wailed. "How am I supposed to rest now?"

"Seeing as how you forgot that you have bad guys chasing after you, I thought a reminder would be appropriate."

She sat up. "Did you and Milo figure things out while I was resting?"

"Resting?" He turned his head and narrowed his gaze. "Is that what you call it?"

And damn if she didn't flush. "Hey, be nice."

He snorted and stretched out, showing his belly. She sighed and reached over to give him a little more love. "I wish I knew what was going on."

"Milo found out a bunch of stuff. Go check with him. And while you're at it, there has to be a mealtime we missed in there somewhere."

"You wish."

"Hey, you satisfied your hunger, now help satisfy one of mine."

Considering he'd been fixed before she ever got him, it seemed a reasonable request. Besides, she could feel her stomach starting to grumble, too. "I'll see." She searched the island hut for her clothes, amazed to find them at odd places but fitting into the scenery as if she truly were there. Once dressed, she stopped at the doorway for a final look and smiled. "Charmin, this island look is perfect for us."

"Only if you bring back the sand."

"Not happening." She partially closed the door as she walked out. The hallway was still the same. She had to wonder why Levi didn't keep the apartment as something more glamorous. Surely it could be a palace on the inside instead of this normal boring old apartment? In the kitchen she found the brothers, heads bent, studying something on the table.

No.

On the table. What the heck? She hurried closer. It appeared to be another computer of some kind. "What is this?" she asked.

Milo lifted his head to stare at her, but his eyes appeared unfocused.

She switched her gaze to his brother. "Levi?"

"It's a new tracking system we've been working on for military applications." He grimaced. "Technically, you're not cleared to see this."

"Oh fun. The problem is, I already have." She sat down beside him on the bench and grinned when it widened to give them more space. "I do love the future, especially the decorating system you have in this place. Although why you haven't changed all the rest," she waved her hand outward to encompass the kitchen, "I don't know."

"Milo doesn't like change. Or rather, we can't agree on a change that suits us both."

Milo turned to stare at him. "I'm not a kid anymore. If you want to redecorate, go for it."

"We tried it once, remember?"

"Hey, you wanted the place to look like some creepy haunted house and I wanted it to look like a science fiction flying ship." He shrugged. "So we did nothing."

Her jaw dropped. With difficulty, she managed to pull herself together. "You can do that?"

"Well, you have to pay for it, but the motto of today's world is that everything is available – for a price."

"Wow. Okay, things have really changed." She nodded to the table that wasn't a table. "Did you guys design this table, too?"

Milo frowned. "Why would I care about designing furniture? That's so old hat. Anyone can do that."

"So this isn't a table – you just designed the computer that sits on top of it."

"Ah, you mean the fact that it's part of the table. Today, you can place computers on any kind of hardware." Levi started manipulating his side of the 3D image again.

"What are you looking for?"

"The missing lawyer. She's the key to this mess. If we could talk to her…" Levi trailed off.

She frowned. "Didn't Charmin find her?

"Yes, but she's dropped off the grid again. We tracked her until she just...disappeared."

The big screen on the side wall opened up, and John appeared to step through. "Levi, are you receiving calls?"

Levi pushed his chair back and walked over. "John. What did you find out?"

"There's no sign of Lina," he said nervously. "We've tried everywhere and nothing. Her mother hasn't heard from her either."

John's face twisted as he said the last part.

Dani stood. John turned to look at her. "I think the answer lies with your wife, Levi. Maybe if I could ask her some questions."

Levi immediately shook his head. "You can give me your questions and I'll see about asking her, but she's not the problem – Lina is."

Milo nudged Dani off to the side. He lowered his head and whispered, "He can't see you here. If you stand in that square," and he motioned to where she'd been on the line, "he can see you."

"Oh sorry. I didn't know." She lowered her voice, "Can he hear us, too?"

"Only if you are in that box."

"Wow." She could imagine the technology being very helpful in many cases, but it sure seemed like an invasion of privacy to her. Or was it? John had asked if Levi was receiving calls. Maybe that was the same as asking permission. "Does Lina live with her mother?"

Milo shrugged. "No idea."

"Maybe we should find out. After all, if she does and she hasn't heard from her, maybe something bad has happened to Lina. Maybe she didn't run off. Maybe she was punished for failing to grab me."

He cocked his head to the side then reached into his back pocket and pulled out his weird fingerboard computer. After tapping on the silver machine for a few moments, he smiled and said, "She does live with her mother."

Levi, distracted by Milo, turned to look at them. "Does that matter?"

"Depends if she's in trouble with whoever she was to deliver Dani to. Chances are, failure is unacceptable."

Levi's jaw clenched. "John, have you checked the hospitals for a woman fitting her description, either dead or alive?"

"Oh dear." John's face twisted up.

Dani thought maybe it was because of the unpleasant media attention his firm might receive if that were the case. Then her attitude toward all lawyers was awful since she worked with Lawrence, the king of all asshole lawyers.

She sighed and tried to remind herself that John was likely a very nice man. Just because Lawrence and Lina weren't didn't mean all lawyers were bad. There had to be good ones out there. She just hadn't met any. Except maybe John. And the verdict was still out with him.

Milo shouted, "Yes! Found her."

Levi turned to face his brother while Dani tried to see what Milo's comp said. "She's in the morgue on Cronan street."

"Morgue." Dani's stomach started to feel queasy again. Lina could have had an accident, but Dani couldn't quite believe it. She was afraid that these people were playing for keeps and failure was not an option.

***

Levi hated the look of fear on Dani's face. He pulled up the information Milo gave him and got into the databanks to give him a visual of the body. Sure enough, it was Lina. He showed the head shot to John, watching the shock, the fear, then the lighting fast calculation wash over his face as he tried to figure out the best way to play this.

"She must have had an accident. Although why they wouldn't have notified me, I don't know. Or her mother."

At the mention of Lina's mother, John's face twisted. "Her mother is going to be heartbroken."

Levi continued to read the file. "She came in with her tags missing and minimal clothing." That caused John's eyebrows to shoot up, "and showing signs of torture."

Silence.

John exploded. "What the hell did she get herself involved in?"

"That's something I expect your help in finding out." Levi continued to read the file. "Her body was dumped outside the hospital."

John dropped his gaze, but his shoulders were shaking. Dani didn't know if he was upset by the news or if he'd had a personal relationship with Lina and was affected on more levels than she'd first assumed. Finding out one of his employees had been murdered had to be difficult for anyone.

"Levi, I have to go do damage control. Let me know when and if you find anything else out." Just like that, he blinked off. Dani stared at the spot on the wall, wondering how long it would take before she got used to that.

"So much for his help." Levi shook his head. "Milo, can you get into the Council files to see if they have any further information?"

Milo walked over to the counter top and brought up the big 3D unit and started clicking.

"Also, didn't we find some of the bad guys' photos on the facial recognition program?" Dani asked. "Did that help at all?"

"We're running the list of known associates, trying to find out where they might be located."

"And then what?" Dani asked. "Do you have police that you can call on for help?"

Milo shook his head so fast, his long Mohawk looked to be in the middle of a major storm. "No. We've crossed the line. We have to handle this ourselves."

"And can you?" she asked, studying his face.

He looked over at her, showing wisdom and maturity. "We have to. There's a lot at stake here."

She didn't know if he meant her or more but decided some information was better left unknown.

She felt helpless. They had so much to do. Normally, she'd have made tea or coffee or pulled together a simple meal, yet it appeared at the moment that she couldn't even do the simplest of things.

She hated that.

She walked over to where Levi had gotten her water the day before. She placed her hand where he'd placed his and pushed slightly. Instantly, a water fountain slid out from behind the wall. She grinned in delight. Now if only she'd watched how he'd made coffee. How hard could it be? Exploring the things she'd watched him do, she managed to pull open the cooler and pull out the fillings for a sandwich. At least, it would be a sandwich if she could figure out where the bread had gone. She'd had some the first meal with a big chunk of cheese and meat. Back in the cooler, she found something that appeared to be meat. She pulled it out and turned to ask Levi about bread. Instead, he stood in front of her with a large loaf in his hands.

She smiled and snatched it out of his hands. "Next time, show me where you got it from." He tapped the counter in front of her, and a cupboard rose up. She grinned. "I do love all this cool technology."

Milo stopped what he was doing, looked at the shelving, and glanced back at her. "What technology? That's a simple cupboard."

She shrugged. "It's more advanced than anything I've seen."

"Right." He gave a small headshake and returned to what he was doing.

She studied the cupboard, looking for other food that she'd recognize. Some were recognizable. Most were not. While the men went back to work, she busied herself opening packages and tasting food. One looked like crackers but tasted like cardboard. Another had brightly colored images of food all over the package but gave no clue as to what was inside. She read the instructions to find it was a synthetic supplement. Yuck. Must be something for Milo.

The bread was good though. She could really use a slice while she rummaged but couldn't even find a knife to cut it with. Finally, in frustration, she began systematically placing the palm of her hand on every surface she could find and giving a light push. Nothing happened for the first few tries, but she persisted and was delighted when she opened one cupboard, then another, and another. She investigated all the contents and realized the third one had a mother lode of utensils. She grabbed a knife and cut herself a slice of bread. She turned to study the cooler but didn't know how to open it. She pressed at various places but to no avail. The door would not open.

Ignoring the snickers from behind her, she said, "Open." Nothing. "Open sesame."

Still nothing, but the laughter behind her was growing. "Open please."

Silently, the cooler opened. She turned and threw an accusing glare at the two snickering males and said, "You just programmed it to do that, didn't you?"

Milo nodded, a wide grin splitting his face. Levi walked over. He reached out a hand and hit a hidden spring. The cooler door closed.

"No, wait."

"Now you open it." She reached out and touched the same place he did. It didn't work. She looked over at him.

"Again." he smiled. "A little harder this time."

Success. She grinned and reached in for butter. "What is this?" she asked about a big package wrapped in paper.

"Steaks for dinner."

"Oh yum." She could really use a steak. "With a baked potatoes and a salad?"

"If you like. Do you need more right now?" He motioned to the thick slice of bread she was eating.

"I'm fine, but Charmin is hungry again."

Levi rolled his eyes. "Of course he is." He walked to a side cupboard. "I ordered this today. It's premium cat food."

"Oh, thank you." She watched him open some kind of odd package and pour a premeasured dose into a bowl. It didn't look like cat food, but it did smell like it. It was an unmistakable smell once you dealt with it more than once. Still, Charmin should approve.

She hoped.

She walked back to the pod room carrying a bowl for Charmin. "I love the South Pacific theme. It's stunning."

"I was hoping you'd like it. If you don't, we can always change it."

"Later," she smiled. "After I'm bored with the concept. If I ever get bored."

"My bedroom is a Swiss chalet."

"Really?"

He grinned. "Let's feed Charmin and maybe I'll show you."

The look in his eyes sent a shaft of heat right to her toes. She murmured quietly, "I think I'd like that."

She'd love to spend a private hour in his bedroom.

As they opened the door to the pod room, she gasped. Instead of her South Pacific island getaway, the room had become a room of cat trees and cat ledges walking up and down the walls. With a dozen cats apparently sleeping on various beds. Overall was a deep rumble of a snoring cat.

"What the..."

Levi laughed. "Hey, Charmin, I don't suppose you were planning on sharing this meal with all your friends."

The snoring stopped. Charmin raised his head, his nose sniffing the air. "Program revert."

While Dani watched in amused surprise, her pod room turned back to the South Pacific hut. "Wow."

Charmin stood, stretched, and walked over to them. "I'm so weak," he moaned.

"Ha. Not so weak as to set yourself up right at home." Dani scooped him up and tried to cuddle him, but he wanted nothing to do with her. Instead, he scrambled out of her arms to land softly on the floor in front of his food bowl. He immediately burrowed his head into the food. Dani took a step back. "Amazing, Charmin. You've picked up everything so fast."

He lifted his head and pinned her with a marble glare. "And why wouldn't I? Nothing here is hard to understand or learn."

She sighed. "Says you."

"It would be easy for you, too. You just need to do things instinctively instead of overthinking everything." With that pronouncement, he returned to eating his meal.

"He's right, you know. Everything nowadays is meant to be intuitive and easier to do, minimizing time and effort."

She shook her head. "Then why is it we haven't sorted out who killed the lawyer and why she was after me?"

He winced. "That's a good point. Let's go and see what Milo has found."

Chapter 14

While Levi went to check on Milo's progress, Dani stayed with Charmin until he'd finished eating, then she bent down to scoop his dish up off the floor when the pod started to make weird sounds. It often made similar sounds when she was in it – but not like this. This one had a weird metronome sound to it. She called out. "Levi? Milo? The pod is making weird sounds."

In seconds, the two men were rushing toward her. "It's probably nothing," Levi said. But his face said otherwise.

Milo circled it, his hands full of his gadgets. "Okay, this is not good. It's a tracking device."

He pushed a button, and there was a weird splat that sounded like a power outage. "Not anymore."

Dani released her pent up breath she hadn't been aware of holding. "Why didn't your bugs pick this up earlier?"

"I think it was triggered after the first one was destroyed. Like a backup system. While it wasn't active, I couldn't have picked it up."

She didn't like the sound of that. "What if there's a third bug that will start when it realizes this one stopped working?"

"It's possible, but not likely. Still…" Milo attached the bug detector, its lights flashing to say it was working, on top of the pod. "That will take care of anything else."

With that, he returned to his study of the pod, looking for the now-defunct bug. "I did tell Levi that the pod was dangerous."

"You said a lot, but you didn't exactly leave me much choice."

"And I for one am very appreciative of the pod." Dani added with feeling. "It's helped a lot. Though I can't say it feels very safe and I'm not sure I want to sleep in here any longer."

Levi tugged her close. "You don't have to."

Milo rolled his eyes. "Can we stay on topic?"

"On topic, I just want to sleep." Charmin said from behind them. "Who can rest with all that racket going on?" he grumbled.

"I thought you were eating," Levi said suspiciously.

"I was eating. Now I want to sle—"

A heavy pounding sounded on the door.

"Milo, I thought stealth was on?" Levi ushered his brother out of the pod room. "Stay here," he said to Dani and Charmin. "Don't come out until one of us says so."

And he closed the door in her face. A final snick made her scoop up Charmin and whisper, "That last part didn't sound very good."

"He locked us in." Charmin stared at the closed door in shock. "That's bad. Like really bad."

"Why is that?" She figured it couldn't be that hard to get out. It seemed like everything was either hand or voice controlled.

"Because the food is on the other side of that door." He turned until his flat face was pushed tight up against her face, his eyes round with horror. "We'll starve."

***

"Milo, find out who is out there."

As usual, his brother was way ahead of him. Being naturally distrustful, Milo had set up multiple programs to keep the world out there – right where he wanted it. He valued his privacy. More than that, he detested the invasiveness of the government.

Levi walked to the front door when Milo said urgently. "Wait. It's one of the men from Lina's office."

Ah shit. Levi froze. "Now what the hell are we going to do?"

"I don't know. They shouldn't know that we are home. Stealth is on and active. No heat seeking, no audio, no power surges being registered. As far as the outside world is concerned, we are not home."

"Unless they were the ones listening in on the bugs, then of course, they know that we are home. And if that last device was a tracker, they'd have traced the pod here anyway."

Levi winced. "Then make sure stealth is on in the pod room and let's see what this guy wants."

"Don't open the door," hissed Milo. "He might have come here to kill us."

That was a possibility as well. But he had other options. He opened the wall com. "What do you want?"

"The girl," came a hard flat voice.

Levi closed his eyes. Damn.

"Give her up."

"Or else what," Levi asked, deceptively calm. He stared at Milo, who was waving his hands in the air in a wild manner.

"She's nothing to you. But she's worth a lot of money to us. You already have money, and with her, we will, too."

Levi frowned. "That makes no sense. She *is* worth something to me. She's *not* worth any money to you. How could she be?" He managed to work just the right amount of helpless confusion into this voice.

"I'm not getting into an argument with you. I have orders."

"Orders from whom?" Levi watched as Milo finally stopped panicking and started calling someone – anyone – for help. He hoped Milo was calling the same people that hassled them all the time. It was only fair.

The big wall screen beside him opened up to show Milo sending a live feed of their visitor to the same department handling Lina's murder case. At the same time, Milo sent a feed from Lina's office showing the same Defino brothers with her that morning. Levi didn't know if any of this would happen fast enough, but if the cops came…he didn't want Dani anywhere around. Or Charmin. And that damn pod needed to stay hidden.

Suddenly, the male outside the door sneered. "Called the cops, have you? That's all right; you can't stay in there all the time. She's the one I want. Give her up and I'll leave your freak of a brother alone."

A frightened squeak behind him said Milo had heard that bit.

Just as suddenly, their visitor disappeared.

Levi turned to Milo. "How long have we got before the police arrive?"

"They're almost here."

And sure enough, the alarms sounded. Within minutes, a small force had arrived at the door.

He had to open up this time. He faced the officers, "Sorry, gentlemen, you just missed him."

"We need confirmation of the material that was sent over."

Of course they did. Resigning himself to a long couple of hours, he opened the door and let the men in. They had ComBots with them. Using combat robots was standard procedure with apprehending anyone considered dangerous. At least the authorities believed him about the thug. If he'd had something to do with Lina's death, then he was very dangerous.

His mind immediately considered getting a ComBot as a security guard to help keep Dani safe just in case he wasn't home.

He waited off to the side as Milo confirmed the video footage and explained via HoloKomp to the Council Security officials how he'd come into possession of the feed and why he hadn't turned it over earlier.

They all appeared satisfied with his explanation about not knowing about the dead woman until her partner called to see if she'd been in contact.

Just when he thought it was over, the person in charge handed over more orders. Both he and Milo were to appear in front of the Council.

Now.

Chapter 15

Dani held her breath as she heard heavy footsteps approach. There were other people in the flat besides the two brothers. It bothered her to be locked in the small room but at the same time, if the stealth mode meant what she thought it meant, no one would see this room either.

That should keep them safe. The pod itself was illegal, so even finding that would cause Levi big trouble. She was a whole new dimension of trouble.

She didn't want that for anyone. If anyone knew the truth about her, she'd never be allowed to stay with Milo and Levi. No, the best thing she could do was learn to blend in. To be one of them.

"Charmin, is there anything that will help me learn how things work here?"

"Time?"

"We don't have time," she said urgently. "I need to fit in. I have this horrible feeling that Milo and Levi are in trouble."

Charmin studied her, but his thoughts appeared to be far away. "There is no comp in here, is there?"

"I have no idea." She spun around. "Comp turn on."

Nothing.

Charmin spoke up. "Audio from the rest of the apartment on."

Immediately, sounds of people moving through the rooms filled the air. Dani shuddered and squeezed Charmin tight.

"We are to take you down to the Council right now."

"Why?" Levi said. Dani shivered at the barely contained anger in his voice. "Why are we going back to the Council when we were just there?"

"More questions need to be answered."

Then there was no more talking as they all filed out of the apartment.

Charmin stared at Dani. "They've gone back to Council without saying anything to us."

"They couldn't," she said absently. "He didn't dare speak to us."

"I will contact Milo then." And damn if Charmin didn't hop up onto the pod and push some buttons on the unit that Milo had left humming away in the background.

"That's a bug finder. Not a com."

Charmin shot her a look. "They are all computers, and here all computers can communicate with each other."

"Oh." Of course they could. It seemed like everything here communicated with every other thing. The damn coffee maker probably talked to the house alarm and vice versa. "So you can talk to Milo?"

"Of course. So can you."

"I'd like to talk to Levi."

"His comp is on silent mode."

"Oh, but Milo's isn't?"

"His is never off. He's receiving my message now."

"Is that safe?"

"Probably."

She didn't like the sound of that. She also wished she could go outside and double check that the apartment was empty. But what if it wasn't?

Then she heard it. The sound of a door opening. She couldn't help herself. She stared up at the ceiling as they heard audio of someone else entering the house.

Charmin froze, his whiskers quivering.

He tapped the comp very gently, as if afraid that the very tiny clicks could be heard. The unit in front of him flashed an answer back. He swallowed, looked at her, and said, "It's not the group that was just here. It's someone else."

She closed her eyes. "That can't be good."

"Milo says to not make a sound. Stealth is on, but…"

She grabbed Charmin, the comp unit, and crawled underneath the pod.

She didn't know who the unknown visitor was, but nothing about this situation was good. "Did Milo say if they were on the way home?"

"They can't yet. He says he's sending help."

She thought about that. "I wonder what that means?"

"No idea." He added slowly, "I wonder if they are bringing food."

***

Levi glared at the Council. "What was that question again?"

"We wish to know where you obtained copies of these videos." Off to the side, the videos of the two badass henchmen entering Lina's reception room were displayed.

"It's obvious where we got it. We do consulting work for John Driscoll's office." Levi didn't like where this was going. Sure, they'd crossed the line by showing it to the police, but as they were looking for a murderer, he hadn't thought they'd crossed the line that much. "Why is this an issue?"

"Because," the speaker said, anger putting an edge in his voice, "If you accessed the private feeds from the lawyer's office, what else might you have obtained and why?"

"Nothing other than the regular security feeds. Which is funneled to Johns security company," Levi tried to stay calm, but he was damn worried about Dani. "I don't understand what this has to do with anything."

"We have a murdered lawyer, who prior to you sending this feed is known to have spoken to your wife before her disappearance."

"No. My wife had nothing to do with this. As we've shown, Lina was still alive when we left. The conversation with those two men prove that."

"Except that as both you and your brother are known to have exceptional skills with anything electronic, you can't actually prove that you didn't doctor this feed." He pointed to the feed frozen on the wall, the henchmen's face stopped with his mouth open. "For all we know, this man was there visiting the lawyer earlier in the morning and you just made it look like their visit was later."

"Good Lord. You actually think that we had something to do with Lina's murder?" His voice rose at the end. "That's preposterous."

"Why is that?"

Levi could hardly formulate an answer. How did one prove that he hadn't done something? "For one, I have an alibi. I've been home with my wife and my brother all day. Besides, what possible reason could I have for hurting Lina?"

"Lina?" This was from one of the other Councilmen. "You have a personal relationship with her?"

"No." Levi shook his head. "No. I knew her before she joined John's firm, but not well."

"But she wanted to know you better? She might have pushed you. Hard. Became a little too pushy. Maybe you told her to back off. Maybe she pushed back. You argued...and things went from bad to worse."

Levi stared wordlessly at the four men staring down at him. He wanted to rage and scream at them for their blatant stupidity. "You have this all wrong."

"That's not what this man says."

Levi turned to stare, shocked as a very sober and sad-looking John walked in. "John? You're the one accusing me of hurting Lina?"

John's dour faced turned even more sober. "I didn't want to believe it, Levi."

"But you just can't help yourself." Levi's cynicism kicked in. "This is your attempt at damage control? Place the blame on my shoulders, then you and your firm don't have to take the fall for a rogue lawyer. Won't have to reassure all the clients that she didn't sell their secrets?"

Milo stared at John. "Wow. Slick move. Of course, it's not going to work."

John's gaze hardened. "And why is that, genius?"

"Because I'm pretty sure if I were to access your office, we'd find a string of communications showing that Lina was alive after we left her office. Your office. The office you have full access to. The office you pay the security company to do whatever you want. The office where you can screen potential clients to do some of your dirty work."

John's face became a picture of innocence. "I had nothing to do with the death of my colleague." He managed to look outraged yet grieving at the same time. "How dare you accuse me of such a heinous crime?"

"Oh, but it's okay for you to accuse us?" Levi was back to being stumped. At the same time, his mind raced in circles looking for something, anything, the one thing that would get him off the hook. "Then let us take a look at your communications." He dared John.

John raised an eyebrow. "Of course. Here." And he dropped his comp onto the table in front of everyone. "I have nothing to hide."

Milo snatched it up, clicked a few buttons, and lifted his gaze to stare hard at John. "It's a brand new phone."

"Yes, sorry. I lost my other one yesterday afternoon."

"Of course you did," Levi mocked. "Coincidental timing, I suppose."

John stared at him blandly. "Whatever."

Milo continued to click and click. Levi hoped he was finding something useful. His brother's head was bent like always when he was focusing on a new project. "Find anything, Milo?"

"Yeah, I did."

John stiffened. "Impossible. There is nothing to find."

"Well, not on the phone. But I tracked it back to the office."

Milo looked up with a smile and hit play. Lina's voice could be heard easily. "You know very well why I'm going to be late for dinner." She sighed. "Dear boy, I need to meet someone. This is going to be an easy open-and-shut deal. No worries."

"Somehow whenever you say that, it works out to be the opposite."

"Then come with me so I'm not alone. That way, we can go to dinner earlier and that will make for an earlier playtime." On that last note, she dropped her tone, oozing a very low, suggestive sexuality.

Milo clicked on something, and the feed froze.

Levi said, "So John, would you care to change your story? After all, you are now the prime suspect. You spoke to her well after we did."

"That means nothing," he blustered. "And that conversation could have happened a while ago. In fact, I'm pretty sure that it did."

"Oh, it probably did when she was always wheeling and dealing. However, by your own admission, this phone links to both your office and home, *and* it's a new phone, so you spoke to her after you got it. Which you said was late yesterday afternoon. So technically, you were the last one to speak with her."

Silence.

Chapter 16

Dani crouched low, making herself as small as she could. The South Pacific theme was open and empty. Kinda hard to hide. She had no idea who walked the hallways outside the pod room, but from the sound of heavy footsteps and pounding on the walls, there was no doubt someone was.

Her nerves were shot with every hard thump on the wall. The intruder were looking for her. She knew it deep inside. And the fear choked her. She couldn't take a breath. She clutched Charmin so tightly to her chest, she doubted he could breathe either. She closed hers.

Thud. Thud. *Thud.* She shuddered and buried her face into his fur. "Please keep us safe."

Thud.

They had to be following the signal from the tracker before it was fried. Charmin shivered in her arms. She squeezed him tighter.

Then the door opened. She gasped silently and shrank lower.

"Bloody hell. Here it is. How the hell did they hide this place?" The stranger walked in. From her position under the pod, she could only see his boots. Leather. Heavy. High. Studded. One of the Defino brothers. The boots were meant to instill fear. And they succeeded. She was terrified.

From the quivering flesh in her arms, she presumed that Charmin felt the same.

The footsteps circled the room one way then returned the other way. Back in front of the door, the boots stopped. "Damn." The boots shuffled slightly. As if he was standing in one place and looking the place over. "Who'd want a pod on an island? Stupid people."

His hands hit the floor and he bent down to look under the pod.

And Charmin attacked.

He flew at the stranger, claws out, slashing and slashing...and yowling.

"Holy shit. What the hell?"

Charmin howled again and dashed away, only to come back and jump up again, this time going after the man's face. Footsteps sounded as the stranger, she thought it was the older thug, raced out of the room.

Charmin gave chase.

A horrible alarm set off, filling the halls and making the walls rattle. Dani cried out and slapped her hands over her ears. "Oh, make it stop."

She scrambled out from under the pod, raced to close the door, and stopped. She couldn't leave Charmin out there alone. He could be hurt. In danger. But the horrific noise was worse with the open door.

"Charmin," she whispered. There was no way he'd be able to hear her with that alarm going off.

Damn. She snuck into the kitchen, but there was no sign of him. Scared to be too far away from the pod room, she snuck back and called for him again.

Still nothing.

On the floor, she found a comp unit. It wasn't one she recognized. She picked it up, wishing she understood how to use it.

After tucking it into her pocket, she went to close the pod room door when she heard, "Hey, open up."

She pulled the door wide open. "Charmin!"

He jumped into her arms. She shut the door with her hip and hugged him close.

After a cuddle, Charmin dug his claws into her arm. "Ow! What was that for?"

"You have the intruder's comp," he said, jumping from her arms to the top of the pod. "Let me see it."

Feeling ridiculous but willing, she laid it down on the slightly rounded top of the pod and held it steady for her cat to use. Boy, if any of her old friends could see her now. They'd lock her up in the loony bin. Then again, she'd have been living there for the last few days anyway if she tried to explain what had happened to her.

"What are you trying to do?"

"See his connections."

She frowned. "As in whom he worked for?"

"And when he last had contact with that lady."

"Lina?" That might be helpful, but she wasn't sure how since she was dead. But if they could find the person behind all this, she'd be happy. Maybe then she could settle in to learn about her new world.

"Do you think the apartment is empty now?"

He shrugged. "I think so."

She walked back to the door and opened it. Everything was quiet. Maybe too quiet? She really wanted to make sure the damn intruder had closed the front door. There were all kinds of security in place – but she was pretty sure the door had to be closed for any of it to work.

Milo said he was sending someone to help them. Surely they'd be here by now?

Leaving Charmin to work the phone awkwardly with his fat paws, she crept toward the front door. And stopped. A man approached the open doorway. Then she realized who it was. Thank heavens.

It was John. Levi's lawyer. Still in his blue outfit.

"Thank heavens you're here," she exclaimed with a big smile. "The place was broken into. We've been trying to reach Levi and Milo and can't seem to get through."

"You did get through. The alarm on the place sent an automatic alert to them. That's why I'm here." He smiled with relief and held out his hand. "I'm so happy to find you safe. Hurry now. I'm to take you to Levi."

"Oh." She was so happy to see someone she recognized. She raced toward him.

He was just outside the door. As she reached it, a clear shield of some kind came down between her and John.

A look of sheer frustration washed over his face.

"What the..." she reached out a hand but realized the shield had a charge of some kind. She'd get a shock. "John, what do I do?"

"Shut it off from the inside." But the peculiar look on his face made her realize this was something she should know how to do.

"He changed it recently," she lied. "I don't know how. He never got a chance to show me the new system."

Anger swept over his face. He turned to look behind him. "You need to hurry, before someone comes."

She studied the wall beside her. She assumed there was another virtual comp hidden in here with the controls she needed. But even if she could open it up, there was no guarantee she could shut this down.

She needed Charmin.

And didn't dare bring him out here where John could see him.

"I can't figure this out."

"What the hell? How could he possibly want you when you haven't got even basic computer knowledge?" His disgusted tone bothered her, but it was the building rage on his face that bothered her more.

She settled back. "You have no reason to speak to me like that. Our relationship is none of your damn business."

He glared at her.

And she realized this shield was all that was stopping him from reaching through and grabbing her.

He wasn't here to help her at all.

He was here to kidnap her too.

***

Levi opened his mouth to answer yet another question from the speaker of the Council. His own lawyer, John, was now under suspicion. John had excused himself, saying he'd be contacting his own lawyer. At that point, Levi had thought that he and Milo were in the clear. That they could go home. He'd been wrong.

His comp went off. He pulled it out, disregarding the frown on the Councilman's face. "Sorry, gentlemen. That's my house security system." He clicked through his signals. Alarm sent shockwaves through his system. "My place has been broken into. I need to go. My wife is alone." He turned to Milo. "Move. Dani is in trouble."

Milo was already heading to the door. Levi ran over to him. "Excuse us, gentlemen…"

With Milo ahead, they raced to the portals. Levi barely made it into the same one as Milo. "Are they okay? Can you contact anyone? Dani? Charmin?"

"I'm trying. But it's not as if either one is trained to override the lockdown system."

Shit. Levi winced. He hadn't done enough to help Dani. She was in a terrible position. And he'd made things even worse. Again.

His heart pounded in his chest. He could only hope they'd make it home in time.

The port opened and the elevator closed. They were back home in seconds.

They raced around the corner, his breath caught in the back of his throat. He stumbled to a stop.

The front door was open.

And the blue shield was on.

Shit.

He came to a sliding stop, hitting the brakes just in time. "Damn it."

From behind him, Milo said, "I'm working on it."

"Work faster..." He tried to peer through the waves of blue electricity and thought he saw something. "Charmin? Is that you?"

He looked around to make sure no one else could hear him. "Milo, is that Charmin sitting on the other side of the field?"

"Give me...one...more...second." A loud click sounded. "Got it."

The blue screen disappeared.

Levi rushed forward, surprised when he heard a new voice behind him.

"And I've got you two. Better yet, I've got her."

Levi came to a confused halt, looking behind him to find John holding a laser gun to Milo's back. Milo, his comp still in his hand, had his arms up high over his head.

"Now Levi, get the girl. I don't have much time."

"What is this all about, John?"

"Did you hear me say I don't have much time? I'm supposed to deliver her within the next fifteen minutes or the delivery will be late. Late does not cut it with these guys."

"Who?"

John's face darkened. "No more talking. Get her, or I'll kill your brother. These guys mean business. Lina failed, and look what happened to her."

Levi turned his shocked gaze toward Milo, who stood helpless in front of him. "Get her."

How could he? How could he hand Dani over? Yet he couldn't put his brother in danger.

"Tough choice, huh? Brother over lover? Too bad. It's not a choice. Hand her over or you die, too."

"He doesn't have to hand me over." Dani's cool voice drifted toward them. "However, I'd like to know who you are planning on delivering me to and why."

John relaxed now that Dani was there with them. "I don't know. And it doesn't matter. They get whatever the hell they want."

Dani stepped past Levi. He reached out and grabbed her. "Wait."

"No. There is no waiting, Levi. There is no choice."

She tugged her arm free and walked to the door.

John grabbed her and shoved her ahead of him while keeping the gun still trained on Milo.

"Don't bother trying to follow me," he snapped. "You don't want to be where I'm going." Bitterness swept over his face. "Hell, I don't want to go there myself. But that bitch put me in the clinch now. So it's you or me…"

Levi stared, his mind racing to find something…anything that would save the situation.

John stepped up to the doorway, shoving Dani outside. With one last warning glance at the brothers, he backed up several steps into the doorway.

Charmin, quiet unassuming Charmin, sprang into action, jumping high up on the wall and slamming a paw into the 3D monitor. Instantly, the electric screen flashed.

As John passed through the middle of the doorway...as the electronic shield surrounded him.

He was fried instantly.

The system flashed and sparked...and shorted out.

Milo raced past him, crying out in horror.

Levi could only stare.

"Jesus," he whispered. "Charmin, did you mean to do that?"

"Of course." He walked closer to what remained of John's body. He proceeded cautiously, then caught a solid whiff and reared backwards. "Oh gross."

Levi skirted the remains on the floor and quickly disengaged the shield. Dani stared at him in horror from the other side.

"It's okay," he reassured her. "It's off."

She didn't look hysterical, but Levi wished she would be – then he wouldn't feel so bad about his reaction. He was shaking uncontrollably. With a cry, she ran inside without looking at the floor and threw herself into his arms. "I was so scared. So scared," she whispered against his neck, squeezing him hard.

"So was I," he murmured, holding her tight against his chest. "Oh God, Dani, so was I."

He backed up, keeping her with him, "Let's get you into the back of the apartment and away from that."

"Gladly," she muttered.

He led her to a big comfy chair that shaped itself around her. "I have to deal with this first. Then you can tell us all about what happened."

"And we need to get something for Charmin, too." Charmin jumped up on her lap just then, and she wrapped her arms around his furry body and cuddled him. "He's my hero today."

"He's everyone's hero. As soon as the police and those...remains are gone, we'll get him anything he wants."

"Food?" Charmin poked his head up over Dani's shoulder. "Food would be good."

"You got it, little guy. I might even be able to get that for you." Levi walked to the wall and opened up a cupboard full of cat food. "What do you want? Salmon, tuna, chicken…"

"Anything," Charmin said, "Anything but…BBQ!"

The End

Broken Protocols 3

By

Dale Mayer

Broken Protocols 3

Dani and Levi Blackburn have slid from being in trouble to borderline hell...

They uncover hints of a dangerous conspiracy permeating the very foundation of their society. And people are disappearing, one by one...

If it weren't for Levi's twisted-genius brother and Charmin Marvin, Dani's talking cat, they wouldn't have gotten this far. At least, not alive.

Only they aren't far enough, because someone is still after Dani – and everyone connected to her.

They need to find a way to expose the massive cover up- and fast... before they are eliminated. Forever.

Dale Mayer
Valley Publishing
Copyright © 2014
Cover model - Mirish (http://mirish.deviantart.com)
Cover designer - Jason Mayer
ISBN-13:9781927461914

Chapter 1

Dani Summerland walked restlessly through the living room and kitchen. Her new life two centuries in the future had taken a strange and ugly turn. The problems besetting her since her arrival should have been over – instead it looked like things were likely to have gone from bad to horrible. Figures. Murphy's Law had somehow followed her to this time period. Like how did that work?

She was desperate to calm the tension vibrating through her. The police had come and gone. As for the lawyer who'd tried to kidnap her, his remains had been removed. Life supposedly could now return to normal. Whatever that meant. She had no normal left. This time jump had come with no warning or preparation.

Life had hit her sideways and she was still sliding. She'd done the best she could, and Levi had been a godsend. Then again, he'd been the reason she'd been plucked out of her nice happy little life into his – as a gift for him – compliments of his uber brainy kid brother.

Since she'd first arrived, there'd been nonstop trouble. From horrible pain to debilitating exhaustion to heated passion between her and Levi. That last part had been a bonus. But between that and the people after her, life had been a dangerous roller coaster.

And she needed off.

As they still hadn't gotten to the bottom of this nightmarish kidnapping scenario, they weren't safe yet. And if anyone found out that the time travel trick had resulted in her overgrown Persian cat now talking like a fluffy Einstein – and getting worse every day…

Was it any wonder she needed a break from this stress?

Determinedly, she turned to face Levi. He sat, his chin propped up on his fingertips. Deep in thought. And she could just imagine what was going on in his incredible brain, one that matched his incredible body. Sex aside, Levi had turned out to be a hell of a good man. She walked closer.

"Are you okay?" She sat down beside him, happy when he opened his eyes and smiled. There was just something weird about knowing that this man was her husband. They'd only known each other a few short days. He'd married her to keep her safe, yet now she couldn't imagine life without him.

Her cheeks heated as she remembered some of their best times together. His gaze warmed. He cocked an eyebrow and murmured, "What are you thinking about?"

She gave a slow intimate smile. "Good times." She paused then added, "And I was wondering about…" She let the words trail off, not sure how to phrase it.

"What?" He reached out and slowly stroked her arm up and down. "If you need something, you only have to say it."

"I need to get away. From here. From all this nastiness."

He frowned and damned if a bit of fear, insecurity maybe, sat in the back of those deep purple eyes.

"Not from you," She reached out to stroke his cheek. The shadow in his eyes lightened, and he sat back to study her. "I was just thinking that I have a lot to learn. There are people after us, and we need time together."

He nodded. "All true."

"I was wondering if we could go away for a week or two. Where it might be safe for you to take me out and show me life here. Where making a major gaffe won't attract much attention. Where we could spend a little time together. Where every move won't be watched. Where I can learn ports, and shopping, and…"

He held up a hand. "I got the idea."

"It's a great idea," Milo piped up. "We could all use the break."

Levi glanced over at her, a question in his eyes. She gave a small laugh and nodded. Of course Milo would come. And there was no way she'd go without Charmin, her walking talking miracle feline.

"A good idea as long as we all go," Charmin said as if reading her mind. "It's too dangerous for us to split up. Besides," he hopped up on the back of the chair and butted his head against her shoulder. "Who'd look after me?" His huge golden eyes stared at her in worry.

"Not going to happen." She stroked his silky back, leaning down to kiss the top of his head. "I wouldn't go anywhere without you."

"Or Milo," Levi said with a laugh. "It's a good idea. We'd both have a few things to take care of first, not to mention deciding on where to go. In theory, we could leave tomorrow."

She brightened. "Thank you. That would be perfect." She grinned, thinking about how easy that had been and added, "Besides, today is almost over."

Charmin snorted. "What time are you on? It's barely after lunch." And he gasped, his eyes rounded into huge glowing marbles. "Lunch."

"No," Dani said. "You had lunch."

"But I had an early lunch, and that means it's snack time." He turned his flat face toward Levi and deepened his tone. "You did order treats for me, right?"

"Wow." Dani rolled her eyes. "It's hard enough for poor Levi to adjust to a talking cat without that same cat trying to order him around. Remember your manners."

"Ha. He's doing fine." Charmin shot a leg into the air and proceeded to clean the back of it. "Soon he might even start obeying those orders."

She smiled and reached out a hand to stroke her four-year-old pet.

"Levi, as much as it's a good idea, I think we need to solve this problem first," Milo said. "The leads are hot right now. If we leave, these assholes are going to go under and we might never catch them."

"I was actually thinking about sending you three away, and I'll stay here and deal with this," Levi answered.

"Oh no." Dani shook her head. "All of us or none of us."

He frowned. "Milo has a good point. This has to stop." He reached over to cover her hand. "If we leave, they're just going to be waiting for us when we return."

"Then we solve this first – then leave. Personally, I'm thinking beach." Charmin dropped and sprawled along the back of the couch. "I'd like some more sand."

Snort. "Maybe you could just get a litter box instead." She exchanged a laughing look with Levi, remembering the last time Charmin had come close to sand.

"If that's the case," she said, returning to the problem, "What do we have to do to solve this mess permanently? I hate the idea of always looking over my shoulder."

"We need to find Johan and whoever was behind my lawyers' attempts to kidnap you. John said Lina had gotten him into this trouble, and they probably tortured the name out of her. So we also have to find her killer. I'm hoping the two are the same man or group of men."

Johan was Levi's friend who lived at the top apartment – or used to. She'd never met him. He was on the run from the authorities now.

"Okay," she said, "That makes sense – but how?"

"That's my part," Milo said around the straw in his mouth as he sucked up something bright green. "Finding them, in theory, is no problem, but stopping them is."

"Because we don't want to involve the authorities?" Dani asked.

"Partly, but they are involved already," Levi said. "There are two dead lawyers. That cannot be glossed over."

He reached out and tugged her into his lap. "We need you safe."

"I need all of us safe," she muttered. "But how?"

***

Levi cuddled Dani close. He'd do anything to keep her from harm. Had already done several things he'd never have believed. But they'd been necessary. "We're good at what we do. We'll find him." He squeezed her gently. "I promise."

When she looked up at him with those huge eyes filled with uncertainty, he repeated, "I promise."

Milo came up behind him. "Sounds like it's time to get back to work." He brought up the big countertop 3D monitor.

"I need treats first." Charmin groaned. "I can't help you until I regain my strength."

Dani laughed. "Ha." She nudged Charmin's large sprawling belly. "You're going to get fat."

"I am not fat. Well, maybe a little, but I'm cuter this way." He stretched out a right paw and offered the underside of his belly for a scratch. When she obliged, he moaned.

Levi shook his head. "He's something else. I'll put on coffee and help Milo."

At the sound of coffee, Dani swung around so he could get up. He laughed. "You are as bad as your cat. Your treat is just in liquid form."

She stretched out on the space he'd vacated and smiled. "In that case, we both deserve treats."

"Finally." Charmin moaned as if in major pain. "Treats. I need treats."

Milo snorted. "How about a booster – whoa, what do we have here?"

Levi raced over. Dani twisted to lean over the back of the chair. "What did you find?"

"I'm not sure." Then Milo pinched his lips and his hands moved faster and faster. Levi stepped back and watched his brother work. It was rare to see him in the zone to this extent. His brother was sheer magic. And when he was on the hunt, he was lethal. His hands flashed. The screens shifted too fast for his eye to see what they were. The monitor buzzed with the speed of the activity. It blurred in front of him. Then Milo made a slashing motion with his hand and everything froze.

Dani made a strangled sound from behind them. Levi could only imagine what she was thinking. There'd been nothing even close to this in terms of home computing in her time. There were bigger, faster, and more complex computers at his office, but not by much. By the very nature of Milo's genius, he needed tools available at all times. And typically the best that could be had. That meant building their own supercomputers. Not a problem, but many of their inventions went way past computing. That's when they got into trouble.

Milo leaned closer. Levi stepped in to look. "What is it?"

"An intersection of paths."

"Whose paths?"

Milo tapped the top of the screen, drawing Levi's eye to the faces. Both Defino brothers' images sat on one side. On the other side sat the two dead lawyers, Lina and John. "So you've tracked all their paths?"

"To this one spot." Milo tapped the monitor frozen in place. "It's at the old shipping docks."

Levi frowned. "That's the turf I'd expect from the Defino brothers, but not the lawyers."

"Except," Dani said, "John said something about not liking where he was being forced to take me to." Dani walked closer to study the screen. "So maybe that's the headquarters. The boss man would be in a location like that, wouldn't they?"

"Only part time," Levi said, "they'd have a home base somewhere a long ways removed from that hellhole. Likely at the top."

Her face fell. Then lit up again. "That would make sense. Could that be Johan? He lived pretty high up. You have no idea what he did for a living, but it sounds like it was just on the edge of legal."

Levi shrugged. "If we could track his path to the same area, then I'd say definitely. But as he's gone underground..."

"What about his known friends and associates?"

"He doesn't have any." Milo looked over at his brother. "Does he?"

Levi looked from one to another. "I don't know. I don't know him that well."

"Then maybe that's where we should start looking. Everyone in his circle. See where those paths intersect?"

Milo raised his eyebrows at Dani's suggestion. After a quick glance at Levi, he swept his hand back the other way, unfreezing the monitor. Immediately, the windows flashed and sparkled as they moved at light speed.

Dani looked over at him. "I guess that means he's on the hunt again?"

Levi smiled. "Seems like it."

"So does that mean coffee and treats are back on the menu?"

With a smile at their tenacity, Levi walked over to the wall where he started coffee. "I guess it does."

While he waited for it to finish, the alarm went off. Dani gasped, her hand going to her chest. He reached out to her. "It's all right. We have company. That's all."

She took a deep shaky breath. "Okay. I'll go back in the pod room then."

"You don't have to." He was already walking toward the door. "Not if you don't want to."

"Actually, I wouldn't mind." She gave him a wan smile, reminding him how tired she was. What she'd been through already today. "A short nap, with Charmin, would be nice. I'm feeling peaky."

"Okay then." He watched her carry on down the hallway; Charmin, somehow knowing what she was up to, followed close behind. Dani looked tired, melancholic. Taking her away from all of this was a great idea. She'd only been here a few days, but they'd been brutal. The alarm went off again.

"Levi? Are you answering that?"

Giving his head a shake, he said, "I've got it."

At the door, he looked outside. Damn, another Council henchman. At least the uniform and close-cropped hair denoted henchman. He could only see the back of the guy's head as he appeared to be looking behind him, as if he was waiting for someone to join him. Not unexpected considering the break-in and death this morning. But he'd hoped it would be over, at least for today. Like Dani, he was tired and fed up. The alarm sounded again.

Gritting his teeth at the visitors' arrogance to keep hitting the alarm, he went about opening the security system. The alarm went off one more time. "I'm coming. You don't have to keep on hitting the damn button."

Finally, he unlocked it and pulled the door open. And stared in shock at the man standing in front of him.

Johan.

Chapter 2

Dani opened the healing pod. Charmin hopped up and froze. His whiskers quivered. She sat down on the side and yawned. She had to admit, she really could use a nap. The morning had worn her out. She slumped backwards, spread her arms, and closed her eyes. She giggled when she felt the pod automatically shift and move under her as it adjusted to her sideways position.

"Nice, huh?"

Charmin didn't answer. She ignored him. She was so tired. The pod was always so welcoming. Nothing like warmth on your back to soothe and ease the tension inside. She was one step away from falling asleep now.

"Dani?" Charmin asked.

"Hmmm?" She rolled over and tucked her knees up higher. "What?" She yawned and felt herself drifting deeper and deeper.

"Did you hear who just arrived?"

"No." And she didn't care. Her body relaxed a little more. Boy, she needed this.

Just as she drifted off, she heard Charmin's response. "Johan."

The word percolated through her brain then slammed into her consciousness. She bolted upright, barely missing the pod lid as it lifted automatically ahead of her movement. She hadn't had a chance to think with so much going on, but on reflection, it seemed like the pod was doing more things. As in learning, adapting to her and her likes and needs.

Nice.

And creepy.

"Did you say that was Johan at the door?"

"Yes." Charmin stared at her, his eyes impossibly round. "Why would he come here?"

"No good reason that I can think of." She sat on the edge and worried about the problem. "Can we hear the conversation?"

"Audio on," Charmin said.

Immediately, Levi's voice slipped through the ceiling. "Johan? I don't understand. Why are you here?"

Milo didn't give Johan a chance. "Whatever his reason, it's a bad idea."

"Milo, give him a chance to explain."
Silence.

A strange lilting voice rasped, "Thanks for the opportunity, Levi. And Milo, for all your brains, you need to learn a little more about human psychology."

Charmin snorted. "Why? He's got brains, and that means he doesn't need anything else."

"That's not true," she whispered. "And we should probably be quiet in case they can hear us."

He just shot her a look of disgust. "Whatever." He lay down, rolled over, and curled into a tight ball.

"Great. You wake me up and now you get to sleep." She glared at the sleeping cat. "How is that working for you?"

"Quite well. If you'd be quiet, I could actually get some rest."

She threw herself down and curled around the bright orange body, hugging him close. "Do you think I should go out there?"

"No. Absolutely not." The alarm in his voice reassured her.

"Right. That's not a good idea, is it? Then Johan will know for sure that there's something odd about me."

He shuddered. From his twisted up position, he opened his eyelids and glared at her. "Do Not Go Out There." He lifted his head as if to make sure she was listening. "Levi will handle it. They know we are here. Let them deal with it."

"But..." she stared down into the flat face, "what if they're in trouble and need our help?"

"Not going to happen." He closed his eyes and went back to sleep.

"It might." She lay her head down next to his. "You never know."

"I know." He snored gently.

"But what if you're wrong?"

No answer. She closed her eyes and relaxed. Before she realized it, sleep swept her away.

***

Levi stared at his old friend and wondered what the hell had happened. The fun-loving guy was gone. This man had a hard edge to him, a well-used look to his face and his eyes – it was as if they'd seen too much. A second closer look showed heavy bruising on one side of his neck. He held himself slightly hunched over, one arm protecting his potentially damaged ribs.

This was not good.

"What happened to you, Johan?"

He winced. "I look that bad, huh? I could use my damn healing pod right about now."

"Sit down. I'll get you a drink." Ignoring Milo's disgust and instinctive wariness, he poured a stiff drink into a glass and brought it over to Johan. "Here."

Johan took it gratefully and tossed it back. He shuddered, and then said, "Thanks, I needed that."

"I can see that, but why?"

His friend slouched back, stiffened, then straightened slowly.

"You're hurt." Levi said quietly. "Is it bad?"

"No. Just took a beating. On an ordinary day, no problem...but I blew my pod up." He gave Levi a lopsided grin. "Don't suppose you'd like to return the favor and let me borrow yours?"

"No," Milo snapped. "For all we know, you're behind the problems we've been having."

Johan's eyebrows shot up. "What kinds of problems?" He looked over at Levi. "I told you to marry her to protect her."

"I did."

"Well congrats, man." Johan slapped Levi on the shoulder. "That's great. You're a married man now." He shook his head like he couldn't believe it. "She must mean a lot to you."

"She does."

"When do I get to meet her?"

"Never," snapped Milo. "Someone is after her. We're going to make sure she's safe."

"Why the hell would anyone want to kidnap her?"

Milo narrowed his gaze. "I didn't say kidnap."

Silence.

Johan put up both hands. "Hey, I'm not sure what's going on here, but I have nothing to do with whatever is happening. I've been on the run and got into a little trouble myself."

"Why?" Levi asked curiously. "What happened to you?"

"I thought I took everything I needed with me. Instead," he grimaced. "I left something behind. I'm here to retrieve it."

"Have you been up there yet?"

"No. I was hoping to use your tube to get there, take a quick look around, grab what I needed, and then scoot back down here undetected." At Levi's surprised look, he added, "I could go through the little rooftop garden you use."

Levi shook his head. "And here I thought that area was private. Secret."

"Nothing is secret anymore." As he spoke, he stared straight at Milo. "Haven't you learned that yet?"

Milo stared back at him silently, not showing any give in his expression. After what they'd been through and the secret experiment Milo had accomplished bringing Dani here – keeping his work private – secret – was paramount. Milo would do anything to protect his inventions. And if Levi didn't quite trust Johan, there was no way that Milo would.

He was suspicious of everyone.

Yet, Levi had to concede, Milo appeared to have taken to Dani and Charmin just fine. More than just fine. Maybe he'd run compatibility tests across everyone's profiles. Yet another thing to ask his brother.

Later.

He refocused on the issue at hand. "You can use the tube to get to the rooftop."

Milo started to protest, took one look at Levi's glare, and shut up. He stormed out of the room.

"He's not a happy chap."

"We've had a rough morning." Talk about an understatement. Levi was half expecting to see more Council henchmen here soon enough. Not to mention cops. They would have more questions. There was no way they wouldn't.

Hell, he had a lot more questions. He studied Johan carefully. "So you had nothing to do with the bug that came in with the pod?"

"What?" The shock was real at least.

"Don't you have an automatic bug sweeper here?" Johan's lips twitched.

"Yes, we do. But the bug was built to detach at some specific time or at a pre-arranged signal, then move to a different location in the room."

That shut Johan up. He sat back and stared. After a long moment, he shook his head. "What the hell. Whose bug is that?"

"Milo is tracking it down. At the moment, we have no idea."

"That's not good." Johan stared into space. "I had mine customized, you know. So it would only transmit specific innocuous data to the database."

"Really?" Too bad Johan hadn't mentioned that fact earlier. It would have saved Levi a lot of worry. "That's a great idea."

"Not good enough. Something still went wrong. It did make me a popular fellow for a long time though." He grinned, a rueful smile of remembered parties and women...so many women. "I had the same person rig it that you bought yours from."

"How do you know who I got it from?"

A harsh laugh slid out of Johan's throat. "There is only one supplier who has the audacity to do something like this."

"Do you have a name?"

"Nope. No one does."

"Damn." Levi walked over to the window. He wasn't getting much help here. If he knew Milo, he'd be out searching the airwaves for information on Johan. There was nothing like siccing someone who didn't trust another to dig out dirt on them. "I need to figure out who broke into my house today."

"What? I didn't hear anything about that." Johan stared.

"Oh, you will soon. My lawyer was killed during the mess."

"Wow." Johan let a long slow whistle slide through the room. "Okay, now that I definitely don't know anything about."

Chapter 3

Dani drifted in and out of the pod's warm healing rays. Some of the conversation going on in the other room filtered in. Not enough to truly understand what was going on, but enough to stop her from going into a deep asleep. Figures. She yawned and rolled over to face Charmin in another attempt to drift off.

He stared at her. And damn, those whiskers were quivering. His large globe eyes stared into hers, and his small ears peeled back along his head as if to hear better.

"What's the matter?"

"Johan says it's not him."

"What's not him?" She blinked, trying to process the short terse message. "None of the mess is?"

Charmin gave a small head shake, sending his fur billowing out. She frowned. "Then who is behind all of this?"

"No idea. And we need to find out."

"Agreed." She lay there thinking when Johan's voice filtered in again.

"Are you sure I can't use the healing pod? Just for a few moments. I'd sure like to feel better. Honestly, besides the jaw, I'm pretty sure a couple of ribs are broken." His painful gasp could be heard.

It didn't sound like he was faking it. And that made her feel guilty as hell.

"Sorry, Dani is sleeping in it."

"Sleeping? Dude, she should be warming up your bed, not snoozing in a healing pod." Amused envy laced Johan's voice. That sounded more like the Johan Dani expected to hear. The sexy party animal looking to score and not understanding his buddy's reticence.

There was a heavy silence. Dani winced. If the guy was hurt, it was the right thing to do to give it to him. Did she just get up and walk out as if she had just woken up? How else would they know she was awake and willing to leave the safety of the pod?

"Chamin, can you contact Milo?"

One eyelid slid open. How did Charmin manage to look insulted? "Of course."

She didn't want to be seen. She didn't want to meet any more strangers. Any more bad guys. "Can you tell him that I'm leaving here and going to Levi's room so the pod is free for Johan?"

"Yes." He stood up and arched his back. "If that's what you want."

"Are you coming with me?" She sat up gently and slid to the side of the pod. "Or are you going to stay and visit with Johan?"

He gave an odd mewl that she took for a snort, then he jumped down. To the speaker system, he said, "Message for Milo only." She stared as he said, "Dani and I are switching to Levi's room. The pod is free for Johan."

He twisted, gave her a look, and when she didn't understand, he sighed. "Open door. Stealth to remain on."

The door opened silently.

Damn. She hadn't even realized the door was voice controlled. Hating the things she didn't understand, she motioned for him to go first. "Lead the way so we can't be seen."

He shrugged. "Configure to keep us in stealth." And he walked out.

She followed, a low burning irritation with a touch of envy washing through her. "How am I ever supposed to get used to you knowing how to do all this when a couple of days ago, you didn't even talk?" she muttered.

"We've been over this. I could always talk. You're the one that just learned how." He groaned. "Now if only you'd learn the rest of this stuff faster."

He ran down the hallway, and she had to pick up the pace to keep up with him. With his tail in the air, he looked like a normal feline. Under that pouf of orange fur, he was anything but.

Still, that mess could be laid at Milo's feet.

Charmin disappeared up ahead. She entered a room and came to a dead stop. The door closed silently behind her. She gasped. She was inside a huge chateau type of room that could have come from anywhere in the Swiss Alps. The open beam structure with log walls and wood furnishing were awesome, but it was the huge bed on a platform beside a roaring fire that really got to her.

"Is that fire real?"

"As real as anything here can be." He padded over and tilted his face up to catch the warm rays. She had to see for herself. It was indeed warm and cozy. She felt safe here. Comfy. She smiled. This was gorgeous and said a lot about Levi. She turned to warm her back and studied the huge bed. The coverings appeared fluffy and light. Maybe down. But she suspected it was as much of an illusion as anything else here.

An illusion she wanted to believe in. The idea of sharing that huge bed with Levi – luscious!

"Pull your tongue back into your mouth." Charmin stalked over the huge bed and hopped up. He sank into the middle and turned around several times before lying down. He yawned. "This will do nicely."

"Ha. Who said that's for you?"

"Losers weepers," he replied, using an old phrase from back in her time.

She stared at him. "How is it you can adapt so quickly? Why are you not bothered about how different things are here in this time?"

He lifted his head. "What's different? Bad guys. Good guys. Kidnappings. Murders. They are the same in both times. The technology is more advanced – and so it should be. But honestly, it doesn't look like humanity improved much. Besides, I only need food, love, warmth, and a cozy bed to keep my world balanced." He closed his eyes, then opened one back up. "It's the same for you."

Was it? She wondered. "I need to be safe."

"And you will be. Soon."

***

Milo clicked away on the comp in his hand, essentially ignoring Johan and the rest of the conversation. Levi studied him for a brief second. Then returned his gaze to Johan. Who looked to be fading. "Do you want to go retrieve your property and come back? The pod will be waiting for you."

He didn't know why he made the offer, but it seemed the right thing to do. He sensed an odd stillness come over Milo before the clicking started in earnest. He was up to something.

Then again, so was Levi.

Johan struggled to stand, his face wreathed in smiles. "Thank you. I surely appreciate that. I'll be back in just a few minutes." He staggered down the corridor to the front entrance.

Levi walked behind him. At the door, he asked, "Do you want company?"

Johan paused to look at him, considered the suggestion, then shook his head. "I'll be fine and it will be better if you aren't seen with me. It will just get you into more trouble. Stay here and stay safe. I'll be back before you know it." And he entered the tube and disappeared. Levi stepped back inside and reset the security.

"How long do we have?" Milo asked from behind him.

"Maybe ten minutes." Levi turned to face him.

Milo had followed them down to the hallway. "Then we'd better get moving."

"Moving where? What are you up to?"

"Setting up video in the pod room," Milo said.

Levi stared at his brother as he raced into the room where Dani lay sleeping. "Why? Wait. Don't scare her."

"She's in your bedroom. Charmin told me they'd moved so Johan could use the pod. Dani felt guilty."

Throwing his hands up in the air, Levi ran to catch up. Since when had Dani moved? "How did they even know about Johan being hurt?"

"Charmin turned on the audio in the pod room. They heard the whole conversation."

"Sweet." He entered the room to find Milo tinkering with the comp on the wall. "How long do you need?"

"More than 10 minutes," he muttered, tapping the console quickly. "I'd really like to know why he wants to use the pod. Oh, he's hurt all right. But while he's in here, is he going to retrieve information on us? Will he send messages from our location? Is he really badly hurt? Or did he pay someone to rough him up to add some weight to his story and get him into the pod?"

"He looks hurt. I'm sure the pod would help heal him." There were any number of pods available, but not as many unregistered. If he used a registered pod, then his name would be sent to the databanks. He could expect a convoy of ComBots and police to be at his side within minutes. Here, he could stay undetected.

"Do you believe his story?" Milo asked.

"No. I don't." Levi added, "But it *is* quite possible that he is looking to retrieve something he missed from his place."

Milo shrugged. "I don't trust him."

Levi said, "Neither do I."

Chapter 4

Dani curled up in Levi's bed. It felt wonderful. And yet so right. Special. Illicit. Which, considering she was married to the man, was just plain stupid. She sank a little deeper into the covers, enjoying the feel of Charmin kneading her belly. They'd had lots of mornings in the past where it was just the two of them. Time together to enjoy a lie in. Time to spoil each other and gain the comfort each offered so freely. Times had changed. In more ways than one. "It's been tough, hasn't it, Charmin?"

The kneading paused. "In some ways."

She smiled. "It's nice that we can really talk now."

"Yep."

"Do you think…" she had to stop. What she was going to say sounded stupid.

"What."

"Nah, it doesn't matter."

"Except if it's bugging you, it does matter."

She gave a small laugh, startled at the wisdom coming out of his mouth. "I shouldn't let it bother me."

"And again, that has nothing to do with it. Just because we shouldn't think about something doesn't mean we don't. And if it's in your mind, then far better to share it."

True. She said in a thoughtful voice, "I just wondered if *any* of the enhancements Milo added to our transport came to me. Or if you got all of it."

"Them."

"Them?" She twisted slightly to look at him. "You mean you received more than one enhancement?"

"I don't know that. I do know he added more than one. It's Milo – how could he resist?"

"Yeah." She sank back into the pillows thinking about it. "He'd think it would all work out perfectly as he planned anyway."

"Of course, and for the most part, it did."

"Does it bother you that you are communicating at the level you are now?"

"Yes. It's just much harder to get my beauty sleep," he grumbled from somewhere in the center of the curled-up ball of fur he'd become. "Everyone wants to talk."

She smirked. "Sorry, I'll be quiet again."

"Yeah, but not for long."

Reaching out a hand, she gently stroked along the curve of his back. "Maybe not, but I do love you, and I'm so glad we're together."

His purr hit diesel engine level in seconds.

Content, she lay there and dozed, wondering what other enhancements Milo had added to the two of them – or just Charmin. And had they worked? Supposedly there was a high incidence of failures with enhancements. Apparently Mother Nature still ruled.

The door opened. Levi walked in and looked around.

"Hey, how are you feeling?" he asked after spying her in his bed.

She realized he had to be worried, considering she could barely be seen under the mound of covers. "I'm fine. Just tired." On cue, she yawned. "Is Johan in the pod?"

"No, he's gone to his place to retrieve something. He'll be back in a few minutes."

"Okay, at least it's ready for him."

"Thanks for that. We did use his pod when we needed it, so..."

"Understood. It's the right thing to do." She shuffled back up against the headboard so it was easier to see him. She was surprised to see him standing in the middle of the room. "Uhm, I hope it was okay to move in here? I know I didn't ask, but I wasn't sure what else to do."

"Of course it is," he rushed to reassure her.

She stared at him, loving the warmth that filled his huge eyes. "Good, then why are you standing in the middle of the room like that?"

The heat in his eyes flared, "Because I don't dare get any closer." His legs brought him a step closer regardless. He clenched his fists.

She raised an eyebrow. Her toes curled.

He dropped his gaze slowly down her face and neck to rest on her breasts, plumped up from the bedding she'd tucked around herself to keep warm. "Because joining you in there is exactly where I want to be, but Johan is going to be back in a few minutes. And Milo is working on something that might need my help."

That made sense, and it reassured her. "You could hurry back."

He swallowed hard. "Working on it."

But he stayed frozen in place. Then with a low groan he said, "I'm leaving. I'll be back soon."

She raised the second eyebrow. He threw up both arms, turned on his heel, and raced out. She grinned. "Nice to know he's just as affected as I am."

"You're both idiots," Charmin murmured. "Now do you think I could get some sleep?"

***

Levi tore out of that room before he jumped into that bed and made love to Dani. He'd dreamed of her in his bed, lying beside him. Lying under him. On top of him. Any position would work as long as it involved Dani.

"Whoa, Levi. What's going on?" Milo stood in the hallway studying him. "Is everything all right?"

He winced. Definitely time to control his unruly thoughts and wayward body. "I'm fine. Just realized you might need some help." Yeah, as lame excuses went, that one topped the cake.

And if the look on Milo's face was anything to go by, he agreed. "Right." He walked toward the kitchen. "Maybe coffee? Or a cold shower?" he murmured as he slipped past his brother.

"Ha. Coffee will be fine."

"I'm not so sure. You don't need more stimulants," Milo said, a grin on his face.

Levi glared at his brother. "No, I don't. But the coffee would be good regardless. I'm sure Dani would love some after all the attempts to get her a cup keep getting interrupted. And maybe we have time for a cup before Johan gets back."

He walked over and pushed the button, choosing an espresso blend. He might not need the stimulant, but he could use the shock to his system. Dani was a powerful drug all on her own.

"Speaking of which, I'd have expected him to be back already."

Levi turned around to face Milo. He frowned as he looked down at his own comp. "How long has it been?"

"Fifteen going on sixteen minutes."

Levi made the mental calculations in his head. "He could have trouble finding what he needs to find. If it's even still there. He's hardly late yet."

He walked over the counter and the big 3D screen. "Did you track his movements?"

"There are no tracks to show how he got here. Unfortunately. Then again, he's spent a lifetime living this way. As for where he went, he did take the tube to the top floor. From there – I don't know."

"Can you hack into the system? See if there are any working computer eyes in his place we can access?" Levi thought about what Johan had said before. "Johan said he had eyes on most of the building. Said he recognized the guy that came to give Dani the tags."

"Did he now? That you did not mention before." Milo got busy. "Would have been good if you had."

"It never occurred to me. We do the same."

"Yes, but he didn't come in today through the normal channels. He's keeping track of all of us but not letting anyone see his tracks. And that's not allowed."

Levi grinned. Milo had a huge competitive streak. He also lived on the airways and knew how to traverse the electronic world better than anyone he knew of. His ability to dig himself in until he found what he was looking for spoke to his stubborn nature. He had a lot of bulldog in him.

A good trait when it came to hunting. Levi left Milo to it and took a moment to check the huge backlog of emails and business issues. He'd been slacking these last several days, and there were some things he couldn't ignore any longer. He buckled down to try and deal with the easiest and fastest of them. It took twenty minutes to take the cream off the top, delegate a huge portion of the other issues to his staff, and skim over the rest. Feeling better now that he knew what was backed up, he turned to the coffee he'd forgotten about. Pouring two cups, he carried one into the bedroom for Dani.

And found her sound asleep.

He stared down at the sleeping beauty curled so innocently in his bed. All he wanted to do was slide under there and curl around her.

She rolled over and opened her eyes.

He smiled gently. "Hey, did you enjoy your nap?"

She smiled sleepily. "Did you come to join me?"

"I wish." He lifted the cup in his hand slightly higher so she could see it. "I did bring you coffee."

Her eyes lit up. "That's a wonderful second place prize." She shifted back and up, and he realized she was fully dressed, not exactly the image his mind had been busy creating. And reminded him of another oversight. "I need to get you new clothes."

She winced. "I'd appreciate it. I've been washing my underwear in the sink and leaving it to dry overnight. But one outfit does not last forever."

"Do you like the style? I can give you others, but that style looks lovely on you. And it's easy to grab you a half dozen of the same."

Her gaze widened. "Yes, please."

"Your wish is my command." He turned and walked toward the side wall of his bedroom, where he brought up the clothing program. He quickly repeated his clothing instructions but switched up the colors. As an afterthought, he multiplied the outfit by seven. That should work for the moment.

As he was stacking up the goods on the bed, he got a transmission over the home security system. The robotic voice said, "A request for help has been received."

He straightened. "What? From who?"

"Johan Strand."

"Damn. Is he hurt?"

"I have no further information from the sender."

"But he's alive?"

"At the time of transmission."

"Well, that's something." He hated that the first thing through his mind was that Johan was dying. There'd been too much death lately. He raced out of the bedroom and into the kitchen. "Milo? I have to go check on Johan. He's sent out an alert for help."

"I'm coming with you."

"No, you need to stay here with Dani."

"Dani is going to be locked in here. You need backup."

That his kid brother saw himself as Levi's backup was touching and funny as hell, but he'd proven that he could be helpful in many situations. Given the choices, Milo was correct. As long as Dani stayed inside, she'd be safe. He could set the security system to alert him if anyone approached. And that was a hell of an idea. "Thanks, Milo."

He ran to the front door, set up the alarm, and stepped out, Milo at his back. The two stepped into the tube and took off for Johan's suite.

The tube disappeared as they arrived at their destination. Johan's door was locked down tight. He motioned at Milo to follow him to the small rooftop garden. They couldn't hear any sounds from the place. That in itself was unusual after hearing Johan's endless parties. He stepped over the small divider and carefully worked his way around to Johan's big rooftop patio. The place was dark and silent. The big double doors stood wide open, also unusual, but good for him and his brother. He wanted to race inside and call out for Johan, but instinct stilled his tongue. There was an eerie sense that they weren't alone.

He knew the layout pretty well. He slipped inside and slid along the wall to the left. Johan's bedroom should be down the same side of the apartment. He couldn't hear anything, but neither could he see anything. The darkness was absolute.

Milo motioned toward a large black bar set near the middle of the room. Nodding, Levi crouched down and made his way over to it.

That was when they heard someone rustling around in the room next to them.

But was it friend or foe?

Chapter 5

Dani sat up, threw the covers off, and slid her legs over the edge of the bed. Beside her was a large stack of clothing. Different colors and designs, all appearing to be pieces of the same outfit he'd given her last time. Levi had dumped them beside her before racing out of the room. He had called back as he left, "These are more the same. Later, we can sit down and pick you out different clothes."

Now she wondered at his words. Sit down and pick out some clothes? Did they have stores anymore? Or only online stores? Did he design something himself? Or did he use a design program? Input her coloring and measurements, and voila, a whole new set of clothes. Hit the print button and there they were?

She paused at the idea. That almost sounded possible.

Spreading the clothing out, she smiled at the bright colors. They were the same design as the one she currently wore, but with a fresh look. She loved them. A deep bronze top and milk chocolate pants were her first choice. The array of matching sexy underwear made her cry out in delight. She dressed quickly. She folded the dirty clothes and laid them off to the side, then restacked the remaining outfits. She looked around and realized that of course there were no dressers or visible drawers that she could see. Everything would be sunk into the walls. Or compressed in such a way as to open upon command. Multitasking space, he'd called it. Cool idea.

And it made for a nice clean line in the room. There was little clutter, just open warm space.

Leaving the clothes stacked on the bed and feeling like every other woman with new clothes, she walked out with a skip to her step.

And found the men missing.

She wandered through the kitchen and large sitting room, and there was no sign of Levi or Milo. She frowned. If they were with Johan, she preferred to stay out of sight. After a moment of indecision, she refilled her coffee cup and returned to find Charmin. In the center of the bed, Charmin opened one eye and stretched out a paw. In a lithe move, he rolled over onto his back.

"Charmin, I can't find Milo and Levi. Can you tell me where they are? Without alerting anyone else in the place."

He rolled over again slowly and sat up. "Audio on."

Silence.

She kicked herself for not having tried the same thing. None of this was instinctive yet. "If they're in the pod room, with stealth on, will you be able to hear them?"

"I don't know." He tilted his head and said, "Audio on in pod room."

More silence.

"Locate Milo and Levi."

A weird robotic voice said, "Levi and Milo are not on the premises."

Dani gasped. How? When? "Where are they?"

Silence. "Oh come on, you must track them," Dani snapped.

"Stealth is on."

"On their personal coms?" She doubted that.

"No."

"Then send a message and ask them where they are." She added as an afterthought, "Please."

Charmin made an odd sound.

She turned to look at him. "What?"

"Oh, nothing. Just good to see you learning how this system works."

"I wish," she said. "Then I'd be able to contact Levi."

Like magic, Levi's voice whispered from somewhere in the ceiling, "Dani, we're in Johan's place. He sent out a call for help."

"I was just worried. I couldn't find you," she admitted.

"We'll be home short—"

And his voice disappeared.

Dani stood beside the bed and called up at the ceiling. "Levi? Levi!"

No answer. "Contact Milo," Charmin instructed the house computer.

"Communication has been disrupted."

"Ya think."

Dani turned around in a slow circle, staring up the open beam construction as if it would magically answer. "What can we do?"

The house system said, "We must wait for communication to be reestablished."

"Can you tell me if their vitals are okay?"

"Their vitals are fine."

Walking toward the kitchen, she breathed a sigh of relief and raised a trembling hand to her temple. "Good, then they aren't in any danger."

"I did not say that."

"No. You didn't." She frowned, her heart sinking. "Are they in danger?"

"I don't know that."

"Of course you don't. Then who does?"

"This might help." Dani turned around, surprised to see Charmin on the kitchen counter. "What are you doing up there? No cats on the kitchen counters, remember?"

His 'get real' look left her gasping. "I'm trying to open the 3D computer. We can track them visually up in Johan's apartment this way. See if they're in trouble. Also see if they're alone up there."

She watched him study the granite-looking counter top. "The problem there is we need a scan of Johan's place with that heat seeker scan thing on."

She looked surprised at the words that came out of her mouth. Then again, so did Charmin. With an odd look her way, he turned and clicked one slightly larger white spot, and damned if the 3D computer didn't form above the counter, with Charmin in the middle of it. His fur filled with static charge and he immediately looked like an orange cotton ball – mega sized.

She laughed. "Get out of the monitor, idiot," she said affectionately.

"Hey, how was I to know it would appear instantly? There should be a 3 second time delay for me to shift position."

"Well, be sure and tell Milo that. He can program that in for you."

"Ha, I'll do it myself."

"Ah Charmin, that might not be a good idea."

"Too late," he groused. "Besides, we live here now. Everything needs to be adjusted for us, too."

"Right." Fascinated, she watched as he closed the system, then tapped the same white dot and moved off to the side.

He beamed at her, marble eyes glinting through the fluff. "See. Not so hard after all."

"Wow. I look forward to seeing Milo's reaction to you tinkering with his computer."

"He'll be fine with it."

She doubted it, but that was Charmin's headache, not hers. Besides, Milo gave the brains to Charmin. If she had received them, she'd have respect and common sense to go with it...she hoped.

Charmin studied the multilayered holographic images in front of him. "Do you know how to find the building?" she asked.

"It is the building."

"Oh," She knew that. *So not*. Now that he'd pointed it out to her, she could see the different floors. Shifting her gaze to the top floor, she saw a myriad of yellow, orange, and red glowing in places. "What are those?"

"I think those are the brothers."

"Maybe two of them are, but then who are the other two?"

***

Levi checked his comp. The house comp was listening in, but he'd gone into silent mode. Undetectable even by the house comp. That meant Dani wouldn't be able to contact him, but any calls from her right now could get them killed. He lifted a finger to Milo and pointed to the right. Milo turned his head and frowned.

Crap, Milo didn't understand. Levi looked around Johan's lavish apartment. They'd found Johan on his bed, hurt and apparently worse than he'd been earlier. As they'd walked across the apartment to him, they'd heard someone approach from the other side.

They'd been in hiding ever since.

"Damn it, Johan, I asked you where it is. If you don't tell me, I'm going to have to hurt you for real."

A weird mechanical voice with a feminine tone. Levi shook his head. How was that possible?

Johan groaned in response.

"If you hadn't set your pod to self-destruct, you could be in there healing by now."

"So you can torture me more?"

"Sure. That works."

Levi couldn't see the speaker, and the voice, although familiar, sounded odd.

Milo whispered in his ear, "Voice mask."

Levi considered that. Did that mean they were dealing with a man after all? That was the more likely answer.

"What do you want to do?"

Damned if he knew. He had to help Johan. He could identify his attacker and maybe they'd finally get to the bottom of this mess. That thought alone propelled him down to the room beside Johan's bedroom. He glanced inside. It was a spare bedroom. Odd that Johan had left it that way. In today's world, he could have turned it into so much more with just a flip of a button, so why hadn't he? Milo joined him, glanced inside, and winced. "Boring."

"And that's what's wrong here. Johan's lifestyle was anything but boring."

"So why this?"

Levi nodded.

Milo lifted the bug detector that he'd grabbed on the way out of their place and turned it on. He ran a sweep, but nothing stood out.

Levi stared at the space and wondered. Then realized it was a holograph like he'd done for Dani's private island. Johan had deliberately made it to look like a dull boring bedroom. So what was underneath? He slipped inside, motioning for Milo to join him. He closed the door slightly so that the flash of the house comp wouldn't alert anyone, then with a half an eye on the hallway, he quickly stopped the cloaking program. Milo gasped. Levi turned to see an incredibly high tech computer layout. He spun around and turned the cloaking program back on. This was what the intruder was after. And if he was willing to kill Johan for it, Levi wanted to make sure he didn't get his hands on it.

A scream split the air. Johan. Levi, knowing it was the wrong thing to do, but couldn't help himself, raced to his friend's aid. He tripped around a corner and dashed into the bedroom where Johan had collapsed. There was a sound of running feet as the intruder bolted outside. Levi ran to Johan's side, but Johan waved a hand at him. "Get him."

And he collapsed again.

Levi followed the sounds of running feet. Time was of the essence. If the person managed to get to the port before Levi... "Milo," he screamed, "shut down the port."

For a small apartment, it seemed to take forever to make it to the front door.

Just as the port vanished.

"Shit." He circled the port area, hoping that the attacker might have left a clue.

"Sorry bro. There's some kind of fail-safe set. I didn't have enough time," Milo's aggrieved tone brought Levi back to his senses.

"Not your fault."

He walked back to Johan. His friend looked bad. Like seriously bad. "Call for a Medivac. He needs more help than a pod."

"He's past it, bro. Look at him, he's not breathing."

"Damn it." Levi checked Johan's vitals. "Come on, Johan, stay alive. Please."

He lifted one of Johan's eyelids, but there was no response. No pulse. No breathing.

Milo stepped up and pressed his comp to Johan's tags. There was no responding beep, only a hum that sounded fainter and fainter…before completely dying away.

"Sorry, Levi, he's gone."

As the words left his mouth, the apartment doors slid closed and a steel cover came down, sealing them both inside.

"What's happening?"

"The system just registered Johan's death. It's gone into a complete lockdown."

Chapter 6

Watching the orange dots on the big monitor was like watching a horror movie, knowing that something bad was going to happen but being unable to stop it. She watched the heat blobs move, crouch, and run. One appeared to be lying down and another one stormed around.

"Can we identify who these people are?"

"Not everyone." He pointed a claw at the two crouching. "I'm thinking those are the brothers. The one lying down will be Johan and the other one…yeah, that's going to be whoever Johan was calling for help about."

"You think he's a bad guy."

Charmin shot her a curious look. "Is there anything in this picture that makes you think this is a good scenario?"

She studied it. "No. It looks creepy as hell."

"That's because…" He paused mid-sentence and leaned closer, his whiskers quivering. "Oh, what's going on?"

She leaned forward. "That doesn't look good." The two men who crept further away had gone down one side of the apartment away from the other two and had stopped inside a room of some kind. She could see a change in the energy field, but then it switched again. "What was that all about?"

"I don't know, but Johan is in bad shape and deteriorating rapidly."

She switched her attention to the prone figure and realized the heat signature, the bright orange and red colors of the others, were muted in his case. Almost faded. Something happened suddenly and all three mobile orange dots were running in a straight line. She gasped as the first man was almost caught, but dove into…something…and disappeared off her screen. "Where did he go?"

"I'm trying to track him, but I'm afraid that might be hard to do."

"And look at Johan. His color, it's almost gone."

"The color itself will last a little while. It will take hours for his body temperature to drop so low that no color will show up."

"I'm presuming that the other two left are Milo and Levi?" At least she hoped so. She watched them go to Johan. Suddenly, as if someone flicked a switch, the entire floor of the building disappeared. It was still there, but now it only showed as a solid black bar. As if the entire floor had disappeared.

"What did you do?" she cried. "Bring it back."

"I didn't do anything." Charmin tapped the console several times, only nothing changed. That floor existed, but only as a black bar. Charmin sat back, stumped. "There has to be something going on up there that the room is no longer visible."

"That's not good. Johan is in really bad shape, he needs help."

"He's actually past needing anyone's help. He's dead."

She gasped. "Are you sure?" she cried. "Maybe he can still be saved. They have wonderful medical advancements here. Maybe it isn't too late."

"Oh, he's dead all right. That's also likely what triggered this blackout. Consider the type of business that Johan was in. If anything happened to him, especially on his premises, there has to be some kind of fail-safe to protect the contents. Or…to catch the killer."

"But the men are stuck inside." With a dead body, and boy did that part creep her out. "Can they get out?"

"Nah, I doubt it. It's probably locked down until someone, a prearranged someone, comes to remove information from the premises."

She stared at him. "Like more bad guys coming to make sure sensitive information isn't recovered by the wrong people?"

"Something like that." He wandered over the counter and sniffed toward the wall. "Is there food in here?"

"Somewhere." She barely listened. Who could think of food at a time like this? "We have to help them. They're innocent, but whoever comes to deal with this situation is going to suspect that Levi killed Johan."

Charmin looked at her. "True, Milo doesn't look like he could kill a bug. Now Levi, that's a different story. That man looks like he could kill."

She shook her head. "What are you talking about? Levi isn't dangerous."

"Nah, of course he isn't." He snorted. "Unless his family or business are being threatened." He motioned with a pudgy paw at the monitor, "If I hadn't seen for myself that Johan was already in trouble and that there was a fourth person there, I'd be wondering if Levi hadn't taken care of Johan himself."

"There's no way he'd do something like that," she cried out. "Where are you getting that from?"

"Uh, maybe from that can-do-what-needs-to-be-done attitude he gives off without even trying." Charmin sat his paunchy bottom down and glared back at the monitor. "I like him just fine, and the fact that he likes you is helpful, but it doesn't change the fact that when threatened, Levi will do what needs to be done."

"That's a good thing," she said gently. "That's something to admire."

"So is killing when killing needs to be done." And he slid down to lie on one side where he proceeded to clean his paw.

She stared at him, his words rippling through her mind. There were times when killing was a good thing, and if Levi was capable of protecting her from the kidnappers, well, it was a really good thing for her. Although she hoped it wouldn't come to that. Even if Charmin didn't think so. "He's a good man."

"Yep, he appears to be."

"It's not like you wouldn't kill for food."

He pinned his beady eyes on her. "I have killed for food. Why do you think I catch mice – to keep them as pets?"

She grinned. "You could go back to that. It would be good for you. A form of exercise and, just think, you wouldn't need to wait on other people to feed you. You could feed yourself."

He made a strangled sound that came from deep within his throat. "If there were mice in this day and age, I'd consider it. However, what I won't consider is exchanging my killer skills for the food that they serve me on a regular basis. Where's the sense in that? I'd do both. Not the one that takes effort at the expense of the one that is easy."

With a shake of his head, he went back to cleaning.

She went back to staring at the blacked-out apartment on the top of the monitor. "We have to help them."

"I agree. Do you have any idea how?"

She winced. "We could go up there and try to open the door."

He hooted. "Really? That's the best you've got? Knowing a little about this system, chances are good you won't even find the place. It's going to be on stealth mode under heavy lockdown."

"There has to be something we can do. They'd help us." She thought about it. "Maybe we could call whatever lawyers are left at John's company."

"They're not going to want to come here after two of the lawyers were killed, one on our doorstep."

"Then we have to go and help them ourselves."

***

Levi had already done a second search for a way out that they might have missed. No such luck. From the furious pounding Milo was doing on his comp and the wall computers, he wasn't having any better luck. "This is not good," Levi said under his breath. "Johan's computer system is our best bet. Plus, I want to see what he was hiding."

"I'm coming," Milo said. "There's got to be an override for this system."

"Yes, but it's likely to be controlled by someone elsewhere. When Johan's tag said he was deceased, this lockdown was instant."

"There has to be something important here, otherwise there'd be no need for all this security."

"Information and possibly items." Leading the way, Levi tossed back, "Let's keep an open mind."

"Right." Milo reached a hand past him and clicked off the mask hiding the room's interior. Instantly, the high tech computer room showed up. Milo whistled. "Like there is some seriously good stuff here."

"Sure, but what was he into? Was it legal? Was he working for himself or for someone else? And if it's someone else, then we need to know who."

"The system might not load with this lockdown happening." Milo had the system booting up, when he said, "Or it might send a signal to someone that we are here."

"I don't want to hear that. We need in. And fast."

"I'm working on it. You take point."

Levi stepped closer to the secondary system, surprised to find it similar to what he had in his place. Johan had to be into something secretive. Had that been what got him killed?

"Hmmm."

"What did you find?"

"This system is connected to another system. It's trying to boot me out."

Levi waited. His brother wouldn't take that kindly. He'd be working his ass off to beat this asshole at his own game. It would also increase the danger of staying here. The need for the other party to secure the place and retrieve or destroy what they needed was now paramount. And...he glanced over at Milo. "Careful in case of a self-destruct order."

"Oh, there will be one, but there's a reason it hasn't gone off yet. The assholes monitoring this place need something from here first."

"Right." That made sense. It also guaranteed that a retrieval team was on its way.

And they were stuck inside.

Chapter 7

Dani strode determinedly over to the front door. They could do this. So what if she didn't know how to use the elevator tube thingy? There had to be stairs. Even in her century, every place had two exits. Stairs made sense. Charmin sat at the door waiting for her.

"Good." She scooped him up and held him firmly. "Let's go."

"Door open," Charmin said. Only the door didn't open. Dani reached out and put her hand on the door. Nothing. "Open door."

Still nothing. "It's not coded to our voices."

"Damn. Now what?"

"We stay here?" he said hopefully.

"Nope." She turned to stare at the wall and the huge computer screen in front of her. "It means you need to add our voices or use an override system."

"Oh great." He puffed up his chest. "As if that is a two-second job."

She smiled. "It would be for Milo."

He spun to glare at her. "That's not fair. I don't know the system, and he does."

With a laugh, she said, "True enough. So how about five minutes?"

But he was already busy on the comp. He spun around triumphantly. "Done."

She hugged him tightly as the door opened. She stepped through, hoping she'd done the right thing. The tube surrounded her instantly. Like how did that work? "Johan's place."

And they took off. "Shit," she said against Charmin's furry head. "I will never get used to this."

He snuggled closer. "It's cool. But a little freaky."

"A lot freaky." And as suddenly as the tube started, it stopped...and disappeared. Looking around carefully, she realized they were alone. Good. She led the way, with a couple of wrong turns, over to the rooftop garden. From there, she could see the whole city ahead of her. She was getting slightly more used to the scene now. It didn't scare her as badly. But it would be much more comfortable if Levi were with her. Just the thought of being left without Levi terrified her. So not going there.

She turned in the direction of Johan's and tried to figure out how to make her way onto his patio. Charmin jumped free from her arms and raced ahead. What was easy for a cat, however...was not as easy for her. But she made it over the cement looking barrier and dropped safely on the other side. With only one scraped knee, she managed to walk across the patio to the large doors. She didn't know how to get in. Steel-looking shutters hid the glass. There were no handles. No levers. No locks. No windows. The place appeared to have locked like a bunker under the ground. She wasn't going to be able to do this.

"Charmin, we're in trouble."

"Ya think?" He trotted along the side of the house as far as they could go until there was no side to be on. The wall dropped away to the vast city below. "That's definitely not the way." He turned, retraced his steps, and went around the other side. Following behind, she realized that led nowhere either. "So where are the fire escape doors?"

At Charmin's odd look, she explained, "The second exit in case of fire so that the inhabitants can get out safely."

"Never heard of it."

"Well, I have."

"Not in the building codes of this time."

"Well, I doubt that they've managed to do away with fire, so there must be a way in or out – especially in these fancy places."

"They'd port in and out. It's fast and efficient."

She stared at him. "You know, that's a damn good idea. I'd have a port in my house, too. Actually, I'm pretty sure Levi mentioned that. So why can't they port out?"

"It won't be coded for them."

"Ah, that tagging thing again."

She backed up several steps to get a better look at the building. Tall peaks and round domes, it looked like part of a duct system from her time. Then maybe a lot of that were actually ducts for the rest of the building. She bit her lip. Could they get in that way? Or better yet, could Levi and Milo get out that way?

"I don't like the look on your face."

She shrugged. "I was just wondering if we could get in there via the ducts or pipes." She waved at the odd structures. "Whatever they are."

"Not a good idea. We could end up anywhere."

"True." She turned to look back at the spot the entrance should have been. "What about us porting in?"

"Not coded for us," he repeated patiently.

"Then how about the vents again…" she studied him. "Maybe you could get in."

He looked at her askance. "What? Why am I the guinea pig?"

"Because you're small, you can get into places I can't."

"I told you to lay off the bread and cheese," he murmured with a sideways look.

"Did not." She glared at him.

"Did too." He moved over slightly as if out of kicking range.

"Yeah, you'd better move," she said in a temper. She considered his innuendo. "Am I getting fat?"

"Oh brother." He plunked his butt down with an exaggerated sigh. "In truth, you could use some flesh on your bones."

"Not going to happen." What a stupid conversation. And with a cat, no less. "And it doesn't change the fact that you can get into places that I can't."

"Agreed, but that also means that Levi and Milo can't follow me back out as they are as big as you."

"Bigger."

And boy, did he give her a look. She loved him dearly, but since he'd learned to talk…she turned her back on him. "True that they can't follow you back out, but you could bring them something that will allow them to break out again."

"It's not a prison, and I can't carry a crowbar. Remember – I'm a cat."

"Glad you remember that." Still, he was right about being limited in what he could carry. "It would have to be something small to fit your back."

"Like a donkey?" His horrified tone made her laugh.

"Exactly – like an ass." Still giggling, she wondered out loud, "What they could possibly use in there that they wouldn't have taken in the first place?"

"Milo's new personal stealth port."

"What's that?"

"It's a port he can take anywhere that is coded for him. So he can move in and out anywhere he wants to."

"Why wouldn't he take it with him yet?"

"Because there was no need for it. And it's not in testing stage yet."

"It might be a great time to hit that stage." She couldn't think of anything better. "It would be a hot product."

"There are some on the market, but not as transportable as this one." Charmin scratched behind his ear. "The portable model is ready, but he's working to interact stealth technology with it. Another military application that will make them a ton of money."

She could just imagine. It sounded ideal for military use, but she'd hate for everyone to get their hands on something like that. No one would ever be safe. "Do you know where it is?"

"Sure. In the kitchen. He's got it on his bug doohickey."

It took her a moment to translate what that meant, but she remembered Milo's unusual little computer. "Wouldn't he have that on him already?'

"You'd think so, but he left it on the kitchen counter." He walked over to a spot in the sun and sprawled down sideways. "Not going to do anyone any good anyways. I can't carry it in."

"But if you could – do you think you could take it to them?"

At that, he slumped to the side and laid out flat. "Of course. But I'm not going back down to get it."

She glared at him. "Well, I'm not being separated from you. The chances of losing you are too great." She bent, scooped him up into her arms, and stormed back the way they came. Thankfully, the door to the apartment was still open. Maybe that wasn't a good thing considering other strangers. She walked straight to the kitchen and turned in a slow circle looking for the item. "Charmin, where is it?"

He reached up, batted her cheek to get her attention, and then pointed to the counter back against the wall. It blended in perfectly. She picked it up and studied it. "It's small. You could carry it if we can figure out a way to fix it onto your back."

"True. That's not going to be easy."

"We need something to tie around you to hold it in place. It doesn't need to stay in place for long."

"A harness would be better than something that ties."

"Ha. It's going to have to be something of a compromise, as I don't know how to make anything here and don't have any tools like a needle and thread so..." and her mind started racing. "Elastic would work."

"Like they have those here."

Dani glanced down at her own clothing. "True." And then she remembered. "But I have old clothing." She raced into Levi's bedroom, but her old clothes were no longer there. Right, the pod room. There in a corner, she found her pile of clothes that she'd been wearing when she arrived in this time. And in that pile...was her bra. The new clothes had one built in. She studied the bra, wondering if there was a way to make it work without cutting it up, but there wasn't as far as she could see. She ran back to the kitchen where Charmin and the small gadget sat. She opened the bread cupboard and pulled out a knife and went to work.

Ten minutes later, she was racing back up to Johan's place.

"I look ridiculous," Charmin snapped, trying to twist inside his quickly tied harness - one bra cup around his belly with the new device nestled inside.

"You look great." She lowered him down on the patio. "In fact, it's very stylish."

"Ha, you're just saying that so I'll do this."

"No, you need to do this to help Milo and Levi."

"I know that." He took several awkward steps, his tail flicking in sharp movements. "But you could have made it so I didn't look fat."

***

Levi had already searched Johan's premises twice looking for a way out. A different control server, something that would allow them to escape. Time was running out. They were going to have visitors soon. And if anyone found him and his brother here, they'd soon find Dani and Charmin. Not good.

He paced behind Milo and bit back the words threatening to tumble free at any moment. Milo had already snapped at him several times.

Levi had searched through Johan's communication center and had been shocked. Something that was hard to do.

He and Milo liked to keep things secret. But this…this was scary stuff. Johan had dirt. Like major dirt on a lot of people. He'd been horrified when he'd found the file that had his name on it, with damn near everything including every girl he'd partied with on the list. Milo's information had been more detailed in that it had a specific set of inventions he'd created and was in the process of creating. That's what scared him. How had Johan known? He pointed the file out to Milo, who went very, very quiet. Next thing Levi knew, the information was streaming at an incredible speed. "I presume you're copying all this."

Milo nodded and held up his comp. "It's downloading on this. We don't have time to sort through it all right now."

"Have you found a way through to shut down the system?"

"The system is not on here."

Levi sat back and thought about that. "I wonder if Johan knew."

"I don't think he did. This system could have gone into lockdown any time they wanted."

"So why didn't they do it before he booked it?"

And then he understood. "They missed it. There'd been no warning. But when he returned looking for whatever it was, he tripped a warning system."

"Maybe, or maybe his death tripped it like we suspected all along. It could also have been set off by the attacker. Once he knew Johan was dying or that we were here, he could have set it off remotely. For all we know, that was only stage one. There are likely to be several other levels of defense to come."

"Or it could be that's all there is. After all, we'd be left here to die of starvation."

"Not likely. It would take too long."

They stared at each other.

"We need to get out of here."

As the words left Levi's mouth, they heard an unidentified sound.

"Shit," Milo said, his fingers moving faster. "I need just a little more time. And why the hell didn't I bring my comp?"

"You do have it." Levi snuck over to the doorway. He set up the same disguise that Johan had originally. Instantly, the same boring spare bedroom shone and damn...he stared in shock...there was no sign of Milo. He quickly reverted the program and Milo appeared again.

Deep in concentration, he wasn't affected by the change. He switched it on once more and Milo disappeared again.

Cool.

Now if only he could manage to do the same.

A long scraping sound came from somewhere overhead. "What the..." he whispered. "It must be a rodent."

Milo's voice came through in an eerie whisper. "We don't have rodents."

"Then what is it?" Levi studied the ceiling.

A crack appeared – and not one as part of the bedroom camouflage, but there nonetheless. And seconds later, Charmin poked his head through.

"About time I found you."

Chapter 8

Dani waited impatiently outside of Johan's place, hating the fear rippling down her body. She hated being alone. She never used to have a problem with it, but now she was in a strange world where so many things could go wrong. And some of the worst ones were running through her mind right now. *Please let Charmin be safe. Please let him find the brothers.*

She blew a strand of hair out of her face, and with her hands on her hips, she slowly counted to twenty. When she hit twenty, she continued to sixty.

"Okay, he should have reached them by now." And if he had – then what? According to Charmin, Milo would be able to port them into their own home from there. What about Charmin? Was he coming back out here or was he going back home with the brothers? And what was she supposed to do? Go back to the apartment or wait here? Damn it. Why hadn't she gone over those details with Charmin?

She shifted her weight from one side to the other and looked around nervously. What if someone else came while she was here waiting? And damn if she didn't hear a sound behind her. She dashed around the side and hid.

The air tensed as odd noises crackled.

Hearing sounds but not being able to see was bad. Her mind conjured up horrible scenarios of all bad things gone wrong. Her breath caught in her chest. She flattened herself against the wall, eyes closed…and something brushed against her legs.

She screamed and danced in place.

"Ouch. Knock it off, will you? Someone is going to hear."

Charmin. She snatched him up and clutched him into her arms. "Charmin," she cried. "You scared me to death."

"Ha, you scared me with your screams," he complained and head butted her.

"I'm so glad to see you." She buried her face in his fur, trying to get her pounding heart to calm down, then she remembered why he'd gone in. She lifted him higher so she could see his face. "Did you make it in?"

"What about me? Are you glad to see me, too?" Levi's warm, caring voice reached her. She lifted her head, saw Levi standing in front of her, and dashed into his arms. They closed securely around her. She shuddered, then realized that Charmin was squirming in the middle of the hug. She let him down before standing up to wrap both arms around Levi. Slightly behind him, she could see Milo grinning like a crazy man. Hell, they were all crazy.

"I was so scared," she whispered.

"I wasn't feeling all that good myself." He dropped kisses down her temple and along her cheek. "Thank you for sending Charmin in with Milo's bug comp – a brilliant idea, by the way." He squeezed her slightly. "As you can see, it worked."

Tears burning her eyes, she tilted her head back. "I'm so glad." She glanced around, realized they were still on the roof, and said, "Can we go home now?"

"Yes, absolutely."

Keeping an arm securely around her shoulders, he led her back around to the tiny rooftop garden and back to the main elevator. Once inside, she breathed a sigh of relief. She held up one shaking hand and laughed. "I hadn't realized how scared I really was."

"To be expected." He squeezed her shoulder gently. "I can't believe that you actually did that."

"Ha. Thank Charmin for that."

"He delivered the comp, but you put it together so that he could."

She smiled and straightened slightly under his admiration. "Glad it worked. I don't know what I would have done if it hadn't."

"We'd have gotten out somehow," he reassured her.

She wasn't so sure but hey, she was willing to believe anything at this point. Everything was good. Well, almost good. "What about Johan?"

He flinched. "I don't know. It's hard to explain to the cops how we found him and not explain how we got out."

"True. Even if you could explain Charmin, you wouldn't want to explain the new port system Milo is developing."

He smiled. The elevator vanished, and they walked to the apartment. "Maybe you could show me how to close this door and open it from the outside," she said. "While we did several trips in and out, we had to leave it open."

"Hmmm. The door was closed when we arrived, so presumably it closed automatically after the time lapse control was triggered."

That made sense. As much as anything here did. Stepping inside, she watched as Levi secured the door behind her, then she opened her arms and collapsed against him. She hugged him tight. "Please, don't leave like that again."

He cuddled her close. "I'm not planning on it." He dropped a kiss on her forehead. "I think you need to sit down and relax."

"I'm thinking a nap in the healing pod might be a better idea. I'm seriously wiped out. Still not accustomed to the time here."

"Good idea. You do that and I'll start dissecting the information Milo stripped off Johan's communication center."

She walked to the pod room, calling behind her, "Was there much information there?"

"Lots. But we don't really know what it all means yet."

"Right. I'll leave you to it then."

At the pod, she crawled inside and sighed as the humming started, lulling her to sleep.

***

Levi watched Dani as she slept. He let out a heavy sigh. She'd done so much with so little and it looked to have completely wiped her out. And they were a long ways from being safe. As long as she was in there, though, he could work on the next step. "Milo, make sure the stealth is on in the pod room," he said as he walked into the kitchen. "She needs some downtime and I want to make sure that she can't be found."

Charmin pinned him with that look he was starting to hate. The look that said he was falling down on the job of taking care of Dani. He could hardly argue. Dani had been in nothing but trouble since Milo had snatched her up. And she'd been the one to save him. His relationships with women had been superficial in many ways. In all ways, if that was possible. Until Dani.

And there was nothing superficial about his feelings for her.

"Hey, lover boy, I could use your help here."

Levi gave a mental shake. "I'm here. What's up?"

"Look at this." Milo said, "It seems like whoever was tracking Johan's tags came from the Council."

"And that would only be if he was a prisoner out on bail."

"Normally, but I've searched the databases and there is no sign that Johan did time or has a criminal record of any kind anywhere."

Levi studied the square holograph moving faster than his eyes could see. "What are the chances that it was wiped?"

"I'm inclined to think so. Considering he was as cagey as he was, his history is a little *too* clean."

"That's what I was afraid of. But why would the Council track him?"

"That's the million dollar question."

Charmin yawned. "Someone in the Council is bad."

Both Milo and Levi stared at him. "And you'd know that how?"

"Think about it." He rolled his eyes as if having to speak to peons instead of peers. "Johan's reporting, willing or unwillingly, to someone in the Council. Only someone with power could wipe his history clean. So someone in the Council is doing this for the benefit of the good, or for the benefit of himself. Knowing people, I'd say he's doing it for himself."

"Listen to him." Milo snorted. "He's actually making sense."

Charmin raised one long-haired eyebrow and peered down his short nose. "Of course I am."

"Besides." Milo grinned. "I'm all for anything that makes the Council the bad guy."

"But there could be other answers. We have to keep an open mind." Although Levi couldn't think of one. And it was galling to think a cat had seen it first. He added, "It won't be just anyone. It will be one person playing both sides."

"Or the Council is keeping tabs on things they shouldn't be, making deals with criminals," Milo suggested. "Or blackmailing criminals into working for them."

Levi tilted his head back and stared at the ceiling, his thoughts a jumble. "If Johan's pod is the issue, then it affects us a lot. If this is something Johan was into by himself, then we are only involved at the edge. And that could mean we can stay quiet and no one will know anything. We're just afraid someone would know something. But they might not know anything."

"The real question is how to know and what do we do to protect ourselves." Charmin added under his breath but loud enough for the others hear, "and our food."

"I'm locking this material from Johan down and keeping it in a deep dark hole where no one can find it."

Charmin stared at him. "Except for you guys, right? It's not blackmail material, but it might keep someone off your back if they know you have this ace in the hole."

"Ace in the hole?" Milo asked curiously.

"An old phrase," Levi said absentmindedly. He pulled out his comp. "The lockdown makes sense if the Council was the one forcing Johan into collecting dirty information. We're presuming he was doing it for them, but he could have just as easily been keeping something back to screw with them."

Charmin sat back. "I like that last part."

"So do I." Milo grinned. "So let's see what else I can find."

An alert sounded through the apartment, followed by a robotic voice saying, "Stephen Cavendish requests a call."

Milo looked up slowly. "Oh? Interesting."

"Yeah, let's see what he has to say." Levi flicked the buttons to open the communication system. Instantly, Stephen's face and shoulders popped out of the HoloKomp.

"Good to see you, Stephen. What can I do for you?"

"Sorry, this isn't a social call. We have alerts coming from your building. A death and rodents."

Milo froze. He picked Charmin up and walked him down the hallway to the pod room. Levi heard the door open and close. "Sorry to hear that. Anyone I know?"

"Johan Stroud."

With what he hoped was a suitable look of shock, he said, "Johan? He's deceased?"

"Apparently. A Medivac team has been dispatched. Someone has anonymously reported the death. But we have no idea who it was."

Levi raised his eyebrows. That alert had to have come from the intruder that escaped. "I have no idea who that would be. I was under the impression that you were searching for Johan, but he was on the run."

"And apparently he returned and was living quietly under everyone's radar."

"What can I do to help?" Levi asked.

"I need to know everyone's whereabouts for the last four hours."

Levi narrowed his gaze and felt his temper simmer. Not to mention the fear. "Are we suspects in Johan's death?" he asked incredulously.

"Not at all. However, the Council wants to clarify who reported Johan as deceased."

"Well, it wasn't me. Or Milo or my wife."

"There are signs that someone from your apartment accessed the rooftop from your elevator. Several times in fact."

Levi tilted his head. "Yes, that's quite possible. My wife's cat got loose today when we were trying to fix the door after John's death. She had taken him up to the little rooftop garden a couple of days ago and she figured he might have gone up there again."

"I need to speak with her."

"And why is that?" His voice deepened with anger. There was no way he was going to force Dani to speak to the Council. "Particularly when the documents are in place for me to speak on her behalf."

Chapter 9

Dani woke up slowly. The heat from the pod was a welcome relief from the earlier stress. It felt like she'd slept for hours. Chances were good though that it was less than a half hour. She felt decent. With a yawn and stretch, she pushed the pod lid open and swung her legs around. The theme was still the Pacific island. She swore she could hear the surf as it rolled out in the distance. Smell the flowers. Maybe they could leave and go to the Pacific for real in a few days

Or somewhere else. Anywhere else would be good. She needed a few days away. Milo and Levi could as well. Charmin probably wouldn't care as long as food came with them.

She smiled at the thought of her baby. He slept, snoring gently beside her. He'd done so well getting in and getting out of Johan's apartment. He'd been quite the hero, saving the day. She hopped off the bed and wandered out to the kitchen. Food and coffee was topmost on her mind. As soon as she'd imagined herself sitting in the island with a cup of coffee in hand, she'd been lost.

The kitchen appeared silent until she made it around the corner and saw Levi in discussion with someone on the HoloKomp. She didn't recognize the male holo image and had to remind herself that he ran a huge corporation that she knew nothing about. He interacted with hundreds of people. He had to get caught up sometime.

A pang of guilt hit her. He was behind because of her. Milo was busy doing something on the big 3D monitor, but both appeared to have an ear tuned to the ongoing conversation.

That stopped her on the spot. She tuned into the conversation. And stopped herself from gasping, slapping a hand over her mouth. Milo grabbed her arm and tugged her over to him. "Stay out of sight and be quiet."

She nodded mutely. "Did they find Johan?" she whispered.

"They know about his death. Presumably, they will be sending someone. They want to speak to you about what you saw."

Her eyes widened, and she shook her head. "Hell no.'" Then she winced. "Unless it helps you guys. I didn't really see anything."

"And if you could tell them exactly that, I'd appreciate it," Levi said from beside her. "I've told them that you went up to the rooftop garden to search for the cat that got loose. It's not like you could see much from there, but if you could tell them the little bit you do know…"

He let his voice trail off and raised an eyebrow. She nodded. And took a step toward him. He held out his hand. "Stephen, my wife Dani."

Dani, suddenly shy, smiled. "Hello."

Stephen's face split into a broad grin. "Hi, Dani. Couldn't believe it when I heard this guy finally found the woman of his life."

Her smiled brightened as Levi wrapped a possessive arm around her waist and pulled her close. "That I have."

"I'm sorry," she said. "I really didn't see much up on the roof. I wasn't focused on anything but my cat."

Stephen nodded. "Understood. But can you tell me if you saw anyone? Anything?

"Oh no. There was no one up there. And the place was quiet." She opened her mouth to add that it was dead quiet and managed to choke the words back. But he looked at her oddly as if waiting for her to say more. Compelled to add something else, she said, "The place was locked down and silent."

"When you say locked down, what do you mean?" Stephen asked curiously.

"It had steel doors all around. The other time I caught a glimpse of it, I saw a lot of glass everywhere. This time I couldn't see any glass."

Stephen frowned. "Interesting."

"It could have been just window coverings inside. It just looked different from the last time I saw it."

"Thanks. I'm glad you found your cat."

Her smile this time was bright and happy. "Thank you, me too."

She stepped away from Levi, smiled at both of them, and said, "I'll leave you to your business."

"You're a lucky man, Levi," Stephen said.

Dani wanted to believe there was genuine admiration in his voice, but she didn't know him. And everyone she'd met here so far had been less than what they seemed.

She backed away and circled around to meet Milo and Charmin, who just arrived. Bending close, she asked, "Was that all right?"

"Perfect." Milo reached forward and tapped the screen in front of him. "Look."

"What am I looking at? I can hardly see what you're pointing out with everything else going on." With every side of the monitor showing different images and all overlaying on top of each other, it was confusing to see what he was pointing out.

Milo made several adjustments, and the monitors on three sides went black. In the center was a series of boxes with orange spots. "That's this building, isn't it?"

He smiled and nodded, then pointed to the spots around the middle of the building. "That's us."

How freaking fantastic was it that he could shift perspective like this? Then her gaze shot to the rooftop and the blacked out apartment. Only it wasn't black any longer. There was an orange dot...on top. "And who is that?"

"We don't know."

"But you can find out." She shot him a sideways look. "With the tags and visual stuff you guys do here, I'm sure you have it figured out."

"His tags appear to be undetectable, and he's wearing a mask."

"Oooh, interesting." She studied the spot. "Maybe he's just running something that interferes with the signal." Feeling Milo's sudden start, she glanced over at him. "What? What did I say?"

"You could be right." He leaned his hands on the counter and stared at display. "If he is running interference, then I should be able to bypass it." He frowned, then his fingers moved faster. "It could take some time though."

"Or don't bother. Wait until he leaves and track him then. Surely you can identify him from that point."

He snorted. "Say what?"

"Why try to bypass it? He had to arrive from somewhere. Can't you track him backwards and check his tags from his earlier position?"

"Only there's no way to know which way he's going to leave and if he ports out, then he'll disappear faster than I can track him."

She shrugged. "True. I thought maybe you gave him only one choice. But then all this is beyond me." She watched Levi end the conversation. The HoloKomp disappeared. She walked toward him, catching an odd look on Milo's face as she did so. She raised an eyebrow in question, but he shook his head. She reached Levi's side. "Is everything okay?"

"As good as they can be." He tugged her into his arms. "You look much better after your nap."

"I feel better." Her stomach grumbled. She gave a tiny laugh. "Sorry. It's been a while."

"I'm hungry too." He turned her back toward the kitchen where his brother worked. Charmin, awake and alert, watched them with hungry eyes. "Yes, Charmin. I'm going to make a meal."

Charmin flopped to his side and rolled over in ecstasy.

Levi laughed. "That's the closest I've seen you to looking happy in a long time."

"You haven't fed me in a long time either," he moaned. "Food."

"Ha." Dani smiled. "Now you can be patient while Levi cooks."

"Shrimp would be good," he said with a long-suffering groan of hunger.

"Cat food is what you're going to get."

"That works." He sat up and proceeded to clean his paw.

***

Levi set about making a hot meal. He'd ordered salmon earlier, thinking that might be the kind of meal Dani would love. He knew that Charmin would if no else cared for it. Dani made coffee and watched him prep the fish.

When the meal was almost ready, she set the table, asking Milo, "Are you going to have a booster drink with us?"

He looked at her blankly. "Why?"

"So you join us for the family meal."

He just stared as if that was a foreign concept. Levi grinned and smacked his kid brother lightly. "Yeah. Come join us."

"Not now. I'm on the hunt."

"Hunt for what?"

"This asshole."

"But you know where he is." Dani walked back over to the comp. "So what's the big deal?"

"Hey, I'm just taking note of your suggestion and taking it one step further."

Levi looked up from plating dinner. "Really? What did she suggest?"

"To only give this guy one escape route so we could ID him." He grinned, that boyish look Levi loved and hated at the same time. "I figured we'd be able to use Johan's equipment to pick up anything we needed to know. Like this guy's com number."

That didn't sound so bad. "And what good will that do?"

"If we can ID him, we'll be able to figure out who he works for."

"Or not, considering the Defino brothers are still out there and one of them is likely to be in Johan's apartment right now." Levi set the plates down. "Stephen is sending a team in."

"When?" Dani asked.

Milo laughed. "Right now from the looks of the orange spots shooting up to the top. Looks like we'll get to see some fireworks soon."

"Except we can't see anything."

"Then come here and watch. I'll plug in the video."

And sure enough, the inside of Johan's apartment showed on screen.

And the intruder, dressed in black, pacing back and forth.

Chapter 10

Dani hated the suspense. They needed to know who was in Johan's apartment. And what that person might want from there. Dani was more concerned about what they might know about her – if anything – and what they would do with that information.

"Dani, come and eat."

She spun around, completely forgetting that Levi had cooked a meal. Then her stomach reminded her. With a last look, she took her place at the table. And couldn't stop staring at the scene unfolding on the screen.

"Milo."

"Yeah?" But his voice was distracted as he watched the screen.

"Bring it over here," Levi said. "Then we can all watch without getting a kink in our necks."

Dani's attention was caught by his words. "Bring it over?"

And sure enough, Milo arrived at the table, and suddenly there was the big 3D monitor at the side of the table where they could all see. "I had no idea you could do that!" she exclaimed. "That's totally awesome."

Levi smiled. "It's fun seeing things from your perspective." He pointed to the see-through image. "We get blasé about our technology."

"You have no idea how much you've advanced." Her gaze was caught by the orange blobs surrounding the top apartment with the intruder still inside. "And then in some ways, nothing has changed."

"The criminals are more sophisticated. But they still exist."

"Crime is everywhere," Milo said. "Then again, what do you expect when the Council is corrupt?"

Dani lifted a forkful of hot food then gasped as she watched the team enter, surround, and attack the intruder. He collapsed to the ground, and darned if that hot spot didn't slowly fade to yellow.

She put her fork down, suddenly sick to her stomach. "It was fascinating to watch – like a movie – but at the same time, I just realized that a person died. It's not so nice now."

"And I'm glad to hear that," Levi said in between mouthfuls. "This monitor allows one to see what wouldn't normally be seen, while allowing the viewer to distance himself from the reality." He took another bite. "But it's not a vid. It's real life."

"Good thing it was a bad guy." Charmin finally lifted his head from his bowl of food and proceeded to clean his face. "And this bad guy would have killed us."

"But we don't know that," Dani protested. "He might have been a nice guy and not hurt us."

The three males stared at her.

She sat back and sighed. "Okay, so that's not likely. But I don't want to be so complacent that someone's death is not a concern."

Levi reached across the table and grasped her hand. "That's not likely to happen."

"Good. Please remind me of this conversation later."

"I will." He gave her hand a squeeze and then released it to resume eating.

"I'll remind you, too." Charmin gave her a fat smirk.

"I can do without your input, thanks."

She polished off her dinner in silence, her gaze watching the rest of the drama in Johan's apartment play out. The team of orange blobs collected the injured intruder and were moving down the building – at a slower pace. "Surely they could move him out of there much faster?"

"Actually, they could." Levi frowned. He got up and walked over to his wall com. Dani watched the orange blobs stop about mid-level. She gasped. "Are they here?"

An alarm sounded.

***

Levi had planned to asked to ask Stephen about the raid…when the alarm went off again. He quickly told Dani and Charmin to go to the pod room.

She had a puzzled look on her face as she scooped up Charmin as requested. At least she no longer panicked as she had earlier. Good. When she'd entered the pod room, he double-checked that stealth was on to keep her presence secret. Then he turned off the alarm to his front door and opened it.

Combots. A robotic retrieval death team. Or as some called them…death squads.

"What can I do for you?"

"Identification required."

"I am Levi Blackburn."

"Acknowledged. We need this man identified." And a body bag was thrust forward.

Levi blanched. "Why me?"

"We need to know if you recognized him from the earlier altercation."

"Let me see his face."

He expected to have the body bag opened, but instead a tablet was shoved under his nose, a large image of a dead man on the screen. "That's Johan Stroud."

"Thank you." And the Combots retreated.

Levi stepped into the hallway. "Wait. Who is in the bag?"

"You just identified him," the leader said.

"No," Levi snapped. "I did not. I identified the face on the tablet, not the body in the bag."

"Same man."

"No." He shook his head. No way in hell they were the same man. He didn't know what was going on here, but they were trying to pull something, and he didn't want his identification to be mistaken.

"I need to see his face."

"We cannot allow that."

"Then my identification does not stand."

"You have already identified him." The Combots were only computers. Advanced computers, but not conversationalists.

"No. I identified the picture on the tablet. I need to see the face on the body in the bag to confirm."

"We can't allow that."

"Yes, you can. And I have Councilman Stephen Cavendish's permission."

The Combots buzzed as if sending the request forward to the Council.

"The Councilman cannot be reached."

"Well, he gave me permission." Levi walked closer. As much as he didn't want to look at the dead man's face, he did want to know who was in the bag. The Combot turned and conversed with another bot. Levi walked closer. He turned his back on the bots and quickly opened the bag.

"Stop. You cannot do this."

"Too late. I have done it." And it was not Johan. "This is Paul Defino. Older brother to Tommy Defino. This is not the man on the tablet. I repeat, this is not Johan Stroud."

He turned, anger building inside him. "Where is Johan Stroud's body?"

"We do not have it. This is the only body that we have collected."

"Why did you not collect the other one?"

"There was no other body to collect."

Chapter 11

Dani had barely relaxed in the pod when Levi opened the door. "Dani?"

She poked her head out. "I'm awake. What's up?"

"That was a death squad of Combots. They have one of the Defino brothers bagged and tagged. Dead."

"So that's who was up there. Interesting."

"Even more interesting, Johan's body was not there according to them. They being robots, they can be ordered to do one thing, then reprogrammed to forget what they did. But it appears that whoever behind this is hiding Johan's death." He walked closer and pushed open the pod lid higher so she could swing her legs around and hop off. "They are gone. I've been trying to reach Stephen, but there's no answer – anywhere."

She winced. "That always sounds so ominous. I was hoping that they'd caught the bad guy, collected poor Johan, and now we were safe."

"I'm hoping that's exactly what the situation is, but I can't be sure of anything at this time. It's almost bedtime."

She walked with him down the hall to the living room. "I am tired, but more wired. Wondering when this will all go away."

"I wonder what happened to Johan?"

"Are you sure the death bots didn't remove his body?"

"They said they didn't. If they did, they didn't let me see it." He slipped a hand up the nape of her neck and gently massaged the tight muscles. "I'm sorry there have been so many issues since you arrived."

"Apparently many were caused by my arrival." She moaned gently as he stopped, turned her around, and dug in his fingers to knead deeper. "Where's Milo?"

"Retired for the night."

Her insides perked up. She gave him a fat smile. "So does that mean we are alone?"

"Not quite," Charmin said. "But I'm heading in to lie beside the fire, so don't mind me."

She laughed. "We won't. Keep your ears shut."

"I'll sleep instead. Just don't wake me."

She watched as her baby cat sauntered toward the hallway into Levi's bedroom. That was where she wanted to go.

"He not only talks but thinks, has words of wisdom, and can solve puzzles," Levi said, "He's quite a puzzle himself."

When Charmin had disappeared from sight, Dani turned around to face Levi. "Now are we alone?"

His smile quirked. "As alone as you want to be."

She ran her hands up his bare arms, loving the feel of his silky skin. "Good. And it's late. So…"

"So…?"

She raised her eyes to his. "Bedtime?"

"Absolutely." A slow smile quirked, lighting a fire in her heart. "Back to the pod or…"

"Or…your bed?"

He lowered his head and kissed her. "Definitely my bed."

In a move that shocked a surprised squeak out of her, he scooped her up as if she were no bigger than Charmin. Snuggling close, she yawned. "You live a crazy life."

"It's your life, too." He walked toward his bedroom, nudging the door open with his foot. Sure enough, the fire was burning bright. Overhead, the big timber ceiling sprawled the length of the room. She shook her head. "This is so amazing."

"Glad you like it. I can change it if you'd rather have a different scene."

"No," she cried. "This is perfect."

He walked over to the bed and dropped her in the middle of the big poufy comforter. She laughed. "I love this. It seems like forever since I actually spent a night in a bed."

"It has been forever." He turned away to lock the bedroom door, then glanced at the big plush rug in front of the fire where Charmin slept. "Charmin in or out?"

All they heard was a heavy guttural snore. "He'll be fine in here with us. He's a heavy sleeper."

"Good. Two's company in the bed, but three is a definite crowd."

"I'd get used to it if I were you. Charmin is used to sleeping on the bed with me."

"Not right now. This is time for just the two of us." He walked to the side, and while she missed what he'd done to make it happen, there was a large series of built-in shelves and hooks where he hung his clothes after stripping them off. She sat up, wondering what they did with laundry. "Do you have a laundry service or do you wash your own clothes?"

He paused momentarily as he took off his wrist com. His shoulders started to shake. He turned with a silly grin on his face. "Haven't you figured it out yet? We don't do any menial work anymore."

Her mouth dropped open. "None?"

"None."

"You cooked," she accused. "And cleaned up."

"Did I?"

She stopped and had to think. No one had washed dishes. She'd assumed that Milo had cleared the table, but she hadn't seen that happen. So really, she had no idea.

"You don't do laundry? Dishes?"

"No. I'll show you tomorrow. Hand me your clothing and I'll hang it up. It will be clean and ready to wear again in the morning."

Her mouth gaped open. "That cupboard will wash your clothes?"

"It's like a mini dry-cleaning service inside." He stood completely nude in front of her, as unconscious of his nudity as she was conscious of it. Then again, she'd have to be dead to not notice. "Do you want to try it?"

"Oh, yes, please." Trying to be as natural stripping in front of him as he was with her, she stripped down to her skin and walked over. He showed her where to hang the items up. When done, he closed the closet and pushed a small button. "Do this every night, and every morning the clothes will be clean and ready to be worn. If you don't do it all the time, it stacks up and you have to stand here and do this over and over again."

"Marvelous." Dani turned to him and smiled brightly. He opened his arms.

She stepped into them, loving that they instantly closed securely around her.

***

Levi pulled back slightly so he could look into her deep blue eyes. She was so beautiful. So natural that he couldn't imagine any enhancements that would improve what Mother Nature had given her. She wouldn't agree, but that he'd found was the way of women. Maybe people in general.

"What are you thinking?" she asked, a small shadow sliding into her eyes. She didn't know him well enough to understand his actions, the nuances of his voice, yet she stood before him, as bare as the day she'd been brought into this world, with such trust, he felt his heart swell.

"I was thinking that I am the luckiest man alive." And damn if his voice didn't drop to a hoarse whisper. He closed his eyes and dropped his chin on top of her head as emotion choked him. "I don't know why I am so blessed, but I truly am grateful that you are here in my life, in my arms tonight."

She snuggled closer, the brush of her nipples against his chest sweet torment, the slide of her arms around his chest a delight. When she laid her head against his heart, he thought he'd cry. Instead, he crushed her against him and held her tight.

She deserved so much more. And he planned on giving it to her. He gently picked her up and carried her to the bed. In some weird symbol, a night in his bed meant the start of their married life. A wedding night for just the two of them.

He flipped back the covers and lay beside her. Instantly, she turned toward him. God, he loved it that she wanted to be here with him. Not just a party where everyone came to have fun with anyone, not because he was wealthy and eligible, but she wanted to be here with him - *because she cared.*

Heat rolled through him. He needed that. Needed her.

Her hands slid up his chest to cup his face. He shuddered.

"Are you all right?"

"Yes," he murmured. "Just a little overwhelmed."

"Same." She kissed him gently. "I came a long way to find you, Levi."

He shuddered again, her words finding all the lonely places in his heart and filling them.

"I missed you all these years," she whispered against his neck, her breath warming him to his toes. "Where were you, Levi?"

She dropped more kisses on his chin, then on his neck before moving on to his collarbone. A trail of heat then ice followed as she drifted her way down his body. He wanted to tell her to stop. Wanted to pleasure her, but the words wouldn't come out. The need to be, to exist, as is, with her like this...it was too strong.

She propped herself on one elbow, then pushed him onto his back and slowly worked her way downward.

"Let me," he said in a low voice, "I want to make this special for you."

"Oh, it will be," she assured him, a tiny smile playing at the corner of her lips. She slid her hand down. "Besides, you promised me."

"Later," he said, and her hand closed around him. He cried out.

"This is my time," she murmured, dropping kisses down his chest and across his ribs. "My turn."

And then she found him with her mouth.

Levi thought he'd died. Dani's mouth was so wet, so sweet, and so damn hot he almost couldn't hold on. He was afraid to move. Afraid she'd stop. And afraid she wouldn't. He didn't want this over too soon. She scraped her teeth down the long length of his shaft.

He lifted his hips and groaned.

Then her mouth was gone. He opened his eyes to find her carefully shifting over him, straddling his hips. She grasped him gently in one hand as she found her position.

And lowered herself. His groan rumbled free. He couldn't help himself. He reached up and grabbed her hips to hold her steady and he lunged upward, grinding his pelvis against her. She gasped and threw her head back, tightening her inner muscles.

He shuddered at the delicate internal massage.

"Oh God," he whispered. "Dani, you feel so freaking good."

She laughed, a wild abandoned sound that ended on a low moan. She leaned forward, dropped a tongue dueling kiss on him, and started to ride.

He was a goner. In heat. In lust. In love.

And that no longer scared him. Emotion overwhelmed him. "Dani," he cried out.

"I'm here, Levi," she whispered. "Just let go."

"Not...without..." he flipped his head back and forth, the tension coiling tighter and tighter. He didn't want to let go. He wanted this to last...forever. "You." And he couldn't hold back.

His body exploded, his hands holding her hips in place as he ground as deep as he could go.

Through the haze in his mind, he heard her cry out, her thighs holding him tightly. He shuddered. When she collapsed on his chest, he held her close against his heart.

"I think I'm in love."

She froze. Then a tiny giggle slipped free. "Only think? 'Cause I don't have any doubt."

He rolled over, still inside her, and pinned her underneath him. He stared down into her beautiful, luminescent eyes, so full of joy, satisfaction and...yes...love.

"Neither do I," he whispered. "I don't know how I got to be this lucky, but I love you, Dani. So very much."

And he proceeded to show her all over again.

Chapter 12

A long time later, warm and happy, Dani rolled over and cuddled up against Levi.

His strong arm wrapped around her and pulled her even closer. He kissed her forehead before dropping back in exhaustion. Good. She'd worn him out, too. She smirked.

"I heard that." Levi murmured against her hair.

"No, you didn't."

"I felt it."

"Now that's possible." She waited, wondering if she should ask.

But he, ever sensitive to her needs, asked first. "What's on your mind?"

She shifted so she was lying, arms crossed on his chest, chin resting on top. Where she could look into his eyes. Where she could see the truth.

In a serious voice, she asked, "Did you mean it?"

His eyebrows shot up in surprise, but his eyes warmed all the way through. Even as satiated as she was, her body quickened at the heat glowing from his heart.

"I meant it. All of it. All the way."

She closed her eyes. In spite of herself, a tear leaked from the corner of her eye. She swore she was done with the bawling, but the depth of the feeling in his voice…well, she didn't think anyone had ever cared for her like he did.

"Please, don't cry." He pulled her higher up on his chest so he could kiss the tear away. "I didn't mean to make you upset."

"You could never make me upset by telling me how much you care." She smiled, blinking rapidly to stop more tears from rolling down her cheeks. "I was just realizing how much I want this. How much I missed when all my friends had loving relationships and I didn't."

"I feel the same. I didn't want to be with everyone and yet no one. I wanted to find someone to love, and who'd love me."

She made a face. "I hate to say it, but it looks like we owe Milo our thanks."

He laughed. A deep rumble that rolled through him, making her sigh with delight. "That we do, but we won't tell him just yet."

He flipped her over, and she whispered, "Tell me again."

"How about I show you instead."

And he lowered his head and kissed her.

***

Hours later, an alarm shuddered through the apartment. Levi bolted out of bed.

Dani woke up beside him, a cry on her lips.

"Alarm on low."

Instantly, the sound stopped.

"Levi," Dani said now that she could be heard, "What's going on?"

"Intruders."

She gasped, clutching the covers to her chest. "What?"

Levi bolted out the door, calling behind him, "Grab Charmin and hide in the pod room."

He couldn't stay to make sure she obeyed the orders. Milo was stumbling through the kitchen when he arrived. "Any idea who it is?"

"No." Milo yawned but brought up the security system. "I also don't know if it's building-wide or just us."

"Find out." Levi headed to the front door and his wall control panel. "The exterior is secure. There's been no breach anywhere that I can see." He called out to Milo. "I can't see what's triggered the alarm."

"Uh, Levi?"

"Yeah?"

"Can you come here?"

Exasperated, Levi gave the panel one final look, but it didn't have anything new to offer. "Coming." He bolted to the kitchen. There was no sign of Dani, so he hoped she'd hidden as he instructed.

In the kitchen, he came to a skittering stop. Milo faced him and so did Dani. Behind them both stood the younger Defino brother, Tommy Defino.

"What the hell?" Levi approached slowly, his hands partially up. "How did you get in here, Tommy?"

Tommy glared, his lip curling. "You're not the only who's good with technology. The world is full of geeks. Just not so full of guys that can get the job done." He smiled a too-shiny grin. "Like me."

"And what job is that?" He studied the man, looking for some weakness. The asshole was cocky, confident. In fact, he looked too damn confident. This wasn't the first time he'd broken into someone's house, even a high-tech one like his. But under that was anger, fear, and maybe a hint…fear…of desperation.

And that made him dangerous.

"Besides, you didn't use technology to get in here. Our scans would have alerted us. So how else?" While he waited for an answer, he studied his brother's face. Milo kept rolling his eyes to the left. Levi casually checked out Dani's pinched face then carried on to the counter where Milo was motioning.

Dani snorted. "When I left the door open earlier. You snuck in then, didn't you?"

Damn. That actually made sense. The system had been off while Dani was out rescuing him and Milo. This kid could have snuck in and found a place to hide until he found the perfect time to come out.

And Tommy nodded and laughed. "You geeks seem to think you're so damn smart. Sometimes the easiest way is the best way to do something."

Milo made a sharp movement with his head. Levi saw the large 3D computer was up and running. The hot spots showed who was where in the building. It took him a moment to realize that Johan's place was once again occupied.

"Your brother already died in this building," Levi said in an even tone. "Are you sure you should be here?"

Tommy narrowed his gaze. "Like hell he did." Tommy turned slightly to look at the shut down HoloKomp center behind him as if wanting to call his brother.

"I saw his body myself. The Combot death squad retrieved him." Levi realized the guy didn't know. "I'm sorry."

"I don't believe you. He's on a job." Tommy shook his head. "He'll check in when he can."

"Except something went wrong." Levi would hate to hear news like that from a stranger. "Sorry."

"Like hell. Paul is good. Better than anyone I know. You're just messing with me." He snorted and waved something around. Levi's gut clenched. Shit. The guy had a laser gun. With a wave of his hand, he could cut a person in half. Dani wouldn't have a hope of escaping. She didn't even know what it was.

"What do you want?" Levi asked in a cold voice. He smiled at Dani to reassure her, but his mind raced. What the hell was he going to do?

He took a step forward.

"Whoa. That's close enough."

Milo made a sharp movement of his head again. Levi glanced over at the monitor screen. He studied the three figures in Johan's place, then motioned toward the moving images.

"Those are the ones that killed your brother."

"What? Like hell." Tommy waved the gun around again and grabbed Dani's arm, pulling her back a step. Dani lost her balance, only righting herself at the last minute when he shoved her forward again.

"Leave her alone," Levi snapped, his voice hard. He clenched his fists.

"Or what?" Tommy sneered. "It's not like you can do anything. She's coming with me."

"Why?" He needed to keep the asshole answering questions. He had to find out where Dani was being taken, not that he'd let her leave...he just needed an opening.

"What about me?" Milo asked.

"I don't know anything about you. Unless you're worth something, you get to die along with Levi here."

"So you know me, but I don't know you. Interesting. I presume you took care of Lina?"

"What do you know about that bitch?"

"Only that she was a bitch," Milo said. He'd shifted closer to the monitor.

"That she was." Tommy pushed Milo slightly. He fell toward the counter and pushed something on the monitor, a move so slight it was almost unnoticeable.

Then the balance of power shifted.

Charmin sauntered into the kitchen. Dani gasped. Levi watched, waiting with a fatalistic attitude, knowing that something was about to give.

Casually, Charmin hopped up on the counter by the monitor. He started to clean himself.

Like any ordinary cat.

"That is one ugly cat."

Uh oh.

Charmin froze. His whiskers quivered. He turned to stare at Tommy. In a low voice, he snarled, "What did you say?"

Levi groaned.

Dani rushed to talk. "Poor baby, you've still got that horrible hoarse voice." She rounded on Tommy. "How dare you say that about my cat?"

The poor guy's jaw worked. He frowned, his shocked gaze going from Dani to Charmin and back again. "Did that cat just talk?"

"You're losing it," Milo laughed. "How can a cat talk? Get too many bangs on the head by any chance?"

Tommy glared. "Shut the hell up."

Behind Milo, a series of weird beeps started.

"What's that? What did you do?" He raced to the monitor. Charmin scurried backwards out of the way. Levi looked at him suspiciously. Charmin gave him a bland look back. What the hell had he done?

Milo studied the computer. Levi caught a grin before he wiped his face clean. So Charmin had done something good.

"Turn it off," Tommy snapped. "Hurry up."

Milo reached over and tapped in a code. Instantly, the unit silenced.

Tommy relaxed. "That's why you shouldn't have pets around computers. They'll fry the circuits."

"This one is particularly bad." Milo smiled. Charmin snickered.

Tommy stared at him suspiciously before switching his gaze to Charmin. "Should throw the damn thing out the window."

"You'd do that?" Dani rounded on him. "What kind of a horrible person are you? Animals are innocent. They don't deserve that type of behavior." She poked her finger into his chest. "What kind of an asshole are you?"

"The asshole with the gun, now lay off, lady." He spun around, his glare angry and frustrated. "What kind of a house is this?"

"A good one," Dani said with a sniff and lifted her nose. "Unlike the one you live in."

Tommy shook his head. "I don't know why the boss wants you. I wouldn't want to be anywhere close to you."

She deliberately stepped closer. "Yeah, how about this close?" She took another step. "Or this?"

"Stand back. I mean it."

Levi watched, fascinated, as Dani, her temper up now, shoved her face into Tommy's. "Why should I? You can't hurt me. The boss paid you good money to make sure you don't. So are you going to go up against the boss?"

Tommy winced at the thought.

"Yeah, I didn't think so."

Levi wanted to wince, too, because Dani wasn't thinking. Tommy could just as easily hurt them…or Charmin.

As if reading Levi's mind, Tommy swung his arm out wide, bringing the laser gun around to bear on Charmin.

And Charmin jumped.

Chapter 13

Charmin landed on Tommy's arm. Claws dug in deep. Tommy screamed. And the laser gun went flying.

Milo jumped for the gun.

Levi jumped for Tommy.

Dani jumped for Charmin.

"Get it off me," Tommy screamed, dancing backwards half bent over and still shaking his arm. Levi pinned him against the counter, twisting Tommy's free arm up and behind him.

"Charmin, let go." Dani tried to pull Charmin off the man, but he was not interested. "Please, Charmin. You're going to get hurt."

"*He's* going to get hurt?" Tommy screamed hysterically. "What about me? I'm the one who's been attacked."

Milo snickered. "Then you shouldn't have threatened Dani. The cat is very protective of her."

"You guys are nuts. Do you hear me? Fucking crazy!" This last bit he delivered at the top of his lungs.

"Ha," Dani snapped. "You're the one that attacked a poor defenseless cat."

"What?" Tommy stared at her in shock. "I didn't attack him. He attacked me. And that makes him anything but defenseless."

"Not the point. You insulted him first." With Charmin safe in her arms, she cuddled him close. "Ignore him, Charmin. He's just being mean." Charmin popped his head over her arm to glare at Tommy, and damned if he didn't stick his tongue out at him. She glared at him. He raised an eyebrow and pulled it back in.

"Did I just see that? Did you just see that?" Tommy cried. "That cat stuck his tongue out at me."

"No. You're really going to need to lay off those recreational supplements." Milo laughed. "Natural is fine, but not in the doses you've been indulging."

"What are you talking about?" Tommy groaned. "You all belong in the nut house."

"Right, and you're the one making crazy talk about a cat," Levi snarled.

That shut him up.

Dani watched from a safe distance as Milo checked Tommy over for weapons and communication devices. When he pulled Tommy's personal com out of his pocket, he stepped back and started clicking away on it.

"Hey, that's mine," Tommy protested. "Don't mess anything up."

Milo rolled his eyes at him. "He's got both Lina and John in his address book, and yes, here's Johan."

"So that means nothing. Johan is behind all this bullshit."

"Then you're in big trouble because Johan is dead," Levi said, his voice icy and hard.

Tommy froze. "What?"

"I said, Johan is dead."

"That can't be. No." Tommy shook his head. "He's the one who told me to come here and grab Dani. Said she needed tags. And we know what that means. Paul had an argument with him about it when he tried to retrieve the information for the Council. He wouldn't tell him where it was. Only there was someone else there. He barely escaped that time so he had to go back."

"That argument finished Johan. He'd been hurt before. You brother must have given the final blow to his injured body. We were the others in that damn apartment. Your brother escaped from me," Levi snapped. "And no, I don't know what needing tags mean – what does it mean?"

Tommy shook his head, trying to absorb the facts as they flew at him. "It means that she's not from here."

"So, she's from somewhere else," Milo said, "What's the big deal?"

"They are eradicating the fringe groups. You know that."

"No," Levi corrected. "They are isolating the fringe groups to live in one area where they can't cause as much trouble."

"Talk about naïve." Tommy snorted. "Look, they just dispatched a large group of them a few months back. When the alert came through on the tagging, they figured she'd escaped. She'd cause them a ton of damage if she spread the word."

Dani stared. "Are you saying someone committed mass murder and they think I got away? And now I'm going to blow the whistle on them?" Oh, this was not good. Like so not good.

"Who did this?" Levi asked in a hard voice.

But it was Milo who answered. "The Council, of course."

And Tommy nodded his head. "They did. And they can't have anyone know what they did."

"Why kill these fringe groups? Were they terrorists?"

"That's what the Council will try to convince everyone, but they weren't. They were people who didn't want to live under the Council rule. They lived a more natural life."

Instantly, Dani felt a connection to them. "Those poor men."

"Women and children, too. They were especially clear about making sure the breeding stock was taken out so the problem couldn't continue."

Dani burrowed her face into Charmin's lush fur. How terrible. Centuries in the future and genocide was still a problem. In her own country, yet. She didn't know what to say.

Levi did. "Do you have any proof?"

"Johan had it. He was trying to make a break from being under their thumb. They blackmailed him into monitoring everyone." Tommy nodded at Levi and then at Milo. "Like you two. He didn't want to tell them about Dani here, but they saw the information from his pod, and they found out anyway."

***

Levi hated the ring of truth in Tommy's words. This explained so much. Tommy no longer looked like a major badass. Instead, he looked like a punk who had made a wrong turn and didn't know how to make the right one to get the hell out.

He took a look at Dani. How she was taking this revelation? True to form, she had tears collecting in the corner of her eyes. He just didn't know why. Fear? Agony for the victims? Something else?

"That's a horrible thing to do," she said in a harsh whisper. "Those people just wanted to live their life their way."

Tommy nodded. "I agree. But you're dead meat regardless. They can't afford to let you live."

That's when Levi realized that Tommy believed she had escaped the massacre, and if he did – others would too.

She was marked. Unless this was solved...and fast...there'd be no end to this hunt. Ever.

Except they had Johan's material. He spun around to look at Milo and realized Milo – as usual – was way ahead of him.

"You realize they killed your brother? They couldn't leave him alive with what he knew. They've already – or someone has – killed Lina, Johan, and your brother."

Grief filled the young man's eyes. "I was hoping you were lying. I haven't heard from Paul since last night. He was on a retrieval mission at Johan's."

"Retrieving what?"

"The data Johan had on the Council."

It all made such terrible sense. "And what are they going to do with you now that you've failed?" Levi asked in a gentle voice. He wondered who had killed Johan. Then again, thugs were easy to find and even easier to hire. It could have been one of many. He doubted Tommy knew.

Tommy shook his head and said in a gloomy voice, "I'm dead already, the final act just hasn't happened yet."

Milo turned to look at him. "Run. Surely you can find a place to go where you can be safe."

Not likely, but Levi waited for Tommy's answer. "No. There's no place to run. All the Councils are connected. I could go to the other side of the planet and they'd find me within a day."

"Unless we find a way to stop them first."

Tommy looked up at Milo, a tiny bright bit of hope in his eyes. "What good would that do? You're just going to throw me to them anyway."

"Did you kill anyone?" Dani asked out of the blue.

"Me? No." He looked shocked at the suggestion. "I'm good with computers," he shrugged, "I've committed many a break-in though. That will get me off-planet jail for life. And it's not fair. We were ditched early in life by mum and had to fend for ourselves after. A little hard to do honestly when you're trying to stay out of the system and have no family to turn to."

And that was the biggest issue. No family to take them in and give them a home. Without it, life could be a little grim. Hell, a lot grim.

Tommy confronted them. "So what are you going to do to me?"

Chapter 14

Dani heard the challenge in Tommy's voice. She carefully placed Charmin on the table with a whispered warning. "Be quiet." He shot her a hooded look. She wasn't sure what he meant by that. She wanted to believe he'd be good, but there was no guarantee.

Ever.

Not with Charmin. Giving him a stern look, she walked over to Levi and slipped her hand into his. He squeezed her hand and tugged her up close. She murmured, "What can you do, Levi?"

"I'm working on it," he said with light humor. "Give me a minute."

She watched Tommy shift uneasily. Milo was back at the big computer. Now that Tommy had been disarmed, he'd lost his bravado. Now he just looked sad. Worn out. "How good are you?"

"At what?" He looked confused.

She glanced over at Milo, whose face had twisted in thought. "Milo?"

"I'm thinking."

She groaned. "Could you two think a little faster please?"

"What difference does it make?" Tommy slouched against the back counter. "There is no going back for me."

She wanted the brothers to step up and give the kid a break, but she didn't know enough of how life worked here to make that happen. Maybe the kid was a major badass and needed to be slung out onto some horrific planet all alone. What did she know?

"Levi, can you help him?"

He glared down at her. "And why would I want to do that? He broke into my house and tried to kidnap you. Where in any of that does it say he deserves my help?"

"Because he didn't succeed, and he really had no choice himself."

"But he did in the beginning," Levi argued, his jaw stiff with anger.

"Did he?" She waited. She didn't know Levi as much as she'd like to, but she knew him better than he thought. He was a good man. With a good heart. A ruthless businessman, but not at the expense of the people. He'd help Tommy if he could. If he saw a reason to.

"Oh no." He started to shake his head. "No. We're not saving the world."

"I didn't ask you to save the world. Just one small part of it." She widened her gaze at him. "We couldn't save those on the fringe."

He closed his eyes and groaned. "Really? You're going to do this."

She smiled. Milo laughed then said, "She has a point."

Levi shook his head. "No. No, she doesn't."

"He's good," Milo said quietly. "We could use him."

"Is he?" Dani asked, her hopeful gaze on Milo's features. He nodded. She switched her attention to Tommy. He was slumped with apparent disinterest, like he'd never known there to be anything but a bad outcome in his life.

"It doesn't matter how good he is, he can't be trusted." Levi's hard voice brooked no argument.

But Dani had to admit to feeling perverse. "How do you know that? I imagine loyalty and trustworthiness are two main requirements of Tommy's life up to now." She looked over at the very confused man staring at her like she'd lost her marbles. "Or am I wrong?"

"No," he said in a rush, "You're not. They mean everything. Or I'd be dead by now."

She nodded. "See?"

"No," Levi said in exasperation. "I don't see." He threw up his hands. "He's a criminal. I can't change his history. The law wants him. The law is going to get him."

"I actually did my time. It's my brother who's...was...wanted by the law. Only the Council said I hadn't done all my time. Only I did. But because they said I hadn't..."

"Juvie?" Milo asked. He was busy clicking away on his damn computer. Dani didn't know if he was helping the situation or playing games, but she wanted someone to do something.

"Milo?"

"Yeah," he answered, distracted.

"What are you doing?"

"Looking at his record."

Tommy started. "You aren't supposed to be able to see that."

Milo snorted. "I'll look at whatever the hell I want to."

Tommy stared from one person to the other. When it was Dani's turn, she gave him a bright smile.

"Milo?" Levi waited for a response from his brother.

"Says he did his time. Was released 4 years ago. Model prisoner. Time off for good behavior."

"And they said that was revoked because I moved back in with my brother, who was a known criminal."

"That's not fair," Dani cried out. "You paid your debt to society. And he was family."

Tommy shrugged. "They said it wasn't enough. It's not like I can argue. They have all the power."

"Too much power, apparently." Dani twisted slightly to face Milo and Levi. "Can you help him?"

Milo grinned. "I don't think Levi wants to. Tommy here was all set to screw with us. You in particular."

"Only because I had to." But he stared at Dani in fascination. "I've never met anyone like you."

"Not going to either." Milo almost danced in place with his secret.

But that was one secret that could never be shared.

***

Levi studied the awkward young man in front of him. He wanted to slug him and hug him. For all that he'd tried to do. Levi couldn't help compare Milo to Tommy. If Milo and he hadn't had the benefit of their extended family, where would they have ended up?

Likely the same damn place as Tommy. Considering Milo's seriously scary computer skills, they could be running the underworld by now. That brought a tiny smile to his face.

But that didn't change the fact that Tommy was dangerous. And alone in the world. "Tommy, how old are you?"

The younger man's eyes narrowed. "Twenty two – why?"

Of course he was the same age as Milo and his older brother would likely have been the same age as Levi. With Paul dead, Tommy was completely alone. But that didn't make him someone worth rehabilitating. His brother had been a hard case. Several steps down the crime path than Tommy. Was it too late for him to be saved?

Dani shifted patiently at his side, and he realized he really wasn't going to have much choice.

"He'd have to give over all the information he knows, sign a contract as to what he would honor, and should he break that contract..." Levi deliberately added an edge to his voice.

Tommy's eyes lit up. "I'm not sure what you're talking about here as an end result, but I'm sure looking for a way not to go back to jail or to have to face the bosses."

"And just who are the bosses?"

He swallowed. Looked from one to the other. "Paul dealt with him. Them."

"But you know who the bosses are, right?"

"They are all on the Council. But one is handling this issue. He's the one we dealt with."

"Who? And is he the one who killed Lina?"

He winced. "We think so. But I don't know who he is. Besides, he commands many contractors. We were supposed to snatch Dani here, but when we couldn't, Lina was blamed. Then they put the pressure on her partner."

"John. Who came here to grab Dani himself after you failed?"

"Yeah, the bosses want her bad."

"Alive?"

Tommy nodded his head vigorously. "They need to know who escaped with her."

"Right. And would torture the information out of her if necessary." *Shit.*

Chapter 15

Dani made coffee. Tommy was hardly a visitor, but the males were sitting at the table discussing what was to be done and would likely appreciate it. And she was quickly becoming addicted to the stuff herself. Tommy was dishing dirt on everyone he knew in an effort to show his good intentions to clear himself. She felt sorry for him. He'd had it rough, he'd done the best he could, but now he was at a crossroads.

What he did from here on out would be dangerous and would change the course of his life. With his permission, Milo had run every kind of scan he could while everyone had watched. And he'd fixed some kind of emotion detector on the poor guy. Dani felt horrible about that one. The last thing she would want was to have her emotions scanned or detected.

That Levi had never mentioned such a thing to her hopefully meant that he trusted her at least that much.

"What's the matter?" Levi spoke quietly behind her. "Do all the tests we're putting him through bother you?"

"Yes," she said with feeling. "Especially the emotion one."

"We have to make sure he's telling the truth. Our lives depend on it."

She nodded. "I understand. I hope you guys never feel you need to do that to me though."

He laughed and tugged her back against him. "Never. You're honest all the way through." His chest rumbled behind her head. "Besides, that's one of the tests Milo already checked you on before."

She stilled. "Really? How could he know?"

"We have much more sophisticated ways to detect stuff like that now," he said easily. "Honesty is big for Milo. And being in business, for me, it's even bigger."

"Me, too," she said with feeling. "Particularly after your blackguard ancestor."

He dropped a kiss on her head.

"What's to do be done with him?" she asked.

"I can't say for sure. Depends on whether we can catch the Council with what they are doing and stop them, or if we have to go on the run."

She tilted up her head. "Really? The latter sounds horrible."

"I am hoping that it won't be necessary. The trouble is finding the information then going above the Council to get them charged with criminal behavior as well as let the public know. Above the Council are only a few older men. They are supposed to be the watchdogs over the Council. But are they really?" Levi shrugged, "We won't know until we get to that point."

"Doesn't Milo have that information?"

"Milo grabbed everything he could off Johan's system, but that doesn't mean he'd recognize the information when he sees it. I'd expect Johan to have it secured and barely identifiable. The material is too dangerous."

That made sense. "So is Tommy going to help Milo look for it?"

"Something like that. We know the material is encrypted. And breaking that encryption is likely to be the toughest part. Apparently Tommy's skills have to do with code breaking. That's how he's been good with breaking into houses. He manages to bypass security codes easily."

She smiled. "Sounds like Milo has found a kindred spirit."

Levi dropped a kiss on her head. "The biggest issue is do we trust him."

"No. Don't do that at this point, but he's got a lot of reasons to expose the Council himself."

"And that's partly why we're running the tests."

"If he holds up his end of this, and we do expose the Council – what about Tommy then?"

Levi shrugged. "I don't know. Maybe if we get a new Council they will give him a medal. They'd certainly look at his criminal past with a more judicial eye than the current one. He's being blackmailed into following their illegal orders now."

"Hopefully he'll come out fine."

"Chances are good." Levi looked over at Milo and Tommy, their heads together as they looked at the huge holographic monitor. He looked like he wanted to say something but stopped.

She nudged him. "What?"

He smiled down at her. "I'm not making any promises, but if he's any good, we could probably use him in the company. Keep your friends close and your enemies closer type of thing."

"So find the information. Blast it out to the world so everyone knows what they did. Make sure it can never be buried as yet another bureaucratic secret. And we need to tell someone about the Council's involvement in Lina and Paul's murder, but who?"

"I'm debating talking to Stephen."

"Your friend on the Council?" At his nod, she coughed lightly and said, "How can you know for sure that he's not a part of this?"

Levi's face scrunched. "I can't. That's why I'm still thinking about it. I don't want him to be involved, but who knows if everyone is or if it's only the four top-tier members."

Tommy twisted around to look at them. "I wouldn't trust anyone on the Council. They're all privy to what goes on there."

"But Stephen is new. He hasn't even gotten full status there yet."

"He's too close to the top to be trusted. His meteoric climb within the Council makes me suspicious."

"You think he's been handpicked to climb that hierarchy because of his involvement?"

Milo piped up. "Everyone in the Council will be involved. There's no way not to be."

"Except they need a fall guy. What better way than to blame the new guy?"

"Or what better way for the new guy to cement his position than to arrange for the deaths of those interfering with the Council's plans?" Dani asked.

"There is that." Levi glared down at the huge computer. "How can we find out who is involved and who is not?"

***

Levi hoped Stephen wasn't involved. This was too important a mistake to make. He walked closer to Milo. "Any progress?"

"A little. I think we found the files, but he's layered it with different encryption techniques. We're still working our way in."

"Okay, I'm going to make some phone calls." Levi headed toward the kitchen. "See if there's anything I can find out on Stephen's history."

"You're probably better off checking the government files and scanning them to see if they've been doctored."

Tommy stared up at Levi. "You guys can do that?"

"Sure. We're just not supposed to."

Instead of calling a few people he knew, Levi walked up to the computer on the kitchen counter. Everything looked normal in the building, and Johan's apartment was once again empty and dark. He might need to make a trip up there.

He bored into the government database and did a quick sweep of Stephen's files. He scanned the information. Everything confirmed what he already knew about Stephen. It wasn't surprising. He'd gone to business school with Stephen, and even then, he'd been full of political idealism. Levi had been the opposite. He'd been full of commercialism and was all about protecting Milo and his inventions.

It was all just as he thought, but this was just surface stuff. Dani would expect him to do more. Damn it, he wanted to prove that Stephan was okay. Beyond any doubt. So he kept digging, using Stephen's middle name and last name. Nothing unusual in any direction. No leads and no flags, which was to be expected. He'd be covering his tracks professionally if he was involved in anything wrong. There'd been a few political rallies he'd been active in as a young man, nothing to raise eyebrows over, just enough to make him 'normal'...and that's what bothered Levi. On second glance, his buddy looked a little too normal.

Scowling, he went deeper.

And suddenly things got interesting.

Dani walked over and handed him a cup of coffee. He'd forgotten she'd even made it. He smiled his thanks.

"Did you find anything?" she asked.

"Maybe." Levi rubbed his eyes. "Signs that he might have had his fingers in a few gambling pots I hadn't known about."

"Bad pots?" she asked. "Or just a little recreational gambling?"

"A lot of money lost." He kept reading the information on the screen. "A hell of a lot of money lost."

"Maybe he had to replace it? And the Council offered him a way to do that?"

"Or they used his gambling debts against him?"

Chapter 16

"To make him go along with their plans? That could be possible." Dani didn't know the man, but it would be nice to think that not everyone here was an asshole.

The HoloKomp beeped. Levi walked over to stand in the weird circle on the floor. Dani watched from a safe distance as Stephen's face came through the wall. From the corner of her eye, she caught Tommy's shrinking motion. Interesting. She flipped back to Levi, who seemed to be carrying on an animated conversation in silence. He must have muted the audio.

She turned around with raised eyebrows. Milo said, "Stephen has the conversation on double security levels."

"So it's serious." She sat down beside them. She leaned toward Milo and whispered, "Can you lip read?" He grinned and held up a finger to his lips then tapped his ear. She realized that he was listening in on the conversation anyway.

Smart boy.

Standing, she walked to the table where she'd placed Charmin. He'd long since disappeared, but she was hoping he was close by. He wasn't. She went to the pod room, but there was no sign of him. Remembering the beautiful fire, she headed toward Levi's bedroom. Her bedroom now, she supposed, only it didn't quite feel like it yet.

"Charmin, you in here?"

"Over here."

She turned to find him balancing on his back legs on the back of a chair, studying the wall computer. She understood today was all about the technical age, but there was literally a built-in computer in each room. She'd never seen what this one could do, but since it was in Levi's bedroom, she doubted it did less than any other one. In fact, as Charmin spiked out a long claw and touched another part of the screen, she realized this one was similar to the one in the kitchen counter. Maybe they were all the same and she only saw parts of them.

She asked Charmin about that.

"Yes, they are actually all part of the same computer. You can pull out a section to look at via holograph at any place. They all have the same capabilities."

"And what are you doing?" She tried to see for herself, intrigued by the different windows he had open.

He said, "I'm looking for a list of those killed in the genocide."

"Why?"

"Because maybe it will give us some idea of who is behind this."

"You think someone did this to their own people?" She shuddered. "That's a terrible thought."

"And yet your species seem to delight in finding ways to hurt each other even more."

"I was hoping that the future would be more developed," she muttered.

"It is, but people appear to be more stupid."

She had to admit from what she'd seen so far, Charmin wasn't far from wrong.

A long list appeared on the screen. "Any names we recognize?

"Not yet."

The list scrolled on endlessly. She hated to think of so many people killed over being different. It was nothing new, but seeing the names of all those people brought tears to her eyes.

Suddenly Charmin reached out and snagged the screen.

It stopped, and one name enlarged supersize.

Stephen Cavendish.

***

Levi had just closed the HoloKomp when Dani dashed around the corner of the kitchen. "Levi, come into the bedroom, please."

He raised an eyebrow, shrugged at Milo and Tommy, and followed her. Once inside, she closed the door so he could see the computer better. And what Charmin had highlighted.

He swore under his breath. "It has to be a different Stephen."

"Does it?"

"It says he's deceased."

"How hard is that to fake?" Dani asked.

"To fake a death? Hard, but not impossible. Taking over someone's life – that's much easier to do."

"And the only reason to do that is to hide who he really is." Dani studied his face. "You're thinking he might have had something to do with the genocide and is now hiding?"

"I'm not thinking anything," Levi protested. "I'm trying to figure this out. There are too many unknowns."

"Then we need to make them knowns," she said. "Bring Stephen here and ask him in private."

"That's not going to happen. Councilmen don't just travel around casually. They come with full Combot units."

"Then figure out how to get him to come alone or meet him elsewhere – just the two of you, so you can find out the truth. It seems like he's at the center of this."

"And yet it might be a completely different Stephen Cavendish."

"Same birthday," Charmin announced. "But everything else looks different."

"It would have been changed to hide his history."

"So…" Dani nudged him.

He ran his fingers through his hair. "I definitely need to talk to him. I'm just not sure how."

"I suggest you send him an encrypted message saying 'I know everything.'" Charmin said, "And have him meet you somewhere private."

Levi stared at Charmin. "For a cat, you're damn smart."

"Only because of Milo," Dani said absentmindedly. "And you're not going alone. Take Tommy to watch your back and Milo to make sure Tommy is actually watching and not stabbing you in the back."

He snorted then admitted, "I hate the idea of leaving you alone."

"We're better off here," she said with a sweet smile. "All hell breaks loose when I leave." She reached out a hand and stroked his forearm. "Better you go, deal with this, and come back."

"Then I'd better get it set up now."

And he headed out to Milo and Tommy.

It was the last thing he wanted to do. But if his friend was involved in this mess, then he was in for an ugly surprise.

Friends or not, if Stephen was involved in Dani's kidnapping, Levi would fry him.

Chapter 17

It was out of Dani's hands now, and she watched as everything happened in front of her eyes. After Milo encrypted the message using a dialogue code common among the Naturals group, Levi sent it off.

They hadn't had time to prepare for the next stage when an answer came immediately.

"Meet at Station 42, zone 6."

Milo immediately searched for that location.

"Interesting. It's an old hangout for the Naturals before they moved out. It's deserted and hasn't been used in decades."

Tommy shook his head. "That's what the records say, but it's not empty. There is a heavy criminal element there."

"Then don't go," Dani cried. "I don't want you to get hurt."

"We don't have much choice."

"Yes, you do. You don't have to go to that location. Change it to someplace safer. One where these two can be with you. And one where you will all be safe."

Milo said, "She's right, you know."

"Make it a public place," she said. "An art gallery? A huge shopping complex."

The men looked at her. She rolled her eyes. "Okay, so I like reading about places like that, but think of something along the same line. Or…" she smiled. "Both of you port somewhere where no one can find you. Go to a ski chalet where you can be alone and talk."

Milo brightened. "I like that idea. Give him the coordinates — a set he can look up — then we'll meet him there."

Tommy got up and walked over to the window. As he passed Dani, she saw pain and grief in his face, and she felt for him. He'd just lost his brother, and now his life had taken a complete shift. Adjusting would be hard.

"Why not just send him up to Johan's place?" Charmin asked from behind Dani.

Dani quickly glanced at Tommy, but he was staring out the window, his back hunched. She turned back to the others.

Thankfully, Tommy was far enough away that he couldn't hear Charmin talking.

Milo turned to Levi. "That's an even better idea. We can track you and everything can easily be recorded."

"And we can help from here." Dani loved the idea of Levi staying close.

Levi nodded. "That's the best plan yet."

"Then send him the message and get it changed." Dani urged. "At least Charmin and I can keep watch from here and help out if need be."

"Remember, we don't know if Stephen is on the good side or the bad."

"True, but he responded — and damn fast, so he's interested."

Milo walked out of the room and returned a few minutes later with a cloud of tiny colorful dots in his hand. "Here. Swallow."

Dani watched with interest. That Levi swallowed the items without asking questions said a lot about them. Tommy had turned around, and even he didn't raised an eyebrow. So this was a common occurrence. She assumed they were trackers of some kind. Knowing Milo, though, it could be so much more.

She sat in the background as messages were fired off and Milo prepped his brother. "I'm going up there and will be in the bedroom under Johan's camouflage. I'll bring my new invention, and I'm setting up a smaller one for you to take as well. In case of trouble, it will be best for both of us to have an escape route."

"I hear that." Tommy said.

Dani loved how Tommy had gone from being a bad guy to a good guy. She just hoped he didn't blow this second chance. The brothers would help him, but if he screwed up...

Levi would kill him.

Hell, she would, too. Dani shifted restlessly.

"Psst."

Damn, that was Charmin. She walked to the bedroom and closed the door. "What?"

"Make sure Milo sets up that emotion scanner for Stephen. Might help see what the truth is."

"Oh, good idea. But I don't think it's portable."

Charmin snorted. "Hell, everything is portable here."

She glanced down at her beloved cat. "Charmin, you look tired."

"Of course I'm tired. It's not like there's any chance to catch up on all our lost sleep."

"I hear you there." She yawned unexpectedly. "I'm really tired, too."

"So let's go for a nap." Charmin's gaze brightened. "They can go do their super secret spy stuff and we can sleep."

"But someone has to keep an eye out to make sure Levi is safe."

"Ha. He's willingly going into that locked-down prison. If he screws up, I'm not going back in there after him."

"You won't need to, Milo is taking that portable port thingy you delivered last time."

"Good. Nice to know I won't be called on to save the day again. Being a hero is tiring." He pinned her with a glare. "And works up an appetite. I'm feeling better, but you're really slacking in the meal department."

"Hey, it's the middle of the night. Not breakfast time."

"It's breakfast somewhere in the world."

"Dani?" Levi gently pushed the door open. "Stephen has agreed to the new location. Milo and I are going up there now to set up. Are you going to be okay here?"

Charmin glared at him. "We'll be fine if you'd let us sleep."

Dani shook her head. "Don't mind him. He gets cranky without his beauty rest." She smiled brightly at Levi, feeling anything but on the inside. "We'll be fine, but what about Tommy? And what do we do if things go bad?"

"I was thinking to leave Tommy here in that case."

He tugged her into his arms. She wrapped her arms around his waist and whispered, "I don't want anything to happen to you."

"Ditto. But I also want a life where we don't have to worry about anyone else coming after us. Looking behind our shoulders all the time is not going to be fun."

"Can you take Tommy with you and leave Milo here?" She bent back to look up at him. "Or send Milo back right away and make them switch places?"

"That's possible. I'll talk to Milo."

***

And talk to Milo he did. Inside, outside, upside, and downside, and his kid brother still wouldn't budge.

"I'm not leaving you up there," Milo snapped. "No way."

"What about Dani?"

"You're my brother. It's your back I'm watching."

"And as your brother," Levi said, concern for Dani a hard lump in his throat, "I'm asking you to come back and look after Dani."

Milo shook his head, the huge Mohawk wafting in the wind. "No. I'm going to make sure you are safe so you can look after her. That's the best thing I can do for both of you."

And that was his final word.

Tommy butted in. "Look, I understand that you don't know me." He paused and winced at the looks from Levi and Milo, "but I do have some experience with this brother stuff."

Now that much was true. Levi could hear the sorrow in his voice and see it in the way he swallowed before continuing.

"I get that you can't trust me, we didn't have a good beginning, but you have your tests and scans to know that I'm telling you the truth when I say I mean you and Dani no harm. I want to find out who is behind all this and to stop it." He took a deep breath and added, "I'd like my life back."

Levi glanced at Milo, who was studying the comp screen in his hand. Milo looked up and nodded. Meaning Tommy was being honest. That helped, but this was the worst time to be wrong.

Still, it's not like he had much choice. Kid brother with no fighting experience and couldn't hide that damn Mohawk to keep himself out of danger, a criminal to watch his back at home, and a girl from centuries ago who was going to be watching his progress with her talking cat.

He had a killer of a headache coming on. And it was only going to get worse. He was also out of time.

"Here, bro. New prototype field equipment. Your new PP." Milo grinned. "No super spy should leave home without it."

Levi stared at him. "My what?"

Milo grinned. "The new personal port. Don't you like the name?"

"It's not the one we're going to market it under."

"That's your problem. I just create this stuff."

"You guys are lucky," Tommy said. "I'd love to be able to invent stuff like this."

Milo looked at Levi, a question in his eyes.

Levi rolled his eyes but gave in…slightly. "We'll see about that *if* we all survive this night."

Silence. Levi glanced over at Tommy and was surprised by the hope in his eyes. The kid was like a big puppy staring at the first bone in his life. And too afraid to hope that it might be for him.

Damn, his life had changed.

Chapter 18

Dani sat in the kitchen hugging yet another cup of coffee. Charmin was in the bed monitoring Levi and Milo's progress from there. He was also monitoring Tommy.

Charmin – her secret weapon. Tommy had no idea what he'd be up against if he attacked her.

She smiled. Then wiped it off her face. There was nothing to smile about. Not until Levi was back again. She should be able to hear his conversation under normal circumstances, but as Johan's place was still in that weird steel lockdown, they wouldn't. She could only watch the figures in the apartment, and that made her insides quiver. Before Levi and Milo left, Milo had quickly explained that the only reason they could see that much was because of what he'd placed inside Johan's place last time. She didn't understand it, but it was all super cool.

As long as Levi stayed safe. She wished he'd made this a holographic meeting, but apparently Stephen had wanted to confirm whoever he was speaking to in person.

It made sense, but it also made the meeting more dangerous. She took a sip of her coffee and watched Levi's healthy orange splotch on the monitor move around. She understood the other weird looking color was Milo and that he'd done something to mask his presence. He'd wanted to get back into Johan's system for another look. The information he might find had to be incredibly valuable…and dangerous.

These two lived a dangerous life and didn't even appear to notice.

A second orange splotch appeared beside Levi. Shorter, not as orange. "He's arrived," she said excitedly.

Tommy leaned closer for a better look. "I wish we could identify him."

"Maybe we can." She shrugged. "But I'm not sure how."

The two splotches seemed to merge, then separate, then merge again.

"Uh, now that looks odd."

"What here doesn't look odd? Are they fighting? Or dancing?" she said, trying to inject humor into the situation even as her voice wobbled.

"I think…" Tommy stopped, then said in a quizzical voice, "they are hugging."

"Really?" Her tension eased. Maybe it *was* Stephen. "He said they were good friends."

The two appeared to be standing, facing each other, talking. She watched and waited and waited. Nothing shifted. Then one started to pace. Stephen. His color darkened and flares fired off his body. As if he was seriously agitated.

Then they calmed down. Stephen disappeared. The light blue colored splotch that was Milo joined Levi, then they both disappeared.

The next thing she knew, she was staring up at Levi's bright purple gaze and his open arms.

She ran into them, loving when they closed securely around her. *Thank God he was safe.*

***

Levi held Dani close to his heart. All that worry and nothing had happened. He'd told her it would all be fine, but until it was over and he was back safe and sound, she wouldn't believe it.

But it was all good now.

"What did he say?"

Levi grimaced. "He thought I was Paul or Tommy here." He motioned at Tommy standing by the far window. "He already knew that these two were doing special jobs for some of the Council, but hadn't figured out who exactly they were working for."

"So he's a good guy?" She waited for his warm smile and nod. "Thank heavens for that."

"So where does that leave us?"

"Stephen is looking at the Council to help clean house." Levi took a deep breath. "He was fast tracked into the Council by the elders to find proof of Council wrongdoing."

"A mole!" Charmin danced gleefully in place. "So he knows that they are corrupt."

"Shhh," she whispered, stealing a glance at Tommy, but he was staring out the window, oblivious to the new voice.

"He knows," Levi said. "He also knows what they did to Tommy and Paul and Johan."

Tommy stood up. "And…is he going to do anything about it?"

"Yes, but not until we get to the bottom of this. He is trying to link Lina's murder to the Council. At least as far as having ordered the hit."

"And by whom?"

Levi winced. "I don't know if I believe him or not, but he seems to think that John did it."

Milo's shocked gasp was loud. Dani turned to him. "Do you agree or disagree?"

"It's possible." He scowled. "But I'm not sure. I found a lot of information on Johan's computer that I hadn't seen because I hadn't realized what I was looking at. It's the background information on the Council members. Johan was trying to research them."

"Did he find anything?"

"John had family in the Naturals group. But he had distanced himself from them years ago – about the same time he was accepted into law school."

"And Stephen?"

Levi nodded. "Stephen was also from the Naturals, but he's years younger than John and was one of the few who left for schooling. He was a teen when he left for school. When he found out that his friends and family had all been killed, he tried to keep his past a secret. He had no idea that he had supposedly died in that genocide, and when he saw his name listed, he just pretended the name was a coincidence and did his best to hide any connection to the group. About a year ago, he found some Council documents sent to him, he thinks by Johan, proving that the Council had killed his family."

"Why didn't he say something to you and Milo? Surely he could have asked for your help."

"He wasn't sure what we were into. Milo got into trouble a year ago for trying to build a time machine, and he blew out all the power in the city. It was a terrible blackout that caused untold damage to various servicers and financial institutes. It was an accident, and they never could prove it was him, but they always suspected. It meant that Stephen didn't dare approach us because we were already under the Council's watchful eye. It would have looked suspicious, and his actions would have been questioned."

"So now what?"

As he opened his mouth to reply, a boom blasted through the room. The force of the noise picked Dani up and threw her against the counter like she was a dishrag. Levi was thrown in the same direction, landing half on top of her. As she gasped for air, he rolled over and jumped to his feet – and stared into the unblinking lens of a Combot standing six inches from him.

His breath sucked in, and he saw the Combot wasn't alone. A full-on tactical team had been sent to his place.

He tensed. That type of action was saved for the worst of the worst.

As he turned to help Dani, the Combot said, "Do not move."

Levi froze. His heart still slamming against his ribs, he stared back at the Combot. "What is your protocol?"

"You are under arrest. For treason."

Chapter 19

Once at the Council, Levi, Milo, and Dani, along with Tommy off to one side, were shoved into the main chamber. Levi stood stiff and tall in front with Dani, knees knocking, slightly behind. She had no idea what the charges stemmed from but thought it had something to do with Tommy's presence in Levi's place. Harboring a criminal or some such thing.

She glanced over where Tommy sat, his arms pinned behind him and a look of defeat on his face. For Tommy, this was bad. Last strike and all that. Her heart was still pounding away in her chest and her palms continued to sweat. Who was she kidding? She was terrified herself. And she was worried about Charmin. She hadn't had a chance to say anything to him before they were ported out of the apartment.

Did he even know what had happened?

She'd never trust the authorities in this time period if they could appear in someone's home, swoop them up, and bring them here without just cause.

Levi had tried to explain that it had something to do with terrorist charges, but there was no way in hell they were terrorists.

He'd told to her to not worry, but she couldn't see how to avoid it. His lawyers were dead and if there were others left to man the firm, they were likely corrupt. His best friend was dead, and he'd been blackmailed into doing criminal activities at the Council's whim and his other friend was part of this same Council that had had them 'retrieved'.

Suspicious indeed.

Yet strangely, Milo had been allowed to keep his personal comp. He'd been working away on it ever since. Levi had also been able to send several messages. If she only knew who he'd contacted, she might feel better.

She hoped it was that powerful family he'd alluded to. They could sure use some help right now.

A commotion at the door heralded the arrival of a dozen suited men. All in black. She almost smiled with relief to see men dressed in power suits and not skin suits.

She stepped forward and slipped her hand into Levi's. He smiled down at her. "It's going to be fine."

"You said that already," she muttered.

He squeezed her hand. "And I meant it."

"What kind of place allows that kind of invasive maneuvers without just cause?" she whispered. Several Combots stood beside her. One turned to explain. "You are changed with terrorism. You no longer have rights."

"Then as you entered our home without warning, without a search warrant or any other legal process in place, you are now charged with terrorism," she snapped.

The Combot looked at her. Then looked at Levi, who was trying to hide his smile, and then back at her. "That is not possible."

"If what you did to me is possible, then what I am doing to you is possible," she cried. "Or have you not heard of citizen's arrest?"

The Combot stared, then lifted his hand unit and asked for direction.

A computerized voice answered. "You are not under arrest. Man your post."

The eldest of the Council members, Levi said his name was Carlson, stood up. "Dani Summerland. Step forward."

Dani whispered to Levi, "Do I have to?"

"Yes." He gave her a gentle nudge.

Fine. Then she'd do it her way. "Dani Summerland following orders like a Combot." And she took two steps to stand front and center. A choked twitter rustled through the room.

"You mock us?" Carlson put on glasses and studied her. After a moment, he frowned and took them off again.

She glared at him. "Can't run your secret scans on me, huh?"

Silence. His face reddened. "You will show respect here, young lady, or face the consequences."

Dani didn't know where the anger came from; something more like rage bubbled up from deep inside. "Respect? For you? For a corrupt Council? For men who ordered the genocide of a complete group of people for no other reason than they chose to live life differently?" Her voice rang out. "A group of men who ordered the execution, the annihilation of all the Naturals?"

The Councilman slapped a hand over his heart. The others gasped, fear and anger building across the group so strong she felt the wave of emotion. Carlson straightened, fury building on his face, but Dani stood tall, not backing down. She'd been ripped out of her home, watched as her cat received the knowledge she desperately wanted for herself, and still she'd made the best of it by finding her love of a lifetime in Levi. She had made that work...now this, this corrupt Council threatened to take it all away from her.

She had nothing to lose.

"You will not hide your murderous soul from me or from the rest of the world. You will not hide your ordering of the slaughter of men, women, and children – the fringe group you call the Naturals – at the flick of your stuck-up, white-ass finger." Shock hit the Council members. She rolled right over them as they opened their mouths, and words ripped out of her from deep inside the pit of her gut, her voice filling the massive chamber. "The world will know of your black heart and even blacker actions. You had Lina Stewart murdered. Because of you, Johan Stroud is dead. And John Driscoll is also dead. You abused your power and position to corrupt this place – a place of goodness – of fairness – and this place full of people who want nothing more than to live fulfilling lives free of your corrupt rule. How dare *you*, sir."

Dani had run out of steam, but ire kept the stick in her backbone in place as an overwhelming silence filled the great hall.

She lifted her chin. She'd be damned if she'd back down now.

Stephen stepped up onto the Council dais. His calm, very serious voice carried in the silence. "Dani Summerland, these are very serious charges. Do you have proof to back up your accusations?"

She smiled directly at Carlson, an icy movement that had the man twitching on the spot, the others cringing from what she'd say next. For all her anger, this was the pivotal moment in history and she, Dani Summerland – no – Dani Blackburn, was going to make sure it was done right. It seemed this world was desperately in need of a champion. And it had found one – in her. "I was hoping you'd say that."

She spun and stared at Milo.

He'd changed her life so much, and she'd forgiven him for everything he'd done these past few days – but if he couldn't produce the material she needed at her fingertips right at this moment, she was going to kill him herself.

The Combots wouldn't get a chance.

He'd be dead before they ever reached him.

"Milo?"

He nodded and clicked away on a few buttons. Instantly, a huge – as in back up several steps before she became part of the monitor display and ended up looking like a female version of Charmin's cotton ball – huge monitor display materialized.

A video of the slaughter, memoirs of the orders, names of the dead, emails and texts, all implicating the four men on the Council in front of her, rolled in an endless display for all to see. A growing murmur of horror swept through the audience.

"Send this out to the world, Milo," she ordered. "Take over every goddamned computer and vid screen in offices and in homes, on computerized ads and any other place where it can be viewed across the world. Let the people see how power corrupts. Let them see how these four men have shamed their position, how they have lied and cheated and killed in the name of their own heartless selves."

"In progress." Milo said, "It's streaming out to the world now."

"Stop him," Carlson screamed. "Combots, stop this. Remove these criminals from the chamber." The Councilman stood up tall, waving his arms around. "Return this chamber to order. I command you."

The Combots stared back but did not move. Dani grinned. Probably Milo's doing. She turned to look at the Combots standing like a solid army at her side. "Good. You should never follow orders that are just plain bad."

She looked around to find everyone staring at the huge display of data. Horrible mind-numbing numbers showing a humanity gone wrong data. She spun back to face the Council and found a team of Combots standing behind the four men on the Council. Stephen stood off to one side. She caught his eye. He gave her a smile and saluted her.

Her gaze widened, and she became flustered.

A sound started in the chamber. First low and quiet, then it quickly built in volume. She didn't understand the noise at first over the buzz from the massive monitor at her side.

Then she recognized it. Clapping.

She turned in a slow movement to find the Council chambers full to the overflowing with men and women of all ages. And they were all clapping. More than that, they were all staring at her.

Her astonished gaze went from face to face. Maybe she was slow, but really, were these people clapping for her?

Her gaze landed on Levi, pride swelling his chest, a proud grin on his face as he clapped harder than anyone. Milo. Tommy. Stephen.

They *were* clapping for her.

Tears crept into her eyes.

Maybe she could do something special in this lifetime after all.

She smiled through her tears and waved.

The crowd erupted into cheers.

***

Levi couldn't believe that calm, quiet Dani was standing up to the Council, talking ... no...berating, as in damn near shouting as she hurled accusations, heaping shame on the Council that had never faced opposition like this before.

The Council had had so much power for so long, they were accustomed to complete obedience, and that had been the chink in their armor. They didn't know what to do with her.

Or how to stop her.

When she hooked Milo into showing everyone the damaging evidence, even the Combots had shut down. Although, he cast a suspicious eye at Milo, he might have been behind that, too.

This Council was finished.

The individual members would pay heavily for their crimes against humanity. Dani was right. These men had defiled their way of life. Committing the ultimate sin in the name of power.

Stephen was a shoo-in for a new Council. That was a good thing. He was a fair man.

Levi had been incredibly angered at being hauled down to the Council like a common criminal. Sure, he'd crossed the line, or at least dipped his toe over the line. He'd had to protect his own. That wasn't justification. It was an explanation. He knew why, and the reason still stood. If need be, he'd do it again.

But to have seen Dani stand defiantly before their most honored – and corrupt – government system and systematically rip them to shreds, publicly exposing the world to their grievous deeds...well, he wanted to thank the Combots for bringing him...them...here.

To see the fall of the Council.

This was a great day.

And to think Dani had brought about the necessary change they'd so badly needed.

Innocent Dani, who'd been dubbed a Natural for no reason of her making...had picked up the cause and sought justice for her fellow man.

He'd never been prouder.

And she'd never live this moment down.

She'd become an icon now.

Milo, he knew, had already sent the video of her speech worldwide. Maybe a dangerous thing to do, but after this, she wouldn't need to hide anymore – except from her adoring fans.

She wouldn't need to cringe when someone spoke to her. Everyone would assume she didn't know much about their world because she had been part of one of the fringe groups. And being one would no longer be a negative trait. She'd elevated the fringe groups to equals. Something they'd never likely understand as they didn't care.

But it was a good thing – especially for her.

Dani had been amazing.

When the clapping started, he'd been one of the first to join in. When she'd lifted a hand in the air to wave, he'd cheered with the crowd. He'd loved her before this, but now his heart swelled and was ready to burst.

To think he'd worried that she would not be able to find her place in his world. Instead, she'd shown the rest of the world what really mattered.

Respect. Honor. Justice.

Truly, he loved her, this beloved woman of his.

He stepped forward, cheers ringing through his ears, and tugged Dani into his arms.

Dimly, in the background, the cheers resounded louder and louder in approval. He picked her up and twirled her around and cried out to the world, "Damn, I'm a lucky man."

She wrapped her arms tight around his neck, her breath warm and sexy against his ear as she whispered, "And I'll keep reminding you of it every day of our lives."

He roared with laughter and squeezed her tight. Just then, his wrist unit beeped. He glanced over to see Charmin's face fill the screen. He smirked again. "Dani, look who wants in on the action."

He watched as she caught sight of Charmin's face, a huge smile breaking across her beautiful features. "Charmin," she cried.

"About time you contacted me," Charmin said, pouting. "You left me all alone."

"I'm sorry. I didn't get a chance to tell you." She rushed to tell him. "The Combots took us away within seconds."

He sniffed the air, his flat nose going sky high. "And you couldn't tell me when you had a chance? Geez, I had to find out from Milo."

"We're coming home," she said. "Soon."

"Sure you are." He scowled. "Like you promised to never leave me alone again?"

"I didn't want to. Honest." She gave Charmin a breathtaking smile so full of love, Levi felt a twinge of jealousy. But he rejected it. There was room in her heart for both of them. "I'll make it up to you. I promise."

The cat eyed her carefully, and Levi frowned. Was something devious moving in the back of Charmin's big marble eyes?

"Okay, I'll forgive you, if…"

She frowned suspiciously. "If what?"

He beamed a huge, crafty smile at her. "If you bring me home something special. Tuna or shrimp would be good. Lobster?" He flopped to one side in front to the monitor. "You've been gone so long, I was afraid you weren't coming back. I'm starving…." He moaned. "Feeeed meeeee."

Author's Note

Dear reader,

Thank you for reading Broken Protocols series! If you enjoyed this book, I'd love it if you'd help others enjoy it as well. Reviews make a difference. There is also Broken Protocol 3.5 – a Christmas novella.

I love to hear from readers, and you can contact me at my website: www.dalemayer.com or at my Facebook author page. To be informed of new releases and special offers, sign up for Dale Mayer's newsletter. And if you are interested in joining my street team, here is the Facebook sign up page.

If you'd like to read about other books I've written, please turn the page.

Cheers,
Dale Mayer

Broken Protocols 3.5

This is book 4 in the Charmin Marvin Romantic Comedy Series. These books are novella length.

When Charmin Marvin wonders when Christmas Day would be in their new time frame, he sets events in motion no one could have expected.

Dani and Charmin lost a lot when they were brought 200 years into the future. But nostalgia brings the possibility of Christmas back into Dani's life - if she can make it happen.

Levi hates to deny Dani anything, but all holidays were removed from his society by the government decades ago. He has no idea what she's talking about - and when he does research and finds out - he wonders if something can be done. And someone outside of their small family wonders, too...

Dani has the best of intentions - but creating Christmas in a world that no longer knows what a holiday is makes her life very complicated very quickly.

It's a Dog's Life – novella

It's the first day of Ninna's job in the local animal shelter...and a dog is talking to her. Not just any dog...a fat, old, smart-alecky Basset Hound who says his name is Mosey.

She can't quit, she needs this job. And then there's the yummy vet. Who turns out to live across the street from her in a much bigger house than her tiny house. Big enough to hold a few animals – including the mouthy Mosey. With all this going on, she doesn't have time to worry about the rash of break-ins and the sense of being watched. She's too busy worrying that she's nuts.

When Ninna agrees to dog sit for the cute vet from work, she sees it as a trial at being a pet owner and a way to build on her budding relationship with the vet. For Mosey, this weekend means time to get to know each other.

For the stalker who's tracking Ninna's movements, it means...opportunity.

About the Author

Dale Mayer is a USA Today bestselling author best known for her Psychic Visions and Family Blood Ties series. Her contemporary romances are raw and full of passion and emotion (Second Chances, SKIN), her thrillers will keep you guessing (By Death series), and her romantic comedies will keep you giggling (It's a Dog's Life and Charmin Marvin Romantic Comedy series).

She honors the stories that come to her - and some of them are crazy and break all the rules and cross multiple genres!

Books by Dale Mayer

Psychic Vision Series
Tuesday's Child
Hide'n Go Seek
Maddy's Floor
Garden of Sorrow
Knock, Knock...
Rare Find
Eyes to the Soul – January 2015

By Death Series
Touched by Death - Part 1 - Free
Touched by Death - Part 2
Touched by Death - Full book
Haunted by Death
Chilled by Death - spring 2015

Second Chances...at Love Series
Second Chances - Part 1
Second Chances - Part 2
Second Chances - Full book

Contemporary Series
Skin
Scars – Febuary 2015

Novellas
It's a Dog's Life- romantic comedy

Charmin Marvin Romantic Comedy
Broken Protocols #1
Broken Protocols 2
Broken Protocols 3
Broken Protocols 3.5
Broken Protocols 1-3

New adult/adult crossover Books
In Cassie's Corner
Gem Stone (a Gemma Stone mystery)

Design Series
Dangerous Designs
Deadly Designs
Darkest Designs

Family Blood Ties Series
Vampire in Denial
Vampire in Distress
Vampire in Design
Vampire in Deceit
Vampire in Defiance
Vampire in Conflict
Vampire in Chaos – April 2015
Vampire in Crisis – August 2015

Non-Fiction Books
Career Essentials: The Resume
Career Essentials: The Cover Letter
Career Essentials: The Interview
Career Essentials: 3 in 1

Made in the USA
Charleston, SC
19 December 2014